About Rose Langshaw

The youngest of five children, Rose was raised mostly as an only child, her parents surprised to add to their brood in their late forties.

This upbringing granted her with a unique perspective, as she was surrounded by adults who loved recounting stories of their youth, not to mention a mother who enjoyed the past and the unexplained. The family often gave her books as presents on the subject. Rose read these avidly.

Her favourite childhood book was The Silver Brumby, with lots of different genres to follow. The urge to write did not appear until her late twenties, after vainly searching for something different, something fun. Something a little out there.

From that search sprung the desire to write. Write what she could not find, and to stick with it no matter what.

About Kane Langshaw

At a time when others loved playing football and cricket, Kane was studying Tae Kwon Do and making movies. On weekends and school holidays, he would badger his sisters and cousins, sometimes friends to stand before his camera, desperate to make a short movie.

As he got older, he became fascinated with special effects, finally completing the study of 3D Animation for film and television in his early twenties. During those studies, he wrote short scripts for an array of projects. It is here his interest in writing was sparked.

Though he still loves film and television, the ability to live another life, write what his mind conjures he finds truly satisfying. One moment you are flying among the stars, talking with new species, the next you're on a battlefield seeking answers to ancient secrets. What could be better than that?

ROSE & KANE LANGSHAW

THE ACTRIX STONE
GLOBAL REACH

EPISODE 1

To all who believe ... this for you.

Galactic Star Key: Kaze Karbroe
Astral Nav-Coordinates: EAS-APL-4
Data Sequence: 1.0

From ink darkness, a digitised voice emerged. "Warning! Spawn-cell re-sequence complete. Cryogenic-sleep terminated, emergency revival protocol activated."

Electrical pulses began moving through Kaze's nervous system, the sensation almost liquid as it flowed from his core into his hands and feet, igniting pain as his extremities found movement.

Again, the voice spoke. "Star-Key uploading, race-caste Hasnirian. Citizenship paired to Northverse Astral State. Identification profile accepted, initialising solo spawn-net."

The acidic taste of cryo-fluid leaving his lungs turned his throat to a rigid column. Fighting to steady his breathing, Kaze took in the oxygenated liquid, even though the action felt unnatural now he was awake.

With a snap-hiss, his spawn-pod's outer seal began retracting, the contact between the air and cryo-liquid creating a chemical reaction that resulted in white vapour.

Skin prickling, Kaze fought against holding his breath, slowly exhaling, expelling the last of the substance from his lungs and feeling his damp clothing and hair dry as his eyes adjusted to the flickering light.

Something was wrong. Jerking himself to a seated position, he spotted a collapsed ceiling beam, compromising the secondary Engineering Chamber. Kicking his legs over the spawn-pod's edge, he halted mid-motion, an unexpected bout of trembling leaving him weak and sweaty.

More destroyed terminals lined the rear wall. Many spewed sparks, their screens fluctuating between different languages and various race-caste profiles.

The sight of his brother working upon a control terminal connecting to the primary Blade Engineering Chamber brought him up short. Zozes was a mess, uniform torn and singed, his usually groomed hair falling in his eyes.

The vocal processor within the Engineering Chamber gave him a clue as to what was happening. "Alpha Blue command-operation uploading."

Alpha Blue? Who's callsign was that? Climbing out of the cylinder, Kaze hung from the side, legs barely able to support weight, face moist with sweat.

It took a moment to understand part of his problem came from the rocking of their spacecraft. Holding tight to the spawn-pod, he worked hard to fight the remnant effects of early waking, his gaze landing on the heavily damaged spawn-pods nearby. A number of occupants were clearly dead, but other hatches were deployed indicating some Blade Officers had been revived.

"Zozes." The name was a rasp. His brother worked frantically on the main operative terminal, loading a series of screens that lit the area around him. Working his mouth a couple of times, Kaze tried again. "Brother!"

"You're awake." Zozes' glance up was brief. "And suffering from post-hibernation sickness. It'll pass, Kaze."

"What's our combat situation?" Kaze could barely keep up with brother's swift movements. His eyes widened when the primary Engineering Chamber beside his brother came online, its three swift moving gyro-rings retracting to the ceiling. "Zozes, are we under assault?"

"I was forced to disengage you from your spawn-pod prematurely."

"What's ..." Kaze fought stray thoughts, striking the spawn-pod in temper. "My skull feels like it's being crushed by a vokking gravity supr—"

"Kaze!" Zozes interrupted. "I need you calm through this to stabilise your vitals. We're both suffering disorientation due to premature waking." Inputting commands via the control interface, he added, "And your consciousness needs to readjust and align itself with memory patterns."

"Calm?" Kaze fought absurd laughter. "As in a subdued lack of emotional feeling?" The wavy image of his brother seemed hilarious. "I'd say your well-natured calm left the airlock the moment you activated my pod!"

"Glib as ever." Zozes shot back. "Some things never falter."

"I'd be more civilised if these fractured memories," his eyebrows furrowed at the absurdity of the situation, "would just hurry up and realign. Argh!" A rush of images seared his mind, each one faster than the last, bringing with them an intense surge of pain.

Without warning, the ship bucked like it was gripped by something powerful. Grabbing for the spawn-pod, Kaze barely dodged incoming debris when a work-station blew out.

Across from him, Zozes appeared to double his efforts.

"Seems like someone's been mistreating our ship!" yelled Kaze.

Before Zozes could respond, the PA system activated, static breaking down the audio feed, an officer on the bridge fighting to make an announcement.

"Warning! Subspace layer-shift in progress!"

"We're crossing subspace?" Still gripping the pod, Kaze looked out an energy-window as the ship lurched a second time. What he saw was not normal space, but the bright translucent waves of subspace, layers of ocean-like currents seeking to crush them as they sank deeper and deeper.

Urgently, Kaze stumbled toward his brother, fighting to stay upright while veering around blown cables, only to be thrown against Zozes at the last moment. Zozes righted them both.

"What's going on?" Kaze demanded weakly as his brother hefted him onto the floor of the Blade Engineering Chamber. Zozes didn't answer. "Zozes?"

"Hold position," Zozes warned, stepping back and hitting the main control. Instantly, the gyro-rings dropped from above to surround him, three rotational arcs of light locking him in their boundary. "I'm using the Engineering Chamber to activate our squad's tactical Artificial Intelligence unit."

"An unauthorised Link-Trone deployment? That's impossible!" Kaze looked around the destroyed bay. "Zozes! Don't you go silent on me!"

Expression taut, Zozes continued working his control terminal, loading an internal bio-map of Kaze while remaining stubbornly quiet, a trait Kaze loathed. When he finally answered, the response was clipped, clearly not inviting enquiry.

"We need the Link-Trone to form a biomechanical network between your consciousness and its control mainframe."

"Wait." As each word penetrated, Kaze's jaw dropped a little further, the gravity of what his brother was attempting slamming through the fog. "You're pairing the AI to my mind? Are you a level beyond insane?"

Before Kaze could say more, his brother activated the Engineering Chamber's Control-Platform, triggering part of the floor to open on his right. Kaze eyed the circulating rows of AI Link-Trone's mounted in their individual compartments, each awaiting an Alpha Blade Officer to call them to duty. But his status rank was not Alpha, not even close.

At the controls, Zozes activated one of the AI's to be released from its compartment, a cylindrical shaped stasis-loader rising through the floor to before him. A second command triggered the device's service-base to materialise their squad's AI Unit within a gravity beam.

Spherical shaped, the tactical AI re-conformed its exterior shell to resemble armour plating, a glossy silver-and-tan surface reflecting the sparks raining from destroyed terminals.

Jerking back to his brother, Kaze fought to think of a way to stop this while the AI's operative systems were still loading. Once it was online, there would be no going back.

"You don't have the authorisation to operate this type of Biomechanical-Instillation, only a Blade Optive does, or our squad's Alpha Chief. The system will abort!"

Those words brought his brother's head up. "Kaze, I've been issued Alpha Command status. After this is complete, you'll be granted it too."

"You're an Alpha?" Feeling caged, Kaze threw back his head, then began hunting the Engineering Chamber for escape. "That's impossible. I'd better be in cryo-sleep, brother, because there's no luck processing this!"

The haze clouding Kaze's mind was slowly clearing, bringing a horrible clarity. If his brother was taking command, what had become of their squad's Alpha?

"Where's the Chief?" he demanded softly.

Pain flashed across Zozes' sweaty face. "She hasn't got long."

The words felt a physical punch, one that locked Kaze's knees and brought on an onslaught of memories — past missions, past battles, and a briefing, one that seemed to connect with this situation ...

"The mission?" Kaze fought off hibernation recall, struggling to focus. "Don't leave me fighting for information, I'll just drown you in questions."

"You'll have to learn on the run," snapped Zozes. "I have to pair you with the AI before we lose the ship."

"Vok that!" Kaze jerked as close as he dared to the rings. "I've got no command training, my spawn-network isn't programmed to control an AI's neural load. The shock to my central nervous system will leave me flat on the deck!"

"You'll have help." Eyes narrowed, Zozes looked up. "I'm establishing a unibind dual-pairing system. Together, you and I will command the Link-Trone, our minds merged. I will compensate for your ... limitations," he said with a shrug.

"A dual-link?" Kaze almost laughed. "Two minds linked to an AI unit as well as to each other? That's not even possible!"

"We're about to find out."

"Vok!" But there was no changing his brother's mind, not once his course was set.

Beyond the energy-window, subspace waves were increasing in force and frequency, the almost iridescent colour shifts telling him their ship was foundering, the creaking sounds of the hull hinting that before long, they would be incinerated. Every phase-shift pulled them deeper into subspace, each layer emitting a stronger radiation field, saturating the ship.

Probably part of the reason his vision was so hazy, thought Kaze. "None of this makes sense!"

Zozes gripped the terminal, fighting to enter commands. "I'm told in time it will, and that this dual-pairing will lead us to the answers."

"So, you're saying the Chief's ordered this? Why?" It appeared his brother was in the dark more than he was admitting. "Sounds like we've got a saboteur on board. Instead of caging me, let's hunt them down."

"Speculation won't stop this," dismissed Zozes. "I need your focus here, completing the Chief's orders. She's reprogrammed the Biomechanical-Instillation to allow for our dual-pairing to control the Link-Trone. It's unique, she said, and over time will start unlocking memory sequences from the Trone, but only when we're ready. Then, brother, we will get our answers."

"Memories of what?" demanded Kaze. "Why not just tell us who sabotaged this mission? Our ship!"

"I don't know!" exploded Zozes, irritably shoving at his hair while clearing sweat from his eyes. "The Chief spoke of repressed memories, truths that should never have been forgotten."

The words made no sense to Kaze. He stared at his brother, wondering if Zozes was affected by the radiation drenching their ship. It could have compromised his judgement, created an elaborate scenario in his mind that did not exist.

Suddenly, the bay filled with light, a golden hue that came from outside the ship. Moments later, a series of explosions detonated. Kaze watched helplessly as a nearby control terminal blew, turning it to melted, charred ash.

"Another shift." Zozes swiped irritably at the sweat dripping from his chin. The temperature within the bay was increasing rapidly. "This instillation can't be interrupted. A power surge will end it before it even begins."

Sweltering in the heat, Kaze shifted in the small space as the floor of the platform illuminated, hinting that a command procedure was being initiated within the Engineering Chamber. A series of blue-tinged cyber-screens appeared before him, the one on his left uploading the Alpha Blue protocol. His new callsign. When the AI Trone lit up within the grav-beam, he saw the system was now updated and online.

Its digitised voice activated. "AI Link-Trone recognises Blade Commando Blue 77-A2."

On Kaze's right, another screen lit, revealing diagnostics of the newly installed command program and stating his Star-Key was being adapted to form a unibind dual network with his brother's to control the AI Link-Trone.

The synchronising of their Star-Keys was nearing completion and so far, nothing had gone wrong. Kaze looked over the cyber-screen display, the telemetry and wave-guide, the latter displaying the positronic mass-drives synchronisation-pulse, which looked stable ...

A sharp pain lanced across his forehead, one that left him tasting blood at the back of his throat. Just as he had thought, mused Kaze darkly. This was much worse than his initial spawn-net instillation, designed to enhance his technological and combat effectiveness upon entering the Blade Mark Two program.

The AI Trone appeared to be having trouble generating the dual sync-pulse needed to connect. Kaze knew both biomechanical networks needed to register to the same frequency, or the AI Trone would reject them. The instillation was attempting to align three pulses, the Trone plus two Alphas.

The AI system signalled again in its stark digitised voice. "Full integration complete; spawn-network established between Artificial Intelligence and Alpha Blue."

"Is it over?" Kaze blinked weakly, then jerked back as a cyber-optic screen appeared over the cornea of his eye, loading a shimmering readout of his vitals. Kaze looked up as another console shot sparks across the bay, and the readout switched abruptly to generate a map of the ship. Disoriented, he swayed on his feet, fighting to control his roiling stomach. Then another surge of pain struck, this time running from the base of his head down his spine. Cold as ice, the pain spread fast, momentarily numbing both legs. Nose dripping blood, he forced himself to breathe deeply, running a hand beneath it.

"Almost there," murmured Zozes, frowning. "Adapting to this dual-pairing will take time and training. The sync-pulse between us and Link-Trone has to form a symbiotic connection. We'll both need to adjust to it."

A hard roll of nausea hit Kaze, so powerful he was vaguely surprised he did not heave on the spot. Laughing weakly, he looked up from a bent position. "You know me and commitment, brother."

"The Chief gave me specific orders to not reformat the Link-Trone's sync-pulse to us."

"Reformat the sync-pulse?" Kaze shook his legs, relieved there was no numbness. "Altering any Blade's sync-pulse could break their connection with the AI. At the very least, drastically weaken abilities."

"That's a standard pairing, one Alpha to an AI. For us, it's a little more problematic." Zozes grimaced. "It could kill us."

"Of course," Kaze nodded, rolling his eyes. "No fun unless it kills you, right?"

Surprised at the tone, Zozes' eyebrows rose. "Aren't you the one who always says we've been through worse?"

"This mission," growled Kaze, wiping fresh blood from his nose, "places all other missions in the anticlimactic category."

"Danger!" The master computer lit before Zozes. "Bio-map signature of Alpha Blue and LT-77 incompatible! Initiating immediate disengagement."

All around Kaze cyber-screens turned from blue to red, information flashing with warnings.

"Vok!" hissed Zozes. "The Trone's sync-pulse is having trouble linking in a new frequency wave to your spawn-net. The Chief said this could happen."

"If this keeps up," warned Kaze, his legs already feeling numb, "you'll be carrying me out of here."

"Cease disengagement process!" Zozes ordered, terminating a series of cyber-screens, before turning to the master one. "Override order Alpha Green 77-A1. Run AI Link-Trone Command Synchronisation Program!"

The digitised voice remained silent.

"I said, run Command Instillation!" Still nothing.

Kaze felt the ship sway, a warning sign that they were approaching another subspace layer. The moment consoles began exploding, he knew their vessel was about to be gripped again. The freq-com crackled to life, a primary message dispatched from the helm of the ship.

"Grid-shield losing structural integrity! Warning, code-red has been initiated! Evacuate ship! All hands to evac-pods!"

Within the grav-beam, the AI unit suddenly activated, its central spawn-well spiralling open to reveal a small construct-dish, the primary power source of all Link-Trones.

Zozes said, "Synchronisation program is realigning into your spawn-net."

Eyes wide, Kaze leaned closer. "I've never been so close to a Blade's source of power. If my body wasn't about to self-combust, it'd be a prize moment."

"The newly established sync-pulse is reconfiguring," said Zozes, "to create Command Biomechanical Probes which your spawn-net controls."

Kaze needed things clarified. "I've access to control command spawn-types?"

"You do." Zozes changed cyber-screens. "Trone cells are for adapting and controlling artificial systems, while sorge cells source your power."

Kaze looked back at the spawn-dish, eyeing the newly formed spawn-cells interacting and replicating. He had a good idea how far along the procedure was when the ship once again shuddered under turbulence.

"Now would be the time to initiate spawn-cell assimilation!" said Kaze, bracing himself.

Zozes nodded, looking up as the Link-Trone's digitised voice confirmed, "Instillation underway, adapting artificial probes to assimilate and replicate new command types."

On a breath of relief, Zozes wiped a hand over his forehead, shoving his hair back while deactivating the rest of the cyber-screens. "Once the Trone's artificial probes are networked to your Star-Key, it will grant operative access to all energy based profiles so you can control the AI Link-Trones sorge-energy."

"Control?" Kaze grunted the word, finding it hard to think past the fire racing along his spine, something his brother seemed to be aware of.

"Once you can stand upright."

"This Link-Trone better be tuned for full control." Eyes watering, he blinked back tears. "I know how much you hate wasting time."

"You doubt me?"

"I'll answer that once the ship stops blowing up around us." Kaze rubbed at the back of his neck gingerly, watching the AI as the grav-beam deactivated and the Trone ignited its anti-grav thrusters, glowing blue.

It was hovering under its own power, waiting for command.

Zozes deactivated the Engineering Chamber's gyro-rings, and the three charged circles of light shot upwards as the dais dimmed.

Free, Kaze jumped from the circular platform, stumbling when the ship rolled suddenly. Fighting to find his balance, he looked around the bay, then out the door, into the corridor, seeing the mist of green-tinged plasma vapour.

"The ship's in worse shape than me," he observed, stepping to the side as the Link-Trone grav-thrusted close, hovering between the two, a series of blue, yellow and red lights flashing.

"Let's move," ordered Zozes, navigating his way through the fallen equipment. He paused at the door.

Kaze followed, only to stumble when he reached his brother, fighting to suppress a groan. A constant stream of images and accompanying sensations filled his mind's eye, both disorienting. One moment he was watching the Alpha Chief finalising a mission briefing, then abruptly shifting to their Blade Squadron preparing to launch from a Galaxy Base ship's hanger bay.

Memories crowded, one jumping clearly to his mind, a cyber-graphic image of a Space Station orbiting a planet.

"The Space Station. That's our mission?" demanded Kaze, grabbing for his brother's shoulder.

Zozes checked the corridor. "Yes, it's a Primordial Installation, built by an Origin race who submerged the Station itself in subspace."

"So the Station exists outside of normal space-time?" Kaze took his brother's silence as confirmation. "Our ship's been modified to land on this thing?"

"There's a plan in motion." Zozes shoved Kaze into the corridor, urging him to move.

Kaze eyed the chaos around him. "By the state of the bulkheads, I'd say free roaming the drift to outer space is the only plan in motion."

Zozes moved to the end of the hall, clearly ignoring his brother's sarcasm. Looking right and left, he pulled back quickly when a fresh blast of plasma vapour shot from the ceiling. "Our Engineering Chamber was initially used to warp-jump our ship through subspace to land on the Station, but the autopilot failed."

"The Link-Trone's lost control of the ship's flight navigator?" Kaze shook his head, wondering how that was possible.

Zozes glanced again before diving out, signalling Kaze to move. "Our Chamber's AI interface went offline, disengaging all automated operations."

Kaze followed, barely avoiding an exposed power relay shooting sparks from the ceiling. "Without the autopilot means—"

"Manual control had to be established by the crew. Now they're attempting to calculate the correct variance shift-lock to move the ship into the same stellar sub-spatial zone the Station resides within."

"Meaning we're trapped in subspace?"

"More like an extension of subspace. Within transverse zones, connecting between dimensions."

"Vok!" Kaze yelled. "A simple 'yes' will do!"

Zozes grimaced, skirting a blown conduit, ducking the vapour it poured. "Emergency protocol was initiated, and the first revived after the Engineering Chamber failed was the Chief."

This meant only one thing to Kaze. "Don't tell me she's ..."

"On the bridge, piloting. She immediately revived senior officers from cryo-stasis and has the engineering team attempting to manually program the magnatronic warp-drive."

"They're initialising for another warp-jump?"

"We aren't getting out of this by measured action!"

Zozes was right, and Kaze knew it. "The radiation?"

"We're all affected. Those revived early won't survive."

"You're saying the Chief ..." Kaze bit his tongue, could not believe any of this was happening. "Alert Medical, place her in a stasis-field, until treatment can be—"

"There's no treatment for them!" Zozes snapped. "Medical was one of the first decks lost. When that happened, she gave me direct orders to get to you, then get off this ship, which I intend to do but only after stopping by the bridge."

"One vokked up plan after another. Have we at least identified the correct sub-spatial zone that the Space Station is in?"

"The less you know the better. I don't need you applying some withered action that'll result in chaos."

"Still flexing that dictative arm." Kaze rolled his shoulders, the unbearable heat shorting his already frayed fuse. "Conditioning of that kind is going to get you cramped up, brother."

The two turned right, finding themselves in a main passage, full of smoke. Kaze manoeuvred around lifted deck plating while avoiding overhead conduits that were dislodged, spewing circuitry, many alive and hazardous.

"Careful," Zozes warned, the two making their way cautiously past. "Your spawn-net still has to align with the Link-Trone's sync-pulse, so it'll inhibit access to any advanced tactical functions."

"You making this harder purposely?" Kaze growled, narrowing his eyes suspiciously.

"LT," Zozes glanced at the hovering AI. "Set navigation identifier to aim us for the bridge, avoiding compromised sectors."

Kaze bit back a groan, waiting for the cyber-optic screen to drop before his eye, highlighting the fastest route around criticality damaged areas of the ship.

"Ready?" Zozes waited for his brother's nod, then ordered the Trone. "Take scout-charge LT."

Immediately the Trone's grav-nacelles engaged, and the three headed off, Kaze fighting to shake off a fresh surge of pain. "Are you feeling any of this? That instillation has got my spawn-net warped out!"

Even basic operating functions seemed to be affecting his spawn-network, making him wonder if it was on the point of overload.

"Remember our training, Kaze, contest the pain," said Zozes. "Push back, otherwise you'll lose objectivity."

His brother was right. Biting down, Kaze attempted to refocus, ignoring the suffocating heat, while blocking the pain riding his spine.

The Trone's route took them through core engineering where Kaze saw a team of technicians working to realign warp-phase injectors, which seemed the only alternative when manually navigating through subspace layers. Kaze listened to the senior engineer yelling orders while others tried to reinitiate the command mainframe.

"Ignition PRO-GRAV-2704–65. Magnatronic Warp-drive restart sequence set."

"You realise this could leave the ship permanently dead in subspace," muttered Kaze.

A muscle ticked in Zozes' jaw. "It's the last resort before the drive goes critical."

The two moved on, weaving through personnel with the Link-Trone in the lead. Once out of core engineering and in the main corridor, they turned left, Kaze realising they were not far from the main bridge.

A squad of Galactic Force Troopers came upon them fast, the Lieutenant speaking swiftly. "Placement orders told us to get to the evac-pods. That last wave took out most of the landing bay. Casualty reports state we've lost over half our crew."

"Understood," said Zozes, both brothers wincing at the severe plasma burn covering the leader's face. "The Chief?"

"Still on the main bridge. Both flight captains are dead. She's taken the helm alone."

Fresh pain sliced Kaze's temple, burning a path into his jaw. Fighting to stay focused, he ignored the blood dripping from his nose, instead forcing his way through the group, aiming for the bridge.

"The Chief is not listening to reason," warned the Commando.

Kaze glanced over shoulder, snarling, "She'll listen to me."

"And," added the Commando, "she's mag-locked the seal-gate, denying anyone access to the flight bridge. She's attempting to manually pilot the ship through the subspace layers and onto the Space Station."

"Get to the evac-pods," ordered Zozes. "Leave the rest to us." He brushed past Kaze, stride shifting to a fast jog.

The Link-Trone led the two up to a main corridor. At the mid-way point, another wave shook the ship, leaving the vessel heaving and lurching. Circuits erupted, service clamps released deck plating, turning each into missiles.

"We're running out of time!" yelled Kaze, the two charging forward, barely evading being hit.

Suddenly, the light emitters died, turning the corridor black, followed almost immediately by artificial gravity failing.

Kaze's cyber-optics shimmered once before switching to night-sight, giving him an eerie view of slowly lifting debris.

Zozes grunted and swore, bumping into a wall. "Find something solid to push off," he ordered. "Use the momentum to bring yourself about then mag-lock boots to deck."

Damaged deck plating joined the debris as they shoved off a side wall in unison to direct themselves down the passage. The moment they could touch down each made a positive magnetic seal.

Each creak and groan of the ship reminded Kaze of a mortally wounded animal fighting to survive. Halfway along the corridor, gravity was reinstated, bringing with it a rain of debris. Deactivating their mag-seals, the two picked up pace, moving through the littered corridor fast, until the vessel pitched and rolled unexpectedly, throwing both against the wall, then back to the deck winded.

On his back, Kaze cast an eye over his brother, noting that blood ran from beneath his hairline, and the corner of his mouth.

The moment Zozes stood and held out his hand, Kaze slapped his in it. "Don't give me that look," he growled, barely stifling a groan as smoke began filling the corridor. "We won't appreciate it unless it's hard."

The two followed the Trone's grav-nacelles, shining like beacons, Kaze bringing up the rear. The moment they reached the bridge entrance, he tried to activate the door, but like the Commando had stated, it was mag-locked.

Furious, he gave it a good thump, while his brother waved a hand over the control panel attempting to scan his Star-Key.

"That won't work," snarled Kaze. "Why does she think she can operate the main bridge alone?"

Setting the control panel for manual override, Zozes pulled the handle towards himself, turning it until the seal lock pressurised before placing it in release position. Activation failed. That left only communication via freq-com.

Kaze had a good idea how that would play out. Eyeing the Link-Trone, he asked, "LT can you establish contact to the bridge?"

"Negative." The AI Link-Trone moved around them. "Bridge lockout protocol is blocking all freq-com channels."

"Vok!" swore Kaze, glaring at the activation panel, fighting to think past the blinding pain racing down his spine. He barely heard the explosion, only becoming aware when he and his brother were thrown to the deck.

"We need to initiate Blade Assault Mode!"

Zozes laughed without humour, jerking to his feet to begin working on the access panel.

"Check your cyber-optics," he suggested. "Until our sync-pulse to the Trone is aligned, all base operating systems to Trone functions are offline. Which means no weapons, no armour."

While Zozes worked on the panel, Kaze backtracked down the hall looking for the emergency armoury cache. Disengaging a side-arm from its hatch, he grabbed a plasma-rod from an ammo case, sliding the projectile into the barrel of the plasma pistol before heading back.

"Step aside, brother, I've got this one." Aiming at the lower chamber of the door, he waited for the rod to heat and charge, knowing it would release a highly-concentrated substance.

Without warning, Zozes jumped forward, shoving the pistol to point at the ceiling. "Are you trying to kill us both?"

Before Kaze could answer, the Link-Trone interrupted. "Positronic mass drives synchronisation-pulse aligned to secondary spawn-network. Blade Dual Pairing is now complete and ready for orders."

Dumbfounded, the two brothers stared at one another, the highly-charged plasma pistol still pointed at the ceiling.

The Link-Trone spoke again, lights flashing. "Blade tactical system loading. Welcome Karbroe 76-A1, callsign Alpha Green. Karbroe 77-A2, callsign Alpha Blue."

"We're aligned?" Slightly stunned, Kaze's eyes widened. "Mind explaining why you're one and I'm number two?"

"Really, you want to discuss that now?" Zozes jerked the pistol from his hand. "We won't be needing this." Disengaging the rod, he lowered the weapon. "Now that both spawn-nets are aligned we can use the Trone to deactivate the mag-lock. LT," he said, swinging to the Trone. "Activate the Trone-slicer to unlock the main bridge."

"Initialising request." A brief pause followed, then, "Placement order accepted, complying." After generating a slicer cyber-panel before the orb-shaped device, the Trone hovered close to the bridge doors to begin realigning the mechanisms within the security nodes. "Mag-lock override complete."

Almost immediately, the door depressurised, seal deactivating to roll back the reinforced door.

At a jog, Kaze followed his brother onto the bridge, shouldering past the Link-Trone, ignoring the unit's high-pitched electrical signal when he came in contact.

He could hear the Chief shouting orders over freq-com, "Bridge to core engineering, there's no more time! The grid-shield's repulse field is losing structural integrity. We have to initiate a manual supra-warp jump on my mark, no matter the risk!"

The bridge was a mess, fallen officers turning it to a morgue, blown-out terminals venting vapour and sparking. When he looked ahead, Kaze felt his stomach drop, not because of the taxed shields fluctuating outside the view screen, but what was beyond it. Subspace, an iridescent cloud of amber, black and brilliant luminescent gold, billowing and shifting.

Absently, Kaze brushed at the blood seeping from his nose, until the pain riding his spine shot like fire then ice from skull into spine then back. Eyes watering, he gripped the back of his neck, certain his head was about crack and spill its insides. There had to be something wrong with the dual-pairing; this was in no way normal.

Most of the operative stations on the bridge looked to have overloaded or were damaged beyond use. Stumbling forward, Kaze almost tripped over a casualty, recognising a Blade Optive's uniform, but between radiation burn and swelling, he was almost unrecognisable.

The first dead flight captain lay slumped at her post, covering most of the blown-out terminal, having caught the brunt of the explosion, while the Chief navigated from the helm, attempting to fly the ship on a hazardous course.

"Chief!" Zozes raced up several steps to the navigational platform, fighting to catch her attention.

Kaze could hear guidance system warnings from the main helm-driver station, the whining sound foretelling. "It's over Chief. The ship's lost."

She barely spared either of them a glance, though she was angry, the tenor of her voice as effective as a shout. "Why are you two not in evacuation bay as ordered?"

"Because," Zozes ground out, "I refuse to leave you for dead piloting this ship."

"Blade, you are not in command here. I can manually navigate this vessel through these final subspace layers, and then eject the escape pods to land on the station."

"Use the automated emergency evacuation launch," said Zozes.

"We're too deep in subspace. If I eject the pods now, no one will survive!"

Kaze came abreast, watching her work the controls. One look and he finally realised it was over. The Chief's condition was critical. Subspace radiation had blistered her skin, one eye was so severely bloodshot and swollen it was barely open, her lips were cracked and bleeding, hands swollen and scarred.

Freq-com crackled to life. "Core engineering to bridge! Standing by to initiate manual warp-window! This'll be our only shot, Chief."

"Understood! Phase-variance set, initiate magnatronic injectors on my mark!" she called, before placing a ship-wide warning. "All hands brace for manual warp-jump!"

Kaze took hold of a nearby console, sparing another glance at the view-screen. Before the ship, an entry warp-window began forming, the eye generating twisting multicoloured spirals that slowly cleared as a hole was punched into another subspace layer.

The Chief muscled the floundering vessel, her weakened state held together by sheer force of will. Multiple electrical strikes began randomly hitting the ship, blowing out more of the navigational flight systems.

"Mark!" she yelled.

The vessel felt like it gathered before surging forward, surrounded by white-hot warp-waves that distorted space in a glowing mass. The heavily damaged vessel fought through the warp-tunnel, moments later re-materialising.

Wide-eyed, Kaze watched the subspace waves dissolve to reveal a planetary size Space Station. The fraction he could see, he could barely comprehend, since its formation was so unique. Different to any station he had ever seen.

"It looks to be a series of interconnecting Space-Rings designed to form a spherical assembly frame." Zozes tone revealed his awe.

"That and much more," said the Chief, her speech noticeably weak. "It's one of twelve, surrounding the planet."

"Surrounding a planet?" Kaze frowned. The planet must inhabit normal space-time and couldn't be seen here, buried in subspace. "Has it been identified?"

"I ..." Holding a hand to her chest, she fought a coughing fit, fighting to relay codes. "Phase-shifting variances match. We're aligned with Space-Ring twelve, astro-way flight tunnel five. Launching evac-pods!" She punched a button.

Kaze eyed the flight tunnel ahead as the Chief muscled the sluggish guidance controls, trying to navigate it safely into the entrance.

"Blades," she drew their attention. "I don't know how long I can keep this vessel together. I need you to both get to an evac-bay launch tube. Now!"

Neither Kaze nor Zozes moved. The ship was entering the tunnel, huge columns either side. Gritting his teeth, Kaze listened to the jarring noises of lost sub-light stabilisers. At least the station's infrastructure was large. The Chief's erratic flight path was anything but standard.

"You realise," Kaze said, drawing her attention briefly, "we're taking you with us."

"Blade, there's only a handful evac-pods left, most have been destroyed when we lost the starboard launch tube. If I initiate an emergency landing, I can save those trapped on ship."

"Chief," Zozes came to stand by his brother, staring her down, "we aren't leaving you."

At a partially working comp-station, Zozes checked the ship's condition as it moved past countless columns and docked ships. Some appeared to be of a very ancient design. "We just passed through the Station's vacuum shield. Ship's stabilisers are correcting, working to align with its artificial gravity."

A major ship marina came into view, too many vessels docked to even hazard a count.

"Look," spotted Kaze, jerking forward. "That's the Planetary Allegiance Task Force's Fleet—" A high-impact jolt faltered him mid-sentence.

"We just lost the starboard magna-nacelle." A series of schematics lit the Chief's display, most flashing red. "Grid-shields are depleted, guidance controls going cold."

Kaze was close enough to hear the energy build-up in her console. Acting on instinct, he threw the Chief to the deck, shielding her body with his as the conduit blew, taking most of helm-drive and half the neighbouring panels.

On her feet before the last overload, the Chief said nothing. Kaze, on the other hand, got up on a snarl of anger. He could see she was already searching for an alternate way to pilot the ship over the energy sparks and burnt terminals.

"We're on a collision course with a Galaxy Ship," warned Zozes. "Can the Link-Trone access the guidance system through core engineering?

"Out of the question," dismissed the Chief moving to the second fight station, attempting to reboot its damaged systems. "Commanding flight controls through AI could rupture your spawn-net, and neither of your bodies can handle that kind of neural strain!"

"There's no more time!" Kaze growled, fighting to stay upright as their ship collected the tail of another vessel before ploughing on. "Issue the order, Zozes, we'll deal with the consequences."

Out of options, Zozes swung to the Trone. "LT, align flight control through core engineering, take over the operation of the guidance system."

Though the Chief fought to countermand this, her words were lost in a coughing fit that left her breathing erratic, face flushing then becoming pale before their eyes.

Several breathless moments later the Trone affirmed, "System flight established."

All of them felt the ship's erratic flight path correct, though the three were still thrown about.

"We've lost inertial dampeners," Kaze said. "This ride is going to get a little more chaotic."

"Land the ship," Zozes ordered, turning to the Trone, "within the Galaxy Ship docking yard, as close as possible to the main marina. And post a priority freq-communication verifying our ship's identification code, making certain the targeted hanger bay is clear."

"Blades!" The Chief slumped at her station, another coughing fit taking hold, this one producing blood. "The only way left … off this ship is through … through the starboard drop ramp. You have to attempt an inflight combat jump."

Jaw a hard line, Kaze looked at his brother. The radiation poisoning was now crippling her motor functions, slurring her words.

"This is it, Blades," she began.

"Don't start with the final words," interrupted Kaze, placing an arm around their unit leader. "Bringing emotion into the equation is something I'm not built for."

"You're coming, Sir, we're with you till the end." Imputing final codes, Zozes got on the other side of the Chief. "Have us court-martialled once we're off the ship."

"I'll do more than that," she grumbled, eyes rolling as she was dragged across the bridge, consciousness starting to fade in and out.

The brothers moved fast, numerous explosions keeping them company. The Link-Trone scouted ahead, relaying the fastest route through the brothers' cyber-optics as the Chief mumbled incoherently, her feet mostly dragging over the deck plating.

"Care to translate what she's throwing together?" Kaze asked.

"I'll leave the deductions to you," said Zozes, noticeably increasing his pace.

"The … planet this Space Station orbits … must understand, need to … liberate … must understand." She groaned weakly, her good eye fighting to focus. "Listen …"

They saw no one as they raced through the ship, until they came to evac-bay, full of the last surviving personnel, most prepping for combat jump.

"Something's wrong with the drop ramp," said Kaze, noticing it was only partially open.

An officer in charge called out over the roar of air. "All evac-pods have been launched, and tele-warp rings are inoperative for site to site transfer."

"The Blade-Gear System?" demanded Zozes. "Has that been initialised?"

The Link-Trone hovered close, choosing to answer. "Negative. That process has been suspended in order to navigate this vessel."

"No combat jump says we're out of options," growled Kaze, staring hard at his brother.

Mouth a grim line, Zozes turned to the engineer, then eyed the damaged mechanism. "What's the issue? Why can't the ramp be dropped?"

"System lock-up. Happened when we impacted that last vessel."

"Help him," ordered the Chief weakly. "Kaze, put me down."

A nearby seat carrier was open. Once she was on it, Kaze activated the manual brace, which crawled over her chest and stomach.

The assembled engineers were only some of the personnel, Kaze realised, as he wound through. If he could get to an armaments cache, maybe they could rig a charge to blow the ramp clear. Opening the first one he came to, Kaze looked inside, noting a series of anti-grav motion bands.

"Blade!" a voice bellowed.

That did not sound friendly. Turning around, he eyed a group of Blade Commandos, noting that none had activated their Blade-Gears, probably due to subspace radiation rendering the devices inoperable.

The leader was glaring at his Link-Trone, shouldering her way through personnel. "Why do you have an active LT unit? Orders were to leave all AIs locked within the spawn-bridge!"

For a long moment, Kaze met her angry stare, then that of her squad as they came to back her up. Death haunted their eyes, a dangerous companion. Before he could respond, an explosion rumbled deep within the ship, sending the vessel screeching sideways, sparks flaring along rear evac-ramp.

"Entering Galaxy Ship landing bay," informed the Trone.

Plasmagnetic fluid spewed from a ruptured line, its toxic smell filling the bay. A nearby power converter ruptured. Stray energy bolts ignited, ripping through the launch bay, taking out half the ramp, the officers working to lower it turned to ash. Two more followed, attempting to save them.

"We're done!" Kaze roared, grabbing the anti-grav motion bands from the locker. Turning, he began handing them out to Blade officers and engineers, watching them silently attach them to their wrists.

"No options left onboard," Kaze called over the roar of air. "Use these for anti-grav flight — watch the stabilisers during descent!"

When he reached the Blades, he handed them over silently before making his way back to the Chief, unlocking her brace. "Your armour, Chief?"

"Blade-Gear is no longer operational." She shook her head. "Prolonged exposure ... subspace radiation destabilises the spawn-net."

"Can you—" A strange sensation moved through Kaze, halting him mid-sentence, a strong feeling of foreboding. It travelled the pores of his skin, surging full blown in his mind, while amplifying his awareness of all that surrounded. He could hear something, a voice, faint, echoing inside his mind. Somehow it was muting surrounding noise, even the screeching metal. Focusing in further, Kaze realised it was his brother.

Somehow, he could hear each word Zozes was speaking on the other side of the bay. Looking across to the drop-ramp, he gauged his brother's position, then jerked when Zozes halted mid-sentence to eye him, clearly surprised.

Kaze looked back to the Chief, attaching the final set of anti-grav motion bands to her wrists, then activating them. "LT, release the ship's flight-controls and commence activation of Alpha Blue and Alpha Green Blade-Gears, we need them operational now!" Pulling the Chief to her feet, he warned, "Keep a tight hold."

His brother was just ahead, waving personnel back before he demagnetised the assembly brace-clamps, then ejected the damaged drop-ramp to clear the opening. Taking several hard, fast breaths, Kaze called on the adrenalin flooding his system, using it like fuel. For an instant, everything felt magnified down to the smallest detail. While keeping a tight grip on the Chief, he raced forward, shouldering his brother through the breach, the three leaping from the crippled vessel.

The moment they did, the ship began to ignite in a series of blasts. Their descent gained speed as a shockwave of heat chased them to the hanger deck.

A handful survivors were leaping, desperate to save themselves, but most were engulfed in plasma flames. Vital systems, jettisoned for recovery, peppered the air. The largest was the Engineering Chamber, blackened and barely recognisable, its thrusters powered to slow its fall to deck. Kaze looked up at the billowing explosion, the brilliant blue-white plume as the ship became a fireball.

The Chief pulled from his grasp, holding out her arms, activating her anti-grav motion bands to stabilise her descent, while Zozes twisted, fighting to regain control of his fall. The Link-Trone relayed a message through their intercom.

"Blade-Gear online. Activating Alpha Blue and Alpha Green."

Moments before landing, Kaze felt armour materialise over his body, dampening the unstable atmosphere and muffling noise. Hitting the hangar deck feet first, he grunted, though his power armour compensated, absorbing most of the impact via its reinforced gravity stabilisers.

"Grab cover!" bellowed Zozes, already running to avoid the flaming debris pelting down. "Chief!"

Kaze reached her first, something was wrong, her body had fallen into an unnatural position. The two grabbed her beneath each arm, pulling her behind the closest barrier as what was left of the ship met the end of landing bay, the vessel's magnatronic drive erupting, a massive blast igniting the entire vessel in a spectacular display of light and energy.

The brothers deactivated their helmets, retracting them into their neck guard. The scents of plasma vapour and burnt metal filled the air, the light alloy of their ship floating like snow. Glancing sideways, Kaze saw that the Chief was watching too, a distant look in her eyes.

"Another smooth landing," she jested, only to be halted by a fierce coughing fit.

"Chief," began Kaze, but she waved his words away.

"It's alright, there was only one way this was going to end for me."

"No," Kaze denied desperately. "Hold on a little longer."

"My legs are shattered, bones turned brittle as glass. The radiation."

Zozes activated his porta-tool, energising a hi-cap glove. "I can at least ease the pain."

"No," the Chief refused. "Leave it. Now, you must listen." Teeth gritted, she fought to stay conscious. "You need to understand why I've done this, connecting you as I have ... through ... the Link-Trone to each other."

The brothers shared a look, Zozes finally asking, "Why, Sir?"

"The planet ... it's because of the planet, Zozes." Her good eye focused. "This Space Station is immense, and it surrounds a young world, one that is important, different from most."

"But—"

"Hear me, Blades. The planet itself is far older than you can understand ... or even comprehend. Only the inhabitants are young." Blinking hard, she bore down. "I know this is difficult ... but the answers will come to you. I've made certain."

"Through the LT?" Zozes glanced at Kaze. "Tell us now, with your own words!"

The Chief's voice was growing weak, but the look on her face was one of resolve, even relief that these last vital moments had not been lost.

"I've found that even a well-intentioned revelation can be deadly. Through your experiences and learning ... what you find and how you find it. That truth will free you." Though spent, the Chief fought on, urgent to say the last. "You must find allies for this cannot be done alone. We may be blood-born Hasnarians, but this fight is for all. We must come together, stand united. Only that will liberate this world, and all it is connected to. Save them. That is my final order. Save ... them all."

Her eyes flared wide as the pain intensified. "Please," she mouthed softly. "Tell your father the ... mantle of the creed was honoured."

With these last words, Kaze watched her slip away, her broken body smoothing out, going lax, no longer held tight in pain.

Gentle, Zozes rested her on the deck.

Kaze watched his brother stand, each movement slow and deliberate. Focusing on the Link-Trone, Zozes asked, "What is this world the Chief speaks of?"

The two waited, Kaze looking at his brother, their dying ship ablaze, sparks and smoke creating a deadly backdrop.

"Accessing data." As lights flashed on the Link-Trone, Kaze stood, the AI unit moving between the two before answering. "Inhabitants call it Earth."

Galactic Star Key: Baden Casteel
Astral Nav-Coordinates: EAS-APL-4
Data Sequence: 2.0

"Check it, Cass! Another missing person report."

Baden glanced back to see Kevin Zheng holding up his tablet computer. "Let's steal a seat over here." Making his way to the top of the grandstand, he turned to look over Freestone College's main oval.

A wide gum tree shaded the corner, giving them both a chance to cool off. Dropping his backpack, Baden unzipped the middle zip, searching for his lunch, while Kevin scanned the article.

"Adele Jones, in her thirties. She was reported missing by her spouse last Monday around nine pm. No one's seen her since."

Baden wiggled his fingers. "Cue the *Twilight Zone* tune."

Kevin huffed a breath, staring at the woman's photo. "If this keeps up, Freestone Valley's gonna end up a ghost town."

Baden checked his sandwich. Ham and cheese. Again. "Anything else worth mentioning? Or are they just peddling the usual song and dance."

"Authorities have not dismissed," Kevin continued, "a connection between the recent disappearances with those of the late 1980s."

Baden leaned back on his elbows and chewed. "Too common to be common sense. I could've told them that."

"How're you still landing a solid joke?" Kevin shook his head. "Isn't your family worried, your mum was one of the first abducted—"

"She returned." Baden interrupted.

"Yeah, but clearly she's in the minority." Kevin grimaced. "My dad would've packed our family up, shipped us out years ago."

"Casteel pride, my man." Baden took a swig of water. "Our land's been in the family since the founding of the Valley."

"Never understood the 'land' thing that's built into your family's DNA. Makes me wonder if the oxygen out that way is a little thinner." Kevin looked back at his tablet computer, taping the screen absently. "We're good talking about this, right? No point me running the mouth off into areas that are a little unsympathetic."

"Your radar's way off." Baden sat forward, elbows on knees chewing. "If it bothered me you'd know, so ..." he gestured, "lay it out, and report in."

"Well," Kevin blinked hard to clear his mind, then dived in. "The local cops have been working in conjunction with Australian Federal Police, but there's also mention of a specialist unit from the Department of Defence."

"Military?" Baden pulled a face.

Kevin nodded. "Might have something to do with the changeover at the old RAAF base."

"That area's been locked down for years," Baden grumbled. "Probably a launch site that's gone nuclear."

"It draws in a lot of attention, so who knows?" Kevin's eyes shone. "I heard it's some kind of experimental facility and has connections with the UN."

Baden laughed, thinking about the Freestone's populace. "Having an intergovernmental organisation taking on the abduction case is gonna set off this town's rumour mill into overdrive."

"Still." Kevin scrolled through to the next story. "Makes you think the two are somehow connected."

"Like we'll ever know." Stretching, Baden relaxed. "So, what's the tally now?"

Kevin pulled out a fork and small thermos cup, popping off the top. Baden leaned over, sniffing the vapour from the hot noodles.

"Hmm. I don't know, maybe about seven or eight people missing."

"Piss on those figures. Got to be at least twenty."

"Depends how far back you look, I suppose. Whatever the numbers are, something's gotta be done."

"Don't I know it, man."

The bell rang, releasing the rest of the students. Immediately the college oval began filling with the usual cliques, many stretching out seeking spring sunshine.

"Midday bell has no hold on us." Baden tipped back his head, eyeing the stretch of blue sky. "Soaking these afternoon rays for an extra half hour is not a bad gig."

"Pot luck I'm your lab partner in science this semester."

"And that Old Mrs Donovan cradles that genius mind of yours. We're so far ahead, she practically shoved us out the door early. Nice way to bend the rules." Baden swigged at his water bottle. "Her kind should be a requirement at this school."

"Perks of who you know, I guess."

Baden straightened to point. "Hey, the heavy hitters are out today."

In the distance, a group of students ran to the end of the field punting a football back and forth. When someone kicked the ball high, a familiar figure went up, using his mate's back to mark it in mid-air.

The instant he landed, he booted the football back down the field. Pulling his shirt over his head, he began sprinting forward, arms wide. Everyone began hollering and yelling.

Baden eased forward, grinning. "Whenever a footy's in his hands, the douchebag-meter goes critical."

Suddenly, the player ripped off his shirt, throwing it to the grass. Kevin winced, shaking his head before going back to reading while eating.

"Ear into this, Cass," he mumbled. "They're talking about interviewing residents, anyone with any connection to those who've disappeared. They're even issuing summonses. Mayor Paul Smart is urging Freestone residents to please be patient, a full-blown investigation commences next week."

"Well, the whole plausible deniability thing can only last so long, I guess."

"That's your uncle's words," said Kevin glancing up. "Has your mum said anything?"

"Nah, our farm appears off limits to the authorites for now."

"Why's this all stirring back up again? There has to be a conncetion."

Baden sighed, heartily sick of the subject, but Kevin would not let it go. "What's with your interest?" he asked. "You're usually focused on your own untried projects."

Kevin tapped his head. "I still keep an ear to the ground, on occasion."

"Nope." Baden turned, detecting evasion. "Wrong answer. Who've you been talking to?"

"No one."

"Kevo, pretence is overrated. Lying is worse"

"So many friends to keep track of." Kevin looked back at the oval. "Some attractive, others genetically impaired, throw in a black dude, and a real lot of Asian ..."

Baden was not deceived. "You're socially retarded. Besides your extended family, the only friends you have in this world are me and Ford." He leaned closer, suspicious. "If you say Alexa ..."

"I won't then."

"No! You know the rule!"

Kevin placed his tablet computer clear of the debate. "Never talk to ..."

"Alexa Noble," Baden cut in. "She's twisted, off her meds. No longer in possession of her faculties and a crazy bitch!"

"You've really got to let the hate go. She's a little quirky, idiosyncratic. In a good way."

"Hah!" Baden leaned back. "Word of the day goes to 'quad eyes' over here. Quirky is a loose term. Since she rolled back into town with her old man, that family's been nothing but trouble."

"That was like ten years ago. I think someone's still riding the judgy factor pretty hard. Your folks were tight back in the day."

"Alexa say that?" Baden leaned forward, running a hand over his head, ruffling his dark hair. "There's enough history between our families to live my life over several times, but none of it's to do with me."

"Alright, I'll make sure I check in with you next time. Mind my own business, remain the awkward little Asian guy with just two friends ... apparently."

"You know what?" Baden punched him in the shoulder. "We gotta find you a chick, someone who'll ... Hey!" He jumped up. "Told ya. Ford'll never learn."

"Detention for sure," muttered Kevin, shielding his eyes, looking at the oval. "That's gotta be his fifth violation."

Baden shook his head watching Mr Robinson, the college computer teacher, march across the football field, back straight while pointing at the shirtless student who came to a halt, throwing back his head in disgust.

Robinson immediately set about writing up an infringement notice, while the guilty student pulled on his shirt, somehow looking pissed and smug at the same time.

Baden sneered. "Guess its Robinson's time of the month again, always giving the world his stink-eye ... everything by the book."

"You're such a homophobe," laughed Kevin.

"I know he's got a life partner, or whatever. That's not my problem. It's his amplified methods of controlling everything that breathes."

"Ford'll attest to that," laughed Kevin. "You hear about his so-called measures to get out of Robinson's class last week?" His hand gestured eerily, "Let me see your computer mouse ..."

"I think I know where you're going with this," laughed Baden. "Robbo's an arse but that is just too far for sense, even for Ford."

"Free will gone wrong," Kevin shook his head. "If only he'd use his powers for good. Do you know he used the same ploy on three other teachers ... in the same week! Old Mrs Gault was not happy when he insinuated her apparent come-on."

"Teachers talk." Baden shook his head. "And the end result?"

"Detention," sniggered Kevin, then added, "three days in a row after school, along with a written letter of apology to all Ford's victims."

"His hand'll cramp!" laughed Baden, watching the sulking student cross the oval. "The sheer volume of after-schools he's scored, you'd think he'd wise up with age."

"Fair to say," declared Kevin, "I want to be around the day he attracts some dude's interest in an actual legitimate sense."

"Creepville Ford, that show'll be priceless."

"If only he was more pedestrian like yourself." Kevin laughed at Baden's dropped jaw. "I mean, you know, an uncomplicated farm boy."

"What's that supposed to mean?"

Kevin grinned, glancing down the steps. "Nice striptease, superhero," he called out. "Did you get Robinson's number?"

Lance Fordham gave Kevin the finger while throwing himself down, stretching out long legs. "He must be on his rags or something."

Baden nudged Kevin. "I guess the love letter of apology hasn't faded the bullseye on his back?"

Lance rolled his shoulders, staring over the oval. "Laugh it up, dudes. If I wasn't around, you'd have nothing to talk about."

Kevin looked at Baden, raising an eyebrow. "You guys spend way too much time together, bringing on the déjà vu. Robbo's not that bad when you learn how he operates."

"Déjà … what? I keep tellin' ya, Kevo. *English*, dude." Lance looked around. "Keep the Chinese lingo thing on the down low, remember?"

Kevin sighed. "Maybe try French?"

"If it ain't in my default vocab, brotha, it ain't a word."

Clearly stunned, Kevin looked at Baden. "Did he really just say that?"

"Seriously, Kevo." Baden started chuckling. "He's reeling you in, *again*."

"But … his argument can only be justifiable to the mentally impaired."

Lance mimed winding a fishing rod before scrunching up the infringement notice, taking aim and shooting for a bin several rows down, scoring a dead centre. Linking his hands behind his head, he leaned back.

"Justifiable enough to me, bud."

Kevin sputtered. "Well, sorry to your African slash American heritage! Half your language is cut up." Kevin sat forward in earnest. "Let's simplify this, you realise only twenty-five percent of the world's population has any kind of understanding of language …"

"And you realise every time you start throwing up facts and figures …" Lance's long back fingers covered his face, "all I'm thinking of is titties."

Kevin immediately puffed up. "Then how does the rest of the world communicate, genius?"

Lance thought for a moment and to Baden's surprise came up with something probable. "Gotta be sign language."

"Okay!" Baden stood, stretching his legs. "We're wasting oxygen on this."

"Like a moth to my flame." Lance looked around, teeth flashing. "Anyway Zheng, you heading out with us on Friday? Annual town festival, it's gonna be double the size of last year. Lots of babes."

"Yeah, but for more reason than chasing skirt." Kevin shoved his tablet computer into his backpack.

"Compared to what? Alcohol lowers the inhibitions." Lance leaned back to slap his stomach. "That's when men of the world take advantage to pull a lady's interest."

Baden snorted, hiding it with a cough. "I was just saying we need to find him some female companionship."

"Plenty of time to mack on chicks at uni in a couple of years." Kevin stood to dump his rubbish in a close bin. "Besides, the type I'm interested in aren't around here."

Lance looked at a group of girls sitting on the oval. "You can't bag out what you haven't tried, man."

Kevin rolled his eyes, but Baden had a good idea what was going through his friend's mind. "You've entered the Youth Inventors contest again."

"Kevo ..." Lance looked around shaking his head, then burst into laughter. "Good to see you're changing things up."

"This is it. My year," Kevin vowed. "I've got it. I know I do. Besides, it's my last chance."

"Sixteen's the cut off?" Baden had not realised there was an age limit.

Kevin nodded. "So, I've got to make it count, which means going all out. Not only locally appealing but globally. First prize is big dollars, too."

"Well, your track record hasn't been consistent." Baden winced, but he had to be honest. "Maybe keep it simple, man. Your overreaching tends to come up a little short."

"Come on Cass, his experiments blow people's minds. Literally," laughed Lance. "Remember when that high-pressure bottle like full on detonated the display stand? CFA loved that unnecessary call in. The adjudicator's hairless from the neck up."

Kevin's mouth flattened. "It was an experimental fuel derived from water and graphite, burns cleaner then propane. It was supposed to be well-suited for cooking." Glancing at Lance, he looked worried. "You serious? Her hair hasn't grown back yet?"

"It's only been a year." Baden shrugged. "She's still wearing a wig and drawing on eyebrows."

"Well it's as they say …" Kevin looked aggrieved. "Experience is a harsh mistress. Give me ten years and I'll make some hair growth product, first prescription for her is free."

Lance brightened suddenly. "Year before that was your attempt to regulate human behaviour. No free will sounds like the way to go."

"It was a biotech system that turns neurons in the brain on and off through cycling different colours of light," corrected Kevin. "I tested it on Bob the rat, and it made him turn in specific directions."

"Damn! Bob the rat!" Baden slapped his leg. "What happened to that furry little sack?"

Kevin's mouth closed.

"Experience is a harsh mistress?" Baden guessed.

"He may have developed some psychosomatic issues. In the end I think he forgot how to breathe."

"Maybe it was a voluntary act to opt out." Lance jumped to his feet. "Good luck this year, homeboy."

"Look," Kevin said, picking up his backpack. "My track record isn't great, but all those were testing grounds. Like Cass's grandma says, 'hard work bears fruit.' This year, the scientific community will embrace a new up-and-comer."

Baden nodded sagely. "Sure. Just don't involve anything that breathes. Or is flammable."

Kevin eyed his friends. Baden felt like he was being assessed. Dropping his backpack again, Kevin yanked out a box, cracking it open.

Lance looked across. "That box looks iron."

"Try lead, and you'll see why." On a bed of dark blue velvet sat a crystalline stone in its raw state, murky white in colour.

Baden shook his head. "If that's Freestone Crystal, you'll lose, man. It's everywhere in the valley, just jump in Freestone River."

"True, but this one's different." Kevin held it up for inspecting. "It was removed from a growth vein over twelve months ago. No erosion, no degradation. Look." Baden and Lance leaned a little closer while Kevin carefully turned it over. "Freestone Crystal with no discernible deterioration."

Intrigued, Baden accepted the crystal shard, turning it over. About the size of a marble, it was slightly irregular in shape. It also felt warm, and had no flecks or particles marring the white. The longer he held it, the warmer it became. Unnerved, he handed it back.

"Independent crystals are really rare," he said, remembering a school project. "Only a handful have ever been harvested because they require some expensive procedure. I guess it's cool, but how are you going to use it as an entry?"

Kevin's smile widened. "Give me your mobile," he said, holding out his hand. After Baden passed it over, he placed the crystal on top. "Now we wait."

Baden and Lance stood watching. Seconds turned into minutes and the pair saw nothing of consequence.

"So, death by boredom's ya plan?" Lance yawned. "Maybe try and pull a swifty and steal first prize when everyone's passed out."

Baden snorted. Kevin didn't respond, but took the crystal off Baden's phone and handed the device back to him.

"Well?" Baden shrugged, turning his mobile phone over. "That's it?"

"Check the battery," suggested Kevin.

"What the?" Baden glared at Kevin. "You've drained my phone to three percent charge. Is this some weird-arse phone hack?"

"The crystal draws in all sorts of energy, even human body heat. I was warned to not hold onto it for any length of time."

"Warned?" Baden's eyes narrowed, already guessing the answer. "Who gave you the crystal?"

Kevin made a job of replacing the stone in the case. "No one in particular."

"Kevo?"

"Now you know why I was talking to Alexa."

Lances eyes widened. "Noble? The weird chick? Where'd she come by that?"

"Well," Kevin shoved the lead box back in his backpack. "She was evasive on specifics, but who cares? I'm going to win. This crystal is the holy grail, fellas."

Baden roughly grabbed his backpack. "This's why I made the rule never talk to a Noble. She'll want something. Be warned, there'll be strings attached."

Lance scratched a hand over his head, pulled at his shirt. "Alexa's old man's seriously loco. Talk around town is that's why he left all those years ago. He was in a loony bin ... some mental hospital in the city. You know the founding town's Fellowship had something to do with it." Suddenly he looked down, lifting his shirt. "What do you know? I'm missing four buttons."

"Speaking of mental stability." Baden leaned forward, eyeing an angry looking cut on Lance's ribs. "What the hell's that, man?"

Instantly, Lance tensed his stomach muscles. "You eyeballing me rippin' six pack?"

"No, that." Pointing, Baden straightened. "Looks like one of Kevin's ancestors time skipped to take a swing at you with a damn Samurai sword!"

"Don't get ya panties in a bunch, it's nothin' but a flesh wound, that's a little fleshier than usual."

Baden grinned, eyeing Kevin mumbling darkly beneath his breath. One thing his mate hated was historical inaccuracy, especially when it related to the Zheng family heritage.

After zipping his backpack, Kevin hefted its weight, intentionally knocking into Baden, who laughed good naturedly.

"Ignoring Cass's creative analogy that somehow connects my Chinese heritage to the Japanese Samurai," he said, pulling a pained face, "do we dare ask how you got that?"

"Haven't a clue," Lance scratched around the cut. "I thought Asians from all over used to do the slice and dice." Pausing, Lance glanced at Baden, "What's that code they used to follow? Sounds ... err ... like 'bushy', but not."

35

"The word's Bushido," Kevin ground out, clearly aggravated.

"That's it!" Lance's white teeth flashed. "The whole 'work equals perfection' thing. It's built into your DNA, man." Yanking down his shirt, he clapped his hands. "History's one complicated mind-bender."

"I guess there's a fine line between perfection and honour ... and it's called Ford," Baden said with a laugh.

"Ford's ability to oversimplify everything," complained Kevin, "makes me wonder how he ever passes a class."

"Maybe intellect combined with physical prowess isn't linked, hey Kevo?" Baden tried removing the fuse since Kevin looked ready to detonate. "Just remember, placing generality over the past removes true historical substance and meaning."

Lance blinked several times, then bowed toward Baden. "Step back, son. Mind equals blown. Probably should write that one down."

"Seriously, Cass?" Kevin did not look impressed. "You're giving him zero hope for academic growth. That much attitude will require years of correction." He started down the stairs before turning and calling back, "And referencing my history speech from year seven? That means my words had an impact on you."

Not waiting for a response, Kevin continued to trudge down the stairs, leaving Baden chuckling as he followed. "It's a good thing I never mentioned your secret weapon for that science fair shindig. Would've got some looks."

Back in form, Lance jogged ahead to shoulder Kevin. "He's talking about ya hidden gun, the sex robot?"

Kevin glared daggers at Baden, before turning on Lance. "No Ford, there will be no sex robot. Stop asking."

Lance straightened, craning his head to look around the seats. "Gotcha, keepin' the sexy machine low profile ... but remember, when ya need a tester." He tapped his chest, winking.

"My presentation's on the crystal." Kevin shook his backpack, hoisting its weight evenly over his shoulder. "I'm demonstrating it as a renewable energy converter that can power any electrical device. At least, that's what I'm proposing. "

Single minded, Lance wiggled his eyebrows. "I can take a shower after using it if that's bothering you."

The sight of Kevin's eyes bulging had Baden holding up a hand. "Ford—" Then the sentence penetrated. "Isn't the idea to take one beforehand?"

"Nah!" Lance slapped Kevin on the shoulder. "Pointless dwags, when I'm done deflowering that thing, it'll be me that's needin a decent clean-up."

"Okay, so many images running through my mind..." Baden shook his head, desperate to clear them. "Descecration of that magnitude would need an inbuilt self-destruct function."

"Damn, what were we even talking about?" laughed Lance, scratching his head. "Talk about detour."

"The Youth Inventors Contest," growled Kevin, clearly at the end of his tether. "And by no chance is it some kind of artificial sex thing!"

When the bell rang, Lance took the lead, Baden and Kevin following.

"Easy, man, it's all good play." Baden frowned, realising how strung out he was. "What I wanna know is how'd Alexa get that crystal? She can't have harvested it herself."

"She talked about some extraction process, used words even I'd never heard. Said the process couldn't be replicated."

"Why?"

"Because the key item's no longer around. It's something I've never even heard of."

Suspicious, Baden pulled Kevin up by his backpack. "What was it? The item that was used?"

"She said it was called a spawn-deracinator."

Galactic Star Key: Zozes Karbroe
Astral Nav-Coordinates: EAS-APL-4
Data Sequence: 3.0

Through a containment screen on the second level's observation booth, Zozes watched his brother move from the decon-bay into medical, passing through a charged purification beam imbedded in the doorway. All contaminants would have been removed.

A quarantine zone had been initialised, dividing the lower level into separate holding wards. All survivors from the Blade Ship were being kept in isolation, med-therapy protocols underway to reverse damage from subspace radiation exposure.

Kaze looked anything but enthused, brown hair sticking up untidily as he ran a hand through it. Obviously, the medical testing was taking its toll. Told to lie down again on the grav-bed, a horizontal scan began shifting electrified waves over his body.

The instant the procedure was complete, he was up again, prowling medical, looking for escape and mumbling to himself.

An older physician walked into the room next to Zozes, Commanding Medical Officer Sinvalo. Glancing briefly in Zozes' direction, she nodded before crossing to a cyber control screen.

Enough with the testing, thought Zozes, recognising the data Sinvalo was uploading was his brother's. He had to speak to someone about their situation. Stepping from the observation booth into the med-lab, he found an unfamiliar face calibrating a hi-cap glove before slipping it on. She set about generating a cyber-trigger over her fingers to connect and control the lab's cybernetic systems. When she looked up, it was with an odd expression, one he found hard to define.

"Lieutenant Gateo isn't on this rotation?" he asked.

Once the cyber-clasp was fully materialised, she shifted, quickly bringing up a series of cyber-screens that displayed his brother's spawn-net. "The MO has been reassigned. Sinvalo is quite particular about project efficiency. I've been called in as a replacement."

Zozes crossed his arms. "So, you're here to save what's left of our crew?"

"It would seem so." The doctor eyed him before adding, "You and your brother presented as ... exceptions."

"The Chief suspended our revival."

"Yes, I read your report." Like she was choosing her words with care, the doctor said, "I fear by the next moon cycle of this planet, most will have succumbed to radiation poisoning."

For Zozes, it felt like he was back on the ship, every system going critical all over again. Grasping the only lifeline he could see, he asked, "But not all?"

"You should prepare, Blade." Looking back at the cyber-screen, she added a few notes. "Interesting how your Chief chose to save your lives over that of the entire crew."

Though her tone was light, Zozes had to reign in a dark response, the faces of those in the evac-bay, those he had served with on so many missions, constantly crowding his mind. "None will survive?"

"Were you close with the crew? I noted your log-in Key to observation level has been accessed numerous times since your arrival."

Zozes took an uncomfortable step back, confused by her question and interest.

"I apologise," said the doctor, noticing his hesitation. "For my curiosity and the harsh assessment, but some may surprise us."

Zozes eyed her blonde hair and young face, his gaze finally settling onto her identifier. "Doctor Venlara?"

"Thaytis Venlara," she affirmed. "I'm going over the telemetry from your brother's scan." Easing back from the generated cyber-screen, she tipped her head smiling. "You disapprove of my appointment, Blade?"

Obviously caught, Zozes stumbled on a reply. "The Galactic Force Medical Department operates their division well enough."

"Do they?" Thaytis crossed her arms. "Why aren't I convinced? Perhaps you'd feel better if you examined my credentials personally?"

"Of course not." Zozes straightened, the movement just short of coming to attention. "That is …"

"Relax, Blade." Thaytis returned to her work running through his brother's bio-map. "Your response confirms that you are the senior Karbroe. I was informed your appreciation for humour is somewhat … slow growing."

"You've been talking to Kaze."

Thaytis smiled. "Earlier this morning. I observed one of his examinations, and he had a lot to say about you, but curiously less about himself."

"You realise why, of course," Zozes crossed his own arms. "That's his way of deflecting. He loathes being tested, or having anything wrong with him."

The doctor leaned over the control terminal. "Believe it or not, I caught that one myself." Straightening, she began running through the main terminal's start up sequence which immediately generated multiple cyber-screens.

She was still wearing an amused expression, Zozes noticed, making him feel like he was the one under scrutiny.

"Commence verbal entry log," began Thaytis. "Kaze Karbroe's spawn-net has again rejected the recalculated blockade system we have added in the attempt to sever his connection as Blade Alpha. It appears all injected medical-bots' countermeasures are being assimilated by his infused spawn-cells, recycling these components to bolster its own replication production. Meaning," she said, looking at Zozes, "the Blade's own biomechanical network has somehow produced defensive countermeasures. All efforts to downgrade his status from Alpha and reinitialise his previous ranking status as a standard Blade Officer have been for naught." Tapping her chin, Thaytis frowned. "This response is something never before recorded." She passed over several screens of information, the cyber-trigger on her hand making the motion almost indiscernible as it separated and moved data. "It's been seven planet rotations since subject began treatment, yet we are still no closer to downgrading his spawn-net or breaking his dual-pairing to the Link-Trone."

"Your idea is to downgrade his system and sever his control over the Trone?" Unnerved, Zozes approached her to interrupt. "Command wants me as sole operator over the Link-Trone?"

"Pause verbal entry log." Thaytis took a moment to study his obvious alarm. "Those are my orders."

"Resistance to injected medical-bots could mean a positive spawn-net has been established between him and the Link-Trone," Zozes reasoned. "He's been stable for days, together we may be able to operate the Trone."

"That's a big leap, Blade. Although it appears the spawn-cell types within your brother are highly active. I admit, I've never come across a central nervous system unibind between two Blades linked with an AI Link-Trone. And adding to that, a pairing that is resisting all disconnection countermeasures. The last option appears to be to alter the Trone's sync-pulse to weaken—"

"No." Zozes said curtly, shaking head. "That's out of the question. I was warned doing so could be fatal."

"Agreed, there is debate." Thaytis sighed, looking at him squarely. "However, not all share that theory."

"My own spawn-net could be compensating for his imbalance, stabilising the pairing between us and the Link-Trone."

When the doctor tapped her chin again, Zozes realised this accompanied deep thought on her part.

"You mean, wait until your dual-pairing fully matures?"

"We're blood, after all."

"Hmm. That's a consideration, and I'm sure a comforting one from your point of view. Perhaps it has merit, one I'll consider." Stepping away from the terminal, she asked, "May I?"

Zozes glanced at her outstretched hand. Confused, he placed his in hers, surprised at how warm they were. Thaytis generated a medical hi-cap glove, covering each finger and palm, right to the wrist. Turning his hand, she began running a finger gently over his palm.

"Don't be alarmed," she warned. "I'm tagging the outer dermis of your skin to connect to the injected med-bots. Through this connection, I can now personally monitor your spawn-net."

Zozes nodded, ignoring the heat building at the back of his neck. He blamed it on the warm energy seeping from the cyber clasp still evident over the hi-cap glove. In the blink of an eye, the skin around his hand flared, becoming translucent. He could see muscle, vein and even the bones of his hand. When she grasped his left hand to repeat the procedure, he was ready, though still uncomfortable, especially at the prolonged silence.

"I assume this won't be permanent." As soon as the words we out, Zozes felt like a fool, to the point he jerked his hand, which she steadied without comment.

While Thaytis worked, Zozes studied her bent head, noting the loose tendrils of hair escaping a lace-braid.

As if sensing his gaze, Thaytis glanced up, a smile playing at her mouth.

"Am I interrupting?"

At his brother's voice, Zozes resisted the urge to snatch his hand free, but barely.

Thaytis obviously felt that twitch, because she spoke quickly into the silence. "Just a little longer."

On a grin, Kaze sauntered forward. "Keep it right there, finish what you started, Doctor's orders."

After what seemed an uncomfortable wait where his brother smirked, Zozes was finally able to stand free. Thaytis dissolved the touch-scan device from her glove before moving to a cyber-screen to upload Zozes' physiological scans.

"Hands looking a little wet ... must have done good?" Kaze said with a grin, bumping Zozes' shoulder.

Zozes fought the urge to rub his palms on his uniform, watching the doctor expand two images on a large cyber-holographic bio-map display. On the left was Zozes' spawn-net in green, and on the right his brother's in blue. A flex of her index finger ignited a control-trigger at the tip. She then began marking points, using the tool to light up individual areas on each bio-map before overlaying the brothers' spawn-nets' layout schematics.

"From your preliminary testing with the Link-Trone, what you can see here is a stable sync-pulse flowing through Alpha Green's superimposed biomechanical network. This newly installed command update has enhanced his central nervous system, thus granting him the ability to control the AI."

"Good." Kaze nodded, eyeing the doctor. "So when is Command going to wise up and reinstate the LT back with our unit?"

"The AI's still in lockdown," Thaytis advised. "We need to verify that you are no longer in danger being paired with it, and that you and it are not a danger to anyone else."

"Huh." Kaze looked at Zozes, eyebrows raised. "At least Command got something right. I am dangerous."

Zozes rolled his eyes; his brother could never resist the opportunity to throw his weight around.

On a sigh, Thaytis interrupted. "Direct your attention here." Activating the control-trigger on her finger again, she began slowly following a line from the brain into the spine, revealing a series of neural pathways feeding spawn-cells into the body.

"Artificial probes are moving through Alpha Green's central nervous system like they are endemic, natural to your body. See?" She activated several more spotter-points, targeting how the spawn-net moved, then enlarged the neural-TECH implant that had been insterted at the base of Zozes' cerebral cortex when he had become a Blade.

"If we move to your brother's, we can see the Link-Trone's sync-pulse that moves through Alpha Blue's neural pathways is clearly out of alignment." She moved to another control-trigger from Kaze's brain down to spine.

Serene, Kaze leaned back against the bio-bed, arms crossed. "I feel fine," he assured, even offering a cocky grin making Zozes wonder how he was not bothered. "The headache's not as bad and fewer bloody noses."

That grin, Zozes knew, often accompanied trouble. Shoving a hand over his hair, he made certain the long strands were held behind his ears.

Oblivious, Thaytis continued her diagnosis. "Your neural-TECH works as a receiver to the Link-Trone's Positronic Drive, programming and replenishing new spawns-cells that are to be adapted into your body's biomechanical network."

It took Zozes a moment to chew over this information. "So, when the Trone's sync-pulse does not align with Kaze's spawn-net, it creates incorrect spawn-cell types that are not adaptable to his body."

"I've a solution," interjected Kaze. "Get Command to release the LT back to us, then it can do its job to stabilise my network."

Thaytis shook her head. "It's a little more complicated than that, Blade."

"Wait." Kaze straightened from the bio-bed. "If I'm understanding any of this, we need the LT to continue programming new, upgraded spawn-types until they fully adapt to my spawn-net."

"In the ideal situation that would be so."

"The problem isn't going to correct itself," Kaze said with a shrug. "After all your attempts, I've still got the same spawn-types warping about my body like they're on some kind of space run. And they're not accomplishing much."

"Let me—"

"No." Kaze shook his head. "This is cannibalised Primordial Technology you're dealing with. I'm not your play study. We need a Blade Optive Specialist, not a doctor."

"Kaze," Zozes jumped in. "We have to work with the resources available, and there isn't an Engineering Chamber on this ship."

"Don't get my mouth running on that fact," growled Kaze. "Because that just gets me wondering why there hasn't been another chamber re-systemised for us and our Link-Trone."

"I know you're frustrated, but there have been developments." Thaytis looked at him squarely. "And you're right, this isn't my exact field but I'm by no means deficient. I've studied the technology, it's always held such fascination. I know I can make a difference."

"She's fascinated?" Kaze rolled his eyes, looking at Zozes. "That makes all this so much easier. Enlighten me on your 'fascination' doctor."

"Kaze, let it go."

"Very well then, Blade," Thaytis interrupted. Zozes decided to give up on the clearly impossible task of making peace between the two as the doctor turned back to her cyber-screen. "I'll break it down further. Spawn-cells are based upon ancient intra-dimensional particles used to control different elements that make up our galaxy." Pausing, she eyed the two. "You both understand that, right?" At their nods, she continued. "Sorge-spawn, for instance, can influence all energy types, biolen-spawn can manipulate all organic ..."

Zozes watched as Kaze started blinking, looking from the doctor to him. He would not have been surprised to see his eyes cross.

"Still have a problem, brother?" Zozes lifted an eyebrow. "The doctor seems qualified enough to me."

Kaze scratched his jaw. "To be honest, I'm space-docked back at the word intra-dimensional. What the vok does that mean?"

"Basics of spawn-wielding," Thaytis said. "Unless the Blade Mark Two program has somewhat softened its research assessments."

"I've a cyber-graphic memory," said Kaze.

Zozes rolled his eyes. "He now crosses the threshold to bring forth a lie."

"Interesting." Thaytis looked hard at Kaze. "I never noted that ability while profiling your Star-Key."

"The Blade Instructors believed it would be unjust to other candidates if I abused it," said Kaze jutting his chin. "No point securing victories on all fronts."

Clearly not amused, the doctor turned back to her work station. Via her cyber-clasp, she reduced Kaze's diagram to open window after window that displayed research on Primordial Technology demonstrating her more than passing interest in the Blades and their spawn types.

Zozes gave a low whistle. "Looks to me she has a more vested interest than the casual observer."

The doctor raised an eyebrow. "Like I said, it's an attractive subject."

"Enough with the dissecting, before you reach some kind of system overload," Kaze said with a wave his hands, trying to halt her. "I'm suitably satisfied you can handle this, even if you're starting to look a little *overly protective* in displaying your grasp on the topic. Still doesn't change that you don't have the resources to deal with this."

"Like an Engineering Chamber for upgrading and servicing Blade functions?"

"Isn't it just my fortune," griped Kaze, while pointedly indicating the doctor, "that my treatment is to be reassigned to a TECH-*jaw* doctor who wrestles an issue to her submission just to prove a point."

Zozes knew Kaze was reaching his limit of what he often referred to as over exaggerated use of technical language to explain a concept, especially when the doctor appeared to have an answer for everything he threw at her.

"An engineering team has been working on modifying a Chamber to your specifications, but developments have halted that," said Thaytis.

Kaze glanced at Zozes. "I'm still finding it hard to believe that out of all the docked Task Force ships on this Station, no other Blade officers are among them."

"Err ..." Thaytis glanced from one to the other. "Who gave you clearance on that knowledge?"

"No one intentionally, that's for sure."

Eyes narrowed, Zozes shifted before his brother. "Who told you this?"

"I overheard it during what they called the 'inducement procedure'. Just before I was placed in a stasis-sleep."

"You could hear us?" Thaytis' eyes rounded. "During your testing?"

"Enough to learn that fact," he growled. "Then everything went dark. You can blame Doctor Gateo for that little breach of information."

It was the first time Zozes had ever seen the doctor look uneasy. "Are there others?" he demanded.

"I'm afraid specifics are classified, Blade. All I can say is that every active Blade officer within the fleet are beyond these vessels."

"You're speaking as if they're on the Primordial Station?" Zozes tried to sift meaning from her words. "They're not on any of the Task Force ships?"

Thaytis nodded. "I can't say more."

"So we're a particular Blade type," Kaze sneered. "Basically, rare and crippled by stand-down orders that treat us more like prisoners. Not allowed to take one step off this ship." He glared at Zozes. "Great time to serve and defend."

"Endure," suggested Thaytis, collapsing the excess of cyber-screens. "Your outcome depends on the testing module program we're about to place you through. Pass that and you will be cleared and granted access to the Station."

"Doctor." Kaze raised an eyebrow. "I know this unibind dual-pairing is a new thing to all of us. Maybe give it some time and a little freedom to move?"

"Time is something you don't have, Blade," Thaytis replied. "Your original solo-operator protocol has activated and is attempting to seize control."

"Wait, what?" Zozes shook his head, momentarily studying her words. "Makes sense that his solo-spawn-net would trigger when we're disconnected temporarily from the Link-Trone."

"I do seem to attract the complications," Kaze said with a shrug.

"It's more than a complication," said Thaytis. "Our issue lies in the fact your spawn-net is fighting between what you were and what you have become."

"I'm still not following."

But Zozes was, and he did not like what it meant. "He could still revert, even without your interference?"

"Partly." Thaytis stood, rubbing her head, pulling several strands free of the braid. "How about I put it this way. You completed the Blade program, acquiring your rank as a non-command operator to a Link-Trone. Meaning you never acquired the skill to command a Link-Trone, only to connect with it, like the rest of your unit. Only Blades who have completed Blade Command training and reached the rank of Alpha can be a Command Operator of something as powerful as a Link-Trone."

"I get that," said Kaze. "But now I am an Alpha."

"Your body does not agree," Thaytis stated. "It's fighting to establish what exactly you are. Do you command or do you follow?"

Kaze clenched his jaw. "Are you asking or telling me?"

Trouble was afoot again. Zozes was surprised his brother had kept up as much as he had in light of his usual wandering mind.

Thaytis ignored the rhetorical question. "Solo-spawns are working against newly established command spawns passed from the Link-Trone."

"So it's a rolling effect," Zozes said slowly. "The sync-pulse forms incorrect command spawns from the Trone, triggering the established solo spawn-net, which also forms spawn-cells in an attempt to correct the issue. One fighting the other."

"I'm getting a headache, but for a whole other reason," Kaze muttered, leaning against the grav-bed. Eyeing the schematic, he added, "This is why we need the Trone now. Command has to trust I can become an Alpha!"

At the annoyed look Thaytis threw Kaze, Zozes sighed. It appeared Doctor Venlara did not appreciate being questioned.

"My orders are to safely downgrade your system and apprise you of the situation as we proceed. That's my duty, Blade."

"We understand that," said Zozes, breaking up the back and forth. "You think Kaze can't handle the pull-and-push on his spawn-net."

"He can't," she stated firmly. "The mixed messages will begin to confuse the brain to the point it may shut down. There are limits on how far I will let this go."

"You're trying to break down my command network?" Kaze demanded.

"Yes. It's the logical course of action as you are not qualified to operate as an Alpha and you did not complete the Blade program to become one."

"That's an opinion," Kaze shot back. "I passed all trials except one, Doctor."

"That's a fact, Blade."

"You're speaking of the Psychological Command Examination," Zozes said.

"Yes." Thaytis eyed the two brothers. "I believe it's one of the most valued components in establishing mental ability, without which a Link-Trone cannot be successfully operated."

Face set, Kaze met the doctor's eyes. "I'm not liking your tone. Do we have a problem here?"

"Yes, we do," she replied. "The spawn operations are opposing one another, fighting between the assimilation and replication processes. Internally your body has become a battlefield, neural pathways are being flooded by copious amounts of spawns and those two very different spawn-types are waging war in an endless cycle."

"That's the reason for the faint electrical sync-pulse?" Zozes asked.

"Exactly," Thaytis said. "This creates a loop where command solo spawn types are focusing upon assimilating and using material for replication to overcome one another. When one spawn-type establishes control, your body will properly align to the Link-Trone's sync-pulse."

"How long will that take?" Zozes asked, eyeing his brother.

When the doctor hesitated, Kaze thundered, "I'm climbing the walls here! Sounds to me like you're no closer to a solution than when this all started!"

"I understand your frustration," Thaytis said soothingly, "but I can't discharge you or put forth a recommendation to Astral Guard Command until this problem has been overcome."

"Astral Guard?" Zozes eyebrows drew together. "We answer to Galactic Force."

Thaytis shook her head. "This is no ordinary Station, Blade. All of us report to the authority of Astral Guard here."

"I see." Kaze clapped his hands like he was mulling something difficult over. "Clearly there's only one option left. A little thing I like to call trust." Zozes groaned. Kaze ignored him. "We've been told a dual-pairing can handle all complications, that my body will adjust."

"Really?" Thaytis crossed her arms. "By whom?"

"Our squad's former Blade Chief, which is good enough for me."

"I can't go on your superior's word alone. We are working on a means to access the instillation protocols from the Blade Engineering Chamber used during the pairing process."

Pairing process? This meant only one thing to Zozes. "You're saying our Engineering Chamber is intact?"

Obviously thrown, the doctor briefly closed her eyes, remaining stubbornly silent.

"Another classified oversight?" griped Kaze. "Your commission on this station is going to be shortlived if you continue to run words without thinking."

Rather than provoke, Zozes tried a different tack. "The emergency jettison system launched vital componenets before crash landing. We saw them during the jump."

"That's standard," said Kaze. "Is it operational?"

"Blades, I've said enough — too much," said the doctor. "In time, you will know."

"So, what the vok are we even doing here? You've clearly made up your mind!" Kaze spat, thumping his fist onto the bio-bed.

"You understand your Chief broke protocol? The Ministry of Defence designates all Official Blade Alphas. What happened on board your ship is an ongoing investigation, one that hasn't cleared either of you," she added.

"Doctor," snarled Kaze, "you and your—"

Zozes moved between the two, flashing his brother a look that clearly told him to back off. He then turned to the medical officer. "So one of the reasons you're keeping us here is because you believe our Chief deliberately compromised the mission?"

"All I know is that the matter is still under investigation."

Zozes felt Kaze's chest meet his hand as he stepped forward, but he could not halt his brother's angry words.

"You're placing blame on the Chief? Accountability and loss of lives to the mission? You have no right to discredit her name. If it wasn't for her, my brother and I wouldn't be alive, nor would those in that medical ward." With that, Kaze moved to the door.

"You're still not cleared," Thaytis called after him.

"Doctor, if I stay here, I'll do something you and I'll both regret," he threw over his shoulder as he stormed off.

An awkward silence followed, before Zozes said, "I'll talk to him later."

"He's very intense," Thaytis murmured thoughtfully. "It wasn't my intention to offend, and if I have, I apologise. I'm just following orders."

"I understand. But you should understand, after losing our parents in the Kadra Civil War, our Chief became ..." Zozes paused, searching for the right words. "More than a mentor and leader. She was like family for both of us, but even more so to Kaze."

"They both took part in the Kadra Civil War?" Thaytis was clearly surprised, her expression almost perplexed.

"Our father served, he was in command of a squad on board a Galactic Force Galaxy Ship. It intercepted a distress call on the border of the Kagar Expanse, and was tracked to the declared Armistice Planet, Voe'ga Five. The ship was seized and most of the crew were captured by a Kadra Outcast Sect."

"They were lured there?" Thaytis shuddered, clearly sickened.

"Yes. The planet had been overrun by Kadra, killing all Galactic Forces. Their Blade Commando squadron on board fought to the last."

"Your father?"

Zozes, nodded. "He was one of the last Blades, amongst only a very few survivors. He was hunted down and executed."

"Do you know who within Kadra Outcast Sect was responsible?"

Zozes fought to keep his composure, but some wounds cut deep. "At the time, it wasn't just the Kadra Outcast Sect. We learnt that the Kadra Prime leader's son, Cedos Garrold, made it his personal task."

"The Garrold name was once a highly respected in Northverse Astral States."

"Once," Zozes muttered, "but no more. Because of those actions, Cedos Garrold became an outcast to even his own kind."

"I'm sorry." Thaytis stepped back, noticing his discomfort. "Your anger is understandable, especially carrying a wound like that. I shouldn't have brought it up."

Zozes sighed, fighting to relax, find the calm that was his inner balance. "Both Kaze and I swore vengeance on all Garrolds that day. It's the reason we joined the Blades."

At that moment, a Galactic Force ensign entered, ending the conversation.

"Can I help you, Ensign," she glanced at his identifier, "Clarkov."

"Acting-Ensign, Sir. Commodore Vae'gon has ordered me to escort the Blades to the missions office."

"I see." Thaytis glanced at Zozes, professional once more. "I'll notify you if I find anything you need to be aware of. One last matter I must speak of. Knowing how well your brother takes new information, it's probably best you explain to him …"

At her hesitation, Zozes tilted his head. "Doctor?"

"If he is cleared for duty and retains Alpha status, he is never again to initiate a spawn-drift cycler with the Trone on his own. Understood?"

Silent, Zozes digested this for several moments. "He explained it was instinctual, that when he jumped from the ship during the crash, taking the Chief and myself, he knew what was about to happen. To be honest, I don't know how he managed to perform such an advanced technique."

"We have our theories," Thaytis admitted. "Your unique dual-pairing opened him to abilities he should not have had access to without proper command training. Be warned, the next time, it—"

"Could kill him." Zozes had already come to that conclusion.

Thaytis stared at him for a moment. "We don't know, but be assured the damage may be irreparable."

"Thank you, Doctor." He nodded before leaving without a backward glance.

Once out of the medical centre, Zozes followed Clarkov along the track-run corridor. After a couple of turns, he spotted his brother leaning against a wall, waiting. Falling in next to Zozes without a word, the three continued on.

Kaze was still angry; he had never mastered the impassive face Zozes had felt it necessary to cultivate.

"Ensign Clarkov," Zozes said, hoping to distract his brother's dark thoughts. "I noticed your identifier's additional tag designation. You're duty-arm to Commodore Vae'gon."

"Yes, Sir. Fourth year in service. It's a challenging role, but well worth it."

"A duty-arm?" said Kaze. "I don't understand why superiors require personal attendants in these times."

"It's an option for the non-commissioned to progress via field-training, bypassing Galactic Force Academy all together," Clarkov replied, seemingly unoffended as he entered the elevator first. "I prefer to learn out in the field." Once the doors closed on them, the ensign swiped the access panel using a porta-pad he detached from is belt. "I did initially complete entry, gaining senior-finest at the Academy."

There was no missing Kaze's surprise or confusion. "Well earned. Why aren't you serving as a Junior Lieutenant?"

Each movement deliberate, Clarkov grav-locked the porta-pad to his belt. "My physical makeup is incompatible with cybernetic neural-TECH."

"Oh." Kaze grimaced.

Zozes nodded in sympathy. "I've heard the odds. Bad luck."

"Yes." Straightening his uniform, Clarkov looked ahead. "I still wanted to serve, do my part. I've been charged with a manual operative porta-pad, but it still does not compare to an automatic networked neural-TECH linked to a subdermal porta-tool."

Zozes surveyed the young ensign with new eyes. "So, you used traditional practices when studying? Memorising data, reading, problem solving to gain knowledge?"

"I did."

"Vok." Kaze pulled a face. "We were both forced to endure traditional practice through the Blade Mark Two program. Not something I'd want to repeat long-term."

Clarkov said, "I understand the initial spawn-net instillation renders all candidates' subdermal implants inoperable until the spawn-net fully establishes."

"That's true," Kaze agreed. "The artificial cut-off effect lasts half the time of the program's operation."

"I can see why the Commodore keeps you close," Zozes said thoughtfully. "You're obviously skilled at retaining knowledge, and comprehending manual-tech operation."

The elevator doors opened and Clarkov lead the way out. "Discussion for another time perhaps. The Commodore is just through that door, Blades."

Zozes nodded, turning to enter.

"Blades, a moment." Clarkov glanced down the track-run corridor ensuring they were alone. Zozes leaned in, Kaze following suit. "Commodore Vae'gon temporarily holds full command over all Astral State Guard personnel on this Station. I'm sure you know that formal protocol differs from that of Blades."

"I've never been one to pay attention to formality," Kaze said. "The rule of order for addressing superiors is best left to the most well-adjusted mediator in this galaxy — my brother."

Eyebrow raised, Zozes asked, "And how many times has that saved your skin?"

"After entering," continued Clarkov doggedly, "it's customary to form at-stance. Do not break stance or show disrespect by engaging eye contact until he has given easement order. And certainly do not speak unless you're directly spoken too."

Before the ensign had finished, Zozes felt a headache brewing. Glancing at his brother, he muttered sarcastically, "This should be easy for you."

"Sounds to me like the Commodore's all about his rank and authority," Kaze declared sourly.

"He's waiting." Clarkov stepped to the side.

Zozes entered the office ahead of his brother, immediately taking at-stance. Kaze came next to him and followed suit.

State Commodore Vae'gon took his time standing and walking from behind his desk. Eyes narrowed, he measured the two, looking anything but approachable.

Eventually he gave the order. "At-easement."

Zozes noticed an Actrix High Priestess standing to one side. She said nothing, expression neutral as she observed, impossible to read behind the adornments of her headdress.

Something else is going on, Zozes thought. He had never before seen a Priestess collaborating with militarised operations.

"Blades. We finally meet." Leaning back against his desk, Vae'gon crossed arms over his barrel chest, the relaxed posture clearly a façade. "All telemetry from the Link-Trone has been downloaded, a report filed. It states that your previous Blade Chief triggered a series of events during a crisis that led to extracting a Link-Trone from its Engineering Chamber without proper authority."

Zozes felt Kaze's swell of anger, knew he was fighting valiantly to stay silent.

"This is fact," the Commodore continued. "And through these actions, lives and irreplaceable assets were lost, including twenty-nine Link-Trones."

Neither Zozes nor Kaze responded.

"I've conducted in-depth reviews of both of your Star-Key profiles." He spun a cyber-screen, pointing at several entries. "These tell me a great deal about your characters."

Vae'gon looked to Kaze. "Let's begin with you. Your last mission ended with you on a stand-down order after an altercation with a Astral Guard Enforcer."

"I don't recall filing that report, Sir." Kaze shoved out his chin.

One of Vae'gon's eyebrows rose as he looked at Zozes. "Your brother did."

Kaze's gaze flicked to Zozes in agitation.

Vae'gon eyed the report. "On several occasions, your brother stated you were of the opinion the Enforcer did not have the experience or ability to take command of a Blade Commando squadron. Colonel Pulmore is a good friend of mine, she has served with merit. I believe you are biased, Blade, that you pick and choose what orders you follow."

From the corner of his eye, Zozes eyed the curl of his brother's lip.

"Sir!" Kaze snapped. "This isn't gender related, if that's what you mean. Our counterparts in femininity excel in duty. Pulmore was a fool and in the way of completing the mission, in my opinion, Sir!"

"Did I ask for your opinion, Blade?" Vae'gon heaved off the desk. "The Blade Mark Two program is still in its infancy yet more and more, I'm seeing reports about officers who are questioning superiors' orders."

The Priestess moved to flank the Commodore, like she was seeking to add weight to the words. Zozes could have told her that Blades would not be intimidated.

"Blades are an effective force," Vae'gon continued, "but it has become apparent your *enhancements*," he sneered, "breed arrogance and disobedience. An infectious trait, one that must be stamped out. Rank equals respect without question, not when you see fit."

Expressionless, Zozes could see the Commodore was working up to something. When he eventually got there, he wanted to be prepared.

"To this end, you should both understand that when this report is discussed with Command, I will be expressing my opinion that the Blade Mark Two program should be terminated." Zozes looked briefly at the Priestess, unable to guage her intention on the matter.

He willed his brother to keep his mouth shut, but Kaze stared from the Commodore's stony face, to the Priestess. "Good luck with that, Sir."

"I don't believe in luck, Blade."

"Cryo-sleep may rearrange our minds, but only on waking. Our Blade Squadron responded to a communications blackout on this Station. Our crew," Kaze continued, "understood it could be a one-way trip, how dangerous our mission orders were, but they still stood. Our orders now are for us to report back to our Galactic Force superior, Commander Vome of the Space Traverse Fleet via the subspace layer map within our Engineering Bridge. Let her know the situation, Sir."

"Such orders," replied Vae'gon, "are now superseded. The Galactic Force has no power over Astral Guard affairs. Commander Vome's mandate is to establish a secondary remote base in this system to prepare for a planet Civilisation-ship."

At that, Zozes swallowed hard, fighting to stay silent himself. The Commodore was looking for a reason, any reason, to lock them both in a brig holding cell.

The Priestess turned to Zozes. "Alpha Green, you have something to add?"

For a long moment, Zozes eyed the Crimson Orb at the top of her staff. He chose his words carefully. "If any wrongdoing was done, I believe our Chief was compromised due to her injuries, the extended exposure to subspace radiation. That is what ultimately killed her, your Eminence."

"That will be taken into account, of course," the Priestess said reassuringly.

"You've already decided where to place blame." Kaze huffed a breath. "No point in dressing it up. I have nothing to hide, my conscience is clear." Looking directly at Vae'gon, he challenged, "Is yours, Sir?"

After a long moment, Vae'gon shook his head, clearly disgusted. "Dismissed." The brothers stood to attention before moving to leave as the Commodore added, "Alpha Green remain."

Zozes shot Kaze a warning look before turning back. As the door closed behind Kaze, Vae'gon leaned against the desk, smiling thinly.

"There's only one reason your brother is breathing free air and not locked within a holding cell. Can you tell me that reason?"

"The Link-Trone, Sir."

"You play things far smarter, Blade, I'll grant you that. Efforts are still underway to undo the damage your Chief has done. However, forcibly disconnecting your brother will not only damage him, but both you and the AI. I am left with one choice — you and the Trone together with your brother as an unbreakable unit."

"I understand, Sir."

"Oh, but you don't. Not yet, anyway. I have one more question regarding your brother." The Commodore glared at the door Kaze had exited through. "Can he be controlled?"

Zozes did not blink. "I'll make sure of it, Sir."

"Be sure you do or, no matter the cost, I will take what action is needed."

"Understood."

"You have an exemplary record, Alpha Green, one to be admired," he said, glancing briefly at Zozes' uniform. "If I had found anything different, we would not be having this conversation."

The Priestess moved closer, the flashing of her Crimson Orb distracting him. Zozes realised she was using it to evaluate his responses.

"These are dark times," the Priestess murmured ominously, "as you well know. Until now, the Blades have been the only thing standing between us and the Kadra. Disbanding them will be at a cost."

Zozes worked his jaw for a moment before saying, "Then why choose this action?"

"Control cannot be an illusion or we embrace anarchy. The Blades must not fall victim to the compulsions that lead the Kadra to turn against us. Your brother must learn control, or he may ultimately become a power that must be silenced."

"Not while I draw breath," he muttered.

The Priestess inclined her head gently. "Your Link-Trone is connected to more than you understand. Your Chief appears to have handed that other responsibility to you."

Zozes finally saw where this had been going all along. Turning from the Priestess, he eyed both her and the Commodore.

"Responsibility? You speak of her mission?" he swallowed before adding, "Sir."

"Yes, your Chief's original mission prior to landing on this Station." The Commodore looked at the Priestess. "In time, this will be revealed to you, but only when you are ready."

"At that time," added the Priestess, "the Actrix Gods will gaze upon your actions with gratitude. You will be their chosen champions. Are you aware that this Station is in fact constructed by the Primordial Race?"

Zozes took in the title, fighting to school his features. There was no way he would allow either himself or his brother to be seen as some type of religious ideal, let alone idol, in the ongoing debate that raged around the Primordial Race.

At least now he understood the size and complexity of the Station.

"It is faithfully written in the Actrix Gods' sacred scriptures, to the Reconciliation of the Twelve Actrix Planets. This world, Earth, will lead us not only to finding, but uniting the Twelve. The people of this planet have no knowledge of this Space Station that rings their world, hidden from them within subspace. They also have no knowledge of its ancient and revered past."

"You mean they're a pre-warp civilisation." Zozes' eyes rounded as he sought clarification. "Do they at least know life exists elsewhere?"

Commodore Vae'gon shook his head. "Which is why the Planetary Allegiance wants to initiate a pre-warp amendment, advancing their knowledge to bring this planet into the intergalactic community. Even as we speak, vital stages within our Astral Guard's Integration Task Force are underway to solidify this commitment."

"Which is, Sir?"

"The commencement of Global Reach. When that is finalised, this planet and its inhabitants will come to know they are not alone."

Galactic Star Key: Baden Casteel
Astral Nav-Coordinates: EAS-APL-4
Data Sequence: 4.0

Baden gave the suitcase a frustrated jerk, hauling it over a street curb. Ahead he could hear music rumbling, its sound echoing down the street he was trudging.

Mobile in hand, he glanced at the time, realising he was over an hour late. He tried to think of an excuse, one that did not sound laughable. Lance was going to have a field day when he spotted him hauling his cousin's hot-pink suitcase.

One of the wheels caught, sending it sideways and spiking his temper further. Yanking the handle, Baden kicked and cursed. The case retaliated by ramming into his heel, almost sending him face first onto the footpath.

For a moment, he seriously contemplated dumping it next one of the old trees lining the street, but Ebony would have the marrow sucked from his bones. His aunt had been very swift in getting him to do this little favour, never once mentioning he would be dragging the monstrosity through the Founders Festival.

And could he think of an excuse on the spot to get out of it? No! Rolling the case through the gutter, water splashed on his leg. Groaning, he lifted the suitcase several steps before dropping it back on its wheels.

No good deed goes unpunished. How many times had heard his grandmother spout that one?

And what was with that smell? Reminded him of the souped-up scent found at some hair salon. Moving faster, he crossed beneath a bright street lamp to the other side of the street where trees older than him led to a back alley, the private entry to Freestone Valley's businesses. Picking up pace, he attempted to jog until the racket of the case slowed him.

At the end, he turned to see the main street was packed. He could hear kids screaming and cheering, and the Ferris Wheel in the distance looked full, multicoloured lights flashing. Maybe if he just barrelled through, he could avoid being seen by anyone from school.

Before he had a chance, his mobile vibrated, signalling a message. Lance was waiting near the fountain at Rock Water Park: *giving you another 5 man*

Shoulders sagging like an old man, Baden glared at the case. He'd just have to suck it up.

The music grew louder as he moved down the street, the clear night had brought out families in droves. Kids dodged around him as they ran, squealing louder than the girl singing on a makeshift stage to his right. She had drawn quite a crowd, a lot of them from his school.

The mood was infectious and even Baden had a smile on his face as he made his way along the footpath. Ahead, Lorraine's Café was lit up, every table full.

"Save the planet! Save the planet! Global Reach is the event that will define this decade. Find out the meaning behind the name on the first of October to become part of this significant event that will unite our planet! This pamphlet," the woman yelled, waving it madly, "will explain how!"

Baden watched as several official-looking people in blue uniforms began handing out brochures to people as they passed by.

The main street had been sectioned off, making room for food stalls, games and rides, countless people crowding around eating and talking. It surprised him to see so many stopping to listen, even to ask questions.

"Have you heard of Global Reach?"

Baden jerked to a stop as the older woman pinned him in her stare. Shaking his head, he attempted to go around. "Sorry, no time—"

"Time is all this world has left, my boy. How you spend it, how you live it, is up to you." She urged the pamphlet into his hand before walking away.

"Crazy old gammer," he muttered as he hurried down the street, trying not to run over people's toes. Glancing at the leaflet's picture, he saw the planet Earth ringed by a kind of Siegel. About to bin it, he noticed that all in the vicinity were overflowing with rubbish, and stuck it in his pocket.

Rock Water Park was crammed with people eating on picnic blankets, large groups of kids kicking footballs. A couple of dozen marquees were scattered over the park, some selling food, others offering tarot readings and other sorts of New Age wisdom that Freestone was known for.

Lance was nowhere near any of those. He was seated on the edge of the memorial fountain before its triple spray system, mobile phone in hand, jabbing out a message.

The moment he spotted Baden, he was on his feet. "What the hell, man?" His jaw dropped as he spotted the pink suitcase.

"Long story," Baden muttered, kicking at it. "Special delivery meant for Ebony's apartment."

"Dude, you must be tripping." He pointed at the case, as if Baden needed more attention. "Why's it still riding shotgun east of your feet?"

"She isn't there. Nina's out too. I was supposed to meet up with Myrick out front of his shop to let me in, but he was a no-show."

Struck with an idea, Lance held up a finger. "Give me a sec. Don't move."

"What're you—"

Lance stepped to the side, then swung back, mobile pointed to take a photo. "You're giving me so much material."

"Nothing like kicking a man when he's down."

Lance paused, taking a sniff of the air. "What's that smell I'm wiffin?"

Baden looked around. "I dunno, it's been haunting me since I was waiting outside Eb's apartment."

"Ugh." He looked from the case to Baden. "Something you ain't tellin' me? You been with a chick?"

"What? No!" Baden shook his head. "It's like a fifteen-minute hike from Eb's place."

"Dude, that's one weak cover story. C'mon, who was it?"

Baden ignored his nagging, glancing across the park. The assembly area was lighting up, a stage its central focus. On the right of that was the science exhibit.

"Let's touch base and see how Kevo's doing," he said, giving the suitcase a bad-tempered yank.

"So," Lance jogged beside him, kicking his heels in mid-air. "Let's hear the deets!"

"Kinda hard when she's a thought in your head."

"Cass." Lance looked ahead. "I need something legit to defend that smell, 'cos anything I come up with leads straight to queerville."

Baden was relieved to finally spot their friend's name printed next to his assigned table space, among about twenty others. Kevin appeared, carrying a load of equipment.

"Man, you ain't done with this yet?" Lance griped, glaring around.

"Nope," Kevin said, yelping as several items started slipping. "If someone doesn't lend a hand?"

Baden managed to catch them, placing them on the table. He'd never seen Kevin looked so stressed.

"Are you ..." Kevin leaned forward, sniffing at the air while looking at him strangely, "... wearing perfume or something?"

Teeth grinding, Baden pulled a face. "You can smell it too?"

With a cough, Kevin stepped back. "Yeah, potent blend. Really singes the nostrils."

"He's either been with a chick," Lance said with a shrug, "or he's heading for a gay bar after this."

Desperate to halt the conversation, Baden moved the suitcase, jabbing it into Lance's shin accidentally on purpose. He looked around at the other entries.

"What's the hold-up?" he asked, ignoring Lance's yelp of pain.

"The final judging was supposed to be an hour ago," said Kevin, starting to arrange his display. "Some kind of mix-up. Xavier Solomon is taking his father's place as Fellowship host for the Crystal Ceremony. Heaps of events have been postponed, and I thought they were going to cancel us, but after I made my case—"

"What's the timeframe?" interrupted Lance, rubbing his shin with his other foot.

"I don't know and I don't care, just as long it happens. The time slot for judging keeps getting pushed back …" When Lance swore, Kevin took pity. "Just head, I'll text you guys later when I find out more."

Baden hesitated until his mobile phone vibrated. Glancing at the message, he saw it was from his aunt. *Baden, I'm coming into town after all. Myrick rang, said he was held up. You can drop Ebony's suitcase at my café. Will be there in ten.*

"Yes!" Baden laughed. "Time to dump this heavy tub of lard. Ford, you wanna come with?"

Lance hesitated. "And be seen with you and your pink friend? I got better things to do."

"I'm dumping it at my aunt's café, man." Baden emphasised what came next, playing his trump card. "Then, we do the rounds."

"Or you can stay here." Kevin glanced up. "Help a brother set up?"

Lance shoved Baden's shoulder. "Family before duty, right?" he said, pushing Baden to the exit.

Baden grinned as Kevin yelled after them. "When I earn fame and fortune through sheer intellect and the power of science, guess who'll be buying new friends?"

The two laughed, making their way through the masses. Baden had to admit, Lance had a fair point, eyes kept sliding to the pink case rattling along behind them.

"You know," Lance grumbled, "the longer you keep that pink bitch with us, the further my rep's dragged down. Tonight's the night we gotta represent."

As if to prove Lance's point, a group of girls from the year level below theirs moved through the crowd.

One called out, lifting her phone. "What a cute couple! I hear pink's the new black, boys."

"Damn, they're taking a photo!" Lance growled, dodging clear. "Probably think we're some kinda unconventional gay couple."

Baden sneered at his horror. "Payback hurts, doesn't it?"

His friend's prattle faded as through the crowd he caught sight of olive-toned, faultless legs. When her head turned, swaying long brown hair in a hypnotic way, he knew, just *knew*, who it was. Only one girl looked like that.

Lance hissed, tripping over the case. "Damn man! What gives?" He followed Baden's shocked stare. "Gwen's back in town?"

Guinevere Solomon was walking with a group of friends that were clearly not from their school.

"Yeah." Baden finally found his voice. "She must be back for the festival."

"Haven't seen her for a couple of years. Damn fine crew she rolls with these days."

"Definitely from outta town."

Eyebrows shooting up, Lance looked from Gwen to Baden. "Still can't believe you got to play with that back in the day."

With an angry jerk, Baden pulled the case onto its end. "I was like eight, man. Had no idea what was what, let alone what to do with it."

"You're both descendants of the almighty Founding Families." He circled a finger in the air. "Hard to process the fact how tight ya folks used to be. The falling out, the big hate session your lot has now. That, I don't get."

"Long, complicated and boring. That's how my Uncle Rickard puts it, anyway."

"Alls I keep thinking is if history had played out differently, you could be having that all over ya body, like right now!"

"Cheers, man," Baden turned away, muttering darkly under his breath. "Always reaching for the inappropriate."

"Inappropriate what? Just sayin' whatcha thinking." Lance roared with laughter at Baden's stiff shoulders.

Baden would never admit that was true. He saw that Gwen's group had stopped at one of the Global Reach marquees and was looking over the information the women were giving out. There were an awful lot of those booths dotted about.

On a breath of disgust, Lance followed his gaze. "More government-funded marquees. Tax payer's money put to good use. Not."

Global Reach spokespeople were moving through the crowd. Realising they were drawing close, Baden started shoving Lance along. "Come on, let's not get caught up here."

"Check your validation code! Check your validation code!" called the representative. "Look for the numbers 1.0/0.1/1.9.4.4. The numbers are located on the bottom right of your pamphlet. They will put you in a draw to win a free pass to Global Reach launch, the event of the century!"

Baden pulled the pamphlet from his pocket, glancing at the number.

"You got one of those?" Lance asked. "I've chucked at least twenty in the last week." But he did a double-take when he saw the numbers. "You lucky son of a bitch!"

Baden crossed to a bin, awkwardly dragging the case around people, meaning to bin it, but Lance grabbed it from his hand, staring at the numbers.

"No way!" said Lance. "People like us never win, then you get the golden ticket."

"Ford look around, it's a play on the date. The numbers represent a date!"

"A date?" Lance stared at the sequence, holding tight when Baden tried to tug it from his hand. "Don't fight it, Cass, we got the numbers!"

As the two fought, the pamphlet ripped in two. Lance had the lower half which had the code. Elated, he ran off grinning.

"Fortune favours the bold, my friend!" Waving it wildly, he knocked an old guy on the head passing by.

"Uncouth youth — watch your arms!"

It was like observing a car crash, thought Baden. Lance was charging forward like the proverbial bull towards a Global Reach booth. With little choice, Baden followed, case trailing.

By the time he reached Lance, his smile of victory had vanished like mist in the morning.

"Whaddya mean we're all winners? This gig of yours better not be swindling me!"

Confused, the representative kept his smile in place. "The Global Reach launch is a free event for all worldwide, my boy! That code in your hand is actually the official date when the Global Reach program roots began, during the Second World War, tenth January, nineteen forty-four. You see?" The representative showed another pamphlet with the same date. "We need passionate individuals like yourself to spread the word for this important cause."

Baden nudged Lance, who looked anything but passionate. "When my friend here commits to a cause, nothing gets in his way. Not even common sense."

"Well, we're happy to have you aboard, young man. I'm sorry I don't have anything else to give you." The representative looked back through the material on the stand. "Only these Global Reach badges and stickers for the kids. Advertising is key, spreading the word to one and all!"

"Stickers?" Baden grinned. "You should know this guy's a man sized child, with a sticker collection spreading the back wall of his room." Since Lance was ominously silent, he saw no reason to stop. "Strange fetish if you ask me."

"Right, I see." The representative smiled, and backed away. "Young at heart's a great way to explore this new world that is to come."

Lance dropped the torn pamphlet to the ground, stalking off. Baden grinned at the representative. "Think you'd better hang onto those."

Still laughing, Baden caught up. "That detour was worth taking. Seriously, the things you get yourself into."

"Sticker collection?" Lance grumbled. "You dick."

"Baden!" The voice was female. "Is that you?"

The crowd parted for Gwen and three of her friends, looking to Baden like a flock of exotic birds, out of place and out of his league.

The smile slid off his face, landing at his feet when he realised they were coming over.

"That it is, ladies." Lance stepped before Baden, his voice deepening. "Hours spent at the gym changes you in a very profound way. Sometimes people have completely mistaken me for another entirely."

An awkward silence fell over the group. Gwen rolled her eyes, the other girls turning to talk to each other while she looked him up and down, "And changed the colour of your skin and tone of your voice?"

Lance looked to the sky. "For the better. What can I say, the sun burns hotter in these parts." Lance ran a deliberate eye over her body. "A concept I can see you're accustomed to."

"Oh, the sun. I see. Well, 'Baden', remind me, what's my middle name?"

Before Lance spoke, Baden could see the end coming. Lance's warped sense of humour knew no bounds. "Err, McTitty?"

Gwen's eyebrows rose as the girls laughed, clearly not believing what was happening.

On a shrug, Lance glanced back at Baden. "Come on, she left that one wide open promoting those luv jugs out in public. Watcha expect a brotha to say?"

Speechless, Baden stared from one to the other, and knew the moment Gwen's gaze landed on the pink suitcase. He groaned inwardly, already guessing what was coming.

"Pink? I recall your colour choice was usually black." Her gaze skimmed the two. "Maybe things have changed over the years?"

On a wild headshake, Baden shoved forward. "No ... no way! It's Ebony's. I've been trying to lose this thing for the past hour."

"Your cousin's?" Gwen laughed, shaking her head. "Nice try. Ebony's case isn't pink."

Baden glanced at Lance, who just shrugged, clearly confused.

"Don't look at me, man. Someone says pink, I just think kinky."

"I know her case from when she's stayed with us in the city," Gwen said. "She's never brought that. I would have noticed, it stands out."

Side-tracked, Baden's curiosity overcame his nerves. "What do you mean, when she's stayed with you?"

"At Fellowship Tower in Melbourne. I thought you knew."

Floored, Baden shook his head.

"She's been staying there on and off for most of the year," said Gwen.

"With you Solomons at Fellowship Tower?" he demanded incredulously.

Gwen's response chilled noticeably. "Yes, with us Solomons."

A kernel of anger bloomed within Baden, but it was not directed at Gwen. No, it was all for his cousin and her secret second life.

"What's she been doing with the Fellowship?"

But Gwen shook her head, obviously sensing trouble. "Look, I don't think I should say anymore. She must want it kept quiet."

"No kidding," Baden muttered. Uncle Rickard would have a fit if he knew Ebony was mixing with Solomons. Tamping down his anger, he searched for something to say.

Gwen led with a much-needed rescue. "Are you Global Reach supporters?"

Lance held up a hand. "We ain't no tree huggers, or whatnot. Looks like a sham to me. Nearly got swindled with some fake tickets."

"A sham? Really?" Gwen turned to Baden. "It's a big deal in the city, there's a Global Reach movement on nearly every corner. There's even a complex built for the launch, but things appear slower here."

"That's country life," he agreed, feeling awkward, his body suddenly not knowing how to stand. "Rolls at a slower pace ..."

"Behind the damn world," Lance grumbled. "When I'm outta school, I'm joining the army. First taking a gap year, doing the backpacking thing."

Gwen ignored Lance, still looking at Baden. "Next month finishes the countdown for the launch. Then we'll all find out what the two years of hype have been for."

"Two years?" Baden looked back at a booth. "I haven't really kept up."

"They're claiming it will unite the world," she added, "so it must be something big."

Lance yawned, interest clearly burning out. "Whatever. I'm thinking a few drinks will make this night much more interesting. We're heading over to White Pier."

Gwen fished her mobile from her purse, reading a message, before turning to her friends. "It's Xavier, we need to go," she said, sounding a little disappointed. "Sorry Baden, duty calls."

As the group walked away, Lance swung back. "Hold on, what just happened here?"

Baden started dragging the case across the park, toward the main street. "We haven't spoken in years. She's different now." At Lance's eye-roll, Baden frowned. "Problem?"

"Right! She wasn't even that into me! That girl's either got the ice-cold bitch act down or she's playing hard to get!"

"Yeah, that has to be it." Baden fused his mouth, praying something would distract Lance. It didn't usually take much. "Hey, there's my aunt's café. Come on."

"Or maybe it was the Ebony connection?" Sticking with the subject, Lance snapped his fingers. "I heard she was thinking of bailing on uni, was even gonna move back here permanently. You know the reason?"

"She dropped back to part-time study about eight months ago," said Baden, "She's been living between Freestone and the city, but I thought she was on campus up there."

"But she's really been shacking up with the Solomons?" Lance's voice rose in tone. "Trading up, man!"

Baden sneered. "Good luck telling that one to Uncle Rickard."

"One would've thought you and your cousin were tight, being cousins. And you grew up on the same farm. Ya seem outta the loop, man."

"Ebony's like five years older than me." Pulling up, Baden rolled his eyes. "We talk, but it's all superficial, keeps the drama level low, you know." Finally, he voiced the only possibility that made sense. "Maybe she's looking into her adoption."

Lance whistled. "Now there's a home-run swing."

"I dunno what else it could be. It's a wonder Uncle Rickard's not spinning off his axis knowing she's staying at the Solomons."

"Maybe he doesn't know."

Lance was dopey ninety percent of his life but every now and again, he hit a bull's eye.

"If he doesn't," mused Baden, "this is bound to blow out into a huge mess." Walking on, he fought to control the growing anger. "She better not be starting something. Uncle Rickard wouldn't piss on Marcus Solomon if he was on fire."

"Whoa, I like the way your mind works, bro." Lance slapped his shoulder. "I get there's a lot of hate for the man."

"Close enough."

A live band pumped out music from inside the bar on the street corner, where even the outside deck was jumping with very happy patrons.

Multicoloured lights strung through the large gum tree

overhanging the deck flashed brightly. About to cross the street to his aunt's café, Baden spotted a waving hand from the deck. Fighting to see through the patrons, he stepped to the side, released a massive sigh of relief when he recognised the owner of the hand, changing direction.

"Yo, what gives?" Lance grabbed his arm. "The old girl's café's over here, bro."

"Come on." Baden kept moving. "Let's drop this anchor at the harbour."

Lance followed, clearly confused at Baden's fast pace. On the deck, the two waded through the patrons until they were standing before a blonde at a corner table. Nina Perkin's mouth dropped open.

"What're you doing with this?" she asked, baffled as Baden dumped the suitcase next to her chair. Then she totally lost it, screeching, "It's filthy!"

Baden felt heat creep over his face as people looked up from their drinks. Nina shot him an accusatory stare as she tried to rub at the velvety material. Tipping it sideways, she gasped as the case slid from her grasp to hit the deck with a thud.

"Yeah, it weighs a tonne," Baden said cheerfully. "And's a bitch to tow. Clearly not designed for a quick getaway."

"Why do you have my suitcase?"

"Your suitcase?" Baden glanced at Lance, who rolled his eyes. "Ebony must have stolen it on a temporary basis. It was at the farm for reasons unknown so don't ask. I was told to deliever it to Eb's apartment, meet Myrick out front, but he was a no-show."

"Aunt Grace?" Nina was obviously fighting to keep up. "Why did she give it to you?"

"I dunno, something was up. She practically threw the thing at me, ordering the hand over."

Lance scratched his head, finally looking interested. "Her apartment's above that new age shop, right? That way-old dude Myrick runs it?" Baden nodded. "Blame it on degenerative sight, probably couldn't flag you down in the dark."

"Nah," Baden looked back at Nina. "Aunt Grace had a change of plans, she's on her way to the café now, where they'll probably meet up. Anyway," he indicated the case, stepping back. "Regardless of the backstory, the thing's now hitching it with the rightful owner, I'm signing off, baggage handling duty complete."

"Why would Eb have taken my suitcase?" wondered Nina.

Jevon Starrik appeared, shoving a pink drink towards Nina, blithely ignoring her angry hiss when it sloshed on the table.

"Ebony took what?" he asked, sliding into a chair beside her, then began sniffing. "What's that smell?" His nose creased. "Kind of a fruitilicious aroma, yet powerful enough to clear all the oxygen around us. You fellas testing a new perfume line?"

"No." Baden glared at the case next to Nina, trying to ignore Lance's sullen face on his right. It would not take much for him to bolt at this point.

On a laugh, Jevon tipped his chair back on two legs, rocking thoughtfully, while eyeballing the suitcase. "Ah, I see the reason."

"No way?" Baden glared at it.

"Yup. Perky here coats anything that's pink in some kind sickly scent. Reckons it triggers certain chemicals in the brain—"

"I've never said that in my life," Nina interrupted haughtily.

"Does for me, head starts buzzing in all the wrong ways." Jevon casually sipped his beer, eyeing Baden and Lance. "Under-agers," he said with a wiggle of his eyebrows. "If you get carded, you'll be tossed, unless you're carrying fakes. In which case ... tsk, tsk."

"Trying to move us along, Starrik? This here can't be a date thing." Lance looked Nina up and down. "You can do better."

"What?" she snapped.

"Touchy." Lance flashed white teeth, while pulling out his his mobile after it dinged. "Saved by a message."

Nina bent, cleary annoyed, brushing fastidiously at the dirt on her case.

"You're rubbing it in," Jevon sighed.

"We need to go," she declared, glaring at him.

Jevon's chair hit the deck. "We just got here. Correction: you dragged me here."

"And now I'm dragging you home. I can't watch this thing all night, especially when it's filthy."

"It's full of Ebony's stuff," added Baden. "Was like hauling lead."

"I'm finishing this." Jevon held up his drink. "Not wasting beer money." Downing half, he eyed her while wiping his mouth, then ruffled his already untidy dirty blond hair.

"Don't worry, I can walk," Nina said before sipping her drink delicately. "Shouldn't take long. You can hold the table."

"There's a reason guys die first." Jevon took another huge gulp.

Lance coughed, looking up from his phone catching the last of their exchange. "Pussy whipped," he laughed. When Nina shot him a withering look, he smiled weakly. "Okay, confirmation ... second ice queen incoming tonight."

"So ..." Nina looked back at Baden. "Grace is meeting you at her café. With Ebony?"

Not about to be dragged back in, Baden started backing up. "Negatory on all specifics."

"Bet she's with those guys again," Jevon mused, sculling the last of his beer.

"Come on, Cass," Lance groaned, clearly over the whole mess. "Let's bounce, Kevo must be done."

"Hang five." Baden eyed Jevon curiously. "What guys?"

"Please don't call on his alter ego." Nina began wiping her hands fastidiously on a tissue from her purse. "Months ago, Jevon drove a couple of guys out to the farm."

"It was three guys," Jevon added, "with thick accents. Outta towners, definitely."

Nina grinned wickedly. "I thought you were sworn to secrecy."

Jevon grabbed a couple of cheese nibbles from a plate. "Sure ... but a lead's a lead, and now," he looked pointedly past her chair, "there's a suitcase and no Ebony. Something's ... suspicious."

"What're you talking about?" asked Baden.

Jevon held up a finger. "Let's start with the suitcase. When did you get it?"

"I don't know, half hour ago, maybe? You think she's in some kind of trouble?"

"I didn't say that. I said something's suspicious. If you'd been in the car with those three guys, you'd think the same. They turned up at Dad's mechanic shop one morning, looking for her. Dad completely wigged out. I got the feeling he recognised them. Then he asks me to drive them to the farm to see your uncle."

"I never saw them or heard anything about this," Baden muttered, scratching at his head.

Jevon shrugged. "Two blokes in their twenties. Third was older, a local."

"Local? Who?" Baden asked.

"Of the older variety. Someone I can't go into detail about."

Caught up, Lance shook his head. "Your tally-wacker below is softer than jelly, Starrik. What's some old dude gonna do besides gum ya to death?"

"You'd be surprised."

None of this sounded good, thought Baden. He had known Jevon most of his life, he and Ebony were tight, first cousins on their mothers' sides.

"I couldn't get a thing outta them, not with those weird accents flying around." Resting his elbows on the table, Jevon leaned forward. "Every time I see Ebony, she's cagey, playing everything close to her chest. I know something's up, and so do you Nina, so don't deny it."

After a look at her case, Nina gave in. "I suppose. She hasn't stayed at the flat much, just sort of breezed in and out during the last month." Thoughtful, she added, "Though I admit she does look uncharacteristically driven, like there's a weight on her shoulders."

"And not one of you asked the girl what's what?" Lance demanded, now clearly interested.

Jevon threw up his hands. "She's like a damn vault. I even called her a couple of times today, thought she might be back in town because of the festival."

"I texted her," Nina admitted. "But nil on the reply."

"I'm really starting to hate her voicemail," declared Jevon. "She never calls back."

Baden pulled out his phone, filing through the list until he found his cousin's name. "I'll try."

"She won't answer," Jevon warned, as Baden listened to the ringing.

"Watch me."

"You're wasting your time." Jevon rolled his eyes.

The pub's band finished their set, announcing they were taking a break which left nothing but the chatter of patrons and an ominous silence between the four.

"Is it just me or is anyone else getting an ear on that funky ass tune?" Lance asked, his gaze finally landing on the suitcase. Kneeling beside it, he grimaced. "So it's pink, smells funny and now makes noises? Bag's a triple-threat."

Baden placed his hand against the suede fabric. "It's vibrating."

"You don't say." Lance winked at Nina.

There was no missing the nasty look she threw him as Baden hauled the suitcase onto the table, quickly unzipping it while everyone crowded around. Within moments, he had Ebony's mobile phone in hand, a list of unanswered calls and texts lining the screen. The charge on it was low, around a quarter. Deciding it was safest with him at this point, he pocketed the device.

"At least we know why she's not answering," he muttered.

"Look at the stuff she's packed," exclaimed Nina. "Clothes, pictures ... this is just bizarre." Sitting back, she scratched at her ear. "What's going on?"

Baden began his own inspection, noting how items were balled up, piled haphazardly, like the pack had been done at top speed.

"Eh," Lance sniggered, eyeing the mess. "Looks like one of my attempts."

"Something's wrong," muttered Baden, feeling decidedly jumpy.

Nina nodded vigorously. "Something is definitely up."

"Photos, jewellery, and of course a book." Jevon waved drawings that looked like they had been done by a toddler. "Why would she pack all this?" He shoved a black box to one side. "It's junk."

Nina grabbed the handmade book, blinking back sudden tears. "I remember this. Ebony and I made it, a book of rules for our club, when we were in year three or four. We even signed it, see? And the rest of this, it's not junk, it's memories. The photos and albums, and this other stuff. Here's her dance shoes from when she won Most Promising Dancer in her first eisteddfod."

"Memories?" Baden looked again, picking up the box. It was heavy and engraved, and no matter how he tried, it would not open.

"You're saying she's leaving for somewhere?"

"Obviously in a rush," muttered Jevon, flicking fast through photos. "Not one of me. That's just cold."

Lance sniggered. "Not feeling the love, huh?"

"I'm calling Grace," Nina declared.

"She texted only ten or fifteen minutes ago," Baden said. "Heading for the café."

Jevon stood on his chair, looking across the street. "The lights are still off. The place looks dead."

"I'm calling her," Nina repeated, pulling out her mobile.

As soon as she moved away, Lance nudged Baden. "Kevo's gonna be waiting. This situation all good now?"

"I dunno." Baden could not shake a bad feeling.

"You're not bitching out on me, not this year. This is all so circumstantial, your cuz's probably tweaked up on sentimentality, some chick thing we'll never get."

"She's family, man. I can't bail, not yet. You go meet Kevo. I'll text when this is done, catch up."

Lance swore, jerking out his mobile to place a call.

The blast of a horn, then belt of a drum, had everyone turning to see the Freestone Marching Band stride into view at the end of the main street.

"Oh man," Lance groaned. "Parade's already starting." A series of long floats came into view, broken up by dancers and other solo acts, many representing businesses and charities in town. Children crammed the footpaths with their parents, waiting for the free gifts that would be handed out courtesy of the Solomon family.

The biggest float was the first, representing the founding of Freestone, depicting three families; Noble, Casteel and Solomon. Baden watched as it slowly filed past, people moving out of the Star Bar toward the street, grabbing their phones to film the parade.

"Welcome to Crystal Cave Parade." A man's voice came over a loud speaker. "Our first float, Frontier Fellowship Brothers, depicts the history of when the primary cave in Skyfall Mountain was discovered. This is a moment in time Freestone Valley historians have documented extensively. Solomon, Noble and Casteel, a lantern their only source of light as they moved into a dark cave.

Freestone Valley was settled well over a hundred and fifty-five years ago, and these families' descendants are now widespread across Australia."

People dressed in 1855 clothing waved, walking behind the float.

Lance reappeared, shoving his phone into his back pocket. "You thinking of joining in, Cass? Get the old boot-legged ancestral dance going?"

"Hilarious." Baden bared his teeth. "The Casteels are like anyone else in this town. Whatever we were back then ended the moment my uncle stepped down from the Fellowship."

Lance shoved him in the shoulder. "I dunno, man. Gwen was sizing you up, unless my radar needs some tuning."

"Guinevere Solomon?" Jevon's gaze turned speculative. "Steer clear of that one, mate. Solomons always have an agenda."

Lance threw out an arm. "Speaking of, cast your eyes left."

Directly behind the first float and its crew came Gwen and her brother Xavier in a red Mercedes convertible.

"Tonight, our Fellowship spokespeople are Xavier Solomon and his sister, Guinevere," continued the voice, "standing in for their father, Marcus Solomon. Please make your way to the staging grounds where they will make an official announcement, one that will put our very own Freestone Valley into a national spotlight."

Nina reappeared, immediately grabbing her suitcase. She began stuffing the overflowing contents back in, forcing the zipper closed. "Grace is having trouble getting through the crowd so she's on foot. We'll meet at the staging area."

Baden glanced at Lance. "Where's Kevin meeting us?"

"Should be around there too."

The group made their way down the main street, past the hordes who were enjoying the parade.

"Did she say anything about Ebony?" Baden asked Nina.

"No, not really. I think something's happened, though. She sounded upset."

A marching band started playing offering a respectable per-formance of the Australian national anthem. A bunch of dancers followed them, flipping and tumbling. By the time the group reached the staging area, a crowd was gathering, people jostling for a front-row position.

Xavier and Gwen arrived fifteen minutes later, their car pulling in beside the stage. Once standing behind the podium, the two waved at the gathered crowd.

Baden noticed immediately how comfortable they both were, almost like celebrities. Xavier Solomon waited for the music to finish before speaking.

"Welcome to the 156th Annual Founders Festival. I know you were expecting the Fellowship Principal of the Solomon family, my father. However, tonight you will have to settle for me as urgent business demands his attention. He sends his humble apologies, realising this has caused cancellations and altered timetables.

"One thing that has not been altered is the opening fireworks. They will commence as always at half past nine. Hopefully, I can bring my own flair, with perhaps a little more fortunate hairline than my father, to Freestone Valley's night of nights."

People smiled and clapped. Xavier glanced back urging his sister forward. "My sister, Guinevere, will have the honour of the first reveal tonight. Then it will be on to the fireworks."

Gwen turned to the screen behind her, switching it on via her smartphone. The Global Reach logo lit up next to what appeared to be a layout design of very large, modern base.

"Many will have noticed the Global Reach booths dotted around the festival. Displayed here is the base that is being built on the outskirts of this town in support of the unification of our world's major nations. Global Reach, ladies and gentleman, has come to Freestone Valley!"

Soft murmurs broke out. Some people looked confused, Baden noticed, while others seemed interested.

"You can bet," Jevon said, "this is the reason the RAAF Base lost that grant to update to a pilot training facility. More than likely it's been earmarked for this development scheme for a while."

"The RAAF Base closing hit Freestone pretty hard," Nina added. "Fewer families moving into town, less cash flow. A lot of people are going to be hurt because of that."

"You're tying that somehow to Reach?" Lance mused. "Kinda

solid, it's all militarised."

"The military and Global Reach." Jevon clasped his hands. "They're in bed together, you mark my words."

"Never promote the details within details," said Baden slowly.

"That's all pure speculation," Nina scoffed. "Melbourne's Global Complex virtually had to build their own airport. The old RAAF base's runways and layout are perfect for development, not to mention its location on the outskirts of a big town like Freestone Valley."

Jevon stared at Nina, his face momentarily blank.

"Shock, horror guys. I do keep up with the news," she muttered haughtily.

Xavier continued his speech. "Further development and updates on this large Global Base will be rolled out from next week, so stay tuned. For now, eyes on the sky, ladies and gentlemen. Let the fireworks begin!"

As it was now well after nine thirty, an ink sky stretched overhead, within it a domain of stars. Three long blasts of a horn preceded the tell-tale sound of rumbling planes. Sparks streamed from each aircraft's wing, a type of firework Baden realised as they crossed overhead. For a few minutes, they twisted and dived, six classic aircraft delivering a display that had the audience gasping and children squealing in delight.

When his mobile phone vibrated, Baden pulled it absently from his pocket, swiping the screen, but the screen was blank, no text message. Then the screen flashed, the phone vibrating, ringing, but there was no caller. He saw a couple of people near him with their phones, staring at them, baffled.

A flash of brilliant white light shot through the night, creating a collective gasp. Then came a heavy sound, a feeling of drawing up, something Baden recognised belatedly: a sonic boom. A strange wave of colour appeared then began dispersing into a circular wave of glowing cloud as two objects burned up in the atmosphere. Baden heard someone nearby scream as twin crashes hurtled into the hills on the outskirts of Freestone.

As soon as the objects impacted, a shockwave blew through the town. Baden fell to the ground as everything went dark, the force knocking out the power grid instantly along with the generators used to power the rides.

One moment paralysed, the next crazed, the crowd began scrambling for cover, a save-yourself-first mentality taking hold, against screams of terror.

Lance dragged Baden up to where their group had taken cover, near the stage amongst other frightened people. Through the shadows, Baden saw Jevon helping an old couple, sitting them on its steps. Every light was out leaving the crowd in panicked darkness. He yanked out his phone to use the torch but the battery was suddenly, inexplicably, dead.

Jevon jogged across. "Did you see that blast? It felt like the air was sucked up and spat out. It was kicking in the burn at blinding speed!"

Baden could hear the festival organisers trying to restart generators, bring some semblance of order. Baden looked around. A lot of people had superficial injuries, like cuts and bruises. Children and parents who had been separated were now calling out for each other, creating a new pandemonium.

In the far distance, sirens wailed. Jevon stood, staring down the main street. Suddenly he took off, and Baden could tell by the way he was moving, something had caught his eye.

"What's he doing?" Nina demanded irritably, trying to tie her hair back in a band.

"He's seen someone." Baden started jogging, not halting until he was next to Jevon at the central Clock Tower, fighting to find the figure he had briefly noticed through the darkness.

"Bro." Lance came alongside, peering also. "Is that …?"

In the distance, a figure was staggering toward them, limping like it was broken, lit every now and again by flickering street lights. Generators began running, ride operators trying to free yelling passengers, but the chaos of the festival seemed distant to Baden. Only the injured figure was real. Baden took a step forward, trying to think what to do, only to find himself paralysed with uncertainty.

Officials rushed to the scene, reaching the figure first, awkwardly catching hold as the person collapsed on the street. Within moments, a police officer was taking control of the situation, forcing the crowd back. Closer now, he and Jevon were part of that group.

Every now and then Baden caught sight of black hair caked in blood. He could hear moaning, wondered how someone could survive those kinds of injuries. Torn clothes that looked burnt, countless wounds seeping blood, darkness adding to the horror.

When an ambulance appeared, lights flashing, they were pushed back even further, paramedics pulling out a stretcher, placing it beside the victim. That's when Baden realised it was a girl, but it was Jevon's sharp breath of recognition that had him looking harder.

"What the ...?" Words dried up, a feeling filling his chest he had no description for.

Fingers clawed at his shirt, someone was trying to get past him. It took Baden a moment to realise that Nina was sobbing hysterically, screaming the girl's name.

"Ebony!"

Galactic Star Key: Kaze Karbroe
Astral Nav-Coordinates: EAS-APL-4
Data Sequence: 5.0

As soon as the seal-gate retracted, Kaze and Zozes entered to find themselves overlooking the main Training Bay on board the Galaxy Ship. Crossing the observation platform, Kaze took in the runways used by personnel when testing different grades of weapons during their fire strike exercises.

Kaze exchanged a glance with his brother at the sound of a constant barrage of energy blasts amidst yells. Following his brother down a flight of stairs, the two jogged to the combat level, a shimmering, high-grade containment shield on their right protecting the area.

The sheer size of Blast Range became apparent, as did the number of personnel engaged in combat exercises. Noticing an armaments prep-zone, the two entered to find the Arms-Master outfitting two squads.

The room was equipped with numerous weapons of all grades, all mounted on magnetised racks connected to a series of stasis-storage loaders. Standing before one, the Arms-Master transported a series of weapon types onto them. Running a hand over her security cyber-controller, she unlocked several, handing out sniper-beam rifles to a four-man Infiltrator Squad. As they left, the unit glanced across, staring coldly at the brothers.

"Feels like a waving moment," Kaze declared, glancing at his brother. "Objections?"

Zozes stepped to the door, watching the squad head off. "Something about this has me questioning the Blades' reputation."

"Got to say," Kaze said as he joined his brother, "those filthy looks aren't about making friends. More like, 'why not use those Blades for target practice?'"

"You sound uneasy, brother."

"Uneasy?" Kaze instantly puffed up. "Give me a handful of rocks and a really long stick …"

"Then you'll show them the meaning of combat."

"Say the words with conviction, brother." Kaze narrowed his eyes. "Otherwise it lessens the meaning."

"One of these cycles, you'll come face to face with what comes out of your mouth."

"You may be right," Kaze said with a shrug. "Until then, I'll have to wait in suspense."

Which was what they were doing now, mused Kaze. Waiting. Glancing across the prep-zone, he saw the Arms-Master was finishing up her prep of the squad of Enforcers. Nodding to each as they headed off, she looked across at the Blades, activating her cyber-controller to materialise a rectangular Blade-class stasis case in a nearby storage re-sequencer.

"Blades," she called, waving them across. "Deactivate all heavy uniform attire in preparation for testing. Standard combat skin-wear is recommended for integration into your Blade armour."

"Nothing like stating the obvious," Kaze muttered beneath his breath.

"Understood," Zozes replied loudly, already programming the subdermal porta-tool beneath his palm, triggering the smart-form fabric to re-bind his jacket into a fine fibre shirt.

Kaze did the same, his gaze returning to the Blade stasis case, which the Arms-Master had set to levitate, activating its anti-grav port.

"Progress brother, about time we re-enter—"

"Kaze!"

"The rip zone!"

The Arms-Master looked up at this, eyebrows briefly raised.

Voice low, Zozes leaned close to his brother. "You realise outsiders don't understand your debased psyche, have no idea it's just your way?"

"Time they learnt the zone us Karbroes specialise in, annihilating all matter beyond the intra-dimensional level."

"You're a sole defender of that zone, Kaze." Zozes shook his head. "Too bad it doesn't include yourself." Both brothers drew to at-stance as an O'Garcian Major walked in.

"No need to stand on formalities, Blades," he said. "I'm Major Rajek Texun. Welcome."

Thrown by the casual, even warm greeting, Kaze moved to easement slowly. The O'Garcian species was known to be aloof, even pompous. Slender of build, the Major's white hair was tied in a lace-band, revealing his ridged ears while pronouncing his dark brown eyes.

"Major Rajek," Kaze and Zozes addressed him together, using the first name instead of last, a formality his species preferred.

"I don't know how much you've been told," Rajek began, "but I'm here to assess your combat capabilities and control over the Link-Trone."

Kaze's friendly feelings began to sour. "Test our spawn-nets' combat stability with active Blade-Gear?"

"Exactly," Rajek said. "And, as an incentive, if you're successful in completing these simulations, your deactivated status will be lifted."

"If our service status is to be officially lifted," reasoned Zozes, "wouldn't we be recalled back to our Galactic Force CO for immediate debriefing, Sir?"

"Commander Vome?" Kaze's earlier bravado appeared to waver.

The O'Garcian observed this with a lifted eyebrow. "Back to the Galaxy Ship of the Hasnirian fleet, *The Nebulon*."

Kaze said nothing more, instead blew a breath, straightening his stance while looking straight ahead.

"I'm well aware of Commander Vome's reputation Blades, and the expectations she holds for those beneath her. Something," added Rajek grimly, "I also hold. However, Astral Guard are in direct charge of this system in accordance with the Overwatch Initiative."

"Overwatch?" Kaze locked onto the word, glancing at his brother in surprise.

Though startled, Zozes covered this by narrowing his eyes. The Major's tone was anything but relaxed, suggesting he was not in full agreement with the directive.

"So they are withholding our duty-right to file a mission report?" Zozes asked, his tone matching the Major's in civility.

"You're in a unique situation," Rajek reminded. "Commodore Vae'gon is evaluating this directly through personal measure."

"So these orders come directly from him?" Kaze shifted on his feet, unlocking his hands. "Think I'd prefer Vome."

"How has Astral Guard authorised this, Sir?" Zozes studied the Major's countenance carefully, searching for a hint. "Wouldn't that require permission from a Galactic Force Official?"

"Legalities regarding Overwatch are somewhat diverse, Blade." Rajek glanced over the Blast Range. "Once it was initiated, all those within this star system fell under its decree. You need to understand the Overwatch Initiative has a far more libertarian manner of governing."

"Libertarian?" repeated Zozes. "As opposed to a Galactic Force standard of protocol, Sir?"

"Seems like this Initiative has one purpose," spat Kaze. "A *'technicality of benefit'* for Astral Guard only if they can control the duty-service of all subordinate officers without the effect of consequence."

Zozes eyed his brother before turning back to the Major. "Once we have successfully completed combat testing will my brother and I be transferring our duty-service to—"

"Astral Guard?" Kaze glared at the Major, every muscle tensed. "I'd rather be spaced! We bear arms in accordance to the Galactic Force—"

"Easy, Kaze," Zozes moved to catch his brother's eye. "Blades are deployed where we're needed."

"They are," agreed the Major, determined to move on. "Success in testing will grant you temporary holding of operation to commence mission objectives for Astral Guard. However, further assessments will be required if you are to attain a more permanent status."

"Permanent status?" Kaze added a hasty, "Sir" at the Major's look. "Do we have a choice?"

"Failure can take many forms, Blade." Rajek eyed Kaze's expression, gesturing to the Blast Range. "Your performance through trial will determine that outcome."

"And I know how you detest failing," Zozes added. "So what's it to be?"

Zozes knew what trigger to pull. Drawing a breath, Kaze cracked a smile, one that felt like the first since being woken within his spawn-pod. "I see what you did there, brother. Challenge accepted!"

At a signal from the Major, the Lieutenant Arms-Master used her cyber-controller to open the unit, generating two circular Blade-Gears. Kaze felt a thrill of anticipation as he watched the familiar tan and silver metallic rims hover in a grav-beam.

Once his was mag-locked on his belt, Zozes nodded to the Major. "Feels like progress just gaining our Gears back."

"Agreed," Kaze's grin broadened. "Been feeling bare-skinned without it, Sir."

The Arms-Master said, "Due to the subspace radiation your ship endured, it was necessary to place your Blade-Gears through an extensive decontamination purge."

"Can't be serious if we're holding them again?" Kaze glanced down at the rim.

"Procedure had to be followed. Blade-Gears' exposure to subspace radiation was minimal. The separation from your squad's AI Trone was necessary to run a series of operational tests, analysing your Gears' status for field duty."

The moment the Arms-Master was finished, Rajek moved things along.

"We're waiting on a couple of others to arrive and," he turned toward the entry, "here they are."

The door opened to admit Medical Officer Thaytis Venlara, guiding a lethal-grade stasis-cart, grav-ports activated. The unit was vastly larger than the stasis case, reinforced armour plating hinting at the danger it held. Beside her strode a tall Devronian female, black hair cropped just shy of her skin. The vertical slits of her pupils momentarily dilated when landing on the Blades. Grim-faced, she halted taking her position, giving Kaze a chance to sight her identifier. He almost sneered upon seeing she was an Astral Guard Enforcer, Lieutenant grade. Before she even opened her mouth, Kaze knew he was not going to like her.

Several security officers followed them, two taking station either side of the entrance, another two beside the stasis-cart.

Before the Major, Thaytis moved to at-stance. "Apologies on the tardy arrival, Sir. Enforcer Noremar wanted to make certain the AI Link-Trone couldn't break containment during transport."

In disbelief, Kaze eyed the stasis-cart. "You've secured the Link-Trone in there?"

Noremar's top lip curled. "You view this ship's safety as unimportant, Blade?"

"I view that," he said, glaring at the holding unit, "as overkill."

Dismissing him, Jenvar looked back at the Major. "The Trone has been secured with a suppression-bolt override, Sir. The strong measure is in direct proportion to the threat level."

Incredulous, Kaze looked at his brother, but could see that Zozes was not surprised for some reason. He eyed the Major. "What's going on, Sir?"

Though Enforcer Noremar looked disgusted at his query, Rajek answered readily enough. "Blades, please excuse Lieutenant Jenvar's lack of consideration."

Kaze smothered a laugh as the Devronian's disgust shifted to outrage, her gaze locking on the Major at his use of her given name. Clearly, she had trouble masking her feelings, which left him wondering if that had been an intentional slip on the Major's part, perhaps some type of test.

Rajek continued. "Always remember, a Devronian by nature is distrustful until loyalty has been proven. Your situation is unique, and the Lieutenant is acting accordingly. I have urged her to grant you each latitude during this time of adjustment.

"Alpha Blue's rank and clearance places him at a disadvantage. I advise patience with added caution when dealing with him particularly."

"Particularly?" Kaze inclined his head. "Good to know I'm appreciated."

"Then let us begin." The Major returned his nod. "We are here to address combat testing. However, necessary contingencies must first be established against any loss of control."

"Sir," Kaze found it necessary to speak up. "I operated Blade-Gears in full combat mode prior to landing on this Station. No issues."

"Brother," Zozes instantly spoke up. "You did not even fire a weapon."

"Which side are you standing with?"

"The one that keeps you alive."

Kaze didn't have a reasonable counter for that. "Traitor talk," he grumbled. "I've full control over this Alpha ... thing."

"Alpha *thing*?" The Major's eyebrow rose haughtily, for the first time displaying his O'Garcian heritage. "That's what we are here to determine, Blade."

"Under strict procedures," added Noremar.

"Doctor." Rajek nodded at the stasis-cart. "You may release the Link-Trone."

Kaze and Zozes watched Doctor Venlara go through the complicated process of deactivating the casket's access port. When the heavily armoured mag-latches released, they disengaged the circular compartment holder, and left the centre of the unit exposed, disengaging the energy-shield.

The Link-Trone materialised within the casket, re-conforming its structure, the tan and silver armour generating while powering its own grav-nacelles. From where he stood, Kaze got a good look at the restraining device on the underside of the AI unit, shaking his head but holding his tongue.

"As you can see," said Major Rajek, "an LT-5 bolt overrider has been temporarily fitted to control the AI units positronic mass-drive."

"Which grants you operational control over the AI," Zozes said. "Meaning you can manually cycle through its Combat Systems to disengage or re-engage the LT when working with us."

"Precisely." Major Rajek activated his porta-tool, generating a screen. With swift movements, he entered a series of commands, the final one releasing the primary suppression protocol used to lockdown the Trone's positronic mass-drive.

Released, the AI shot forward, flashing yellow and blue lights, hovering closely between Kaze and Zozes. The action was so unexpected, Kaze almost laughed. How could a mechanical device look disgruntled? In a strange way, he understood how it felt. He too was tired of the relentless testing to see if he was what they classed as 'safe'.

The portable Blade-Gear on his centre belt suddenly lit up, indicating that the Link-Trone was establishing a unibind pairing to both brothers' spawn-nets. With that pairing came a cold shift, the now familiar wash of ice down his spine.

He knew Zozes was also lit, but the pairing was stable, his brother easily handling the neural load.

The Link-Trone spoke. "Dual-pairing complete. Welcome Alphas."

"Before we begin." The Major's gaze switched from Zozes to Kaze. "You are well-aware of the lock-order against activating spawn-drift?"

"No need to battle through another lengthy discourse, Sir." Kaze was prepared for this. "My brother hasn't cut short on the responsibility, something I call an ongoing debrief since I was discharged from medical bay. Before our ship crashlanded, I know I somehow triggered the spawn-drift moments before our combat jump."

"Your brother's right, Blade." Rajek stepped closer. "We believe the reason you could initiate drift is because of your unique dual-pairing. You now have access to one of the deadliest abilities in the galaxy. It can't be used on a whim. Combat hours and training to perfect something as powerful as a drift can take a Blade Commando their entire life. When you commit to the Blade program ..."

"You commit for life," Kaze finished. "I know what I signed up for, Sir."

The Major nodded, like something had been cleared up for him. "For now, the LT-5 bolt override will lock you out from accessing that ability. Once your Star-Keys are cleared for duty, the responsibility will be placed upon you."

"Whatever makes Astral Guard more comfortable, Sir." Schooling his features, Kaze looked straight ahead.

"Then we should move on to our first weapon's discharge examination." Rajek raised an eyebrow momentarily softening his

O'Garcian features. "Alpha Blue, I'll handle your assessment myself while the Arms-Master will evaluate Alpha Green's capabilities."

The two were escorted through another set of doors, where they were shown to a firing zone. A clear grid-shield of octagonal beams connected like a net, separating the brothers' firing booths.

The Trone had been hovering close to Kaze, so when the grid-shield separated the two, its lights ran through a sequence of colour flashes, pausing briefly when Zozes glared at it. Kaze grinned. It was like his brother was accusing it of turning traitor.

The Arms-Master moved to Zozes' side, silently working on a porta-tool, looking up every now and again.

"Blades," called Major Rajek. "Gear up."

Both brothers pressed the Blade-Gear located on the centre of their belts, activating its tele-warp function, the Gears transporting power armour over their bodies.

"Next," the Major ordered. "Tele-warp sorge-pistol."

After initiating the process, Kaze looked down at his hip to see the cyber-graphic outline forming inside the holster, signalling a tele-warp in progress. Keeping his hand clear, he waited for it to finish, knowing disruption would cancel the process. The moment it was solid, he drew the pistol, watching as Zozes did the same half a beat later.

Silently, Rajek input data on his porta-tool. "Blades," he called. "I'm activating the Link-Trone's sorge-spawn energy type for first analysis. Stand prepared."

A series of red targets materialised at the end of the firing range. Rolling his shoulders, Kaze drew his weapon, peering through the barrel's sight, waiting for the Major's order.

A dark figure suddenly appeared among the targets, features shadowed, unrecognisable.

Eyes bulging, Kaze jerked back, fighting to collect himself. No one else noticed; he could tell he was the only one.

"The Link-Trone is designed," Rajek began, breaking Kaze's attention, "to calculate every situation it encounters within tactical analysis."

When he looked back, the figure was gone.

"Blade? Are you alright?"

"I ... yes, Sir!" Kaze looked again at the Major, schooling his features to appear neutral.

Thoughtful, Rajek stepped closer. "We are in unknown territory Blade, you need to be honest. It's one thing to be connected as a non-primary, as you were to your previous Alpha Chief, but you are now both Alphas. Your brother's command training means he is more prepared for this transition."

"You'll be surprised what I can do." Stealing himself, he looked back, reassured to find no figure standing silently among the red targets.

"That remains to be seen, Blade. You are yet to understand what being connected truly entails." Stepping back, Rajek resumed. "Tactical analysis is broken into numerous categories. For this exercise, I want you to order the Link-Trone to initialise threat evaluation."

A moment later, the cyber-optic overlay appeared before Kaze's eye, displaying the individual site-lock coordinates of each target and a tracking motion guide. There was also a rundown on each target's composition and dimension, and the best weapon to deactivate them.

Looks like we're fully paired with the Link-Trone, thought Kaze, knowing that now was not the time for distractions but unable to contain the thought ... had Zozes seen the figure?

When his brother initiated a sensor scan of the Blast Training Range, Kaze shook off the question, focusing.

"Threat evaluation in process, sensor sweep underway," the Trone intoned. "Calculating ... training facility detected. Generating armaments for non-lethal weapons testing."

Everything was working. Kaze took aim, energy pistol comfortable in his hand, breathing light and steady.

"Let's begin first to fifteen blast-targets," suggested Rajek, signalling the Arms-Master to prepare Zozes.

Weapon held lightly, Kaze studied the blast-target in front of him. Almost immediately, they began deactivating and reactivating.

"We'll be cycling through different Assault Modes," Rajek said. "If the Link-Trone's threat evaluation registers a class-one target, immobilise-strike will be initiated, paralysing the target with non-lethal rounds." Rajek took another step back, generating a final row of blast-targets. "Weapons primed. Live fire exercise in three, two, one!"

Kaze fired on the first cyber-graphic target but missed, the device deactivating before he could land a hit. Redrawing, thought into reflexes, he fired several more shots, this time striking a couple mid-motion, both dispersing. Focusing was harder than he had anticipated, but he hadn't factored the shadowy image still in his mind.

Instantly, the figure reappeared almost halfway up the tunnel, seeming to jolt into existence. Disorientated, Kaze blinked while his heart pumped a tattoo, sweat beading his forehead.

Why was he seeing it? Who was it? What the vok was going on?

"Focus, Blade!" ordered Rajek, "Your brother has only three blast-targets remaining."

Unnerved, Kaze glanced at the Major, who was frowning at him. He obviously did not see the figure. Glancing across at his brother, he saw he had now finished firing.

"Karbroe?"

There was concern in the Major's voice. Mentally, Kaze shook himself, forced his mind to calm, his breathing to level while looking at the deck. Failure was not an option.

When he looked back down the tunnel it was clear, and he could now see the pattern the blast-targets were following. Through his cyber-optic overlay, he marked their positions, taking aim and firing a series of bolts that knocked out each target as it appeared.

"Disengage exercise," Rajek ordered the Arms-Master. "Well, Blade, not a bad end. Once you discovered the targets' cycle pattern you didn't drop a shot."

He barely heard the Major, still watching the firing tunnel. "Run the test again, Sir, the warm-up's done."

"Not necessary, the examination was to test your reflexes, focus and connection while using the Link-Trone. The targets are designed to deactivate upon detection of an energy-round. In order to hit the targets, you had to fire before they materialised."

While Rajek reprogrammed his porta-tool, Kaze looked at Zozes. It was hard to tell what his brother was thinking, his expression not giving anything away.

"Activating Link-Trone's next Assault Mode. If the Trone's Threat Evaluation registers a class-two target, fire-strike will be initiated. Charged sorge-rounds will become lethal that can wound or kill a pursued target."

From the moment the next lot of targets appeared, these ones yellow, Kaze felt the power chamber of his side-arm heat in response.

"Alright, let's see if your spawn-nets are assimilating and distributing the correct yield to each sorge-round from your weapon. Alpha Blue, I want you to fire first."

Weapon ready, Kaze took aim. This blast-target was different, protected by a kind of stress-shield that could measure and calculate his weapon's discharge. The moment he pulled the trigger, the sorge-bolt moved through the firing tunnel, dispersing into a white flash-burn explosion. Almost instantly, Kaze felt a corresponding pain, mild but it was there, much like when he had first been paired with the Trone.

Rajek eyed the stress-shield, calculating the sorge-round's output yield.

"Fire again," he ordered. "Three rounds."

Each time Kaze fired, the pain increased, a wash of ice and then fire moving through his spine until his jaw felt welded in place.

"Disengage firing rounds."

On a head shake, Kaze kept his eye trained, determined to keep going until he felt the Major's hand on his arm. "Karbroe."

"Major." Kaze refused to look at his brother. "Commando Perfection over there is more than trigger lucky, firing with no problem."

"That's the difference between operating a command and a solo spawn-net. An adjustment period will be required, where you master the amount of control necessary. Your brother is the embodiment of this as he doesn't overstimulate his neural pathways while centring his concentration on the task at hand."

Despite the situation, Kaze laughed. "Doesn't overstimulate. I think you just summed up my brother's life in two words."

"You cannot force the process, Blade," the Major said. "Now, prepare to commence next firing round."

He had to appease the Major's concerns, Kaze thought, deciding to slow the rate of fire. Almost immediately, the pain eased and he finished without gritting his teeth.

"How do you feel?" Rajek looked at him, clearly pleased.

"I ..." The figure reappeared with jerk, this time standing directly behind the Major. It was so close, Kaze could have reached out and ...

"Karbroe?" Rajek glanced over his shoulder.

"Yes, Sir!" Kaze forced his eyes back to Rajek. "The pain was minimal, Sir."

"There's a few things you need to be aware of. If the Trone believes you are unfit for duty, or impaired in any way, it will lock you out. You will not be able to access any of its tactical functions."

All through that speech Kaze watched the shadowy figure, and for a moment its facial features began to lighten, like they were coming into focus. Then he blinked, and it was gone.

Rajek was looking at him expectantly. "Understood, Sir."

"You can't deceive a Trone. They're linked with your central nervous system. You must comprehend that the spawn-types you have access to are one the most powerful and potentially devastating advancements in the Planetary Allegiance. Link-Trones are the gatekeepers of that power, so it can never be used or abused beyond the means or orders."

"Yes, Sir." Kaze nodded. "Understood, Sir."

"Good, then let's continue with the last Assault Mode. If the Trone's Threat Evaluation registers class-three targets, Havoc Strike will become available. This is only authorised against powerful or numerous enemies breaching through heavy defences."

As Rajek reprogrammed the Link-Trone, Kaze watched his side-arm reconfigure to form a triple barrel. As the chamber of the weapon began priming, Kaze could feel the sorge-energy build. Taking aim at the new range of blast-targets, these orange, he pulled the trigger.

Almost immediately, all sound and light was drained from his surrounds as the sorge-pulse beam shot out, hitting multiple targets in a mass explosion, one that erupted at the end of the blast-range ... and his spine burnt like fire.

For the first time in days, blood dripped from his nose and his vision began to blur, but only for a moment. As the pain faded, he tipped his head back, breathing deep, the iron taste of blood at the back of his throat.

"It doesn't take as long as it first did," he murmured. "To adjust."

"I believe it will get easier each time," Rajek said, nodding to the Arms-Master working with Zozes. "Let's disengage."

As they walked back in the prep-zone, Kaze realised that Thaytis had been assessing their bodies' responses upon a bio-map cyber-screen throughout the exercises. Telemetry for her examinations to determine their suitability to operate the Trone, no doubt, he thought nastily.

"I'll organise a meeting with Commodore Vae'gon," she said, gathering her equipment, then walking to the door.

"What will you be recommending?" asked Zozes.

"I've got to say, results are beyond projections." Pausing, she looked back. "I'll be recommending a return to active field duty for both of you to Commodore Vae'gon."

"And I'll be seconding it," added the Major. "Your performance here should suffice for what is to come."

"For a Galactic Officer," Kaze said, "you seem well-versed in Blade protocol."

"I've a feeling," Zozes added, "that's come from first-hand knowledge. Trone-Hybrid?"

Stunned, Kaze stared at the Major with new eyes, noting his attire was in fact Galactic Force, custom-grade, a clear indication of accomodations to rank, permitting a personalised status. "You were part of Blade Mark One program?"

Rajek nodded. "A long time ago."

Kaze scrambled to remember the statistics. "Only a handful of candidates survived Trone Cell integration, it was said to be fatal back then."

"I lost many good comrades," the Major said quietly, carefully closing his porta-tool. "We believed in what we were doing."

After a long look, Zozes gestured to his body. "How much of you is left?"

Rajek shrugged, pausing in packing up his personal gear. "Vital organs, central nervous system. Everything else, down to my hair and skin, is synthetic."

"What about ..." Kaze wondered if was too personal, but then again, he had to know. "Your physical sense?"

"Gone." The Major looked at both Blades, his expression neutral. "Replaced by artificial responders." Lifting his arm, he ran his opposite hand over it. "Physical stimuli, for want of a better term, is controlled by pressure triggers. These activate electrical currents within my synthetic skin grafts which then move into my neural pathways."

"You mean," Kaze was trying to keep up, "it's like a mild electrical shock every time you touch something?"

"In a manner of speaking." Rajek eyed his reaction. "But very minimal, though it took time to adjust. I have triggers over my entire body that can be activated and deactivated."

"Kind of puts my bloody nose thing into perspective," Kaze muttered. What the Major had been through ...

"The Second Galactic War," Zozes said. "That was a different time. It demanded much of everyone, but at least now spawn-infusion is illegal. The loss of life, and the suffering. For a time, the Planetary Allegiance lost its way, falling victim to the same power that turned the Kadra against us."

"Illegal for very good reason," Kaze said, watching the Major, wondering at the pain caused by every movement. "Parts of our anatomy are all about touch, and should remain whole with our full senses intact."

"The way I look at it," said Rajek, surprising both brothers, "is that for such regulations to be formed, they first must be broken. I am a product of those consequences. Without such sacrifice, the second generation of Blades would never have come to fruition."

"That's true," Zozes said. "Did you serve with the Archetype?"

At that question, the Major smiled, surprising both brothers. "You speak of Nyron, the first Blade."

Enforcer Noremar interrupted. "Sir, when you are ready, we need to move."

The three turned, eyeing her impatient Devronian stare. Kaze smirked, and the slits of her eyes narrowed.

"However." Major Rajek re-established control over the Link-Trone via his porta-tool and the LT-5 bolt overrider, disengaging the Blades. "That discussion must wait for another time."

Annoyed, Kaze triggered his Blade-Gear to disassemble his combat equipment, tele-warping it off his body and into his Blade-Gear's stasis-loader.

Noremar watched as the doctor prepared the portable stasis casket, activating the access port and tele-warping the Link-Trone back inside the unit.

"Once you've both been cleared," the Major added, "the Trone will be able to stay online permanently."

Relieved, Kaze nodded, watching as his brother looked around the prep-zone thoughtfully.

"Has Command assigned us to a deployment squad, Sir?" he asked.

Clearly impressed at Zozes' suspicion, Rajek nodded. "They have Alpha Green." He nodded to the doctor, then the Enforcer. "You're looking at them, including me."

Noremar watched Kaze's reaction, her expression flinty. "Objections, Blade?"

"None. If that's what it takes to get us back on active duty." Kaze met her cold stare, letting his words soak in. She broke first with a snort of disgust and stomped out, the doctor following with the stasis casket.

On a more traditional route, Zozes nodded. "Looking forward to serving with your team, Major."

"Indeed." The Major moved off, following the squad down the corridor.

Kaze pulled his brother aside as soon as they were gone, glancing up and down the corridor. "You saw it? That figure back there?"

On an exaggerated eye roll, his brother tried to walk on, but Kaze pulled him up. "Zozes!"

"What?" Jerking free, Zozes eyeballed his brother. "All I saw was you goading the Enforcer with your—"

"No!" Kaze cut in. "No warping of subject. I know you saw her out there."

"Residual effects from the Trone's sync-pulse, that's all. Must have triggered some form of cognitive-visual response."

"A waking memory?" Kaze scrambled to keep up. "I've never heard any reports of that."

"Regardless," Zozes said, seemingly relieved to have defined it, even to himself. "This needs to be kept between us. It will pass with time as our dual-pairing matures."

Kaze chewed on the idea. "Like the Major said, we're in uncharted territory now."

"I couldn't agree more." Zozes tried to walk on, groaning as Kaze pulled him back. "What?"

"The last time I saw her ... I could have reached out she was so close ..."

"Kaze," Zozes interrupted. "She's a memory now, nothing more."

For a long moment, the two battled in silence, glaring at one another.

"We have to let her go, both of us." Resigned, Zozes began walking down the corridor. "It's what the Chief would have wanted."

Galactic Star Key: Zozes Karbroe
Astral Nav-Coordinates: EAS-APL-4
Data Sequence: 6.0

As the tele-warp doors parted, Zozes passed between, Kaze at his side. No operator was in sight, and he could see most of the room's primary functions were powered down. Even the warp-block was not lit up.

His brother began to prowl the small area, clearly annoyed, before finally halting to stare at the warp operator's console. "Either we're early for a change or in the completely wrong warp-bay."

"I'll check." Zozes refreshed his cyber-optics' overlay, watching the information fall before his eyes, scanning the navigator link-up sent by Major Rajek.

"We're ahead of schedule." There were no seats, so Zozes leaned against the wall. "Relax."

Boredom already setting in, Kaze joined him. "You know me. I live for the voyage, not the destination."

Dramatic as always, thought Zozes rolling his eyes. When the doors opened, he straightened, nodding to Rajek. "Sir."

"Well ahead of schedule. Good start, Blades." Major Rajek strode into the bay followed by Thaytis Venlara and an Astral Guard Tele-Warp Operator.

Thaytis gave Kaze an odd look as he slowly straightened, before returning to the cyber-screen on her porta-tool. "Making yourself comfortable?"

"Always." Kaze fought off an exaggerated yawn, like he was making a point.

Annoyed, Zozes restrained the urge to give his brother a swift kick, instead watching the Operator move to the waist-high control terminal, activating several cyber-screens and initiating a start-up sequence for tele-warp jump. One glance back told him that Kaze had just noticed this too, and was eyeing the Operator's pre-warp diagnostic warily.

"Now that your duty status has been reactivated," Rajek said, "your Star-Keys have been granted official access to the Interstellar Station this Galaxy Ship is docked on."

On a ripe grin, Kaze nodded to the Major. "We've travelled more than enough light cycles, Sir. Stepping foot on that Station's been playing on my dreams."

"Dreams?" Zozes barely restrained a laugh. "That's far tamer than your usual flights of imagination."

"You know me in isolation, brother. It affects the mood and subdues the senses. Freedom, that's the best stimulation for up here." He tapped his temple. "Keeps the mind apt for all situations."

"Subdues the senses?" Thaytis tapped her chin thoughtfully. "So, if you were taken captive, you'd presumably request execution ruling?" She glanced at the Major. "Best I log that in his Galactic Star-Key."

"Me? Taken prisoner?" Kaze barked a laugh. "Not while this spawn-net's still firing."

"With an attitude like that," Thaytis sighed heavily, "I'd best issue you with a portable tissue-welder." Tone condesencing, she added, "However the item's complexity would likely bewilder, resulting in not the best consequences."

Eyes narrowed, Kaze viewed her warily. "There she goes again, phasing in the TECH-*jaw stigma* to overcomplicate common medical practice—"

Thaytis wiped pointedly beneath her nose, stopping him cold with a grin. "I was only recommending you include a reserve set of ray-sheets in your stasis-loader for when exertion breaches common sense."

Outwitted, Kaze hit back in the only way he knew how. "There's only one place I need ray-sheets to wipe over."

Zozes stepped in. "Regardless of bloody noses, it'll be good to have our boots touchdown, something we can all agree on."

"You'll understand the restrictions placed upon this Station soon enough." The Major accepted their impatience readily. "Generally, we like to begin with giving new personnel a tour, but that must be postponed. Your mission takes priority."

"You make it sound like we won't be remaining on the Interstellar Station," Kaze said.

Rajek climbed the two steps and took position on the dimly lit teleportation block, turning to face the room. "You won't. There's been a new development."

As Thaytis took position beside him, Zozes stepped up, then turned to see his brother's hesitation.

"Let me guess." Thaytis sighed heavily. "Your brother has a problem with tele-warp."

"Problem?" Kaze glared at her, then the warp-block, visibly gritting his teeth. "Not me, no problem here."

Zozes rolled his eyes, belatedly noting the doctor's vivid gaze turned his way.

"Alpha Green?"

"He's never placed much trust in any form of tele-warp technology. A misguided fear of something materialising ... out of place."

"Really? Another impairment to add to his Galactic Star-Key." Thaytis' eyebrows rose. "You do realise you use this technology each time you generate your Blade equipment onto your body?"

"*Onto* my body," Kaze ground out. "There's a difference between that and tele-warping my entire body to a whole new transit-site."

"Well," Thaytis said thoughtfully, absently flicking through something on her porta-tools generated cyber-screen. "I wouldn't concern myself, Blade. Anything non-vital that might be misplaced can always be removed. I'm more than skilled with beam-scalpel."

On a huffed breath, Kaze opened his mouth to respond, but Rajek halted the back and forth. "Alpha Blue?" he intoned expectantly.

Kaze clambered up the steps, grimly taking position. Zozes knew every movement was torture for his brother after being cut off a second time.

"New orders have been issued," the Major said, "to deploy a ground team on Earth. We are to assist the Astral Guard in an investigation involving Global Reach."

Zozes chewed on the information, hiding his surprise. "Astral Guard's Bureau of Security doesn't usually issue joint operations."

"Agreed, this is a rare occurrence." Rajek nodded. "But the mission has grown since its conception, so several divisions are being sent by the Planetary Allegiance to achieve the objectives."

"Good." Kaze rolled his shoulders. "Means there's something worth hunting planet-side."

"Be careful what you covet, Blade." The Major's face hardened. "As it may come true."

The Tele-Warp Operator made the final adjustments on his terminal, the virtual screen flashing a set of coordinates.

"Ready, Sir!"

The Major drew the squad to attention, giving him the go ahead.

"Everyone hold position," the Operator ordered. "Tele-warp coordinates locked. Ignition begins on a count of three, two, one ... and warping."

The grip of the jump was instant. Zozes felt the extreme pull as his body was broken into radiant matter orbs.

Every tele-warp Zozes had experienced, he felt deaf and weightless, yet his mind able to account for each moment, how he was aware of passing through the ship's bulkhead, out onto the Space Station, where he was reconfigured, each cluster of warp-patterns igniting in randomised bursts, materialising bone, muscle, skin and clothing.

The instant Zozes was whole, he could hear the sounds of teeming personnel, his boots firmly planted on a mobile tele-warp block that overlooked the busy Space Station's internal docking zone.

It looked like the entire Integration Fleet. The docked Galaxy Ship from which they had just tele-warped was positioned next to a landing platform holding a squadron of Pentar Star-Jets.

"With me." Major Rajek led off, striding quickly down a wide tele-warp deployment ramp designed for large volumes of incoming and outgoing personnel.

"From what I can tell," Zozes said, looking around, "this Primordial Station's internal cityscape circulates the entire planet?"

"In a manner of speaking," agreed the Major. "Its infrastructure conforms to numerous formations. This Space-Ring alone is part of twelve modules."

"A little excessive," Kaze said, squinting. "Without the aid of trone-optics, most of this station's cityscapes are barely conceivable. All I'm seeing is blurry shapes on the far horizon."

"Something to be explored much later," Rajek said, moving forward purposefully.

A lot of uniformed personnel filled the platform, many of them working on ships, replacing taxed systems. Others were working at cyber-terminals, looking over ship schematics, obviously preparing their teams for system maintenance.

Some of the larger cyber-screens, Zozes noted, displayed the Space Station's layout, the design highly progressive. Pausing, he stepped closer to look over a virtual control screen, obviously Primordial in origin, observing the foreign communication markings that seemed to represent a language. Complex, parts of it appeared almost hieroglyphic.

"Astral Guard," continued the Major, "have established transit outposts through the entire Astro-Way Landing Zone. These are networked so personnel can safely operate mobile tele-warp rims, but of course you need clearance to do it."

"I advise becoming accustomed to this mode of travel," Thaytis said.

"Agreed," seconded the Major. "We use it a great deal."

"Work-shy talk for convenience if you ask me." Kaze rolled his shoulders, clearly disgruntled. "Nothing more gratifying then placing a sturdy foot forward and trekking to your destination."

Kaze always felt it necessary to justify an inadequacy, thought Zozes, and usually via his smart mouth. "With no tele-warp, Kaze, we'd still be aboard the Galaxy Ship, decks away from the deployment bay using your conventional method."

"And time," Rajek interjected, "is a limited commodity, Blades."

"If it's efficiency you want," Kaze argued, "my combat suit's grav-thrusters could boost me here in less than half the time."

Eyes narrowing, he swung around to face the doctor walking backwards. "Care to log that one into my Star-Key?"

"That's a bizarre state of reasoning, Alpha Blue, especially if you think I've nothing better to do than chase you around."

"You sound doubtful," Kaze goaded. Zozes willed him to shut up.

"Of what?" Thaytis inquired.

Kaze jerked a hand toward the ceiling. "Feeling my thrusters' force as they break the gravitational pull, leaving you mid-air and motionless."

"You're delusional."

"I'll be jetting forward in style, while you're floating in zero gravity, your only company the rules you live by." He turned and walked after the Major.

Thaytis briefly glared at Kaze's back, before also starting after the Major, who had doubled his pace. Bemused, Zozes rounded a spacecraft, neatly avoiding a spilled engine and several flight engineers.

Now that his squad was silent, Rajek spoke. "Establishing and maintaining a tele-warp transit system is a necessity when dealing with a Station of this size, so I suggest you both get used to it."

Kaze was going to have to get used to it, Zozes thought, and hopefully before he annoyed anyone else. Focusing his attention on a much larger tele-warp system ahead, he watched as a power-armed contingent of Astral Guard Enforcers materialised on it. At shouted orders from their Captains, the newly arrived squads moved off, falling into formation.

"Looks a little heavy on Enforcers for an Integration effort," Kaze said, eyeing the same squads. "Are we expecting trouble, Major?"

Zozes tried to ignore his brother's not-so-subtle fishing, wishing it was coated in a little more courtesy.

"The wise never seek trouble, Blade." Rajek glanced at the Galactic Force's base infantry units, his expression serene. "The effort and scope needed to secure a Space Station of this age provides many complications and," he paused briefly, "this particular Primordial Installation has been catalogued as the oldest and most advanced superstructure in the galaxy. When it was seized during the Second Galactic War, our adversaries left behind an array of countermeasures to hinder our efforts in stabilising this world."

"You speak of the Kadra." Even saying the name made Kaze's lip curl in disgust. Zozes understood the feeling well.

"Their reach has been deep." Rajek gestured below. "Right into the bowels of this Installation."

"A difficult fact to believe," murmured Zozes.

"Their presence still lingers," assured the Major. "Remain vigilant, for this Station holds not only those countermeasures, but secrets that could lead us to the Star races."

"Star races?" Zozes paused, turning to the Major. "As in, where all life came from?" he asked cautiously.

As usual, Kaze spoke without thinking. "I didn't take you as a believer of the Actrix Emanation Theory, Sir."

"Over time, much of my life has been stripped away." Rajek lifted a hand, looking at it in a way that suggested he was seeing something different. "But none can take away my faith."

For some reason, Zozes found this reassuring, right up until his brother ruined the moment.

"Sir, your legs are going to get tired chasing that theory. The Star race are long dead, it was their time." Kaze gestured to the high columns coming into view, adorned with alien hieroglyphics, similar to what Zozes had seen earlier. "That's the reason they left these Primordial Superstructures behind, a keepsake that boasts of their achievements, so we'll never forget."

"That sounds a little simplistic to me," Thaytis said.

"In my mind," Rajek said, "it's a question of how one defines living."

Kaze glared from Thaytis to Rajek. "Don't do that, answer a question while asking another. It leads nowhere."

Amused, Zozes raised an eyebrow. "Or does it?"

Kaze mumbled words under his breath that were better kept to himself. Zozes fought a laugh.

"For now," Rajek said, "our focus needs to be on how we bring about the Integration effort of the world, Earth. Every move we make must safeguard its inhabitants, that is our highest priority.

It is very important they become part of the Planetary Allegiance. No complications will be tolerated. Remember that, Blades. Earth and its inhabitants are our highest priority."

"We understand," Zozes assured, briefly glaring at his brother, who nodded.

"And the Troop deployments?" Sounding anything but convinced, Kaze openly trawled for information. "Care to share the specifics of these countermeasures left behind by the Kadra?"

At the blatant question, Thaytis shook her head, obviously exasperated. Zozes eyed the stiff set of her shoulders, smiling to himself. Kaze certainly knew how to get under someone's skin.

"For now, Blade," the Major said, spearing Kaze with a look, "that information is classified."

While his brother huffed at the reproof, Zozes followed Rajek through to the transit zone, where they came across a mass of networked tele-warp base units interconnected. These were larger, moving great volumes of material which were primarily used as a supply line. Personnel were loading cargo onto grav-carts, then loading them to storage depots.

The Major paused to speak with a distribution officer before moving to stand near a platform's access gateway.

Kaze jabbed Zozes in the side, pointing to the left of the marina, to what looked to be its heart. A horizontal stream of pure white energy was bouncing back and forth between a series of power conduits. It was quite a sight.

The Major was studying a small access terminal beside a gateway. It was wide enough to admit several personnel at once. The configuration of the terminal was unlike any Zozes had ever seen, obviously Primordial in origin. When Rajek moved his hand, Zozes caught sight of the converter device attached to the terminal's side, which looked to be Galactic-issue.

"Retro-formers?" Kaze asked, eyeing the Planetary Allegiance equipment design.

The Major nodded, activating it via his porta-tool. "These converters have been configured to control Primordial Systems."

"No small feat for the Planetary Allegiance, managing to bridge that gap between our technology and that of Primordials."

Zozes eyed the converter, which suddenly changed from red to blue, obviously coming online.

"Astral Guard are responsible for all that you see here. Development has had its reasonable share of setbacks, but of late it's been a fairly effective operation." Rajek began imputing commands into the console. "Retro-formers are the only way for us to operate Primordial technology. Without these convertor units, we're locked out, can't even access the most basic of functions."

"It takes some adjusting," Thaytis added. "The retro-formers operate differently to a standard terminal. You'll both need a quick course in operating the network. Service patches constantly need updating to align this station's systems to that of the Command Mass-Trones."

Zozes nodded at this information. "How many command AIs have been established here?"

Major said, "Twelve on one Space-Ring alone."

Critical, Kaze eyed the technology. "What use are they, if none of them can make any of this retro tech self-automated? Another useless skill that I don't care to acquire."

The doctor's gaze landed on Zozes. "I'm not surprised, Alpha Blue, though your brother appears to be someone who is good with his hands."

"When LT's finally reinstated within our squad, that'll count us out of the senseless manual hardship." Nudging his brother, Kaze added, "You know, this Alpha thing levels us with some specialist perks."

Barely aware of Kaze's ramble, Zozes' mind was back analysing the doctor's words. Had there been a double-edged meaning to that offhand comment? Not game to look at her, he kept his eyes on the converter, inwardly groaning when Kaze suddenly piped up again.

"Doctor, remind me of that old native Hasnirian adage from the colony region of Vegita's second moon? 'An effort without struggle is an effort without appreciation'?" Bait dropped, Kaze waited for her to bite. "Or something like that."

"You managed to maintain your attention long enough to glance over my Star-Key's service file. Congratulations." Crossing her arms, she looked Kaze up and down.

"You can congratulate my brother." Kaze slapped Zozes on the shoulder, rocking on his heels. "Looking it over at great length, he was. Wouldn't want to miss anything." Kaze raised an eyebrow, doing a fair imitation of the Major. "Would we, Zozes?"

Clearly surprised, Thaytis went from haughty to amused in the blink of an eye. "I see."

"It was ..." Zozes swallowed, thinking fast, "standard procedure. I always review the team members' backgrounds." Relief flooded him, though it did not crush the urge to throw his brother off the nearest platform.

"No judgement." Kaze held up a hand. "I just don't recall you reading the Major's in quite such depth or so intimately ... err ... I mean intently. Wouldn't want to make anyone uncomfortable."

"Of course not." Zozes' stare pinned his brother. "You never do."

He could feel the doctor's gaze on him. Keeping his own trained on his brother, Zozes fought to appear patient and unaffected.

"Oh." Kaze backtracked grandly. "Clearly I misread the situation."

"Getting back to our previous discussion," Thaytis said. "Despite your aversion, Alpha Blue, it will take a diligent mind to understand and work with retro-formers. It's one of the main reasons I still prefer to work on board the Galaxy Ship."

While the doctor elaborated, Zozes edged back discreetly, trying not to appear he was doing so, since he was finding the scent of her hair distracting. Kaze grinned, eyeing his every move while leaning against the wall, arms folded.

Major Rajek turned from the terminal. "Operating zones on the station are slowly being established and fitted with retro-former converters and adapters."

Kaze reviewed the one the Major was working on with a critical eye. "No adapters, no access. Wouldn't want to be stranded outside an operative zone anytime soon."

"Sounds simple enough." Zozes eyed the retro-former. "You just have to follow procedure."

"I get the feeling," Kaze murmured, "that you and the Major are going to be fast friends."

The terminal suddenly powered, its interface generating micro-beams that formed into solid fractal mesh that had the ability to interchange into numerous shapes and patterns. Zozes realised then that the access panel was not solely operated by cyber-graphic technology, as the interchangeable material restructured the surface of the console before his eyes.

For a moment, Rajek watched it. "Zones not fitted with retro-formers are on lockdown, Blades, for obvious reasons. We don't want anyone getting stranded in a non-serviced area."

Zozes eyed the large structure ahead, recalling what he had learnt. It was called the Pulson Dome, an advanced teleportation structure. The dome was a separate structural island, not connected to the docking platform and suspended a good distance away, supported by an active graviton ring.

"Almost there," the Major said, eyeing the interface. The fractal mesh reconfigured into a diagram that looked to form a bridge. "Now it's verifying my Star-Key, allowing access to the Pulson Dome."

On his last words, the Major opened one of the rear security barriers on the docking platform, allowing it to retract. Zozes stepped forward, eyeing the bottomless drop on the other side, a gentle breeze ruffling his hair and dragging a few strands free to fall over his eyes. It came from the depths of the station and was cool on the skin. Breathing deep, he looked across the expanse, feeling he was just beginning to understand the scope of this Primordial Station.

"The Pulson Dome," the Major said, "is where our mission will commence. Giving us a means of transportion to Earth."

"Is the access bridge down, Sir?" Kaze looked across, then eyed the drop. "If you're asking me to jump this one, I'll need a good run up."

The Major turned to them both, his expression unreadable. "Patience, young Alphas." Rajek looked again over the cavernous distance, then stepped off the platform.

Zozes felt his heart drop. Shocked, both brothers lunged, their hands closing over nothing but air.

"Major!" Kaze bellowed.

"Blade?" answered a voice.

Zozes pulled his brother back, the two finally seeing the Major standing just below, looking over his shoulder with his usual raised eyebrow. He was standing on floor panels that had materialised from the platform generator port, reconfiguring as he took each step.

A soft laugh from behind told Zozes that this play had been performed before.

Thaytis touched his arm. "Practical ruse served best on newly stationed personnel. Welcome to Former-lane technology."

Annoyed at being taken in, Kaze grumbled before stating, "Wasted effort if you ask me."

"I was under the impression that you would appreciate that type of creative will," the Major mocked gently. "Your Star-Key states as much."

The former-panels finished configuring, joining with the edge where the Major stood.

Kaze kicked at it with his booted foot. "You say creative." He stepped out watching the former-panels materialise. "More a touch certifiable. Sir."

Thaytis joined them, looking back at Zozes, still on the edge. "It's quite safe, Blade. Former-lane fractal assembly units bind to reconfigure en route. Your proximity makes certain they will generate."

Zozes stepped out and the group began to move across the bridge growing before them. With each step taken, more panels reconfigured beneath their feet.

The Major indicated right. "Advanced users can manipulate flooring panels to alter their directional pathways. I suggest starting slow, though."

Zozes looked ahead to the Pulson Dome which was large and multi-faceted. It was built out of off-set segments that reflected the light, giving the structure a look of depth and mystery. Beneath it, the graviton ring shone brilliantly, supporting the Dome's weight seemingly effortlessly. Zozes could see a vertical beam of light shooting from beneath. Power output seemed to be directed toward the core of the Space Station itself.

Thoughtful, he stepped from the former-panels to the deck of the Dome, which appeared similar to the assembled former-panels of the bridge. The technology incorporated the same type of binding process, fractal-units. These seemed to be permanently fixed.

The Major approached another round-shaped Gateway entrance, activating the retro-former interface to grant them access to the Dome.

"Getting here's a lot of effort," Kaze said, eyeing the super-structure.

The interface's micro-beams formed into fractal blocks, reconfiguring the panel, then the door, which Zozes realised were comprised of similar material. Before them was a wide entryway with several access tubes leading off it.

"Indeed." Rajek stepped into the entryway. "Professor Marzden oversees the Dome, and he ensures strict security measures. Only select personnel are granted access. His experience with Primordial technology is extensive, making him invaluable. He takes his duty status very seriously."

"Magel Marzden? " Zozes triggered a clasp activator within his left hand, generating a small porta-tool screen. Ring pointers appeared over his right fingers, allowing him to load the Professor's Star-Key. Checking his current serving status, he deactivated the device, glancing at his brother. "Magel may be a possible connection with Dignitary Marzden of New Moncove. The family line has a long service record in the Civil Federation."

Kaze ran a hand over the stubble of his chin. "A redirection of duty service to science over political establishment? Nothing more controversial then breaking family tradition, if you ask me."

The squad followed the Major into one of the tubes, Zozes glancing behind to see the former-panels reconfigure, closing the doorway.

"In short," the Major said, "don't touch anything."

"Hmm." Kaze glanced at Zozes. "I've a feeling that was for my benefit."

"Go with the feeling."

The access tube curved to the left, disappearing as they walked forward, in a similar way to the Former-lanes of the bridge. There looked to be many levels within the Dome from what Zozes could see, with countless staff handling Primordial technology.

"The professor has a large staff at his disposal," Zozes said, watching a group of female science officers pass them, the leader operating a hover-cart transporting stasis units.

"He certainly does," Kaze agreed, jauntily saluting one of the rear female officers who looked back. "This place is an understatement of varying complexities. I don't see the need to keep these hands on stand-by."

The Major frowned. "Stand-by is where they will remain, since not all require your expertise."

"I wasn't referring to the Dome."

"Neither was I."

Zozes barely restrained cuffing his brother, especially when Kaze glanced again at a dark-haired Junior Lieutenant trailing the group, grinning and mouthing something to her. He hoped the Major missed the action, but doubted it. Probably a wise course of action was to just ignore Kaze, a practice he needed to master.

The squad left the tunnel, coming into a large room with a vaulted ceiling. At the centre was a pale, luminescent beam of energy moving vertically between power conduits, smaller than the one in Astroway Marina, but identical in design.

These beams had to be some type of energy source, thought Zozes. Probably connected to or in control of Primordial technology. Turning further, his jaw dropped a little as he spotted a Spawn Chamber on his right, surrounded by Astral engineers.

Stunned, Kaze stepped forward. "That looks like our ..."

"It is. We managed to salvage your Blade Engineering Chamber." For a moment, the Major eyed the blackened frame. "Where your Link-Trone was released from."

Scorch marks marred the unit's armour-plated surface, and many of its components appeared to have been stripped.

"It's well maintained from the deployment protocol mid-jump, before the ship crash landed."

Stepping forward, Zozes eyed the interior casing, which looked heavily charred. "The sorge-shield held? Protected the Chamber?"

"For a time," Thaytis said. "The extraction team was able to secure the Chamber before irreparable damage was sustained. The outer holding shell and external components are damaged, pretty much beyond repair. The bridge holding the Link-Trones, however, is operational."

"You're saying all the Trones are secure?"

"And accounted for," Rajek added.

"So, our mission wasn't in complete vain." A weight he did not know he was carrying was lifted for Zozes, a liberating feeling of relief.

"No, Blade." Rajek rested a hand on his shoulder for a moment.

His brother was on a completely different track, clearly irked. "Why keep this from us?"

"Your reactivation had to be verified first."

Kaze looked even more irritated. "You're saying we may never have been told if not cleared?"

"Kaze ..." Zozes said in a warning tone.

One hot look was all he spared Zozes. "Have you any idea how many Blades sacrificed their lives in the attempt to map the subspace transverse layers so we can freely move on and off this station?"

"They understood the mission's risks when volunteering. As did you." Unruffled, the Major crossed his arms. "Command issues orders beyond our control. These must be followed without emotional attachment. A skill you must acquire, Blade."

Mouth fusing, Kaze let the subject drop. Zozes avoided his brother's gaze but was saved as a disturbance near the rear of the Dome caught everyone's attention.

One of the engineers spun around, pushed by someone barging through. A young Moncovian female almost fell, caught at the last moment by another officer.

A wild-looking man appeared, white hair sprung up in all directions. He was operating a type of twin porta-tool system, a device implanted in each palm. Above his left hand were several schematics, his bulbous eyes looking them over. Opening his right hand, another set of diagrams appeared, and when he tapped his hands together, the schematics joined, several parts beginning to light up, realigning.

Suddenly, he looked up, yelling at several engineers, "Link-Trones twelve, thirty and fifty-seven are out of alignment. Move! This is our last attempt! I'm uploading new algorithms which will establish an effective chain-beam to enhance the network between each of the AI units."

Engineers scurried, some dropping equipment, scattering it around the Blade Engineering Chamber in a bid to complete his orders. The scene was almost comical, but Zozes knew just how serious it was, attempting to bring the collective back into alignment. They had arrived at a critical moment.

The Major walked forward, clearly confused. "Command ordered there be no system retesting."

Sweat beading, the addressed engineer held up a hand, silencing the O'Garcian Major as he activated his subdermal porta-tool. The moment a cyber-screen appeared, generated above his palm, it displayed all operative systems coming online.

"Opening data-feed line, Professor." The engineer's face glowed. "Your upgraded chaining-beam has re-established connection. They're coming online!"

Looking pleased, the Professor activated a control-trigger around his finger, marking areas on his porta-tool's main cyber-screen. "Good, good! Now eject the Spawn-Chamber's memory core and generate the re-calculated variance pattern of this planet's sub-traverse zones. Finally, finally we are achieving!"

"Underway, Sir!" The Moncovian engineer changed cyber-screens, his hand tapping information transferring data across instantly, updating his porta-tool.

Like he was coming out of a trance, the Professor turned, eyeing their squad. "Fajek? Is that you?"

Cold water tossed in the face could not have been more insulting. Zozes surreptitiously kicked his sniggering brother.

The Major was serene. "Rajek. Major Rajek to you, Professor."

"Rajek?" The Professor blinked, his round blue eyes appearing to finally focus. "Are you certain?"

"Without question." Rajek stood aside, indicating the brothers. "Blades, may I finally introduce you to our last team member."

"Blades, you say?" The Professor ran an eye over Zozes and Kaze. "Ah yes, the Commando replacements. So, they've finally been cleared. Now let's see if you can live up to who came before."

This meant only one thing to Zozes. "You worked with the Chief?"

"Feeling intellectual, are we, conjuring a realisation?" Heaving a breath, Magel returned to his porta-tool. "Yes, Blade, extensively.

She was no fool. It's something of a rarity to attain intellect, beauty and boldness all associated in one delightful package."

"Professor." The Major sighed heavily. "The restart?"

"Yes." Shrugging off memories, the Professor pondered the question. "Secondary testing had to be issued."

"Command rejected your request, Professor," Thaytis said. "The original testing figures have been evaluated and cleared."

"Oh, this is an interactive event? Even more opinions!" Magel waved her words aside. "They have no comprehension, no vision, and even less intellectual relevance." He pointed vigorously at the AI chamber. "Do you have any comprehension what is truly taking place on this Primordial Station?"

"I'm well aware of your concerns, Professor Marzden." Obviously, Rajek had heard all this before. "We're all very well aware."

"Then value — better yet, treasure! — the knowledge. This Station's a puzzle, each Space-Ring is comprised of an intricate piece, all of which is shifting deeper and deeper into subspace." He looked Rajek up and down. "Even *you* can understand what that means."

Before the Major could respond, Zozes spoke. "You think we're losing the Station?"

"Blind fact, I tell you. All this," Magel looked around, "will shift beyond our reach, crossing into a dimension beyond, laws, time and reasoning."

"Command has gone over your projections," Rajek said, "and rejected them."

"Simpletons." Magel cut through their arguments like foam on water. "Dismissing claims, altering my findings to serve a fool's errand. Frivolous proposal, using the Stellar Spawn Relays upon Earth, like a tether? Anchoring something this size in normal space time? The very concept is dangerous and the action itself?" He waved his hands agitatedly. "I can't even begin to calculate the outcome!"

"Are you ..." Kaze whispered to his brother, looking around the room, "actually keeping up with this?"

"Enough to know it's not good."

The Major turned to reassure Professor Marzden. "Your observations and requests have been noted, but the mission must get underway. Is this Space-Ring's Spawn Relay synced to the Dome? We need to get to the planet."

Magel eyed the Major for a long moment. "It is," he said finally. "I've aligned your jump coordinates to phase-jump outpost thirty-two. Due to the Global Base lockdown status, they are currently not accepting incoming traffic."

"Understood." Rajek lifted his eyebrow. "If you will, Professor."

Magel led the group to the Spawn Engineering Chamber. Zozes could now see it was connected to a series of strange-looking Primordial Rings, a series of vibrant colours weaving in a pattern as they spun, charging.

"Professor Marzden," called an engineer. "An update of the traverse zone map has been compiled from the Blades' Spawn Chamber. We were just about to eject its memory core."

Zozes viewed the mapping coordinates that would see the squad shift safely from the station's transverse zone through layers in subspace to reemerge in normal space-time on the planet.

The engineer input a series of codes into her porta-tool and a large cylindrical device shifted, shunting forward then back before the mechanism could lock into place, at once depressurising. The moment the circular hatch opened, vapour poured from the port.

Magel ignored this, reaching in confidently to pull the memory core free, the round device protected by a carrier stasis case.

"Excellent." A delighted smile lit the Professor's face. "Now transfer the mapping coordinates to phase-motion Gateway Three. Use it as a guide so the squad can phase-jump personnel from the station to the planet."

"Phase-jump?" Kaze's eyes rounded. "Why do I get the feeling this is still in its experimental stages? And yet we're saying goodbye to tele-warping?"

Major Rajek smiled. "There's no way for a standardised teleporting system to operate beyond the depths of subspace. However, as this is a Primordial Station and its systems are designed to operate spawn technology, we have a second option."

"Phase-jumping." Zozes chewed on the term. "Only a few Blades have been able to master pulson-spawns, and that was during the Second Galactic War."

"And," added Kaze swiftly, "I remember something about pulson-spawns turning Blades insane. You ask me, this plan has some questionable aspects."

"Blades." The Professor's tone was condescending as he waved both observations aside. "Think of this technology like an advanced tele-warp device, one that has no restrictions. Temporal-motion physics is but one of the aspects discovered within omni-force effect. Access to Primordial research opens countless new possibilities."

"Enough." Kaze rubbed the back of his neck, a sure sign of tension. "Just tell me I'll be put back together."

"And in the right order," Thaytis added, smiling at Zozes. He ducked his head.

"Sir?" An engineer drew the Professor's attention, sounding confused. "Shouldn't the calculations be transferred for command overview?"

Magel waved this aside. "I'm uploading my Star-Key for the override. This time I want to initiate the preliminary testing phase myself, then I'll compare the proposed calculations for anchoring this Station to my own." Grim, he added, "Then they'll see who's right."

"Understood, Sir." Obviously still confused, the engineer queried, "Phase-motion Gateway Three, perhaps we should deactivate the alignment before …"

"If you don't mind?" Magel snapped, clearly agitated. "How am I to run a proper subspace Pulson test?"

"Err, well, it's just that … it's against regulation. A subspace navigational map first needs Command to run overview." The engineer stood to attention. "That's Astral Guard orders, Sir."

"Then find a duty you can attend to."

There was no missing the suspicious look the engineer cast the Professor as she moved off, clearly holding her tongue with some effort. When she joined her co-workers, the group began an animated conversation, going over readouts on their porta-tools.

"Professor." The Major stepped close to the Chamber. "That engineer's right. Gateway Three should be shut down until Command clears your results."

"She's young and inexperienced," Magel argued.

"Shut it down, Professor Marzden. That's an order," the Major stated. "We don't want any accidents due to exuberance."

"There won't be any." Magel activated his left-hand porta-tool, pulling up a schematic and adding information too fast for Zozes to track. "Initialising a power down will take time, but it is underway, as ordered, Major."

The Professor then swung to the brothers while initiating a small stasis hatch to open on the Spawn Engineering Chamber.

"Very well, Blades. I believe it's time we disengage your Link-Trone unit from its access port. Wouldn't want to be Trone-less phasing down to the planet!" He chuckled at his unfunny jest. "It's also well placed common knowledge that I'm the only one aboard this station who can effectively control and manipulate an artificial chaining-beam cycle between a multitude of LT units. It's a similar action to an active spawn-drift."

"Seems to me," Kaze whispered, "the load-count of personnel on this station believe they're clear of reproach."

"You think the same of yourself." Zozes said with a shrug, though he privately agreed with his brother.

"I know how to rein in my limits."

"More often those limits rein you in, right into a security brig."

"Simple misunderstandings. Always cleared up," Kaze snapped his fingers, "fast."

"One day, brother, you'll learn there are always consequences."

"You're just jealous because you've never faced any," Kaze smirked.

Their AI Link-Trone materialised, halting Zozes' response. It restructured its outer shell to one of armour, at the same time activating the dual-pairing. His cyber-optic overlays appeared as a flood of information about the Primordial technology surrounding them assailed him.

Rajek broke the silence. "You now understand that these are transport Gateways where we will initiate our phase-shift jump."

"Yes, Sir." Zozes looked over the columns with their subdued lighting. "It seems the elusive pulson-spawn has finally been mastered by you, Professor."

"Keying in the score chart on victories?" Kaze observed. "Are you certain you're not a Blade?"

"Me? Huh, I think not!" Obviously diverted, the Professor eyed Kaze. "All your enhancements could not entice me, living as you do beneath the weight of those above."

"Professor," Thaytis snapped, her expression unusually hard.

Equally annoyed, Rajek took a surprising step forward. "Rule of order is a system that cannot be broken, as well you know. The authority behind every command is respected and passed down to each officer."

"Just as accountability flows upwards," countered Magel. "I need no lecture on your militarised 'rule of order', Major."

"Don't you?" Rajek laughed, but levity was not present. "Best you remember who stands before you in the future, for they are not as lenient as I. Words have consequences, Professor. Remember that."

Surprised at their reaction, Zozes pondered the exchange, which on the surface seemed only a reprimand, but there was more here. Perhaps a lot more.

After mulling on the Major's words, Magel nodded, moving on. "Every accomplishment is stored safely right here." Magel pointed to his temple. "These advanced Primordial Stations are something of a mystery, and without those that built them, our knowledge is hard won, our skills slowly mastered. Unlike conventional transport devices, pulson-spawn connects into this solar system's natural temporal-motion cycles, which are dictated by its central star. Pulson-spawns vibrational effect can shift physical matter through subspace transporting it to materialise in normal space."

Magel tapped the Engineering Chamber, his hand staying there briefly. "Now that we have the correct subspace map provided by your ship's AI Trones, these two principles can be combined as an effective means to move between this Station and planet Earth."

"I'd much prefer to fly a ship, if there's a choice in the matter," Kaze grumbled.

"Well there isn't," Magel sneered. "There's no other option due to the premature disengagement of your Link-Trone. The collection of Trones were in the process of mapping the sub-spatial transverse layers, but that calculation was broken. The map's variance-locking coordinates between all layers are not complete."

"Which means," Rajek added, "the only way on and off the Station is phase-jumping using these Primordial transporters."

"Slow the intel for a moment." Kaze rubbed a hand over his hair, ruffling it in a way Zozes recognised as discomfort. "You're saying we may never be able to pilot a ship on or off this station ever again?"

Magel shrugged. "My current projections suggest that may be so. That your ship made it through is rather astounding due to the shift variance the Station is set within."

"At a great loss of life," Zozes said stiffly. "You're saying all ships on this station are trapped due to the disengagement of one Link-Trone?"

"Debatable, Blade. Much peculiarity and coincidence surrounds that subject, and even more so on the question of your survival. From what I understand, you two are the only Blades who can carry on your Chief's mission."

Zozes bristled, but Kaze responded instantly. "Your meaning, Professor?" he asked, tone dangerous.

"Enough." The Major closed the subject, voice emphatic. "That question is for another time. Remember your place, Professor Marzden."

"Of course," Magel said with faux sincerity, his gaze sliding over phase-motion Gateway Three.

Zozes had a feeling there was more going on here, and when the Moncovian engineer returned, her words did not dispel that feeling.

"Professor Marzden, Gateway Three just went unresponsive."

"At ease, all is as it should be," Magel said, smiling as a central part of the Dome opened before the squad. "See?" Motioning them forward, he eyed the Blades' Link-Trone, which was now moving about freely in a curious manner. "Ahead is the Gateway you are to use, and it's just coming online."

Zozes looked over the line of phase-motion gates, noting their pulsing blue-white energy was at a low intensity. The third Gateway, however, looked different, a glow coming from above, washing down in a wave of iridescent sparks.

"Sir!" called the Moncovian engineer, voice full of alarm. The way she jogged hurriedly back, Zozes knew something was wrong, especially as she was flanked by a senior. "The Third Gateway has not been disengaged, mapping coordinates are still uploading."

"It seems," the senior engineer added, "a set of coordinates have brought the gate fully online."

"Online?" Rajek glared at the Professor. "I ordered it to be deactivated."

On a heavy sigh, Magel shook his head. "Major, Major. It seems pretense is at an end. I simply cannot play-act anymore."

For a moment, the group looked at him in total confusion, until Rajek drew his side-arm, the brothers and Thaytis automatically following suit.

"What's your intent?" the Major demanded.

"Intent?" The Professor watched the Link-Trone warily. Zozes felt it begin generating a threat analysis while activating an immobilising strike.

At that moment, the Third Gateway went from low level glow to fully charged, a brilliant column of swirling energy producing a phase-portal within the chamber. "Why Major, you know me. Full of intrigue and mystery."

Alarmed, Zozes glanced at his superior. "Sir?"

"He's got the stasis case holding the memory core," Thaytis said, her voice rising. "We can't lose that information, it could very well strand us on the Station permanently!"

"We're not going to, Doctor." Rajek measured the Professor for a long moment. "Place that case on the deck slowly. You're not going anywhere, Professor."

"I'm not?" Magel smiled thinly. "I warn you, don't discharge those weapons near a pulson-spawn event horizon. The result would be … regrettable." He took a step back, shuffling awkwardly across to stand before the Third Gateway.

"Then why force our hand?" Rajek said. "Let me speak to Command, we can come to an arrangement."

Magel drew himself up while activating a porta-tool screen, inputting data. "If Command won't help me to save this Primordial Station, then I'll find someone who will."

The gate's swirling energy altered, seeming to gather as it received information, the Professor triggering a cyber-optic shield to cover his eyes, while powering the porta-tool to produce a ray-flare.

All within the Pulson Dome were instantly dazzled, not even Zozes' cyber-optics able to compensate, fighting to make out a rushing figure moving at surprising speed, provoking him into immediate action.

"LT!" Zozes ordered, sprinting. "Activate Blade-Gears now!"

Kaze was a couple paces ahead on his left, the brothers' armour generating around their bodies as the portal began closing. Activating his suit's grav-thrusters, Zozes propelled forward, the Link-Trone at his side.

The pull of the portal widened his eyes, violent streams of colour swirling as he entered a tunnelling vortex, its intense grip stealing his breath, locking him in instant pain. He had never experienced anything like it when tele-warping.

Moments later he was rolling and tumbling across the ground, another wave of bright light hitting his eyes. Gasping for breath, he became aware of gravity, how it was different to that of the Space Station. Pushing himself upright, Zozes eyed the grass and dirt, the distant roll of hills covered in trees. Retracting his helmet, he took a breath of fresh, oxygenated air.

Kaze jumped to his feet directly across from him, retracting his own helmet. "That jump was more than vokked! We're planetside?"

Via his cyber-optics, Zozes viewed the drain on his power armour shields. The phase-jump had been vicious. A strange vapour was evaporating into the atmosphere, something he and his brother had been coated in during the jump. Without their power armours' shields active, they would most likely be dead which begged the question, had the Professor survived?

"You see this?" Kaze asked, gaining Zozes' attention.

At their backs was a weathered phase-motion Gateway, hidden well within dense bush.

"Looks as if the Professor's been planning this for a while," Zozes said, watching the Gateway slowly shimmer away. "Multi-cloak device must be active. LT, open your sensors and start gathering what readings you can."

"At least the air here is fresh." Kaze rolled his shoulders. "There better not be any side-effects from that jump."

"Agreed." Zozes shook off the last of a sick stomach. "Like no ordinary tele-warp, that's for sure." A ping on his cyber-optics alerted Zozes that the Link-Trone had located the Professor's Star-Key signature. "The Professor survived the jump, and he's close. LT, set trace-lock on that signal!"

"He won't get far on foot," Kaze growled, setting off.

The brothers moved fast, running down a steep incline, cutting around trees, forcing their way through thick scrub. Numerous times, they caught sight of native fauna, startling it into either bounding away or flying high.

At a clearing, they found Professior Marzden, bent double and breathing heavily. Weapons drawn, they flanked him. Zozes taking note he was carrying the stasis-unit on his left.

"Pass it over, Professor." Zozes held out a hand. "We're going back."

"You move fast, Blades," Magel gasped. "But I think not." He tossed a mobile tele-warp rim before him, jumping through its field, warping from sight leaving only misty blue vapour in his wake. The tele-warp rim disappeared moments later.

"A mobile tele-warp rim? This vokker plays it well!"

A strange crack on the far right edge of the clearing and the rim materialised mid-air, teleporting warp orbs configuring the Professor. The way he staggered, fighting to stay upright, spoke of disorientation.

Instantly, he began lurching down the incline, aiming his porta-tool at the tele-warp rim, restructuring its size, locking it to his forearm's control unit.

"There's a river ahead," Zozes called to Kaze, both taking off. "And hold fire, the phase-jump disrupted his vitals. An immbolising strike may induce cardiac deceasement."

"Vok it if his heart seizes up! We need to lock down that case."

"That's an order, Kaze! Excute counter solutions to subdue him."

The Professor's abrupt reappearance seemed to have changed the gravity in the immediate vicinity, turning it heavy. It reminded Zozes of moving through water. He put that aside when the Link-Trone began relaying trace-lock, a wave-path the two used as a tracking guide upon their cyber-optics.

"The Professor's tele-warp unit must have been damaged during the phase-jump to Earth," Zozes realised, breaking through bush.

As they moved, the foliage changed, thinning to include rock and boulder as a river came into view. The Link-Trone's wave-path led them around a bend, to find Magel standing on the edge of a cliff, rushing water disappearing over the edge, landing far below if the distant rumble was any indication.

"Professor Marzden!" Zozes called. "Stand down. It's over."

Magel glanced over the cliff. "This case has a genetic seal-clasp installed, separating the device from myself will result in a regrettable end to us all."

Kaze murmured softly to his brother, "Lies, let me take the shot."

On a grimace, Zozes shook his head, searching for an alternative. "You can't transport through a damaged tele-warp rim! You'll risk breaking your own warp-pattern signature."

On a smile, Magel shook his head then wagged a finger at Zozes who was edging forward. "I've survived much worse. I'm prepared, Blade. More than you can know."

"You'll end up a liquefied pool on the ground!" Kaze yelled.

Without hesitation, Magel leapt, jumping off the cliff as the brothers ran forward. For the briefest of moments, they caught sight of a body being swallowed into another active tele-warp rim.

Grim, the two holstered their side-arms eyeing the vacant space which left the sting of ozone zapping the air.

The Link-Trone hovered close. "Star-Key trace lost."

"Over there." Kaze pointed past bush, toward the country flats. "There's some type of settlement in the distance."

Still eyeing the settlement through his Trone-optics, Zozes ran a hand over his face, before pushing back his hair. "Try calculating the signal-lock of the last tele-warp exit window."

After several moments, the information was relayed to both brothers. "Signal-lock verified. Loading last known position coordinates."

"So much for withdrawing my target shot." Kaze looked over the land, a smile tugging at his lips. "The signal ends in that remote settlement. Is it time to visit the natives?"

"It would seem so," Zozes sighed. "LT, what's this place called?"

It took the Trone several moments to reply. "Freestone Valley."

Galactic Star Key: Ebony Casteel
Astral Nav-Coordinates: EAS-APL-4
Data Sequence: 7.0

The fight to wake, to leave the darkness of her mind, took everything she possessed.

Eyes closed, Ebony tested the air, wrinkling her nose at an unfamiliar smell, almost sterile. The moment she moved she was gasping, intense pain ripping through her shoulder into her neck, even down her back.

Her shoulder was in a sling. Cracking her eyes, she took in the white ceiling. Was it day? Turning her head very carefully, she noted the serviceable bedside table carrying a water jug and glass. Next to these was flowers, a mix of colours and varieties.

There was also a grey armchair and a window displaying treetops and blue sky. She was in a hospital, a private room, and this was not the ground floor.

The murmur of voices caught her ear, someone approaching the door. Spotting movement, she watched as it was pushed open, barely catching the end of the conversation.

About to call out, she grit her teeth and instead tried to sit, which left her weak, head spinning and body prickling with sweat. Nausea dug angry fingers through her stomach, curdling it sickly.

As her father backed into the room, talking quietly with someone over his mobile's loudspeaker, she breathed a sigh of relief. Now she would get some answers.

Grace followed him, looking tired until she glanced at the bed. "She's awake!"

"Mum?"

Her mother raced across the room, gripping Ebony's free hand, while hugging her as best she could.

Rickard spun around. "Duke, I'll call you back."

"What am I doing here? What happened?"

Her father moved quickly to the other side of the bed, eyes briefly meeting his wife's. The shake of his head was subtle, but Ebony did not miss it. "Dad?"

"Everyone just hold up," Rickard said sternly, looking pointedly at his wife before making his way across the room. "Remember the procedure, Grace. I'll grab Doctor Walker. Bonnie, you just slow down, stay calm."

"Calm?" Ebony swallowed, frightened to move. "Doctor Walker? I don't know any Doctor Walker."

"Be patient," her mum insisted, brushing at her eyes. "How are you feeling?"

"You're crying!" Ebony could not believe it. "What's going on?"

"I'm just happy to see you awake." Grace smiled shakily.

But it seemed more than that. Then Ebony noticed how bedraggled her mum looked, nothing like the woman who ran the local café with straightforward efficiency. Bruised beneath the eyes, Grace's blonde hair fell around her face, and she had lost weight, her usual cuddly figure gaunt. Even the clothes she wore were rumpled, like they had been worn through the night.

"I'm so glad you recognise us," Grace murmured softly. "It means more than you know."

"What? Why wouldn't I recognise you?"

"You're still healing." Grace lifted Ebony's free arm, indicating injuries. "Physically. Your memory's been more complicated, that's all."

For the first time, Ebony noticed the scrapes and cuts, dried but still sore. "I was in an accident?" Brushing at her face, she searched for further injury. "My shoulder?"

Grace nodded. "We've been here every day."

"I …" Words momentarily failed, Ebony's mind fighting what felt like thick fog. Instantly, her stomach clenched like a fist. "I don't remember. What happened? What happened to me?"

Her father pushed open the door, distracting Grace before she could answer. A female doctor stepped smartly after him.

Ebony eyed the woman cautiously. She looked around forty, dark hair piled into a bun on top of her head. Offering a small smile, she appeared no-nonsense, almost corporate, and not overly friendly.

"Hello Ebony, I'm Doctor Walker." Placing her clipboard on the nightstand, she folded her hands. "It's nice to see those dark brown eyes of yours. How do you feel?"

"Stiff and tired." Ebony winced, trying to push herself up. The doctor had an English accent. Before she could ask, her shoulder jerked painfully. "God that hurts."

"Yes, it was dislocated." She adjusted the sling as she spoke. "We should be able to give you a little more freedom soon. It's healing quickly."

"Dislocated?"

From the corner of her eye, Ebony saw her mum grip her father's arm. Rickard rubbed his own hand over hers, bending to whisper something in her ear.

Ebony was glad they were there, but couldn't help but feeling frustrated. The way everyone was looking at her it felt like they were waiting for her to detonate.

The doctor wrapped a blood pressure cuff above her elbow. As she was taking the measure, she said, "I understand you have questions. In your place, I'd have them too. However, I'd like you to answer mine first, which might in turn answer yours. We can stop if you feel overwhelmed. Just let me know."

"What kind of questions?" Ebony chewed her lip.

"Just standard procedure. No need to worry." The doctor jotted down the reading. "For example, what's your full name?"

Ebony rolled her eyes, but the doctor merely waited, as did her parents.

"Ebony Rose Casteel."

"Your date of birth?"

"Seriously?"

"Seriously. How about we sit you up?" Doctor Walker indicated it was okay for her father to help, while she secured the pillows at

Ebony's back. "There, that looks more comfortable. Now, what's your date of birth?"

With her good arm, Ebony pulled her hair over her shoulder, fiddling with the ends.

"My birthday's March fifteen, nineteen-ninety-six."

"Sounds about right." After taking her temperature, the doctor jotted it down. "Okay, how about your parents' names?"

"Why are you asking such obvious questions?" she blurted, chin jutted.

Grace stepped alongside. "Please, honey. Just a few more. It won't take long."

Her eyes flicked to her father. Though his face was impassive, she had a feeling his calm was an illusion since his hands were balled into fists in his pockets. Wide-shouldered and tall, only those that knew him well would realise he was agitated. Almost as agitated as she felt.

"Rickard and Grace Casteel," she said finally. "And I have a younger brother James, he's eight." Before the doctor could open her mouth, she added, "Let's skip the fact I'm adopted, if you don't mind."

"What year is it?"

Ebony eyebrows shot toward her hairline. "2016."

Silence filled the room. The nurse that walked in paused, then kept walking at Doctor Walker's nod. When she started setting up to take blood, Ebony looked away.

"Okay," she griped. That's when she noticed her parents' blank expressions. "What? You know I hate needles."

"It's not that," Grace said.

"Ebony," the doctor claimed her attention while the nurse took hold of her arm. She winced as the needle stuck her, the doctor completing an eye check. The whole procedure took no more than a few minutes, but she was glad for the distraction.

As the nurse left, Doctor Walker asked, "What's your last memory?"

She shrugged without thinking, her shoulder protesting angrily. "Moving back to Freestone Valley after I left Melbourne. Nina helped, she was with me on the drive back. Jevon—" A horrible thought stopped her mid-sentence. "Was that what happened?

A car accident?" She fought to straighten, ignoring the pain. "Nina and Jev? Are they alright?"

"They're fine," her mother said, moving to her side. "Ebony, relax. No one else has been hurt."

After making another note, Doctor Walker spoke quietly. "I want you to take your time, be very sure that is your last memory. Nothing about the Freestone Festival?"

"Freestone Festival? Why would ...?" A series of staccato images halted her, racing before her mind's eye. Nothing she could control, let alone understand ... a dark street ... jarring music. A ball of fear, icy cold, formed in the pit of her stomach.

"W-what was that?" Breath hitching, she stared at her parents, stared at the doctor, eyes swimming with tears.

"I want you," said the doctor calmly, "to tell me."

"I—I don't know. I saw ... the main street. I was hurt ... collapsed." She could see it, but the images felt distant, like it was someone else. Trying harder, she focused on the street, fighting to see more, see the buildings, but the image pushed back, collapsing in on itself. Swallowing, she tasted blood.

Ebony felt a mild strain bleeding inside her mind. The more she tried to focus, the more pressure she felt.

"Go on."

"There were people. I think I heard Nina. She cried out and then ..." Ebony's throat closed, but she forced herself to keep remembering until a cold sensation spread out from her spine, her arms and legs going numb, an insistent tingling taking control of her body.

Alarmed, she swallowed repeatedly, fighting to regain control, when just as suddenly the cold sensation receded back.

"I don't know, I don't know! I'm ..." She gulped. "What's happening to me?"

The doctor watched her silently, not in the least unnerved. "What year is it, Ebony?"

"What year?" Ebony shook her head. "2016! Why're you asking that again?" Through the silence, she looked hard into Doctor Walker's eyes. They were an intense blue, incredibly bright.

Her mother's hand gripped hers. "This is a good sign, honey." Grace looked at the doctor.

"From the first couple of days, her condition has greatly improved."

Her father, strong and silent, stood at the foot of the bed.

"Cases vary," said the doctor, "no two are alike. Ebony's suffered something extreme, so I'm not going to jump to conclusions or make promises I can't back up. You'll need more tests, a lot more. But," she added, "I'm pleased with the response so far."

"What happened? Was I at the Festival?" For some reason, she was fixated on the point. "How was I there?"

Doctor Walker glanced at her parents. "The truth is we don't know, Ebony. The only option now is to evaluate how your body and mind have reacted."

"You don't know what happened to me?" Ebony stared at the scrapes on her arms, the sling. "How long have I been here?"

"Seven days," Grace answered quietly.

"A week? I've been unconscious for a week?"

"Not the entire time," Doctor Walker said. "We quarantined you for the first three days. Your immune system was low, fighting a foreign fever, one that antibiotics could not treat."

"I was sick?"

"Your body fought off the infection, but it weakened you. That's why we placed you in quarantine. Anything could have been lethal, even the common cold."

"Why do you seem more concerned about what I can remember than the infection itself?"

Doctor Walker laughed softly. "The recovery stage for your body is a short-term issue, however the condition of your mind may take some time to heal."

When her lip trembled, Ebony bit it hard. She felt on the verge of tears, but was determined to not start blubbering.

"So I'm stuck here?" She stared down the bed, toward her father. "I can't go home?"

Rickard looked away, his face reddening noticeably.

"Honey," Grace intervened. "We need to be cautious. This isn't the first time we've had this discussion."

"What do you mean?"

"You've woken before during the week," said Doctor Walker.

"How many times?"

"Four. Each time, you had trouble establishing a connection with who you are. For the first three days, we couldn't get near you, not with the fever. But after, an attempt to reach you was made. We brought in your family and friends to help with your rehabilitation."

"We've a lot to thank Doctor Walker for," added her mother.

Rickard stepped around the bed. "There was other help. Don't forget that, Grace."

Clearly uneasy, Doctor Walker eyed Rickard before looking to Grace. Ebony waited for someone to enlighten her. When no one did, she looked at her father, who remained stubbornly silent. He was the proverbial closed book, a character trait that rode alongside his inability to suffer fools, often acting as a sharp axe, whittling a person's logic with a few choice words.

Doctor Walker tugged at her medical coat, like she had been on the receiving end of that axe. "I think you've made considerable progress," she said brusquely. "Let's leave it at that."

"Even though I can't focus my thoughts?" Ebony huffed a breath. "How long will this last?"

"Think of it like this," the doctor said. "Until today your mind has had difficulty processing past and present memories. For the first few days you had no, what I call, self-identity. That blew out into severe stress and anxiety." Looking down at her notes, she added, "At one point, you didn't even recognise your own reflection."

"You're joking!"

The doctor shook her head. "It was on the second day and your words were ..." She looked through notes, "'Looking upon my reflection, I'm haunted by a ghost, a stranger. She feels somehow familiar, something lost in my past.'"

"I said that?" Ebony looked down at her hands, pulling a face. "Sounds like I was heavily medicated. Maybe it was the drugs or the fever?"

Grace ran a soothing hand over her head. "It's nothing to worry about."

"There's no brain abnormality," the doctor said. "No physical injury. CT and MRI scans can back me up. We've also completed an

EEG, not to mention a battery of other tests." She tapped Ebony's head. "Up here is physically clear."

Relieved, Ebony blew another breath. "I'll take any good news."

"There will be more tests — there always is. The blood the nurse just took, though I'm not expecting anything new. None have shown any residual infection, or nutritional deficiency."

The image of a dark main street flashed before her, Freestone Valley's, together with laboured breathing... Frustrated, Ebony pulled at her hair. "I hate this! One moment there's this blank space, the next jagged images that make no sense."

"We'll begin a neurological assessment to determine the full extent of your memory loss, that should go a long way to calming your anxiety. Our evaluation so far indicates that you are suffering from a rare form of psychogenic amnesia."

"Which is?"

"Severe emotional shock that leaves its victims as you are. It's often associated with people who have suffered violently, from natural disasters to sexual abuse. Soldiers involved in combat can suffer it too."

Ebony's mouth dropped open. "So basically, the worst possible things a person can live through."

"Unfortunately."

"Maybe it's best I don't remember."

"It seems your mind has already made that choice."

"The doctor's spoken at length with your father and I," Grace said. "She's very confident with her diagnosis."

Uncomfortable, Ebony moved her aching body, wishing she could do the same with her mind. "What if I don't want to remember?"

"That might not be possible," the doctor said. "If I released you with no further treatment, you might live a normal productive life and adjust to the gap within your memory."

"Sign me up, doc."

"Then there's the other side of the coin. Your memories could flood without warning, the complications disastrous."

"Can't we face that then?" Ebony countered angrily. "Isn't that my choice?"

Rickard rested his hands on the bed end. "Ebony, we know you've had a shock, but the way you act is the way you will be treated."

Tears welled at the stern words, leaving Ebony staring at the ceiling, wrestling frustration. She had never felt so helpless.

"Sorry, it's just a lot to process at once," she managed finally.

Doctor Walker shook her head. "Nothing to be sorry for, I know I'd be frustrated. Let's agree to be ready if that traumatic episode resurfaces, an action plan we'll call it. I don't want you placed in further harm."

"What if it never comes back and we're waiting for nothing?"

Rickard had an answer for this. "You could be down the street and smell something, or taste meal, see an object, and then game over. You need to be prepared."

"Also," the doctor said, "your form of memory loss often ties to a situation-specific amnesia, as part of post-traumatic stress disorder."

"I remember studying something about that in psych. You're saying certain things may cause flashbacks, or even nightmares?"

"Like your father said, a situation or even smell or sound. We just don't know."

"And there's no way to know how long this could go on?"

When Doctor Walker looked at her parents, Ebony got the feeling she was gathering herself. "We aren't going to lie to you. A lot happened in the first days when you were brought in. Right now, I think it's best to tackle each day as it comes, step by step, as they say."

"What happened?"

"Nothing for you to worry on," Rickard said firmly. "Doctor Walker was here within twenty-four hours. She came straight from England to help."

"I noticed the accent," Ebony murmured, digesting the news. "Thank you."

A voice came from the doorway. "We were more than happy to place one of our private planes at the doctor's disposal."

Ebony stared wide-eyed as Xavier Solomon walked in. She had not seen him in a long time. He had two men with him, easily recognisable as private security. The bald one in his early fifties indicated for the dark-skinned one to wait outside the door as a guard.

"I hope no one minds the interruption," Xavier said, sounding anything but concerned. "But when I heard our VIP patient was awake, I dropped everything to come to see her personally."

Grace glanced at Rickard, who remained stonily silent. "Of course," she said. "You're welcome to come in."

Xavier stepped to the bed, his grey suit looking as if it came straight from a fashion magazine. A smile played around his mouth. "Well, aren't you looking much better?"

"Err, thank you." Nervously, she looked between her father and Xavier. Glancing at the doorway, she eyed the bald man whose gaze remained watchful.

"Don't mind Axel," Xavier said with a laugh. "He looks fierce, but under that gruff exterior, he's pure marshmallow."

Rickard's lip curled in disgust, which Axel did not miss, saying, "Still riding that infamous temper, Casteel? Would've thought control came hand-in-glove by now, but I see the passage of time clearly hasn't seasoned you."

Rickard sneered. "Just like I thought all that Solomon arse-licking would've grown a crop on your bald head."

"Rickard, please," scolded Grace. "Not here."

"Fine." Stepping to Ebony's side, he kissed her forehead. "I'll grab you a coffee. When I get back," he speared a look at both Xavier and Axel, "you'll both be gone."

As her father left, Xavier sighed, his gaze resting on the empty doorway. "I'd hoped your husband might stand beside a Solomon after all that was done. Maybe even clasp a hand of friendship."

Grace picked up a water glass, filled it from the jug and handed it to Ebony to sip. Ebony took it. Knowing her mother; she would allow Xavier Solomon to say his piece, then want him to leave, taking his henchmen with him.

The silence lengthened, Xavier watching her expectantly. Grace's manners forced her to speak. "Your father and Rickard have a long history," she said. "I don't think my husband's capable of separating you from your father." Her look included Axel. "It's too big a leap."

"I am not Marcus Solomon," Xavier said flatly. "I can see it'll take time to prove this to both of you. I was foolish to believe this crisis might have chipped anything off the boundary he's erected. Still, I'll pit that against his cynicism."

Grace shifted uneasily. "Your help has been appreciated, even if he can't show it."

"You know I can do more. If you and Rickard need financial support, or maybe labour to work your property?"

"Casteels farm their own land, always have," she said, an unmistakable chill in her voice. "Though I appreciate the offer."

For a long moment, Xavier was silent, his face inscrutable. Tension rode the air, though Ebony had no idea why. It was like they were circling some issue she had no knowledge of, stepping over and around it.

"Well." Xavier turned to Ebony. "I can see your condition has much improved, thanks to the talents of Doctor Walker. Perhaps you're not aware, but she's one of this world's top neurologists."

"No." Ebony looked at the doctor with new eyes. "I wasn't."

"I go where I'm needed," the doctor said with a nod.

"Your case demanded the best," Xavier said. "And as it's unique, some of what she suggests may seem a little abstract, so don't be alarmed. She's a physician within the Fellowship. Her techniques are quite advanced."

"Oh." A piece of the puzzle fell into place for Ebony. "Is that why you've come? The Fellowship?"

"In part," said Xavier. "One thing I do ask is that you keep the treatments you receive between us."

Ebony lifted her chin. "Why?"

"Because," Xavier paused, seeming to choose his words carefully, "not all treatments have been released to the public yet, though they are fully tested. The Fellowship has supported Doctor Walker's career and her research. We like to choose when those findings are released, and how."

Wary, Ebony narrowed her eyes. She had no trouble picking up what he was not saying. "You want me to remember," she said. "Why?"

"Huh." Xavier's eyebrows rose, a smile twitching his lips. "Nicely deduced, Ebony. My family believe you are a part of a twenty-year-old mystery, one that began when you were very young." Pulling a mobile phone from inside his suit jacket, he searched for something before handing it to her. It was an article in the local newspaper, *The Freestone Times.*

"Teenagers kidnapped," she read out loud. Scanning the first paragraph, she looked back at Xavier. "You think I'm connected to this?"

"Twenty years ago, a series of disappearances took place, and they're happening again. Granted, not on the scale of back then, but random disappearances have been occurring." He looked across at Grace, who was fiercely shaking her head.

"That's enough," she warned.

"Grace, I'm sure she knows, just like everyone in Freestone, who the three are. It's common knowledge."

Ebony felt her stomach clutch. "Of course I know. My Aunt Eve, Dallas Noble and Marcus Solomon. Your father."

Xavier looked again at Grace, who pinned him with a cold stare. "We're running out of choices. If she doesn't make the right one like my father, she'll suffer the same fate as Eve and Dallas. Do you really want that for her?"

"She's been through enough. They made their choices. Ebony—"

"And they are now paying the price," Xavier interrupted. "Her healing must take precedence. We cannot allow our families' past animosity to interfere with what needs to be done now. I know Rickard disagrees, but isn't the truth the first step?"

Mouth tight, Grace's glare warred with Xavier's. "That's for her father and me to decide."

"You're suffocating her."

"I think that's enough," the doctor cut in.

Held silent by the exchange, Ebony found her voice. "What's going on? Mum?"

"Ebony," the doctor said in a warning voice. "Keep yourself calm."

"Things have changed," Xavier said, drawing her attention. When Grace frowned, he held up a hand. "It's alright, I'll take care. The abductions have started again, and we need to know what happened to you to see if they're linked."

Ebony glanced at her mother, watched her push at her hair, glaring at both Xavier and Axel. She got the feeling she was on the point of ordering both from the room, but something was holding her back. What hold did Xavier Solomon have over her parents?

When she looked back at Xavier, at the intensity of his stare, she wanted nothing more than for him to leave. But he wouldn't go.

"What is it you want?" she asked cautiously.

"You already know."

"You think I was abducted? That I somehow managed to escape?"

At this, Grace clutched Ebony's bedsheet, her knuckles whitening. Not a glance did Xavier spare her.

"They are the three who returned, and now so have you. Somewhere, locked in your mind, is the how and why." His gaze was sharp and it burnt into hers. "Will you help us uncover it?"

Ebony chewed at her lip. "But I can't remember."

"You will," Xavier said firmly, almost like an order. "Stay strong, Ebony. Help us, and the Fellowship will help you in return."

Galactic Star Key: Zozes Karbroe
Astral Nav-Coordinates: EAS-APL-4
Data Sequence: 8.0

Zozes studied the collection of vessels lined before Freestone Valley's police station.

At the sound of the station doors sliding open, he looked up to see Major Rajek jogging down the steps, garbed in what Earth inhabitants termed 'civilian clothing'. The dark suit was similar to his own, right down to the tie circling his neck.

The Major's dermal-graft simulator had altered his appearance to hide the sharp O'Garcian features and shorten his light blonde hair. He now appeared human, even down to the mannerisms, Zozes noted, watching him glance at the round face of the device circling his wrist.

As he came alongside, Zozes enquired, "You understand what you're looking at?"

"It's called a watch." Rajek turned his wrist to give Zozes a better view. "Humans use it to chart the motion cycles of the planet. Not as accurate or useful as a time-cycler, but it's competent enough."

"Charts time?" Zozes glanced from it to the large central clock which he could see between buildings to his right. "I've seen many worlds outside the Planetary Allegiance record time in various ways, but nothing quite like this."

"Commonality amongst pre-warp worlds." Dropping his arm, Rajek adjusted his sleeve. "Time dictates many worlds, while others believe it has no effect." Though the Major's face was impassive, Zozes did not miss the hint of steel entering his tone. "Where's your brother?"

137

"Kaze was meant to arrive before all of us," he admitted.

After a pointed look up and down the street, Rajek glanced back lifting both eyebrows. "Indeed."

"Maybe I'll try posting another ..." Zozes fumbled his response as the Major's eyebrows rose a little higher, "call over SS freq-com."

"See that you do." Looking back at the door, Rajek eyed the comings and goings. "I believe it would not matter what part of the galaxy your brother resided within, distraction seems to find him." Thoughtful, he studied an Earth vessel as it slid into a nearby parking bay. "We cannot afford that here, not with so many eyes on us. I can assure you that time is a lesson I will have him respect by the end of this assignment."

"Yes, Sir. I'll get the message across."

Zozes followed the Major's gaze, watching two occupants exit the Earth vessel. The male blew smoke from his mouth, a grey stream of stench he could smell from this distance. Tapping ash from its end, he finished his conversation before crossing to the station steps, dropping the smoking end in a receptacle.

"Similar habit to a stim-pipe." Zozes eyed the curl of smoke. "Well used on Nova Trade worlds."

"A parallel concept," agreed the Major.

"This planet seems to thrive on habits that shorten their lives," Zozes observed darkly.

"Debauched customs can be righted when new understandings are offered." Like he was seeing something more, Rajek surveyed the surrounds. "Give them a cause, something worth striving for."

"Intergration cannot be forced, Sir, for good or bad. To me, it should be earned," Zozes said.

"Perhaps walk among them first. Our place is to evaluate their true standing, not pass swift judgement." Rajek looked at Zozes. "A sole review of humanity's Chronicle Index is not that. Us concurring with this integration is also not required, though I do believe they have potential."

Zozes could see the Major chose his words very carefully. He watched the doors slide closed behind the male, then glanced back observing the female who crossed toward them.

"What's her interest?" murmured Zozes, straightening.

"Actually, she's one of ours. Lead Inspector Roccna on assignment here. She was working in conjunction with the previous Alpha Chief," said Rajek.

"Astral Guard Superintendent in command of the joint operation with the humans?" Zozes asked, eyeing the woman.

"She is very experienced," Rajek said. "Handpicked by Commodore Vae'gon personally."

Zozes blew a breath. "A joint-op between us and the humans will only slow things down. Like you initially stated, our duty-service transfer to Astral Guard is on a short-term status. Best we use the time allotted to complete this assignment before it expires, Sir."

"I see it differently," Rajek countered. "Humans cannot be pushed aside, Blade. They have a responsibility, not to mention a right, to defend their world. In regard to your termination of status on Earth, there are contingencies to remedy this."

Zozes had a good idea what they would be. "The launching of further assessments through the Overwatch Initiative?"

"Of which you will be advised of in time."

Both fell silent as the Inspector walked toward them. Zozes took note of her formal attire, the dark suit that resembled theirs minus a tie. Dark brown hair tied in a knot, fixed at the base of her skull.

"Gentlemen." She acknowledged each with a nod.

"Inspector Roccna." Rajek's greeting was equally formal. "This is our new addition—"

"Zozes Karbroe," she interrupted.

After a brief nod, Zozes straightened his stance.

Roccna squinted at him. "So, you're the second-generation combat specialist to the Major. The Blade sent to keep things in line."

"When necessary." Zozes did not miss the mockery coating her words.

Rajek's sharp gaze moved from Zozes back to Roccna. "When holding the line alone ..."

"... we stand together," she finished over the Major.

"You know our words?" Zozes could not have been more surprised.

"I spent time with your former Alpha Chief," Roccna affirmed. "Her last official charge duty was on this world, before her recall order."

Zozes scrutinised Roccna, trying to gauge how she felt. "The details surrounding this assignment are somewhat unclear."

Her stance stiffened, picking up the dissatisfaction in his tone. "Am I detecting an issue, Blade?"

Surprised at her venom, Zozes looked at the Major, who was leaning silently against one of the vessels.

"None," Zozes replied in a clipped voice. "I'm here on the Commodore's orders."

"See you remember that," Roccna said. "He has placed full authority on how this investigation is conducted with me. When I deem it necessary, you'll be apprised of further details and orders. Is that clear?"

For a long moment silence held the three. Zozes again looked to Rajek, who was watching Roccna, his expression thoughtful.

"Agreed," he relaxed his stance. It was obvious Roccna had issues, but was it with the mission or the Blades?

Her next words answered one point. "Blades have a tendency to become overzealous. We're working a covert operation on a world that is on the cusp of a new beginning."

"Securing the pre-warp amendment through Global Reach will gain Earth the ability to advance their technology while moving them into the stars," he said, schooling his expression to remain neutral.

"Precisely. During the transition period, there is very real danger. A single misstep could lead to a drastic change in events. I will not allow that to happen."

"You have to agree that the Blades' Galactic Star-Keys speak for themselves," Rajek interjected calmly.

"Their duty records?" Roccna laughed without humour. "Do you include Kaze Karbroe? Will you vouch for him as readily?"

Neither Rajek nor Zozes responded.

Roccna smiled slowly but it was more like a bearing of teeth. "I believe we now understand one another."

As she stalked toward the station, Rajek watched her. "We certainly do."

"Another Vae'gon?" Zozes hazarded.

On a deep breath, Rajek straightened his jacket. "Roccna's issues are known only to herself."

"So they're personal."

"Perhaps," Rajek said, watching several Earth vessels enter the lot. "Has your brother updated his Star-Key? I don't plan on waiting here indefinitely."

Zozes activated his cyber-optics, adjusting for the readout to drop before his eyes. He controlled these actions through his neural-TECH's link, uploading his brother's latest entry log.

The last line left him baffled. "Found some nice wheels," Zozes read aloud. "Catch you at the station after a test drive."

Rajek's mouth firmed in annoyance. "I see the young Alpha's adjusted to this region's native colloquialisms in less than half its day."

"So it seems." Zozes moved irritably to crush the still-smouldering smoke butt within the tray, imagining his brother's face. "Sub-words hold his interest. The predominant populace in our local speak what is called English. A derivative of this is something referred to as 'slang', a concept he was concerned with grasping."

"Slang?"

"The simplifying of a term or phrase."

Rajek swore softly beneath his breath. "Sub-verse words are a common affliction on pre-warp worlds."

"EAS Integration effort will cleanse Earth's languages."

"Yes. A necessary prerequisite," Rajek said, though he looked anything but hopeful. "Humans will need to create standardised dialect if they wish to successfully communicate with other space-faring civilisations. Your brother knows that."

"He does. We can rely on the neural-TECH's voca-translator for anything else."

"It appears we'll need to. Humans' use of sub-verse phrasing is … frequent and disruptive."

"Then Kaze's fluent understanding may prove useful in acclimatising to Earth's culture."

"Doubtful." Rajek's clearly could not be persuaded. "See it doesn't follow him off world. I'm done waiting, we're going in."

The two made their way across the parking lot toward the building. As Rajek moved up the stairs, Zozes paused, a throbbing rumble catching his ear.

A dark vessel rolled into a nearby docking area. Zozes felt a creeping of trepidation. *It can't be*, he thought.

Every human in the vicinity turned, an elderly couple shaking their heads. Other Earth vessels attempting to leave were forced to pause and wait for the pilot to navigate the vessel's bulk into a one of the designated holding bays, marked with white lines.

The vessel's impulse-drive powered again, ignition thrust echoing long and loud. The instant the throaty rumble halted, the window in the pilot's door slid down to reveal his brother's wide smirk.

A look Zozes knew all too well.

Furious, Rajek stepped back to his side. "Shut that thing down and get him inside!"

The fury behind the words had Zozes moving fast. By the time he got there, Kaze was standing by the vessel, its impulse-drive finally powered down.

"You've gotta give this hot little number a try brother!" Kaze winced at his brother's flushed face. "I ain't casting a fake hook, it's time to reel in the catch and test out its limits."

"Test *what*?" He could almost feel his voca-translator scrambling to decipher the sentence.

A half-smile pulled at Kaze's lips before he began chewing on something between his teeth. "Earth lingo. Gotta play in it."

"We're supposed to keep exposure to a minimum, and you're ..." Zozes' mind momentarily drew a blank, staring at the vessel his brother was leaning against, "doing the complete opposite!"

"Clearly you haven't heard the phrase," Kaze pulled a curved black shape from his pocket, "hiding in plain sight." Casual, he slid the visor over his eyes, chewing again.

Zozes tried to ignore his own reflection staring back from the twin lenses. A buzzing started in the back of his head, hinting he was hitting his limit.

"How did this even happen?"

Kaze ran a hand over the vessel. "Isn't she a beauty? I got here over an hour and some..." he scrunched his eyes, "odd minutes ago."

"Earth time permitting ... And?"

"I had some time to kill."

Face blanching, Zozes jaw dropped. "You killed what? We've just landed here!"

Chest heaving, Kaze laughed out loud. "If you're gonna survive here brother, you gotta understand the beauty of this world's language."

Nostrils flaring, Zozes fought to control his boiling temper. Snatching the visor from Kaze's face, he crushed it in his hands, relishing the crunching noise. "I can't think with you wearing those things."

"Well." Kaze heaved a sigh looking at the ground. "Aren't you just my favourite person today."

"Either the focal-lens or you."

"All good." Kaze pulled a second pair from his pocket, casually flicking them open. Keeping his distance, he slid them into place. "Thought something like that might happen."

Mouth falling open, Zozes waged an internal battle before gritting his teeth. To kill or not kill his own brother. "You were saying?"

"You're well aware waiting is no strength of mine, so I started going through the Alpha Chief's Star-Key." Kaze faced his brother, clearly excited. "Zozes, it was information overload. Forced me to do a lot of skimming. Then I stumbled on one of her previous mission targets." He punched at his brother's rigid shoulder. "The mother lode, brother. The mother lode!"

"The ... what?" Wising up, Zozes shook his head. "Just explain to me how glancing over her Star-Key," he gestured to the vessel, "led to that."

"Well." Kaze ran a hand over the front of the vessel. "The mission target was located at a service facility which repairs—"

"Transport vessels," Zozes guessed.

"They're actually called vehicles," Kaze said. "And that gave me an idea to help us blend with the natives. The Chief documented all kinds of information on humans. This form of transport is commonly used by young males and is called a ute. Custom-restored from manufacture, very high quality. I questioned the owner and his son. LT detected nothing of consequence."

"It's loud," Zozes said. "The impulse-drive's exhaust suppression is clearly malfunctioning." Irritated beyond thinking straight, he added, "Acquiring defective resources is not blending." Then another thought occurred, one he was almost afraid to voice. "How did you claim it as your own?"

His brother's grin re-emerged. "It was up for trade, so I bought it."

"Bought?"

"Exactly!" Delighted, Kaze folded his arms, stepping back to admire his purchase. "This entire planet is virtually controlled by the alternative exchange system. Here it's called a 'monetary policy'."

Zozes had a bad feeling. "A currency-based world."

"A strange concept," Kaze said. "It rules the majority of the world's populace. Performing task duties in exchange for currency is their policy." Pulling a folded pouch from his back pocket, he displayed thin rectangular material with symbols. "Currency."

"How did you acquire that?"

"I had LT scan funds being traded," said Kaze. "He used his replicator to generate fabricated material through replication resequence."

"Am I to understand," an ache built in Zozes' temples, "that you traded fraudulent tender for this?"

Kaze waved the material beneath his brother's nose. "How can something I'm holding be fraudulent?"

"That isn't the point. Where's your respect for this world and its customs?"

"You're looking at it!" Kaze tapped the vessel proudly. "And I gave the owner a lucrative tip."

For a long moment, Zozes looked the cumbersome vessel over, trying to imagine climbing inside the tight space, travelling with that vibrating noise.

"I can see you're impressed." Kaze smiled happily. "No applause needed, the owners I traded it from own a local mechanic shop, Starrik Motors. Interacting with them taught me about exchange. The kid, a young male, kinda reminded me of myself when I was younger."

Zozes tucked a length of hair behind his ear, resisting the urge to pull it out. "No one is like you, Kaze, no one. I'll deal with this later, and the complications you've created."

"What you call complicated, I call living."

"Where's LT?" Zozes demanded.

"Take a look." Kaze opened the vessel's door, pointing inside. "Run your cyber-optics thing, its multi-cloak is active."

Before ducking to look in the cockpit, Zozes glared at his brother. "Aren't I fortunate to have you here to tell me these things." Activating the overlay, he eyed the Link-Trone which was sitting in the centre of the passenger seat.

However innocent it looked, Zozes knew what it could do. As did his brother, supposedly.

"It's all taken care of." Kaze flashed his brother a grin as he stood.

"We're not here to have fun, and that is not a toy."

"It's not my fault it thinks it's one of us."

"It acts like that because you don't have full control over it," Zozes snapped. "A Link-Trone adapts their positronic-drive to our state consciousness through its sync-pulse."

A group of uniformed police walked past, a couple eyeing the two openly. Zozes grit his teeth. How did his brother manage to make him forget everything, even their surrounds? When the group had driven off, he turned back to Kaze, who was obviously still thinking about the Trone.

"You're saying it's becoming more like me?"

"Regrettably, yes. I've never seen it to this degree. Spawn-nets connected to the Trone are meant to only adjust to our thought patterns and neural pathways. Not our personality traits."

"Makes sense. Now I know why it doesn't always listen to me," Kaze said thoughtfully. "Not unless I really mean it."

"Well, it'll listen to me." Zozes leaned down looking through door, glaring at the Trone hovering above the seat. "LT form up. Form a shadow-run with us through the coming meeting."

When nothing happened, the Trone remaining in low power mode, Zozes felt the final thread of temper snap before Kaze tapped his shoulder.

"Where's your civility, brother? You know, try a more formal request. With a please tacked on."

Zozes looked back at the AI, growling, "Please."

The Link-Trone shot up, pushing past Zozes to hover between the two brothers, lights flashing in a manner that agitated Zozes beyond words. Barely resisting the urge to thump it, he looked toward the station. "Now that we're all accounted for, I'll reactivate myself back into the LT's system."

"You mean you're taking back operative control?"

Mute, Zozes started walking toward the police station, knowing it would be better not to answer.

"Well, that didn't take long," Kaze muttered, coming alongside.

"Command Training doesn't look so useless now, does it?" Zozes said. "Also, it's the best defence to keep you away from trouble."

"And cripples the learning process," Kaze argued. "I'm finally getting a feel for this."

"Feel?" Zozes glanced at his brother. "You can't gauge this progress on feelings alone. This is far more complicated."

Kaze waved a hand of surrender. "Don't give me another rundown. I live by instinctual means. More knowledge at this point just blocks everything up."

"Look." There was no missing his brother's set expression. Not wanting things to blow out, Zozes fought for patience. "Your lack of command training makes it dangerous to leave you two alone. That's a fact. It can change if you listen and open up to what I can teach you."

On a snort, Kaze started up the stairs. "Nothing happened. My spawn-net's more stable than a constellation dancer gyrating around a grav-pole."

At the top of the stairs, Zozes paused. "That's because I locked off LT's tactical analysis to prevent overstimulating your network," he snapped. "You saw what happened earlier on the Blade Ship, and in the Training Bay." The look on his brother's face said he was anything but convinced.

As Kaze shoved past, Zozes grabbed his arm. "You think I'm wrong?"

"Your lack of trust in me is what's wrong."

For a long moment the two eyed each other. Zozes knew words would not be enough. Kaze usually had to experience pain before a lesson was learnt.

"You can't do this on your own," Kaze said finally. "I think ... no, I know, we're meant to do this together."

"Then let me teach you, Kaze."

"Forget it, you've pissed me off now."

As his brother stalked through the automatic doors, Zozes swore roundly. There was just no reasoning with him sometimes. Adjusting his jacket, he fought to shake off the tension. Where was his calm? He needed that now more than ever, especially on a pre-warp world where the majority of its inhabitants believed that no life existed within the stars.

As soon as he entered the station, Zozes saw his brother standing by a door at the end of the room, the Link-Trone hovering near him, multi-cloak still active. Major Rajek was sitting on a seat, a piece of Earth material in his hands like he was studying its contents. Several humans waited, spread out at random points around the waiting area. Some cast cautious glances at the Major and his brother, like they knew they were not civilian.

On the opposite side of the room was a long counter. This separated those who entered the station from those that worked there. Several uniformed officers sat before operative terminals, tapping away at keypads with symbols.

The layout looked sterile, the scattered seats generic. More material was pinned on boards, displaying the Earth language and pictures, some of them sad, he noted, some gruesome. More were folded in display holders.

A door near Kaze opened, a uniformed woman sticking her head out. "If you'll follow me, I'll take you through."

After a nod to the woman, Rajek dropped the material he had been scanning back on the table. "Please, lead the way."

Zozes followed finding himself in a long corridor with numerous closed doors. The officer led them around a corner into what looked like a main hub. Rectangular in design, it was filled with many sub-offices, most in use.

Very active, he could tell that the stationed officers were interested in what they were doing, as well as who these newcomers were. Furtive glances were cast openly in their direction, a sizing-up he found thorough and admirable.

The female human paused at a door near the end of the room, flashing her identification card over a disk near the handle. He heard a click before she swung it wide, stepping back so they could enter.

Zozes spotted Thaytis immediately. She was sitting at one of the long rows of tables, dressed in the human attire of pants and a jacket. Her blonde hair was loose, eyes covered in a clear visor similar to the dark pair now resting on the top of his brother's head. Why he had placed them there was beyond imagining. Thaytis was talking to someone next to her, but she glanced up briefly when they entered.

That distraction had him bumping into the officer ahead, mumbling an apology, only then realising the room was half full of personnel. Some were uniformed police, others clad in the same attire as himself and the Major.

The three walked around the edge until they came to seats near Thaytis, each taking a chair.

Thaytis leaned forward, pointing at Kaze's neck. "What's happening here?"

"You talking about the thing that supports my head?"

"I explicitly told you to wear a tie," she said.

On a sigh, Kaze pulled a length of fabric from his jacket pocket. "Not going to happen. Can't work the thing."

Before he could jam it back in his pocket, she grabbed it. "Come here, you look like a fool without it."

"Wait." Kaze tried to stand.

Annoyed, Thaytis shoved his chest, forced him back down. "Stay!"

"Well, when you put it like that." He wiggled his eyebrows. "I can play that game anytime you like, doc."

Thaytis met his grin with one of her own, tightening the knot at his throat. "The thing is," she said, her glance landing on Zozes, "I play it better."

"Not a chance." Kaze lifted a hand to loosen the knot, which Thaytis immediately slapped away. Frustrated, he leaned back to sulk, glaring at his brother. "Well, isn't this going to be fun."

Zozes adjusted his own tie, looking to the front of the room. Inspector Roccna was seated next to a woman in her forties, red hair cut to chin length and swept back. She seemed to be constantly scanning the room, dark eyes shifting. The woman looked impatient, almost ill at ease, like she would rather be anywhere else. Zeroing in on her uniform tag, Zozes made out the name via his optics: Senior Sergeant Mara Perkins.

Suddenly she stood, taking position at the head of the room, full of authority.

"Gentleman, ladies!" Voice slightly raised, she called for silence. "I'd like you to take a moment and watch this before we begin." Immediately the lights faded, and the room darkened.

An overhead digital display materialised above her on a square of white material at the head of the room. Information filled the screen, pictures of those who had gone missing, Zozes realised.

Then the forward display altered to the geographical overview of Freestone Valley and the analysis for this case. A uniformed officer began circulating the room, placing files before each person. It was a copy of the list, coupled with their bios.

Zozes knew enough of the human language to read three names with aid. Eve Casteel, Marcus Solomon and Dallas Noble.

"I'm Mara Perkins, Senior Sergeant of the Freestone Police Station."

Pausing, she seemed to gather herself. "You have all been called here today to work in conjunction with a Specialist Task Force," she nodded briefly in their direction. "However, formal introductions will have to be set aside until later. As you know, there is an event in the works that will change this world and how countries interact with one another. That event is Global Reach. The official launch for this is almost upon us and it will be our job to keep the peace. To that end, I'm placing this station on high alert."

An older, grey haired officer raised a hand. "None of this has been conventional, all counter-insurgency measures have been conducted within the Valley through to Ridge Falls. We still have no idea what terrorist faction you are primarily concerned with?"

"The factions in question are known only to myself and my senior staff. The rest of you will be briefed before the launch. Global Reach will define our generation, and there will be those who oppose what it represents. We must be prepared."

Zozes watched that same officer lean across to make an offhand comment to his neighbour. The Link-Trone moved around the perimeter of the group in cloak mode, profiling everyone in the room while Senior Sergeant Perkins continued her address.

"Because of the launch there will be changes on how our station will operate. New training schedules for all officers are being announced." Mara paused, brushing at a stray hair. "These changes are to be implemented immediately."

A disgruntled murmur rumbled through the officers, one that slowly gathered volume. An officer near the front rose a hand. "This is ridiculous, what changes? I'm a year off retirement!"

Mara held up a hand, indicating for quiet. "I know this has caught you off-guard, but after the announcement you'll understand why it has to be this way. You'll also learn what will be required of you if you wish to remain an officer of the law."

Another officer raised a hand. "What does the Valley Disappearance Case have to do with Global Reach?"

"There has been new developments and evidence released to us. The victims," she indicated the overhead display which was once again active, "are where I'll begin. On the night of 1 November 1995, three people disappeared. Each happened to be a member of one of Freestone Valley's Founding Families." She pointed at the display as a picture flashed on the screen. "A Casteel, a Solomon and a Noble. They were found, but that only led to more questions.

"Each of these families' histories runs deep through Freestone Valley. Their connection to it, and this twenty-year-old mystery, turned them into minor celebrities for a time, locals referring to them as 'The Returned'.

"From case evidence, we all know how this first incident sparked a string of disappearances far different to the Returned. These victims sustained excessive exposure to an unknown form of radiation that always resulted in death." A brief pause followed this, Mara gesturing for the slides to advance on the display. "The disfigurement on some was so severe it was difficult to recognise them as human."

A heavy silence filled the room, each officer obviously shocked at what they were seeing.

Via his cyber-optics, Zozes scanned and tracked the evidence presented, correlating each image with a cyber tab identifier for later review.

The last victim caught his immediate attention. Adele Jones, age thirty-one had been found dead by a self-proclaimed … his mind tripped on the term 'bushranger'. A human male, Corbett Starrik, who lived in the alpine region of Lake Rockway, east of Skyfall Mountain. The victims family had not yet been notified pending the results of her post-mortem examination.

"I see," Kaze caught his attention, "the latest victim has peaked your interest."

Zozes noted his brothers log-in via his own optics. Kazes Star-Key now paired in, granting access to the marked tab identifiers for overview.

"Her exposure," he said, "registers as an unidentified type of ionization."

"Subatomic particles?" Kaze looked again at the screen. "With a strange sense of humour altering her molecular structure. She's been sized up considerably."

"These humans," Zozes eyed the noticeably pale faces around him, "are in uncharted territory. 'Novice to assignment', is by no means an effective approach, they're clearly not ready for this."

Kaze uploaded via his cyber-optics the dimensions of an average humanoid female frame, overlaying and comparing it to the victims.

"Probably a good thing that she's deceased. Anyone walking around that size would not only spook the locals, but send shockwaves across the globe."

His brother was right. Furthering Zozes frustration was the fact that all additional intelligence was classified, his clearance level blocked via Global Defence security net.

That left the 'bushranger'. Corbett Starrik was in his mid-forties, a recluse who rarely visited any town. The Starrick family still resided in Freestone Valley, Charles Starrik owning the local mechanic shop.

"Radioactive mutation doesn't sound half bad," murmured Kaze. "This case isn't looking so tame now."

"Are challenge and danger the only incentives that keep you tuned in?"

Grin cocky, Kaze looked again at the female. "Who knows, give it some time I might surprise you."

Zozes further studied the victim noting that extreme alteration began at a molecular level. What had caused her genetic structure to rapidly deform her entire make-up? In parts it appeared to be rough, thickened skin tissue flaking and weeping. He noted the puncture along her abdomen, how it exposed darkened muscle and sinew. At the centre of that wound looked to be fine black filaments netted together, covering the bone.

Officers were now murmuring to each other, shifting in their seats uncomfortably.

The rest would have to wait. Minimising the profiles into suppression tabs, Zozes lent back deciding on later analysis.

"Freestone was not the only target," Mara continued loudly. "Clearance has come through the UN Specialist Division to reveal that these abductions were in fact tied to a global phenomenon. Isolated pockets in different countries experienced similar abductions to those in the Valley. The total count here was six deaths with twenty-two still unaccounted for."

The Senior Sergeant's gaze told Zozes how invested she was. "The police and detectives that worked the investigation during the 90s were silenced by the same department in government, people connected with the organising of the Global Reach launch. All evidence gathered here was handed over to the Specialist Division," Mara made a dismissive gesture, "and to my knowledge, that division has been operating covertly ever since."

Her glance included Roccna. "The Inspector and others in this room are part of that Specialist Division. They will temporarily take charge of this investigation, collaborating and mentoring this station's officers on how to deal with the unique circumstances that surround this case and our area."

Kaze leaned back, tapping Zozes around Thaytis to get his attention. "Glad we aren't part of that little set up."

Mara signalled a female police officer to advance the screen to new images.

"Let's move on to an overview of the case. You will be divided into groups. An Inspector from Specialist Division will take you through the evidence, the case details, practices that will connect with the launching of Global Reach."

Via his optics, Zozes brought up the information, covering it quickly. Lifting a hand as he had seen other officers do, he queried, "That report speaks of the three original abductions at length. You believe these families are somehow involved? Am I understanding the information correctly?"

Mara lifted her chin, the movement arrogant, challenging. "Yes, that's an angle I've been looking into for a number of years. A theory not well received until recently, but my findings have now gathered support. Inspector Roccna and I will talk about that in further detail."

"The Returned?" Zozes said.

Again, she indicated the view screen. "Eve Casteel, Marcus Solomon and Dallas Noble. These three were found wandering the Princes Highway with nothing but the clothes on their backs. No memory of what happened, exhausted and hungry. Fast forward twenty years." The display changed. "We now have Ebony Casteel, twenty-one years of age.

"She's a Casteel, though an adopted daughter. Ebony was found stumbling through the main street during the Freestone Festival after nine in the evening. Her injuries were far worse than those of the Returned and have been detailed for you to read. Her reappearance is part of the reason we are all here today, re-opening the Valley Disappearance Case."

Mara waited for the overhead to change, then went on to describe previous cases, the information gathered, documented.

Zozes looked around the room. She had every officers' undivided attention, all were sitting up straight, taking in what she said.

"I've made promises to families in the past," she said. "Told them justice never sleeps, that answers will be found. It's affected this town, its people, my people. We will not stop until the perpetrators are found and held accountable."

"LT," Zozes murmured quietly, opening the file on the table. "Mark that Senior Sergeant's profile for later analysis."

As he flipped through the documents before him, an image caught his eye, that of a deceased male. Something about the shape of face, the expression, even look in the eye made him pause. Glancing at the name, he made out the Earth language via his cyber-optic: Karl Christian Perkins.

Zozes immediately relayed the information via neural-link to his brother's spawn-net, downloading all available intelligence on the humans.

After scrutinising it, Kaze leaned back and whispered to Zozes. "Mara Perkins was married to Dallas Noble, who is one of the Returned?"

"And," Zozes added, "her brother Karl was one of those abducted, later found dead. An autopsy revealed the same exposure to an unidentified radiation source, one that drastically mutated the molecular structure of his physiology."

"Mutating appears to be the theme here. Question is ... into what?"

"Classified," ground out Zozes, "via Global Defence network."

"And now her and Noble are divorced," Kaze whispered. "That's what this world calls the dissolving of a rite-bond. If you ask me, this link will cause trouble."

"Her dissociation with him dates to days after his return."

Kaze whistled softly. "Like always brother, you don't miss a beat."

The Senior Sergeant's voice drew their attention. "You may believe this is unconventional, and perhaps it is, but times are changing. These joint briefings are for your benefit and will continue. Please remain seated until your name is called to be assigned to a Global Defence Inspector."

Lights brightened and the screen deactivated. Zozes kept an eye on the officers, watching them murmur between themselves.

At the front, Roccna signalled for their group to come forward by catching Rajek's eye.

Zozes could hear individual names being called as officers were divided by rank and position into new investigative units.

Before they could leave the briefing room, Mara Perkins waylaid Roccna, a careful scrutiny in her eye as she looked over Kaze and Zozes.

"Inspector, I wasn't aware this station received additional operatives from your Specialist Division. You two seem," she looked them over, "different."

"They're part of our Tactical Unit," Roccna answered politely.

On a smirk, Kaze intoned, "You got a problem with me being special?"

His brother was getting ruffled, Zozes noticed, but only those who knew him well would have known.

"I see this one has a sense of humour." Mara did not back down, she even stepped forward. "Tactical Unit? That's a part of criminal investigation?"

"It is," Roccna replied.

"Full disclosure was the arrangement between your superior and me."

Kaze met her step forward with one of his own. "Why don't you try rolling with the punches."

"Excuse me?" Challenged, Perkins shoved him back, hand on chest.

Zozes groaned, uncertain how to defuse the situation short of moving his brother out the door, and that was bound to be noisy.

"Just because you're a woman doesn't mean you can get physical," growled Kaze. At his brother's glare, he tacked on a grudging, "ma'am."

"That's quite enough." The Inspector moved between the two, an angry crease forming between her eyebrows. "Mara, you need to trust me on this. I was just informed that their unit would join the briefing. It was never my intention to keep you in the dark. Their presence here was just cleared."

"Not by me," Perkins said darkly, but she stepped back. "Just another happy surprise."

"Senior Sergeant," Zozes stepped before his brother hoping to smooth the situation. "We're all here for the same reason."

"Really?" Perkins looked him up and down. "The way I see it, you have to be part of this community to understand what it's been through."

"We understand that." Zozes inclined his head. "Commitment and service is what we'll be for you."

"Mara." Inspector Roccna pulled her aside noticing the odd look she gave Zozes, one that made him wince inwardly. His choice of words was clearly the cause, setting apart their speech patterns. "They won't step out of line, I'll make certain of it. Right now, we all have work to do."

"Yes, we do. Maybe you should get on with it." Stepping back, she waited pointedly.

Roccna moved off first, while Zozes shoved his brother after her, briefly inclining his head at Perkins while following the group into a private room. Rajek closed the door as soon as all were inside.

Disgruntled, Kaze began prowling the conference room, circling the few tables while pulling at his tie. "She's got a lot of confidence for someone that short and human."

"She's been a problem," Inspector Roccna replied. "And harder to deal with as the investigation progresses, but she is a fine officer."

"Does she know what we are?" Zozes asked. "Do any of them?"

"Not yet," the Inspector said. "Adjusting to what is to come, that life exists outside this world? It'll be hard for people like her."

"Overwhelming," Rajek agreed. "Such closed minds become very conditioned, and hold tight to their ideals."

"Just keep her off our backs, and those like her," Kaze said. "Give us a chance to do our jobs."

"Agreed." Roccna moved them on. "Now it's time we focus on the matter at hand. I presume your LT's security field is online?"

"Operational since entering this building," Zozes said. "The taping surveillance devices in here have been disengaged. All systems are now under its control."

"Excellent." Roccna eyed something on her porta-pad, obviously designed to blend in with human technology. "It's my understanding you have access to intelligence surrounding the crash zones?"

"We do. LT," Zozes turned to the Trone, "disengage multi-cloak, activate rundown mode."

The Link-Trone materialised in the centre of the room. Its base structure plate retracted to reveal a cybernetic rim that loaded multiple cyber-screens around the Trone as it slowly spun.

Zozes took a step closer, using his hands to manipulate the information, enlarging some screens, deactivating others so the group got a good overview of the information, the cyber-ray projections casting all in a green-blue hue as they scrutinised the intelligence data spread.

The Inspector indicated two screens of interest and Zozes restructured the layout to focus on the crash zones. "These are the mission targets for now. Separate objectives are linked to each site. These are to be undertaken by your squad. We will update you further priorities in due course."

"Understood." Rajek stepped closer, eyeing the two screens. "I think we should divide the squad. Doctor Thaytis and I will go over the evidence that has been transferred to the Global Base from crash site one. Blades, I want to you investigate crash site two."

Via his cyber-optics, Zozes expanded the generated map. There did not appear too much of the vessel left. It was hardly recognisable as a ship, blackened and engulfed in what he assumed to be plasma fire.

At his side, Kaze pulled down another file, one that was currently lockdowned, coloured red. "What of the girl?"

His brother was looking at the girl's image with a great deal of zeal, Zozes noticed, coupled with a wide smirk.

"Leave that job to me, Major." Kaze wiggled his eyebrows. "I'm raising a hand to investigate this one personally."

No one bothered answering.

Frustrated, Kaze looked at Zozes. "It's important to me."

For form, Zozes rolled his eyes. "Anything female is important to you." Turning to Rajek, Zozes asked, "Are the two events connected? This girl's abduction and the crash?"

"Her recovery has been complicated," Rajek said. "For now, Ebony Casteel is off limits. Thaytis and I have been ordered to transfer her to Global Base for further questioning after our survey."

Inspector Roccna stepped in to answer, her attention on the cyber-map, in particular the crash site. "Your orders are to assist Astral Guard within the joint operation, site one and two, understood?"

Kaze crossed his arms, plainly aggrieved. "How is this relevant compared to Professor Marzden's escape? He still holds the stasis case, is probably kicking up his boots free-roaming across this world."

"Blade," Rajek cautioned, "we've already been over this."

"An Astral Guard Enforcer unit stands as nothing compared to the potential of our squad, Sir. It's a Blade principle to finish what we began."

Roccna instantly got her back up. "The Enforcers are more than capable of handling such a duty. Remember your place, Blade."

Zozes could see his brother was not in agreement, and neither was he. Overlooking someone as dangerous as the Professor could very well cause complications for not only this world, but the Station in orbit of it.

"Professor Magel Marzden," he began carefully, "holds a vital asset to stabilise transporting personnel to and from the Station, Sir. We may need to prioritise accordingly. You yourself stated you barely made it to this world."

"Yes." Kaze nodded in agreement. "I like the flow of your words, brother. Magel's a greater threat, pure and simple."

"This is not up for debate," said Rajek. "We have been ordered to maintain course and unless our orders are rescinded, that is what we will carry out. There will be no deviation or action to detach from our objective unless issued by command." The hard look he cast each brother left no room for argument. "Is that understood, Blades?"

Zozes and Kaze eyed one another before answering. "Yes, Sir."

Satisfied, he turned to Roccna. "Very well, let us begin."

Galactic Star Key: Kaze Karbroe
Astral Nav-Coordinates: EAS-APL-4
Data Sequence: 9.0

With the setting sun casting streams of light over the hills, Kaze swung his ute from the main road onto what looked to be a gravel track. Overcorrecting, he got a thrilling view of the tree-lined edge, while skidding on loose stone.

"Grab something!" he yelled, muscling the wheel, ignoring his brother's hiss while bracing an arm on the dash. Once the ute was back on track, Kaze glanced in the rear-mirror, spotting a plume in their wake. "Now that's one sexy looking dust cloud!"

Hurriedly winding up his side-shield, Zozes swatted at the particles filling the cab. "Since I can barely breathe, or see, I figure you're trying to remind me how unconventional this vessel is."

"Vehicle!" Kaze glared at him. "So, tell me what're you feeling?"

"Don't start that again."

Kaze ran a hand over the steering wheel before thumping it. "The authenticity of living on a pre-warp world, brother."

"You're going to feel my fist's authenticity if you keep on about this planet!"

"Challenge accepted ... hmm, is that lights ahead?" Squinting, Kaze peered into the thick vegetation and growing darkness.

"We're coming onto the crash zone. I believe this world's military will have formed a blockade."

"A lot darker in and around these trees." Scrutinising the switches on the dashboard, Kaze hovered a finger while looking for the correct one. "Err ..."

The front wheel bounced in and out of a pot hole.

"Kaze!" Zozes grunted as his head hit the ceiling. "We could use some powered light-reflectors about now."

"Right, I'm certain it was on this handle." Taking a guess, Kaze flicked a switch. The wipers activated, squirting water that turned the windshield dust instantly to paste.

Zozes sat and fumed while the Link-Trone hovered, its operative signals chirping merrily between them.

"Hang on, vok!" Kaze cursed considering a different dial. "I think it's …" Music screamed from the speakers. "Nope! Not that."

"I thought you knew how to operate this thing?"

"Activate your cyber-optic night-sight," Kaze tapped the side of his head. "It's not like we need the vehicles lights to see."

"Don't think I haven't," Zozes growled, clearly fed up. "I'm done with you're unrestrained approach to this assignment. LT—"

"Just give me a moment to feel this out," cut in Kaze, leaning forward for a better look.

Zozes threw a hand forward, bracing against the dash. "The humans ahead will not understand any non-native reason for us seeing in the dark!"

A wash of light streamed ahead. "There you are!" Kaze breathed a sigh of relief, not about to tell his brother he had accidentally tripped the mechanism. "We're no longer advertising our off-world status so freely." Waving a hand, he added, "We're blending, brother."

Around the next bend the two came across the military ground force which was spread out, lights glowing between numerous groups of temporary shelters. The area looked heavily fortified and filled with personnel. Several officers turned at their approach, a couple squinting and pointing.

"They seem agitated," murmured Kaze. "Probably eyeing my rims."

"I believe," Zozes said, shaking his head, "they want us to stop."

Kaze pulled up, eyeing the group of military personnel headed in their direction. An older officer was in the lead, and it was he who tapped at the window.

"Retract the screen," ordered Zozes.

"Relax." Kaze slowly bought the window down, smiling widely at the officer. "How's your station of task-duty, my authoritative friend?"

Immediately, Zozes shoved his identification past Kaze's face. "We're Specialist Global Defence Officers."

"Hmm." The officer accepted the documentation dubiously.

"No need to worry," Kaze assured the stony-faced human while handing his across. "Validation to the law."

Baffled, the officer stared. "Excuse me?"

Zozes murmured beneath his breath. "Keep your tongue universal, brother."

"Genuine, not a copy of ... questionable origin," Kaze added.

"We're on a tight schedule," ground out Zozes. "Superintendent Roccna sent us here to examine the crash zone."

"Just a minute." The officer took a couple steps back, talking into a radio attached to his combat vest. Eyeing the badges, he read out the ID numbers.

After a moment, he nodded. "You're cleared to move through," he said passing the documentation back, while pointing to the largest of the shelters. "Sign in at HQ."

Kaze drove the way indicated, eyeing everything he saw via his cyber-optic overlay, updating and screening different types of personnel within the outpost. It was a hive of activity, especially around the main headquarters.

The smaller temporary accommodations dotted near it were even busier, the humans entering them wearing strange garb covering them from head to feet. His cyber-optics identified the suits as chemical protection wear. The ones dressed in white jackets were scientists from a range of different fields.

"There's Inspector Roccna," said Kaze, eyeing a group ahead as he pulled up. "Why's she on-site?"

"Good question," said Zozes, opening the ute door. "Looks like we're about to find out."

Roccna was looking toward them, expression decidedly chilly, a hand shielding her eyes. Those standing with her were doing the same.

After turning off the vehicle, Kaze joined his brother, their Link-Trone hovering close in multi-cloak mode.

The Inspector cast them a brief glance while finishing her conversation with a scientist. Turning on her heel, she disappeared into the nearby shelter.

That scientist, an older woman, walked over, pointing at their vehicle. "Next time you drive through a crowd, try dipping the lights, genius. That's what low beam's for."

Stumped, Kaze glanced at his brother. Rolling her eyes, the scientist walked off toward a smaller shelter.

"What's low beam?" asked Zozes.

"No idea." Kaze scratched at this head, shrugging. "Directing them at the ground would defeat the line of sight."

"Humans." As if this said it all, Zozes headed into HQ's shelter.

Still puzzling on it, Kaze ducked in after him to be greeted by the strong scent of moist air choking him immediately. "Nice smell of mildew permeating in here."

"Still embracing pre-warp authenticity?" Zozes glanced at the working humans. "No one else seems to mind. I'd say these structures have been used elsewhere." He zeroed in on the rear. "The Inspector's back there."

Busy personnel crossed Kaze's vision as he looked across. Headquarters was a moving mass of officers, many gathered around work stations, inputting data in terminals.

At the rear of the structure stood a large display featuring multiple images of the crash zone. Inspector Roccna was conversing with a human male dressed in uniform. Every now and then she would indicate a spot on a topographical map, obviously making a point.

"He looks impressed," muttered Kaze sarcastically.

"Seems she doesn't discriminate between us or them." Zozes indicated the senior officer.

After signing in, the two began manoeuvring their way through the personnel to join the Inspector. Roccna continued her conversation with the older, grey-haired officer.

"None of what you propose is conventional, Inspector." It was obvious he was the human in charge. "How are my people to further examine this site if you deny all direct access?"

"The safety measures have been put in place for your protection, Commander Hagen. Your people's protection. The radiation levels are too high, even for my personnel."

"So you say, but we've detected only minimal radiation that..."

"It's clearly beyond your scientists' expertise," Roccna interrupted.

Silence briefly greeted this, before his eyes narrowed. "You realise I have people alive down there!"

"Who are now my concern, Commander." Roccna looked down her nose. "You may consider your efforts concluded. No one is to proceed into the quarantined area surrounding the crash zone without my explicit authorisation. Is that clear?"

For a long moment the Commander eyed her, his jaw moving up and down like he was chewing on words he knew better than to utter.

"Now that we've got that sorted, I have further orders." Roccna glanced at a hand-held computer. "You are to withdraw all personnel and maintain the outer defence perimeter."

"I see. That's to keep up an appearance of our involvement." The Commander cast an icy look toward Kaze and Zozes, then back to Roccna. "So you're effectively taking command? If you told us the truth from the beginning all of this could have been avoided."

"You seem inclined toward the melodramatic, Commander. You were never in charge to begin with."

Obviously stumped, the Commander snapped his mouth closed.

"Good," murmured Roccna. "You're dismissed."

The Commander pushed between Kaze and Zozes, his shoulders rigid with an anger that propelled him out the shelter at double quick time.

"I thought the objective was to work in conjunction with the humans?" enquired Zozes.

"Two hours ago, that would have been the case," she agreed.

"What's changed?" asked Kaze.

Barely sparing them a glance, Roccna closed down her porta-pad. "You're both with me."

As she walked off, Kaze glanced at his brother finding his expression difficult to read. Once the three were outside, Roccna headed over to a breach in the trees where the crashed ship had taken out and broken up the bush.

Kaze noted the multi-cloak emitters set around the perimeter of the crash zone generating a terrain cloak that covered the scarred land, felled trees and dug up dirt, concealing the crash.

When Roccna began speaking with two security officers, Kaze pulled his brother to one side. "Take a look back there."

Behind them black vehicles were pulling up on either side of his parked ute. The people getting out were dressed in dark uniforms, clearly non-military.

"Undercover Astral Guard personnel," judged Zozes.

"While all the human personnel are being escorted out of the quarantine zone," he added, then followed his brother back to Roccna.

As soon as there was a break in the conversation, Zozes spoke, "Pulling all human military back to the outer perimeter may produce issues."

After dismissing her security staff, Roccna looked at him. "Are you questioning my methods of operation, Blade?"

"If we're to establish trust, shouldn't they stand beside us, Sir?"

"Not when they give me no choice."

"But this will create division—"

"Tell me, Blade," she interrupted. "How many worlds have you seen integrated into a pre-warp program?"

Zozes fell silent.

"I thought as much. In my service, I've successfully taken part in over thirty-seven, so I'll keep my own counsel."

"Trust can be garnered," Zozes reminded, "in many ways."

"By the look on those humans' faces," Kaze took in the disgruntled military personnel being shifted, "trust is the last thing on their minds."

"Astral Guard neither requires, nor requests your opinion, nor does it need your sanction. As for me, I'm governed by one fundamental rule."

"Which is?" asked Zozes.

"Obedience. Abide by this rule and my operations run smooth."

Kaze smothered a laugh, which he tried to disguise as a cough. One of her withering looks came his way.

"I fail to see how this educates the humans to stand on their own," said Zozes.

The Inspector's lip curled, disgust coating each word. "They have a saying on this planet. 'In order to stand, one must first learn to crawl.' Humans are but youths embarking on a journey that will take them into the stars. To succeed, they'll require a firm hand, one that gives them no room to make the wrong choice when many are presented."

Kaze wondered how the humans would react to be preached at. He knew he hated it, already deciding her type of insight was stifling and of no use to him. So, he focused his attention on the Astral Guard officers, as they went about fortifying the quarantine zone.

When the Inspector fell silent, his brother did also. The silence grew uncomfortable to the point Kaze was forced to respond. "Time we move on, Inspector."

"It was foolish of Command to grant humans any type of responsibility," she mused, more to herself than them. "A mistake that I will not allow to be repeated."

"They might have to come up to speed sooner," said Kaze approaching the impact delver. "Looks to me like what's out there is coming here, they have no choice anymore."

A long channel scarred the earth leading to a deep crater where the highly-crippled flight craft was partially submerged in dirt and other foreign matter. Intermittent plasma fires flared, brilliant blue and yellow.

"What's happening down there?" he asked.

The Inspector moved to his side. "That military Commander deployed extraction teams into the quarantine zone against my explicit orders." Looking from the crash to his brother, her eyebrows rose mockingly. "Still believe I'm treating the humans unfairly?"

Zozes said nothing.

Even at a distance, Kaze's optics localised on the human bodies frozen where they stood in mid-motion. All wore chemical suits which they believed kept them protected and safe.

How wrong they had been.

These humans had no way of knowing that the power source used for space travel was a means of slipping through space-time. A magna-drive achieved this effect, reaching warp speed, but when these vessels set a magnatonic self-destruct, everything changed.

Kaze eyed the multiple magna dilation currents that had been triggered, breaking down into temporal warp bubbles.

The captured humans had no idea they had been enveloped, let alone how to escape.

At his side the Link-Trone's multi-cloak suddenly disengaged. One look around told Kaze why. The humans had all been moved to the quarantine zone. The Trone moved ahead of the group, performing readings. "Magnetic charged plasma signature, detected. Calculating radiation level."

Grouped back from the edge, the three looked over the impact crater.

"Humans lack the knowledge to detect magna dilation currents, and the radiation they produce." Roccna laughed softly, the sound mocking, holding no humour. "Let alone understand that it can lock them in a temporal pocket. Faster than light travel in space and its complexities are beyond them."

Via his cyber-optics, Kaze eyed the dense magna layer, how it thickly coated the air, made everything within seem to wave in and out of focus. Almost gelatinous from a distance, the blue cloud smouldered behind the perimeter shield. No native fauna flew over, or hung around the edges. Not even crawling insects were evident, he mused, kicking at the silty dust.

The entire area appeared a vacuum, held victim by this one event.

His brother continued to remain silent, a treatment Zozes favoured when irritated. Kaze had been on the receiving end more times than he cared to remember.

This time it was Roccna's problem, he thought, though he doubted she would even care that he disagreed.

"Do you think the Earth Commander had any idea what he was sending his people into?" Kaze asked.

"No." Roccna's answer was clipped. "He knew it was a matter for Global Defence. Sending his people in came down to arrogance, him believing they could handle the situation. I'll make certain he's held accountable for that transgression."

Before she finished speaking, Zozes was walking away. Standing next to the Link-Trone, he watched as it ran through its scans.

"Inspector, was the magna drive's self-destruct protocol issued?" asked Kaze, noting his brother turned back at the question, waiting for her answer.

She looked at him before answering. "We've confirmed it was."

"And?"

"You mean was someone trying to cover their tracks?"

Kaze nodded briefly.

"We believe the magna drive's self-destruct protocol was initiated for one reason, to break down all the ship's material."

"Leaving no evidence to be traced." He chewed on that for a moment. "Isn't that function only installed on Planetary Allegiance-classed ships?" Kaze waited, but she remained stubbornly silent forcing him to ask bluntly, "Was it one of our own that did this?"

"Reports," she began grudgingly, "have been relayed over private channels through Astra-Com that there's been escalating developments of an ongoing civil war within the Kadra Realm."

Kaze remembered seeing similar reports before being deployed to Eastverse Astral State. "The Planetary Allegiance have made many enemies after the shift of power from the Second Galactic War."

"Of course." Roccna looked over the crater. "But what I'm referring to is a little closer to home, survivors of the battle of Insurrection."

"Kadra sympathisers." Now it was Kaze's turn to sneer. "Those that turn from the Planetary to support Kadra?"

"And their so-called 'Assultra Rebellion' which was believed to have been disbanded after the conclusion of the Galactic War when its Leadership members were executed for high treason."

"So," Kaze eyed the wreckage. "This could be the beginning of their return."

"The Kadra will never have an open presence in this galaxy again," she spat. "Any force they bring forth will be crushed, just as it was."

"If an Assultra Core rebel faction stole this ship," pondered Kaze, "why come to Earth? What were they hoping to gain?"

Zozes walked up. "To sabotage the pre-warp signing."

"Speculation," said Roccna. "But plausible at this point."

The Link-Trone hovered between Kaze and Zozes. "Scan complete. Detecting charged plasma bonds generated by ship's drive core explosion. Magna radiation level reads between stages one and five, expanding and contracting within field.

Temporal-motion bubbles weave on dilation currents, varying in diameter and complexity…"

"Time before temporal convergence?" interrupted Zozes, eyeing the dense magna layer.

The Trone's lights flashed in uncharacteristic annoyance. "Unknown, due to unstable properties present."

"And the humans?" Kaze looked at the trapped figures held immobile. "Have you got readings on them?"

"The rate of exposure is calculated presently at stage two and rising. Converged magna radiation currents trapping humans in temporal pockets has not reached critical."

Speculative, Zozes looked from right to left, examining the perimeter. "So it hasn't gone fatal for them yet. They'd survive if we got them out now."

Roccna made a noise, but Kaze and Zozes ignored her listening for Link-Trone's response.

"Correct. Extraction must be completed before stage three is reached. Human cell regeneration can be undertaken if …"

Incredulous, Roccna spoke over the Link-Trone, glaring at Zozes. "You realise that's a magna dilation field governed by laws beyond even our understanding."

"I'm aware of that, Inspector. I don't plan on becoming magna-fied due to radiation poisoning."

Roccna stifled an oath. "Entering without a dilation chart of the area is suicide. You'll end up trapped in the field!"

"When that count passes stage three," said Zozes, "most of those humans will be dead, beyond help. I intend to be out well before then."

"I've a decon team inbound," she snapped. "We will launch our scout probes to map the current those temporal-bubbles traverse while establishing a mobile site-to-site tele-warp disc."

"And by the time those currents are mapped? Your team's set up?" Zozes walked away, not bothering to state the obvious.

"Blade, you're not dismissed!" she yelled furiously. "We don't have the equipment to operate within a heavily charged magna field. Not even a military-based combat-issued grid-shield can counter magna effects."

"Inspector." Zozes looked over his shoulder. "A Blade sorge-shield can."

Kaze wondered at his brother's strong belief. Ignoring Roccna, he stepped before Zozes. "I know you're having a bit of a moment here brother, but what're you doing?"

"We can do this, Kaze."

"Of course we can." Feeling jumpy, he eyed the crash site, the trapped humans. "But if our armour's shield drops less than a micro-count, our bodies may not agree. First stage exposure alone can cause long-term effects. I'm kinda fond of where my hair is."

"Our power armour's sorge-shield will give us enough time to get in, and we have LT to map the area, lead us around the devastated zones. We can extract, save, those humans," Zozes assured, "while maintaining your less than attractive grooming habits."

"Last I checked, only Blade Optives have the service expertise to regulate and measure what our spawn-well can and can't do."

"So you're afraid," Zozes scoffed.

For a long moment, Kaze eyed his brother. "That's pretty low. You know the deal, not to use that against each other. Things can get out of hand."

"Just say that you are. I'll go in on my own." Zozes started down the crater.

Resigned, Kaze followed. "Have it your way, hero. Lead on."

"We've wasted enough time as it is. LT, prime your spawn-well's construct disc, increase replication volume for combat operations."

"Are you insane?" Roccna demanded, still standing at the edge. "You have no right nor authorisation to enter this quarantine zone."

Kaze spared the Inspector's dumfounded expression a brief glance, realising he had completely forgotten her presence.

At the delver's deep edge, Zozes activated his power armour, clearly having heard her. "Those lives down there give me every right, unless you want to try and stop us."

Lip curling, she advanced a couple of steps, halting only when the two pinned her with a narrow-eyed look of solidarity.

"How am I supposed to explain your entry to Command?" she demanded.

"I'm sure you'll think of something, Inspector." Kaze triggered his power-armour, then demagnetised the sorge-rifle from his back, enjoying the feel of its weight in his hands. "Isn't boot-licking reported high on your Star-Key?" Before she could respond, he activated his helmet, moving to join his brother.

The moment his cyber-optics linked with his helmet's tactical visor, they generated a cyber-graphic display of the terrain, compensating for the thick magna-layer, though the schematic of the area was somewhat distorted, no doubt due to the temporal bubbles.

Shoulder to shoulder the brothers stood on the edge overlooking the chasm, Zozes casually demagnetising his sorge-rifle while calculating the depth of the drop.

"I've a few ideas how to get this done, so pay attention," he said. "Once in there, the crash site's temporal field will be attracted to our energy signatures, so don't shoot or expel power from LT's spawn-well, unless you have no other option."

"Not that interested in becoming a permanent resident," Kaze assured, eyeing what was left of the mutilated craft. "And our shields? Won't they attract it?"

"The short answer's yes. LT is already readjusting our shields' radial fields to emit a low repulse frequency."

"LT's weakening our shields?" Kaze digested this. "Curtailing our only defensive will make this a very short run."

"My suggestion is move fast, that's our best protection. I know we can do this."

On a shoulder roll, Kaze cricked his neck. "So much for the pep talk."

"I'll take scout-charge." Zozes prepared to jump. "You bring up the rear. LT, initiate recon-mapping, localise each bio marker of a survivor and overlay dilation currents, where each temporal bubble is shifting within that manga field."

"Affirmative." Lights flashed as LT activated its grav-nacelle thrusters, flying ahead. At the Trone's signal the two took the leap, landing at the crater's bottom, kicking up ash but only marginally, due to the change in atmosphere which was heavy, something Kaze felt immediately.

The density of it was like another layer weighing him down. Automatically, his power armour's mobility stabilisers began compensating, bringing up its thrust. At a hand signal from Zozes, the two began jogging across scorched earth toward what remained of the craft.

The Link-Trone was extrapolating dilations within the field, updating the brothers' cyber displays on current directions, high spike areas of temporal energy, how they were likely to shift. The AI generated a wave-path through its map-scouter, displaying several spatial feet-treks ahead of his movements. Keeping a sharp eye on the magna radiation gauge, Kaze's main concern was avoiding any hot zones.

The destroyed craft had created a deep trench, littering a vast area, larger than Kaze initially thought. Bowed structural beams, torn hull plating, even random steam pockets, all this tested the two as they fought their way ahead, making their way to the safest section of the destroyed craft.

The victims were just ahead.

In sharp detail, the Trone highlighted each on his visor, illuminating them in yellow. Frozen, trapped in a temporal pocket just outside the craft, they were locked there, time slowed to such a degree they appeared to not be moving at all.

The Link-Trone's sharp voice broke into his concentration, flashing a warning on his visor. "Marking dilation anomalies ahead. This current's polarity shift reversed within pull trajectory."

"Brace yourself!" yelled Zozes over the received the alert.

A clear, moving stream, the current collected Kaze's right shoulder, its power a crushing blow that he could feel but not see, only his armour's energised repulse-field protected him. The severity of this wave tested the power of his shields, their output level driven to the limit. Then came the pull, the undertow, dragging him hard and fast, fighting the power of his armour.

Mid-attack, an image snapped to life, randomly appearing within the currents. Barely visible, but definitely there. Eyes narrowed, Kaze fought to stay upright and focused at the same time …

… he saw the ship rising up out of the delver it had created, leaving the earth unscarred as it had once been, and the pilot …

At that point, the image began distorting and he was thrown out, head reeling. Ahead, Kaze watched his brother fighting the stream, pushing hard off the ground. Following his brother's example, the two made their escape, reaching the other side.

There they breathed, waited for their Blade-Gears to stabilise. Kaze glanced at his radiation gauge, grimacing. It was climbing steadily.

"What just happened?" He focused on his brother.

"Temporal motion transference?" Zozes glanced back at the current. "I've heard the theory, never believed it."

The Link-Trone hovered close. "You experienced residual transference, of a reversed polarity within a temporal stream phase motion. In that current, you experience a reversal of events."

Kaze watched the distortion slowly fading, becoming a clear wash. "So that was a past event."

"A sequence where the ship crashed, but in reverse," added Zozes. "Without our armours' shields, that current would've become a temporal pocket, and we'd be trapped."

"Best avoided." Problem was, thought Kaze, there hadn't been enough warning to do that. The further they went into this magna field, the more volatile and unpredictable these temporal dilation currents would become.

The crash seemed to have created not only temporal streams but temporal bubbles that floated like great boulders, trapping and locking a victim. The streams appeared to weave through the shattered vessel, branching out in numerous directions. Some dragged you into the past, others flowed forward carrying you through to the present.

The Trone marked another dilation current on Kaze's optics. Rippling ahead, this displacement of flowing energy rode off the ground. It seemed to be part of an explosion at first glance, a massive flash of light firing repeatedly. Another push and pull current that was trapping the exact moment of a blast, vibrant blue-white energy bouncing back and forth.

The Trone flew beneath it, disappearing from view. Zozes followed, timing his roll to avoid flame and gases, avoiding draining his shields from connecting. Kaze brought up the rear, but knew immediately he had misjudged his entry and was forced to drop to the ground then power slide underneath the swelling cloud.

That mistake forced him to activate a short grav-boost, speeding up his slide, in the process throwing up ash and dust. Below the anomaly, the roll and billow happening above him was in slow-motion, fluid and gas meeting, erupting in a brilliant blue flame, the resulting explosion trapped within the singularity.

Momentarily dazzled, that brief pause cost him another boost, this one jerking him to his feet. Jogging on, he looked back, then almost fell over his own boots. That same current was closing in on him, attracted by the brief bursts of energy.

"LT!" he bellowed, swinging back hefting his sorge-rifle at the billowing mass.

"You activated your grav-thrusters!" yelled Zozes, turning also.

Kaze grimaced, only then realising the truth of his brother's earlier warning. The two brief thrusts had caused the current to lock onto the radial signature of his suit's thrusters.

As he was about to fire, Zozes held up a hand. "Trigger hold!"

The wave unexpectedly pulled away, leaving the trapped explosion where it was.

"There's why it changed its direction," pointed Zozes, but before he could elaborate, the Trone interrupted.

"Alert, alert! Dilation maelstrom detected."

Both brothers turned, Kaze's eyes rounding at the sight of a temporal rift detonation washing toward the trapped humans. It was coming from inside the ship's magna-drive.

They had much less time than had been estimated on entry. The ship's magna-destruct detonation appeared to be expanding from the centre of the magnatonic drive-core, temporal currents washing constantly from the ship.

"Move!" bellowed Zozes as plasma flames burst to life, blistering heat waves striking their shields.

His brother cut a fast route around the wreckage, entering a torn maintenance tube. Close behind, Kaze was almost stepping on his heels as they sprinted through the tunnel, both skirting a damaged section to come upon the humans. Only then did the two realise the extent of their entrapment.

The Trone was already scouting the survivors from the perimeter of the temporal bubble. One female had been caught, her companions trying to pull her free resulting in all of them becoming trapped.

"Her arm!" Zozes indicated the injury, fighting to be heard over the noise.

It looked fractured to Kaze, almost displaced, lodged between the push and pull streams from inside the temporal pocket. "If we pull her out—"

"—she'll lose it," finished his brother.

"Then what?" Fighting to think, Kaze blocked the approaching maelstrom. Heat, radiation, everything was building, including his own anxiety.

"We'll rework their locked condition to what happened earlier." Zozes swung to the Trone pointing above the survivors and indicating a damaged beam. "LT, calibrate a pulse-dart yield to generate a delayed sorge-burst on point of contact."

Alarmed, Kaze shook his head. "That'll draw it to us faster!"

"A pulse-dart set on delayed contact activation should attract temporal currents to change course. Remember how the wave altered direction, was drawn towards your grav-thruster's radial trail?"

"That sounds like guesswork to me. When'd you become a magnatonic physicist?" Kaze felt like his temper was building as fast as the oncoming maelstrom. "For all we know, you could detonate this entire area!"

"Not if LT calculates the correct yield. I'll get in, extract the humans."

"No, I have to go. If the current's polarity changes, you have a better shot at accurately calculating the yield for an additional pulse-dart through LT."

Pushed for time, Zozes looked at the maelstrom then nodded. Weapon in hand, he waited for the Link-Trone to prepare a shot.

Kaze needed focus now, nothing to disrupt or shake it. The survivors became objects, he no longer saw their stark expressions, or felt the ferocity of the approaching explosion.

"Hold ready," called Zozes, taking aim with his sorge-rifle. "Firing on my mark."

Stance lowered, Kaze took several hard, fast breaths, bracing for what was to come.

"Firing!" The dart left Zozes' weapon, hit the beam, bathing the survivors in a brilliant pale glow. Instantly the temporal currents fluctuated, warping the dilation field toward the glowing pulse dart.

Flung into motion, unaware of what had happened, the humans resumed pulling at the woman who was screaming in agony.

Arms wide, Kaze charged toward the three, shoving them clear of the immediate area. Kneeling, he lowered the female who was now unconscious, face white, her right arm missing. Picking her up, he moved again at his brother's yell.

"Current's dropping! Get out of there!"

Kaze felt more than saw the current warp. Bracing the unconscious woman, he dove toward the deck, landing on his back while protecting her. The wave billowed above, striking the ground next to him in a violent blast that spread dust and debris. Rolling up, he breathed a sigh of relief. Looking down at the unconscious survivor, he gently placed her on the ground, eyeing the injury. She was wearing one of Earth's protective suits. It was melted, fused to the skin where the mutilation was exposed.

Zozes was keeping the rest of the humans still, trying to control their obvious shock. "Stay calm, we're here to get you out."

"Her arm's bleeding out." Kaze knew they had no time, but if he did not dress the wound, she would be dead from blood loss. "I'm applying a MED-Band."

From the utility case on his belt, he took a circular cap placing it on her arm, pressing its centre it formed a rim, ringing the wound. Kaze watched as the band tightened, an energy window forming over the missing limb, activating a blood extraction sample which could then release tissue foam matching her anatomy, temporarily stemming blood loss while numbing pain.

The woman's eyelids fluttered during the last part of the procedure as she groggily stirred.

"It's alright, we've got you," Kaze assured. "I need you to stand so—"

The Link-Trone's shrill voice broke in. "Detecting additional bio-signature!"

"Where?" Zozes demanded, swinging to the Trone.

"Localising source." Lights flashing, it indicated another wave path. "Signature generated from inside craft."

Kaze did not have to be a mind-reader to know what his brother was thinking.

"Don't say it," he growled, urging the woman's companions to help her. "Don't even think it."

"Lead the survivors to an extraction point," Zozes ordered. "I can do the rest."

"You see that?" Kaze jerked a thumb over his shoulder indicating the again growing temporal maelstrom. "Once the magnatonic particles are expended, that explosion will engulf this entire area."

Zozes moved close by Kaze. "LT, remain with the survivors, assist Alpha Blue to escort them to the quarantine perimeter."

Before Kaze could respond, Zozes took off, racing toward the craft. Torn, he looked from the survivors to his brother, the last image of him entering that damaged vessel etched in his mind.

The Link-Trone started relaying a wave-path for him to follow, his tactical visor lighting up with the safest route. Saving time, he picked up the woman, carrying her while urging the others to start moving.

The trek out of the crash zone seemed to have dramatically decreased, many currents having readjusted into normal space-time, telling him the temporal pocket's external boundary was receding back towards the ship, most of the affected area appearing to have disintegrated. Smoke billowed across scorched ground, only matter-dust remaining.

"Keep close," Kaze ordered. "Place a hand on the person's shoulder before you."

The Link-Trone was guiding the group fast through a thick dust storm billowing out from the magna-drive's core as it collected all within its path. This meant two things to Kaze. The journey back was cut in half, and Zozes was in a lot more danger as the craft was on the point of collapse.

When he spotted the approaching decon team, Kaze urged the humans toward them. The lead decon officer began placing tele-warp badges on each survivor. Activating a tele-warp rim, he threw it high, generating a teleportation window of static. The humans fitted with badges immediately began to breakdown into warp-orbs disappearing into the device.

As the last badge was placed on the injured woman, Kaze stepped back watching her warp out.

"Your Link-Trone has been authorised to connect your Star-Key with the outpost's tele-warp engine," said the officer. "Now that the magnetically charged field comprising tele-warp is collapsing, site to site warp is active. There's only you and your brother left."

"Understood." Kaze glanced back toward the craft. "But I can't leave. Alpha Green's in there searching for a last survivor."

"That maelstrom's growing because the magna-drive's on the point of going critical. Once it blows, magna particles will level this entire crater, syncing all temporal pockets and phase motion currents back in time with this planet ... the only thing left will be matter-dust. You have to warp out now!"

"I don't have time to argue." Grabbing a tele-warp badge and mobile rim-disc from the leader, Kaze added, "Keep scans open for our Star-Key signatures, and for this badge identifier." He held them up. "If I know my brother, he'll have that last survivor."

Kaze took off fast, the Link-Trone hovering ahead so he could avoid any remaining temporal currents. With the magna drive going critical, the temporal maelstrom's pull was so strong that the stabilisation thrusters of his power-suit were now kicking in repeatedly to steady him.

Random temporal streams seemed to be rolling toward the craft, through the crash site, like they were converging. As he skirted these, his brother's signal was refreshed by the Link-Trone, showing Zozes moving fast, deeper into the ship.

The explosion itself appeared suspended within the pull and push trajectory, the right side of the ship exploding then restoring, repeating like it would never end.

Forced to fight his way in, Kaze waited impatiently for the Link-Trone to extrapolate the safest route through the ship, sending him a wave path. The heat was dramatically increasing, plasma flames engulfing large sections, and what was not alight appeared eaten away or engulfed, collapsing into matter-dust. Kaze pushed at the wreckage unable to believe the change in such a short time.

When his visor's readout was disrupted, cyber-screens moment-arily powering down, he paused, gritting his teeth, realising the magna radiation was interfering with his Blade-Gear functions. It was only a matter of time before his power armour's shield would be fully compromised.

"LT," he called, "how far?"

Before the Trone could respond, a dilation current formed in the coming corridor, the stream pulling and twisting as it washed toward him. Diving for the deck, he missed being caught, but barely.

"Zozes!" he yelled, activating SS freq-com channel in desperation. "I've just entered the ship's command bay, respond!"

As the current dissipated, it took most of a wall with it, forcing Kaze to move even faster. The strain on his nervous system, the constant wash of spawns from the Trone, was now taking its toll on his body.

At the passengers' quarters, Kaze looked inside. "LT, what ship class is this?"

"A deep space Warront Craft."

There was a series of crew quarters, the first two altered, resembling training bays, which made no sense. Moving on, he raced into the third, finding it different again, a combat training cache containing weapons he had never seen …

… a sensation moved over his body, one he recognised feeling briefly on the training range. Blinking, he saw the Chief on his right, near the end of the bay. She was standing with three young boys. They looked strange to him, then the image shifted, altering to the boys following her as she pointed at something he could not see …

Head pounding, Kaze fought to look away, but something held him in place. Not even when his nose began pouring blood. Fighting the sensation, he forced himself to turn, knowing if he did not, he would die. In the corridor, he leaned against the wall, breathing hard, waiting for the pain searing his spine to ease.

What had he just seen? The Chief? Who'd she been instructing … and why had the image been so clear?

Static interrupted the moment, freq-com firing. "… ze … found … keep … order … now!"

"LT!" Kaze turned to the Trone. "Track the source of that communication!"

The Link-Trone's grav-nacelles ignited, moving it along the corridor, Kaze following at a sprint, ignoring how much of the ship was crumbling around him.

When the Trone paused at the entrance of the medical bay, Kaze knew why. Here the temporal currents swirled violently, much of the room appearing in flux.

At his side the Trone informed, "Temporal fields converging on maelstrom, all currents are reintegrating the crash zone back into normal flow of this planet's temporal motion cycle."

"Which means the ship's about to go nova," ground Kaze, eyeing the multiple currents moving before the entrance of medical bay.

"LT, calculate a sorge-dart charge output. One that'll give me as much time as possible." Weapon in hand, Kaze took aim above the entranceway.

"Sorge-dart signature set."

He hit the target dead on, instantly warping the currents into violent action, drawing them up away from where he needed to pass, but only temporarily.

His brother was in the next room, trapped in a temporal current. He had opened a med-stasis capsule, and was attempting to get someone out. Whoever it was, they were unrecognisable, mutated, burnt, but still whole, gripping some type of device in their hand.

"Two more rounds," he ordered the Trone.

This time he fired the sorge-darts either side of the stasis-chamber, splitting the warp currents around his brother. The instant Zozes was freed, he swung to Kaze who was placing a tele-warp badge on the burnt body.

"Don't you ever listen?" Zozes demanded.

Kaze levered the body up, throwing it over his shoulder. "You know me."

As they crossed medical bay, he could see the current returning to engulf the scorched deck.

In the passage, they had to fight to stand, plasma flames burning out conduits above and on the wall, vibrating the deck, pulling it apart.

"Collapse imminent," informed the Trone.

"She's buckling!" Kaze yelled.

As the brothers cleared the final corridors, jumping the damaged ramp, Kaze gasped a desperate order at the Trone. "LT, mark the safest zone to reach site-to-site tele-warp."

He did not want to look back, could hear the violent sound of temporal currents being absorbed into the maelstrom. The craft was buckling around them, hull plating collapsing and compacting, caving in, being pulled toward the magna core.

Then abruptly, all was silent, not even the sound of matter-dust shifting beneath their boots could be detected as they raced on, trying to leave the eye of the storm before it ignited.

There was no escaping the coming shockwave, and when it hit, the three were sent rolling across the ground, almost buried in the dirt and ash. The instant he was still, Kaze became aware of the warning on his visor. His shields were close to collapse, but remarkably still held. Turning his head, he saw Zozes checking the survivor's body, and that unbelievably the arm was moving weakly.

"He survived without protective gear?" Kaze gasped.

"Move!" Zozes yelled, standing to throw the body over his shoulder. "This isn't over yet!"

Kaze jumped to his feet, activating the tele-warp disc above the three, watching it fully expand while it was priming, fighting to get through the disturbance. "LT's marking the tele-warp site through the mobile device unit."

The Trone indicated where each was to take position. "Uploading tele-warp request."

Around them plasma flames continued to burn, looking innocent, almost playful within a fog of dense grey dust. Silence reigned, but a rumbling could be felt, the final build-up of a dust and ash, a storm that would engulf all in its shockwave, first the push, now would come the pull. Without warning it struck again, casting radial ash over the three, pounding their shields. The brothers activated grav-thrusters to keep them stabilised in place, could see the rolling barrage of plasma with the magna detonation. Neither could take much more.

"LT," Kaze roared desperately, "it's getting a little hot in here!"

The tele-warp disc window activated, gripping his body fast and strong, warp-orbs surrounding it. The sensation of moving through the warp-corridor was welcome, his surrounds seemed to illuminate into a blur of motion before being transported, and released, ultimately materialising at the outpost covered in dust and dirt. As that cleared, Kaze crossed to his brother who was placing the survivor on the ground.

Inspector Roccna approached, immediately signalling the Astral Enforcers to generate their armour and draw weapons while taking aim at the disfigured body.

Confused, Kaze looked to Zozes who had stepped back, expression guarded.

"What's going on?" Kaze asked, watching his brother kneel beside the survivor before cautiously picking up the arm, watching the limb move.

It was then Kaze remembered seeing something gripped in its hand on the ship. Kneeling beside his brother, he felt the Link-Trone hover close.

The moment of realisation hit him hard. Jerking upright, Kaze spat, "A zaphna rod?"

Zozes let the disfigured arm fall to the ground, before standing slowly. "It's a Kadra."

Galactic Star Key: Ebony Casteel
Astral Nav-Coordinates: EAS-APL-4
Data Sequence: 10.0

With every jerk of the zip, Ebony's shoulder pulled, the suitcase almost sliding from the bed. Her accident was no dream, no matter how much she wanted to believe it had been. She had the aching body to prove it.

Now she was being discharged, finally going home. It was all she had thought about since waking, so why was she anxious?

Confused, she perched on the bed. At least here, she was insulated from the world. Outside these walls would be gossip and looks, the locals asking questions.

Questions she could not answer.

"You ready, Bonnie?"

"Hang on, Dad." She opened the bedside drawers, double-checking she had everything. "I think so, just let me ..." She fought with the zip, cursing.

Rickard took over, eyeing her speculatively. "Good to see nothing's changed, still living life like a bull at a gate."

"Ha ha." Ebony watched him zip it up, place it on the floor and pull out the handle. "I have to admit it took a little longer than most for common sense to kick in."

"Like several years?"

"I've matured!" Ebony glanced around the hospital room, grimacing. "Somewhat."

"Oh, definitely." Rickard took the handle himself. "No way I can forget your wondrous teenage years, living life with that no pain, no gain mindset."

Ebony chewed her lip. "Don't even think about bringing up the water skiing incident."

"Been reminiscing over your glory days all week, it's my parental right."

"Fire away." Ebony sighed in resignation. "Not like I've a choice in the matter."

"Well, that landing was pretty spectacular. Someone who hadn't skied in years attempting to cut through water like a professional on slalom ski."

"Yes," she agreed, thinking back. "That cut was pretty ambitious."

"The effort was. The tumbling across the water like a cannon ball, not so much. That splash alone could have watered a ten-acre paddock."

"But the graze was small, barely noticeable."

Rickard leaned close. "Grazes don't usually need eight stitches."

Ebony gave up. Her dad was deflecting, hoping to ease the tension by kidding around. One thing he had was an endless supply of sarcastic comments.

"Hey, I'm just out of my teens, so I can't be anywhere near that bad."

"Actually," Rickard said, touching her shoulder lightly as she sank onto the bed, "you're twenty-one."

"Seriously? I'm twenty-one?" Ebony looked out the window, not seeing the blue sky, only the lost time.

"From the evaluation," Rickard grimaced, finally admitting, "it seems like several months are still missing from your memory."

"Months?" Ebony swallowed hard. "How many?"

"You want an amount?" Rickard thought on this. "I'd say around eight. Maybe a little more."

"That's why Doctor Walker went on about the year so much." Ebony thought of the date, what year it really was, trying not to freak out. "I had a birthday that I don't remember."

"Everyone will give you time to catch up, Bonnie."

"How am I supposed to do this?" She thought of the two-page list the doctor had given her. "All of the appointments, living, and what about giving the police a statement? I can't even remember my age!"

Rickard pulled her up, set her on her feet. "Like a Casteel. Casteels stand together."

"Dad, I can't expect you or mum to help me the whole time. You've got your own life and the farm, and mum's got the café."

A moment's silence fell between the two.

"Grace told you," he guessed.

Ebony said nothing, instead turning to check the second drawer of her night stand, opening and closing it just as quickly. "She may have mentioned something about another milk price drop, the second in two years. How're you expected to live on that?"

Mouth tight, Rickard paced to the end of the bed. "Farmers are slaves to the cents per litre the milk factories pay us. Most often half of what our product's worth, but holding out the carrot of better pay to come. It's an endless cycle, keeps us crawling back year after year."

"Great lifestyle for a family." Her father's connection to the land was deep. "Why don't you try a petition? Get some numbers together?"

On a bark of laughter, Rickard shook his head. "Back in the day, when I had little more go, maybe. I'll leave that to the young guns coming in."

"Mum said something about how a lot of big corporations are buying everything up, turning small independent farms into some type of super-farm."

"She sure gave that mouth of hers a workout." Rickard sighed, seeming to turn philosophical. "Life never stays the same, Bonnie. I remember a time when a handshake was the seal on a deal. Modern age changes all that, loyalties, friendships. That's the past."

Thoughtful, she secured the latch on her bathroom case, then stuffed it in her shoulder bag. Bringing up a certain name was a risk, but it was out before she could stop it. "The Solomons said they could help."

Face flushed, Rickard's eyebrows locked together. A passing nurse paused at the door, but moved on after noting the tense atmosphere. "I'd rather deal with the bank, and you know how much I like them."

"Yes." Knowing she was entering dangerous waters, Ebony swam out regardless. "You're still part of the Fellowship though. I know not officially, but maybe it's an option?"

Rickard crossed his arms, facing her. "The day I can describe the taste of water is the day I'll consider that tragedy."

"Dad, what happened? Why did you leave?"

On a sharp snap, Rickard collapsed the tow-along handle again, picking up the suitcase, stalking to the door. "It's enough to say I stand apart from them."

"Was it to do with Aunt Eve's condition? Why wasn't she treated, like me?"

As the silence lengthened, Ebony grew impatient. She knew he hated talking about his twin sister, but her aunt's rapid deterioration was something she really needed to know about.

"Dad, please ..."

Head tipped back, Rickard eyed the ceiling, shaking his head. "Let it go."

"Xavier and mum were talking about it," she pleaded. "They said Aunt Eve's condition could have been treated, that Marcus Solomon was treated."

Her father shook his head, holding out a hand. "Bonnie, all that history is complicated. Each suffered differently, their memories of the incident still remain a mystery, despite what Xavier Solomon claims or thinks. His father returned a changed man. They all did."

"If he doesn't ..." Ebony swallowed with difficulty. "He seems to think I share a similar problem, but from what I understand, my symptoms aren't the same."

"I'm not here to influence your choice," said Rickard, deflating a little. "I have my own reasons for what I do. Doctor Walker seems competent enough, she'll show you what needs to be done, and when you're ..." he tripped over the next words ever so slightly, "going through it, you can decide if her methods are for you."

"You mean if I'm prepared to do what she suggests?"

He offered only a curt nod.

What could this mystery treatment be? Why had her aunt chosen to not go through with it?

As they moved down the hall toward reception, the two were quiet. Even speaking with the nurse, her father seemed subdued as he made certain all the appropriate discharge forms had been taken care of. Ebony searched for the courage she had seemed to have in abundance during her youth.

"You're all set," the nurse said, smiling reassuringly. "Take care of yourself, Ebony. You've had quite a doing."

"I will, and thanks again."

Every step toward the exit, her anxiety grew. Why was she so afraid to go out there? Staying here, vegetating and withering away, was no option. Veering from the lift at the last moment, she walked to a window, looking out into the busy car park, hugging her shoulder bag. People were hurrying about, some walking past on the footpath, heading for the local park's walking track.

"Bonnie?" Her father drew alongside.

A question was circling her mind, one she knew her father would hate, but it had to be asked.

"Do you think I could talk to Aunt Eve about her treatment?" She looked at him, trying to read his expression. "Would she mind?"

"Well." Rickard seemed to mull this over, dumping the case next to him. "I wouldn't recommend it."

"Why? There's so much she could tell me."

"Her condition's taken a toll over the last year. What you'd get might not be what you're looking for." Pulling out his car keys, Rickard fiddled with them absently. "Grandma May moved in six months ago, something I guess you don't remember. Evie needs help now, to look after herself and Baden."

"Oh." The information formed a lump in her stomach, one that was hard and uncomfortable. "Things really have changed."

"And some things haven't." Rickard mustered a grin. "Your old nag's still chewing down every blade of grass she can."

"She is?" Misty-eyed, Ebony smiled at her father. "I missed that horse so much when I was in the city."

"Your gas ball's just the same, scared stupid of her own farts, which is nothing new."

"Probably thinks I've abandoned her or something when I left for uni."

"Ha!" Sliding his hands into his pant pockets, Rickard looked out the window. "As long as there's grass and sun, she's happy jamming more kilos on that rump of hers."

"Mum promised she'd ride her."

"Good luck with that. Every spare minute she's got, she's been tapping away at that side project of hers."

"No! Are you saying she's finally finished her book?"

"Never said that."

"So the never-ending story still isn't finished. At least I didn't miss seeing her get published."

"After fifteen years, I wouldn't hold my breath."

Something in her father's tone had Ebony tipping her head. "You don't think she'll go through with sending it in?"

"She can bloody well write. I think she's waiting on something or someone." Shrugging, Rickard tapped the window. "There they are."

"What?" Ebony looked around. "We're waiting for someone?"

"Nina and Jevon, they've just pulled in. The two have been insistent about driving you to your apartment. Something about a home tour."

"Oh, I didn't realise." As her father's words sank in, Ebony clenched her hands, her chest suddenly tight. She lived in an apartment now, not with her folks at the farm. She had moved out during the year. "My apartment. I live with Nina."

"Chin up, remember the controlled breathing exercise Doctor Walker showed you. Hold ten seconds, then release. Helps reset the mind to ease the anxiety."

It took a few moments, but slowly, the tightness in her chest waned. "This is weird, going to a place that I've lived for the better part of a year and I can't even picture it."

"You'll be fine. It's just a visit. When the tour is done, grab what you need and we'll all meet back at the farm."

"Right. I need to get my mobile too, it's weird not having it on me." Ebony leaned across to hug her father. "Thank you. I don't know what …" Her voice choked, throat closing.

"You're doing fine. Don't forget your appointment at the cop shop, it's at three. Mara will be there to guide you through it."

"Okay." Spotting Jevon getting out of the car, she nodded. "Thanks, Dad."

"Don't worry so much, Bonnie." He pressed the button to call the lift. "You'll catch up, probably faster than you'd like."

Galactic Star Key: Rickard Casteel
Astral Nav-Coordinates: EAS-APL-4
Data Sequence: 11.0

From the window, Rickard watched as his daughter left the building. Jevon accosted her and lifted her up, spinning a circle that had her hitting him until he finally set her down.

It was good to see her smile, watch the strain drain from her face. As the car drove off, Rickard picked up the case and headed for the stairs.

At the reception desk, he paused. "Can you send a message to Doctor Walker, please. I need to remind her to email my daughter's entire documented examination, from day one to her discharge today."

"I see." Though obviously puzzled, the nurse nodded. "I'll pass that on to her."

"Thanks." Rickard tapped the desk, offering a smile before moving off. "Enjoy your afternoon."

"I didn't take you for the fraternising type."

At the sound of the gravelly voice, Rickard tensed. "If you're here for your shots, I'd try the clinic down the street," he said, turning. "The Vet centre specialises in your kind."

Axel smiled, getting to his feet. "You know why I'm here, Rick."

"Stay away from her," Rickard warned, approaching the bald man to stand toe to toe. "I'll only tell you once."

"The longer you keep treating Ebony as a mere child, the longer it will take for her to come to terms with all of this."

"She'll come to terms in her own time." Glancing around, Rickard raised an eyebrow. "Aren't you straying a little far from your boy boss? Solomon doesn't usually loosen his leash."

188

Like he was engrossed in the task, Axel folded the paper he had been leafing through. "My agents and I have been temporarily reassigned. Wherever your daughter goes, we go."

"The hell you do!"

"Careful, Rick. Don't let that temper of yours land you in a situation we'll both regret. I'm doing you a courtesy, telling you how things are."

"Who's 'we'?" Rickard demanded.

"Agent Canon is on detail as we speak."

"May agreed to this? Without consulting me?"

"Your mother seems to be the only Casteel equipped to understand that Ebony's safety comes first."

"Looks like she and I will be having a little chat."

"She has sound reasons, Rick. There's been a development, a Special Division unit has been brought in to investigate the crash zone."

"Special Division?"

"You've been out too long, Rick. Let the Fellowship watch over her. Keep out of their way." Leaning forward, he pulled Rickard's coat closed. "And mine."

For a long moment the two eyed one another.

"You really think that'll work on me?" Casually, Rickard shrugged out of his jacket, tossed it over his shoulder. "My family, my rules. We are her caretakers. All decisions go through Grace and myself. Understand?"

For a long moment, Axel seemed to measure the situation. "Xavier made it clear to keep our presence hidden for now. My concerns are for her safety, that's all."

"And my concerns include all. She may not carry our blood, but she's a Casteel and she always will be."

"For now, you can cling to that infamous caretaker title," Axel said with a theatrical sigh. "When it's severed, and it will be, you will become nothing more than a man who chose to live the remaining years of his life as a coward."

On a snarl, Rickard stepped forward, hands clenched. Axel raised his chin, practically daring him. "Tell me, Rick. What is it that makes you hate us so much?"

The question was a cold wash on Rickard's anger, his face at once smoothing out, expressionless.

Axel shrugged and stepped back, contemplative. "If memory serves, not too long ago you and I were not that different."

Rickard watched Axel's retreating figure before glancing at his right fist, still tightly clenched. Spreading his fingers, he stared at the palm before sliding it into his pocket then resumed walking to the hospital exit.

Galactic Star Key: Ebony Casteel
Astral Nav-Coordinates: EAS-APL-4
Data Sequence: 12.0

Sprawled on the back seat of Nina's red Mazda, Ebony tried to get comfortable. Her cousin Jevon kept turning around in the passenger seat, his expression unusually earnest.

"Enough with the staring," Nina ordered, turning a corner, then slowing for kids crossing to the skate park. "She's alive, and she's fine."

Jevon hunched back. "Can you blame me? She's the talk of the Valley."

"Great." Leaning forward, Ebony watched a couple of joggers running with their dogs. "Everyone's jabbering about the freak show that is my life?"

"That's one way of putting it." Jevon eyed Nina briefly before adding, "Coverage seems to have expanded beyond the confines of our small locality."

"Beyond Freestone?" She'd expected this, Ebony reminded herself. "How far beyond?"

"Let's just say the global eyes of the planet." Over Nina's glare, Jevon blurted, "Weighing in with vested interest."

"Jevon!' Nina hissed, glancing at Ebony in the mirror. "He's exaggerating."

"It's alright," Ebony mumbled. "I had a feeling. I guess my introverted tendencies are going to get a workout." Drawing a breath, Ebony held it, and then began counting as the doctor had ordered, to control her anxiety. Barely managing to make it to five, she noticed Jevon staring at her oddly. Feeling like a pricked balloon, she released abruptly. "The press will get bored and move on if I just—"

"What?" Her cousin jabbed at her. "Go subterranean for the next month or two?"

"Yeah Jev," growled Nina. "Withdrawing from normal life's clearly the healthiest move for her right now."

"No funny bone to be found in that strung-up body, Perky," Jevon rolled his eyes. "I guess oversensitivity comes in pairs today."

"We were told," Nina paused at a 'give way' sign before turning right, "last week at the hospital, remember? Don't rush her."

"That's right," Jevon slapped his head. "So many rules before stepping foot in your room." He started ticking them off leaving Ebony open-mouthed. "Don't approach too fast. Speak in a relaxed calm voice. Don't make physical contact and—"

"Don't turn on the TV," Nina cut in.

"Is that why it wouldn't work?" Ebony thought back to the stale hospital room. "Dad told me it was broken."

Nina laughed, nodding. "More like the cord was pulled, and you can thank Jev here for that."

"Come off it already," Jevon said. "We were in there for over three hours, a guy's mind needs stimulus otherwise it'll shut down. How was I to know it was such a big deal."

"Doctor Walker was emphatic about no contact with the outside world," reminded Nina, tapping her head. "Not until you could handle it up here. No shocks."

"Right, no shocks." Ebony digested the information, for the first time understanding the extensive precautions taken to help her mind recover.

"And behold, the proof a week later, no harm no foul." Jevon swung around holding up a copy of the *Freestone Times*. "The local paper's been headlining it all week. You've more than broken through the ten-minute fame barrier now!"

"If you're looking for applause," Ebony eyed the paper darkly, "you're in the wrong car, Starrik."

"That's not helping." Nina knocked the paper down.

Ebony grabbed it from the console, the headline jumping out at her. 'Reopening of a Twenty-Year-Old Case, Freestone Valley

Disappearances.' A grainy photo of her accompanied the article — from school!

Jevon laughed, snatching the paper back. "Damn, that's shwag using your graduation photo from college. Gotta frame this one."

"Whatever." Ebony slumped back. "Just add it to the list of crazed circumstances I'm currently living through."

"It's not a bad pic," soothed Nina, glancing at Ebony through the rear-view mirror. "Maybe you're a little dark around the eyes."

"You mean stoner-ish," laughed Jevon.

"Hey!" Ebony jerked forward. "I'd been sick all week before that was taken, there's only so much concealer can do."

"That's right," Jevon looked at the photo. "You'd had the flu. Weird, I can count the times you've been sick, and then right before graduation ... boom!" He flicked his fingers. "I believe that's called irony."

"You really know how to drag something out."

"Okay, moving on." Jevon shoved the paper on the floor. "What time are they expecting you to swing by the police station?"

Onto something worse, thought Ebony. "Around three. At least Mara will be a familiar face."

Jevon turned immediately to Nina. "You get anything from behind the scenes from your mum?"

"No, so don't ask."

"Got it." Temporarily thwarted, Jevon narrowed his eyes before needling, "Really difficult imagining that you and Mara are related."

"Why? You got a problem with women in power?" Nina asked with a smirk. "Or is it the fact my mother runs the police station?"

"I believe," Jevon said with a wide grin, "it's me wondering if you're a true blonde, her being a fiery redhead and all."

Nina gave him a pitying look. "So I've been dyeing my hair from the womb?"

"You said it, not me." Jevon tapped the dashboard rhythmically. "If that's true, I'd say the Perkins' beauty gene must really bomb out around the thirties, don't you think, Eb?"

Ebony scowled. "Leave me out of this!"

"Then it must come from her old man," Jevon concluded. "Bet him being blond saves you a few dollars."

"Do I have to beat it into your head?" Nina cut him a serious look. "Don't bring Dallas up around me, alright?"

"When the parentage title is downgraded to first name only, trouble's brewing." Jevon held up a hand while debating. "To step out of the danger zone, or not to?"

Nina glared at Jevon. "For our benefit or your own?"

"Thought I'd put a positive spin on this," soothed Jevon. "Was just going to say that the rift between the Nobles and Casteels never stopped you and Eb being BFFs. Guess your loyalties to your father aren't *noble enough*, and when I weigh in your mum's acceptance of Ebony, shows that you're truly a *perky* all the way," he added with a wink.

"That," Nina shook her head in amazement, "must've taken some time to work out in the delivery."

Jevon said, "The choice to be a Noble or a Perkins has now come full circle."

"You know," Ebony called from the back, "it's times like this I'm happy to have been adopted."

Jevon said, "It's the words that bind us ladies, no point expressing ourselves without a little imagination."

The car fell into an awkward silence, Ebony realising there must have been a development over the last months between Nina and her father, and not a good one if she was using his name in that tone.

Tender-footed, she waded in. "Neen ..."

"Don't worry about it. Mum will behave," Nina said, quickly pushing aside any attempt to talk about her father. "Jev and I have already given our statements. I think the cops were actually happy when we left."

Jevon glared at her. "Don't drop the name."

"Question Boy," she whispered, laughing. "Mum summed him up in two words, priceless and unforgettable."

"You don't think they'll grill me?" Ebony asked.

"Why would they?" Nina straightened primly while driving. "You're a victim, and you've got amnesia. Just don't do a Jev and ask a tonne of questions. Because that would be ... what's the word? Stupid."

Jevon sighed dramatically, his lean body seeming to sink into the seat. "It's not a one-way road when you're dealing with a Starrik!"

It was obvious Jevon and Nina had been through a lot lately. Chewing her lip, Ebony tried to decide if she wanted to know more.

Jevon made a noise. "We were bystanders, Perky. Witnesses to what happened. You were the victim," he said, glancing back at Ebony. "They will want to literally read her mind."

"But since this is the real world, and that's not possible," Nina snapped, "they'll just ask some questions."

Ebony leaned forward, grimacing as her shoulder pulled against the seatbelt. "Who questioned you?"

Jevon shuddered, indicating Nina. "Senior Sergeant Perkins herself. Mara's part of the investigation. But there was also this uptight suit woman, she was weird, standing in the background the whole time. Some kind of specialist."

Specialist? Ebony frowned over that. "You don't know who she is?"

"Perkins called her Inspector. I got the feeling she's the one in charge. It's a rare thing to see Mara become someone's bitch."

"Jevon!" Nina looked appalled.

"Your mum's damn hardcore on authority, keeps having Constable Donnelly nailing me with tickets for my back tail-light."

Nina eyeballed him. "Then fix it. You're a mechanic."

"Priorities, Perkilicious."

"Fine." Nina elbowed him. "Don't forget we're supposed to go easy. Ebony needs time to adjust, so quit dumping everything on her when she's just got out of hospital."

"She asked me!"

A shut-up-or-else look cut across the car, making Jevon slump back. "Alright, alright, but I've been hanging out for today all week!"

Eyebrows raised, Nina looked in the rear-view mirror. "See? You've been missed."

"It's kinda nice listening to you two go a few rounds."

Jevon turned in his seat, pulling at the belt crossing his shoulder. "I can't get over how normal you look. If it wasn't for your shoulder, no one would ever guess all you've been through."

Totally confused, Ebony looked at Nina. "What now?"

After checking the roundabout, Nina drove through, turning onto a side street where she slowed her speed.

"Um." She glanced briefly in the mirror. "Well, you've healed faster than we expected. Which is a good thing."

"My arm's still in a sling. That's not fast," Ebony said slowly. "Unless ... how bad was I?"

Jevon drew a breath. "You were literally lights out in the street drenched in—"

"Shut up!" Nina poked him harder.

"Right, no need to sweat the details." Jevon hunched back in his seat, then turned again, saying fast, "Just think of classic horror flick, guts and blood, decapitated head rolling down the street with paramedics chasing after it. The works."

"Does your mind ever process a rational thought?" Nina eyed him disgustedly. "Like ever?"

Jevon frowned. "Inventive thought—"

"Well, since I barely remember anything," Ebony interrupted loudly, "nothing penetrates. Kinda feels like a bad dream, all disjointed." Shuddering, she added, "An overshadowing that I don't want to look too deeply into."

"There!" He nudged Nina. "I told you she would remember some stuff. Serves you right for calling me ignorant on that."

"We're here." Nina swung into a car park before the Newage Store, effectively finishing the argument.

When the two unclipped their belts, Ebony leaned forward. "We're where?"

Nina pointed to the second storey of the shop while opening her door. "That's our flat, right up there."

"We live above some crazy soothsayer shop? Are we forgetting the list of things that freak me out?" She ticked at her fingers. "Clairvoyants, palm readers, tarot whatever, and, top of the list, mediums."

Nina and Jevon stood before the car, waiting.

"Alright!" Annoyed, she shoved open the door. "This just gets better and better." Climbing out, she glared at Nina. "How'd you talk me into this, let alone afford the rent?"

Clearly amused, Jevon leaned against the car. "You just repeated everything I said eight months ago, except the mediums. What's with them?"

"They see ghosts! Don't you know anything, Question Boy?" She looked from one to the other, almost afraid to voice the question. "Whose idea was it to live here?"

"Well, if want to get technical," Nina pulled her onto the footpath, "it was kinda yours."

"Mine?" Nothing made sense. It was as if someone had taken over her life and made decisions she never would for eight months.

Nina and Jevon walked up to the old wooden and glass door, opening it. A brass bell rang cheerfully, announcing their arrival. Hanging back as they entered, Ebony eyed a plaque with strange letters. Everywhere she looked was old and rundown, more like a worn down second-hand shop. It felt eerie, and it was smelly, some type of incense burning that was sharp on the senses.

"Why're we going through the front entrance?" she whispered, not wanting to attract the shopkeeper's attention.

Wide-eyed, Jevon glanced back. "Usually this is how one enters a building. Besides you gotta do a meet and greet with old mate Myrick."

Looking at her watch, Ebony squirmed. "We'll be late for the police station. Can't we just slip through to the back or something?"

In the lead, Jevon gestured for her to follow. "Come on, you love the old guy. Or you used to, didn't she, Perks?"

"He's different," Nina admitted, "but good different."

Ebony followed slowly, head swinging right and left until a collection of what appeared to be differently shaped dreamcatchers caught her eye. Elaborate in design, they swung gently in the breeze of the open door. Books filled shelves beneath them, next to an assorted collection of strange statues and coloured stones.

Though she could not remember being in the shop, the place made her feel strange, her skin prickling in a funny way, like when she had been questioned by the doctor at the hospital.

"Forget it, guys." Nervous, she started backing up, sweat prickling her body. "Walking in here feels like the time I stumbled across a huntsman's nest in the machinery shed back at the farm."

"Childhood reminiscing!" Jevon laughed, instantly miming the experience. "Splitting the web to release its junior leg crawlers running every which way."

"Yeah, a loving experience with nature." Ebony took a couple of steps toward the door, then spotted the look on Nina and Jevon's faces. "What?"

A wave spread outward from her spine, holding her in place. It was the only way she could describe the sensation, an intense pressure centralising at the back of her neck moving quickly down her backbone. The next moment, her legs went numb, like they had forgotten how to hold her upright, the floorboards suddenly looking inviting.

"Eb?" Jevon grabbed her hand, sliding an arm around her body. "Whoa, your body's all locked up."

Nina looked horrified. "What's the matter?"

"I ... I really don't know how to describe it."

Jevon grinned, but it looked forced. "You're pulling one hell of a poop face, that's for sure."

"Sit her down," Nina urged.

"I just felt so strange."

"Here." Jevon looked around for a chair, finally shoving her onto one that was joined to a dusty side table. When he stood up, he laughed, looking at her locked legs. "There's a natural pose."

Slowly, her legs began to relax and muscles release. Sitting forward, she breathed, working her jaw a couple of times. "What the *hell* was that?"

"Beats me," Jevon said. "You looked like a strung-up doll."

"A doll?" Ebony wiped sweaty hands over her jeans.

"Has it happened before?" Nina asked.

That was too hard to explain. Ebony shook her head, getting to her feet. "Whatever it was, it's gone now. Give me that exit."

She pushed Jevon, Nina hovering worriedly at her side as she walked to the door. Grabbing the handle to open it, she felt the same strange sensation moving down her spine, locked muscles holding her in the doorway.

"Round two?" guessed Jevon.

She couldn't speak! Caught in a struggle for control, her sweaty grip slipped on the knob when she abruptly turned, launching back into the shop, knocking the hovering Nina into a nearby display shelf. A glass bowl tipped, layered coloured sand from the Freestone Caves coating her jacket sleeve and jeans.

Dumbfounded, Jevon stood aside watching both girls fighting to stay vertical. "I should be videoing this, no one's gonna believe me."

Agitated, Nina rubbed furiously at the white material. "Maybe you need to go back to the hospital."

Frightened more than she cared to admit, Ebony shook her head. "No, I'm alright, but I think I need to stay. Should definitely stay."

"Amnesia's made you weird," Jevon declared.

"I don't even know what that was." Grimacing, Ebony watched Nina rubbing at her jeans and jacket. She felt like a complete idiot. "Are you okay?"

"It's alright, just dead-legged me when you launched yourself back around." Shaking her leg, Nina laughed darkly. "Probably won't be dead-lifting this afternoon."

Jevon shoved the door closed, making both girls jump.

"A tad jittery, aren't we ladies?" He grinned at their dark looks.

As they moved through an arch into another area, Ebony heard a type of meditative music playing, almost tribal. It gave her an odd feeling, right in the pit of her stomach.

There was also another type of incense burning. Weirdly, it seemed to match the music, somehow relaxing tense muscles, even easing the headache that had been building since leaving the hospital.

How can it be familiar?

Nina leaned close. "Different to out there, huh?"

"I'll say." In fact, this part of the shop looked fully restored.

Polished wooden floors and architraves, painted walls, gorgeous sculptures and paintings filled the room. Intricate light fixtures hung from the ceiling, as well as more dreamcatchers.

Jevon leaned close to a painting. "It's got a kinda Japanese-cross-tribal feel, don't you think? All intermixed."

Ebony examined a bunch of strange old scrolls, eyeing their elaborate script. Books lined a nearby shelf, thick and old, the page corners yellow with age. On her left was something she did recognise, white crystals from the Freestone Caves. They were placed in a large tank filled with water to help preserve their quality.

"Check this out," Jevon called from around a bookshelf.

"Jev's in here every chance he gets," Nina whispered. "Much to Myrick's irritation."

The moment she walked around the bookshelf, Ebony gasped in surprise. A large, dark polished rock fountain stood pride of place. Walking close, she glanced into the well, eyeing the sides and bottom. Each was covered in white pebbled crystals. They appeared to be placed carefully so that the water poured in a certain way, lighting each of them in a sparkling glow.

High in the middle stood a statue, water pouring from different parts. Twelve people gathered there, men and women, each holding out a hand, trickling water.

"Wow." Ebony searched for words. "It's …"

"I know." Nina ran a hand over the rock. "Stunning and unique."

"Whose work is it?" she asked. "Not anyone local."

Nina looked at her oddly for a moment. "You'd be surprised."

"Myrick," Jevon enunciated the name broadly. "He's pretty out there. Probably had a hand in many trades back in the day."

"So he collects all this?" said Ebony looking around. "Fixed it up on his own?"

"Mostly. He's had plans drawn up, and started in this area." Looking directly at Ebony, he added, "You spent some time down here helping him."

"Me?" Gobsmacked, Ebony stepped back. "You're not serious."

Nina frowned at Jevon. "Maybe we shouldn't be talking about this."

"Why?" he challenged. "She asked. You lined the bottom of this fountain, but you'd never tell me how you did it or what it meant."

They weren't lying, thought Ebony. She could tell when Jevon was telling a lie or prevaricating.

"It's like I've lived a double life. Can either of you imagine me doing something like this?" She pointed at the Freestone Crystals, the way they were placed. "The most I know about these things is that they break down when they're cut from their growth vein."

Nina leaned over the well. "They say placing them in water dramatically stops erosion."

Tentative, Ebony ran a hand over the rim, then down over the Freestone Crystal. "They're fixed to the bottom."

"That's what gets me the most." Jevon touched a couple. "How'd you fix all these pieces? It's Freestone Crystal, that's like impossible to work with since it erodes so fast, especially out of water. Then add chemicals? Well, that's a whole other story."

"Jev." Ebony gave him a long look. "You're well aware I don't possess an artistic bone in my body. Can you imagine me doing this?"

"Well, you have a hidden talent," Nina said soberly.

"I keep asking Myrick his secret but he just won't give it up," Jevon grumbled. "Then he gets all mysterious, answering a question with a question that leads to another question, until I can't remember what I asked to begin with."

Ebony used Jevon's sleeve to dry her hands. "That isn't too hard to imagine."

"He's got skills," Jevon said, shoving her back, annoyed. "I'll give him that."

"Sucks you in every time," Nina said, walking down a long aisle. "The old moth to a flame. Or maybe he's working some voodoo magic on you."

Nervous, Ebony started chewing at her lip. "You think?"

Jevon burst out laughing. "You know I embrace the weird and unexplained. He can lay down as much mojo as he likes as long as he answers the questions."

"You start levitating off the floor," muttered Ebony anxiously, "I'm running, not helping."

"And you know just who to run too," called Nina, walking down a long aisle.

"Where's she going?" Ebony craned her neck trying to see.

"Myrick must be in. Come on." He headed off, not waiting for Ebony.

When she got there, she saw that Nina was laughing, leaning against a glass counter as she talked to an older man. He was on the short side with a mixed ethnic appearance and was completely bald, not even eyebrows. As soon as he saw her, he came around the counter, taking her good hand.

"My dear, my dear, look at you!"

Unexpectedly, he held her face lightly in both hands. "There's not a mark on you."

Like a statue, Ebony stood. Why was this old man touching her?

Then, just as unexpectedly, he stepped back, hands clasped. "My apologies, I detect a shift in your body's energies. I forget my place, that your personal space is important to you, something that takes time."

At sea, Ebony looked at Nina and Jevon, making them both grin.

From the counter, Myrick grasped a long dark stick, one that had been smoking on a stand in a pot. Holding it between them, he smiled before blowing smoke in her face. The instant the smoke made contact, she felt blinded. Trying not to gag, she gasped, her head slowly clearing.

He waved a hand through the smoke, still smiling. "This will aid in a rebalance, a cleansing of your senses. It will also help remove all negative impurities."

"Okay," she said, coughing harder. "A little warning would've been nice."

Jevon grinned like a fool. "Got a kick to it, hey? Give it a sec."

Her body suddenly became lax, all tight muscles loosening between head and feet, the sensation unnerving. "What's in that?"

"It isn't artificial." Jevon studied the smoke, leaning against the counter. "Some type of natural herbs, essences, probably pure oils and such."

"Young Starrik, you do amuse me!" Myrick touched his shoulder. "Have you been researching?"

Delighted, Nina clapped her hands. "The internet's his best friend."

"Ah." Myrick looked close into Ebony's eyes. "I see we're much better now, aren't you dear?"

Over his miff, Jevon jumped, sitting on the bench, legs swinging. "The amount of times I've been smoke blown, you'd think I'd be the most chilled bloke in Freestone. He doesn't like negative or, what was it? Unbalanced energy in the shop."

"Wow." Nina grinned widely. "Smoke blown, really?"

Ebony watched their banter, feeling like she was standing at a distance.

It took Jevon a moment to catch on, but after scratching his head, he made the connection. "Yeah, that didn't come out right."

"Seriously?" Nina shook her head. "The things you learn about a guy."

Even though supremely relaxed, she could feel Myrick's gaze on her, a fixed stare that did not waver.

"Your arm?" He gestured to the injury. "I may have a remedy that can increase your healing factor." Rummaging under the counter, he returned with a small circular container, unscrewing the lid. "Nice, yes?"

An experimental sniff was all she managed, the odour strong and unfamiliar. "I don't think I—"

"No, it is good!" he assured. "This particular blend will suffice. Very potent, very special. Harvested when the moon was full and ripe, this extract can even repair nerve damage." Lid on, he held out the jar, a shrewd expression crossing his face when she hesitated to accept. "Come now, I know you have more sass than this. You don't suffer the affliction of low blood pressure? Symptoms of dizziness, blurred vision, nausea, or irritable bowel syndrome?"

"Err, not recently."

"Take it and be well, my dear." Myrick tapped the lid. "Massage ointment into affected areas not once, not twice, but three times a day. You comply?"

"Right, three times a day. Gotcha. Thanks"

Out the front, the doorbell jingled merrily, signalling a new group of customers. Ebony could hear footsteps and the murmur of voices. Moving a little, she aimed a look through the arch. A well-dressed woman with blonde hair was wandering the aisles with a tall man. He had a coat thrown over shoulder and was examining something on a shelf.

No way were they locals, she thought, turning back. Myrick was looking too but his gaze was hard and flinty, a world away from the welcoming she had received.

"Okay, so—" she began.

Myrick moved off, turning back at the arch briefly. "Excuse me."

She watched him walk down the aisle, slightly baffled. He was tidying things here and there, but there was no doubt in Ebony's mind he was heading in the couple's direction.

Jevon tapped her good shoulder. "Earth to Ebony." When she glanced around he predicted, "I think those two are gonna change our afternoon."

"What do you mean? Who are they?"

The man was looking toward them, his expression intent.

"They were at the police station," Nina whispered, pretending to leaf through a book. "When we gave our statements."

"That's right," he agreed. "I bet they're with some organisation in the government. At least that's the vibe I got."

"Vibe?" Nina rolled her eyes.

"Meaning internal sense ... gauging a gut feeling ... reading a situation if you will," he elaborated unnecessarily.

"No uniform doesn't automatically mean that, Jev." Though she could reason this, Ebony still chewed her lip. "Vibe or not, they're probably your everyday detective."

"Maybe." Nina repositioned herself for a better look, book still in hand. "They're definitely not local, or even regulars to Freestone Station. Mum did mention your investigation has drawn a lot of attention from Melbourne."

"Your blood really doesn't run blue," Jevon grumbled. "With all the perks of Mara practically running the show downtown, you still know next to nothing."

Annoyed, Nina took a step to the side, placing her heel on Jevon's foot. "Sorry, I didn't catch that last part? You were saying?"

Jevon shoved her to the side, face red. "If you're a part of this clique, you gotta contribute!"

Tired of their bickering, Ebony looked back to see Myrick was now speaking with the two. When he turned suddenly, leading them in her direction, Ebony felt her stomach clutch.

Behind his counter once again, Myrick watched the small group like he was the one in charge.

The tall man spoke first, his voice clipped, a definite accent present. "Ebony Casteel?"

Uncomfortable, she nodded stiffly. "Yes?"

Instantly, the two pulled out badges, showing their identification while relaying names she had never heard before. Ebony had no idea what she was looking at or if the badges were authentic.

"We are officers within Global Defence, Specialist Division," said the man.

"Global Defence?" repeated Nina, startled.

"Yes." The man nodded in her direction. "An international organisation working within the UN."

"Time trip it back." Jevon interrupted now. "You're saying the United Nations have an interest in Ebony's abduction?"

The man appeared to study Ebony. "Indeed, your incident may connect to a network that spans far beyond Freestone Valley."

The last three words sounded ominous. The woman offered nothing, though her eyes never left Ebony, making her feel pinned and out of options. Myrick was watching too, though his expression seemed undecided.

"Beyond Freestone?" Jevon repeated.

The woman spoke finally. "That's what we're here to determine. Speaking to you will gain us insight, Ebony. Once we properly identify your status, we can then implement the proper course of action."

Something was up with how they were speaking, almost like it was foreign. Ebony shook her head. "Maybe I should—"

The man stepped forward, no longer relying on tact. "From this moment on Ebony, the truth is your only ally. Suppressing any vital knowledge will only endanger yourself and everyone you know."

"Okay," Ebony replied slowly, looking from the male Global Specialist to the female, her mind racing. "What exactly do you want?"

"You were asked to give a statement today." When she nodded nervously, he added, "We have been sent to escort you personally on behalf of the Inspector in charge of your investigation."

"I was told it wasn't until three," she said in a rush. "Down at the police station, and I'd be giving it to Senior Sergeant Mara Perkins."

The woman smiled, holding up a hand. "Please do not be alarmed, there has been a change in location, that's all. Senior Sergeant Perkins will still be present for your comfort and assurance."

"I see." But Ebony really did not. "Why another location? What's with the change?"

The man answered. "Things have developed. Your case is gaining traction, which has made your presence urgently needed."

Gaining traction? Ebony looked sideways at Nina and Jevon. What the hell did that mean?

"Can I at least get my stuff? I'm staying at my family's farm, and was just about to go up and pack some things."

The woman cast an impatient look at her partner. He, however, nodded in understanding. "Of course, and once this is done, we can take you there."

Ebony chewed her lip fiercely, tasting blood. "Alright, I'll be down soon."

"We will wait there." The male nodded toward the footpath. "When you are ready."

Myrick watched the interaction silently, his eyes flicking over the group. Ebony felt him weighing everything that was happening.

"Go, dear, I will attend to our guests, see if anything within my humble space can open their mind's eye. We are all part of the same nature, are we not?"

"Come on," Nina said, guiding Ebony around the counter to a door in the corner. "Let's introduce you to your apartment."

As they climbed the narrow staircase, Ebony watched the two officers move off with Myrick. All the tension that had drained following the shopkeeper's 'smoke blowing' was now back. Rolling her good shoulder, she pulled at the sling, wishing the day was over.

"So," said Jevon, glancing back, "you guys hear what they just said?"

"Nope," Nina snapped, pulling a set of keys from her handbag to unlock a door at the top of the stairs. "I'm not earwigging like you."

"Location change."

"I don't care." Ebony sighed heavily. "Once this is done, I can leave it all behind and get on with my life."

Jevon pulled a face, clearly doubtful.

"What?" Ebony snapped. "You don't think so?"

He shrugged, looking at Nina who was pushing open the door.

"Welcome home!" she called loudly.

Ebony walked in, looking around the small lounge with its couch and flat screen television, as well as a small table and chairs. There was an adjoining galley kitchen, fit for one, that looked to house all the major appliances.

"Any of this old-school crap sparking something?" Jevon asked.

"Nope, but it's different to how I'd imagined."

Nina moved to a door. "This is your room."

On the threshold, Ebony halted, utterly speechless. If the lounge had been different then this was beyond words. For a start, it was circular.

"This is my room?" she repeated, needing confirmation. At Nina's nod, she said the first thing that came to mind. "I have a round bed?"

"Alternative, isn't it?" Jevon bounced into the room, pick up one of the round throw pillows, spinning it in the air. "Not boring like the Sergeant-Major's next door."

"Ha ha." Nina grabbed the pillow from him, tossing it back on the bed. "Keep that up and your eating privileges here will be revoked."

"What's with the bedside tables?" Ebony asked, counting four. Each was curved to sit at points around the bed. She could also see what she assumed were wardrobe doors hidden in walls where the corners would be.

"It's better than crashing with the olds." Jevon waved a hand before her face. "Right?"

"Okay, laughing boy," taunted Nina. "When're you taking the jump, moving out of home to, you know, embrace adulthood?"

"All about the cash, Perky," sneered Jevon. "Not like I can afford to feed myself on minimum wage. Give it another year when the garage ups my pay."

"Yeah, just keep telling yourself that, home boy."

Barely listening, Ebony wandered the room, picking up photos, studying jewellery boxes and knick-knacks.

She spotted a garish pink suitcase, asking, "What's with this?"

"Um." Nina looked at Jevon uncertainly. "That's the suitcase you packed just before the accident. You must have borrowed mine for some reason."

"Oh." Ebony stared at it for a long moment.

"Be back in a moment." Nina took the opportunity to back out of the room.

"Where're you going?" Jevon asked.

"Bathroom!" Nina hissed. "If that's okay with you."

"No, you're not!"

"Starrik!"

Jevon glanced at his watch. "It's coming up to three, so I'd lay odds you're packing the old gym bag. Can't miss a training bout, huh?"

"So what if I am?" Nina huffed.

"This day must really be killing you. The break in routine, not knowing the end point."

"I'm fine," Nina said, standing by the door, arms crossed.

Jevon stretched out on the bed. "You know, after Ebony gives her statement, we should all head out to Star Bar, kick back and sink few brewskies, aim for happy hour."

Nina's eyes widened, baring her teeth, "Great idea, Jevon. Glad to have you around." Spinning, she stormed out of the room.

"Do you have to do that?" Ebony asked tiredly.

"Keeps her on her toes," he said with a grin, jumping up to close the door. "Her entire life is measured by the minute hand. Makes her a little," he spun a finger beside his ear, "regimented."

"Why're you closing that?"

"I'm not supposed to push your whole memory thing." He grabbed the pink suitcase, dumping it on the bed, then began rifling through the haphazard mess. "You just have to do this one thing for me."

While he searched, Ebony began picking through contents. Holding up a picture drawn by Nina when she was a kid, she shook her head. "What's with all this stuff? What was I thinking?"

Like he had found gold, Jevon held up a black box. "Open this."

"What is it?"

Desperate, Jevon pushed it at her "Don't get me started on the box that cannot be opened."

Ebony turned it over in her hands, eyeing the engravings. They looked eerily like some of the ones she had seen downstairs. "I've never seen it before."

"Ah! So no luck with it, right?" When Ebony shook her head, Jevon dived back into the case, pulling out the mobile phone. "And this."

"My phone!"

"Nothing gets by you." Jevon rubbed at the screen, trying to clear his paw prints. "And it's fully charged, ready to be unlocked. There's messages and missed calls."

Ebony eyed the display screen hesitantly.

About to blow a gasket, Jevon ran a hand through his constantly messy hair. "Just try to keep up. This here could be the holy grail, clues to what happened to you."

"Or it could be nothing." But she could see the number of missed calls and messages.

At Jev's pained expression, she took pity, swiping the screen but Jevon grabbed her hand. "Hold up a sec. I might have tried a couple of times and failed at guessing your pin."

"Of course you have."

"So, there's most likely only one attempt left before you're locked out."

Carefully she input her PIN, ignoring her cousin's nervous hovering and insane expression. At the fail tone and vibration, Jevon grabbed his head, the image of someone trying to prevent it from doing a three-sixty spin.

"That did not just happen!" he wailed, grabbing the phone. "You put in the wrong pin!"

"Well if *someone* didn't touch my stuff, I'd have more than one attempt to do this!"

"How could you not remember?"

"Maybe," she ground out, "I changed it during the last eight months. How do I know?"

"Damn! I had a lot riding on this." Jevon slumped onto the bed, staring at the blank screen. "This wouldn't be an issue if you'd just updated. The new phones have fingerprint ID for easy access."

"Easy access?" Ebony echoed, confused.

"Don't you wanna find out what happened to you?" Jevon asked, suddenly serious.

Cornered, Ebony snatched her mobile from him. "This is ridiculous," she said, staring around the strange room. "How am I supposed to pack when I don't know where anything is?"

"Wait one hot minute, I'm having an idea."

Ebony threw back her head, covering her eyes. "Please! No more."

"Baden's mate Kevin has an IQ that's off the chart. The power of his mind is like throwing a hundred of me together."

"Jev ..." Ebony looked him in the eye. "The added volume won't help you get your point across. So far I'm not impressed."

"He could fix this faster than we could explain it!"

The door swung open. "Why's this closed?" Nina demanded, looking at Jevon suspiciously.

As soon as she stepped into the room, Jevon pointed triumphantly at the gym bag near the front door. "Bull's eye!" He mimed shooting a gun at Nina. "I do believe we've established that this bag is actually a person."

"Sure is, and the relationship we have could never be understood by you."

Jevon leaned in, sniffing. "Hmm, musty..."

Nina stepped to the bed, looking at the open suitcase. "Well?"

At Jevon's sheepish look, Ebony knew their friend had no knowledge of his obsession with her phone.

"Jevon's being Jevon," she muttered, shoving the mobile onto the bedside table.

Nina eyed the phone as Jevon leaned over to whisper, "Slip it to me on the down low. I'll get it sorted."

"I think you've done enough," Ebony warned him. "I'll get it sorted myself. Now can you two please help me pack something before those Specialists come and drag me off?"

"Sure thing, hon." Nina cast Jevon a withering look.

As she started opening drawers, Jevon made a dive for the mobile, but Ebony was quicker and the two began to struggle.

"Let it go," she demanded, feeling her one-handed grip slip.

Victorious, Jevon held up the phone happily. "I could do this all day."

A shudder moved along her spine, washing up and out to cover her entire body, stiffening her muscles. Taking Jevon by surprise, she twisted his arm behind his back, shoving it up with a jerk while flipping him face down on the bed.

For one stunned moment, Ebony held him there, knee resting on his back, wondering how it had happened.

"You mind taking that knee out of my back?!"

Her phone was on the carpet beside the bed. Releasing him, she grabbed it then retreated, keeping her stance low.

Jevon rolled onto his back, resting there for a moment, head craned looking upside down in obvious shock. "Damn, Eb, you nearly dragon-clawed my arm off."

"No, I didn't!"

On a backward roll, Jevon slipped off the bed and stood beside it, rubbing his shoulder. "Yeah, you did."

Ebony stood to her full height, fighting to relax her body, then noticed how tense her hand was. Fingers held at odd angles, even her thumb. Giving it a shake, she looked away.

"Looks to me," Nina said with a smirk, "like those self-defence classes you took in the city have stuck. Need an icepack, Starrik?"

"You took self-defence classes?" he demanded.

Ebony shrugged, not having a clue. There was no way she was saying she'd barely been aware for the whole episode, on automatic pilot.

"That was full-on Shaolin style," Jevon mused. "The way she shaped up looked to be the way of the dragon."

"And you're an expert in identifying different martial art styles?" Nina laughed loudly. "Too bad it didn't stop you ending up face down."

Jevon opened his mouth to speak, then his eyes flared. "Eb! Your phone's lit up."

The moment she lifted her hand, the lights in her bedroom started flickering, an instant before the phone rang, deep distorted tones, nothing like her usual ringtone.

The three stared at the flashing screen, locked in place. Alarmed, Ebony held the mobile out.

"Answer it!" Jevon said, surging into action.

"No!" Ebony backed up immediately. "There's no caller ID."

"Here, I'll do it." Snatching it, he answered before she could think, switching to loudspeaker while urging her to speak via gesture.

Out of options, she gave in. "Err, hello?"

For a moment silence reigned, then a man's voice, warped just like the ring had been, distorted by long gaps and a strange crackling. "Locate … it … are you alright?"

Ebony looked at Jevon, noticing his eyes were now bulging with excitement. "Um, I'm okay. What's wrong with the line?"

"... had to ... the line ... can't contact you ... couldn't make it out ... is alive?"

Ebony looked at Nina, fighting to make sense of what was being said. Holding a hand over the mouthpiece, she glared at Jevon. "I can't keep this up, it's freaking me the hell out!"

"Ebon ... stay ... Myr ..."

Suddenly, another voice yelling in the background. "Tracer identified ... picking ... dropping the ..."

More distortion, scrambling the rest of the words. At the same moment, the bedroom light started flashing again before failing completely.

The two voices continued arguing, clearly in disagreement about ending the call. "Be ... contact ... rescue."

Rescue? mouthed Jevon.

More distortion and arguing. "... frequency dropping ..."

The sound of static filled the room then the line went dead, leaving an ominous silence. No one said a word until the overhead light flickered back on, producing a shriek from Nina, who started patting her chest with a trembling hand.

"Sorry," she whispered.

Ebony stared at the mobile, watching the phone reset, the screen going dark. Dropping it on the bed, she looked back to Jevon, his expression going from ecstatic to determined in the blink of an eye.

"We gotta find Kevin," he declared, and kept right on talking, ignoring Ebony's wildly shaking head. "We need to unlock this so we can call them back!"

Clearly freaked, Nina stepped in. "Are you insane? Ebony almost died last week, have you forgotten that?"

"Of course I haven't."

"Damn right. We're civilians, not meant to get involved in this sort of thing. We need to go downstairs," she said, pointing wildly at the door, "and tell those officers what just happened!"

"Those guys are no cops!" Jevon grabbed the phone. "Who says they're the good guys? We'll never know anything, they'll just feed us a bunch of half-truths. Probably less than that." Taking his time, he held up his hands. "Alright, I'm going to lay it out. We're all involved now, whether we like it or not. The truth, that's what we need! What's been happening for the last eight months? This phone holds the answers."

"What we need," Nina said, "is protection, police protection for Ebony, and that," she pointed at the phone, "it's not happening, Jev, no way. Next thing I know you'll end up like Ebony, or dead, having gone off on one of your tangents, ignoring any signs of danger."

"Give me a day," he pleaded.

"I'm not giving you another second. Hand the phone over now!"

On a sigh, he pulled the awkwardly stashed mobile from his pocket, staring at it.

Nina hissed in exasperation. "Can't you see sense, even now?"

Ebony jerked to attention, jumping between them. "Stop! Just stop!"

Nina and Jevon spun around, obviously shocked by her outburst.

"Eb ..." Jevon began, but she shook her head violently.

"No! Nina's right, it's too dangerous. I almost ended up dead, and if that happened to either of you ..." She swallowed hard. "You just can't be involved."

"Thank you!" Nina reached over to grab the mobile from Jevon, but Ebony beat her to it.

The feel of it in her hands gave her the creeps. "But Jevon's right as well. I'm sorry, Nina, but if I give this to police, I'll never know what it holds." Nervously, she eyed the box on the bed, the one that would not open. "None of this is normal, Neen."

Nina slowly sat on the bed, rubbing her head. "You think you can go this alone, Ebony? You can't even pack your suitcase."

"I thought I could avoid the past eight months, just pretend it never happened, but I can't." She looked around the foreign bedroom. "What I can do is give myself time. I'm back, maybe not all of me, and if the rest turns up," she said with a glare at Jevon, "I'll deal! Don't force anything, like the doctor said. Just let nature take its course."

"And if your memories don't come back?" Jevon demanded.

"Then they don't. They're my memories, not yours, so leave it alone and stop pushing this."

Expression unreadable, Nina eyed the mobile. "So we're doing nothing?"

"You know," Ebony said as she looked at the scrollwork on the black box, "I really don't care right now if I never remember the last eight months. But if things change for some reason, I'll decide what to do." Sitting on her bed, she faced the two. "I want you guys to know my last memory. It was of us driving home from Melbourne. I remember feeling great, the best I'd felt in a long time. Coming home to Freestone."

"You're wrong in this, Eb." Jevon shook his head, unusually sombre. "That call sounded like a warning."

"If something else happens," Nina said, "she goes straight to the police. They'll be all over it."

"Sometimes, doing nothing can be more dangerous than taking action," Jevon said. "If that phone call was anything to go by, it let us know two important things."

Ebony frowned as Nina demanded, "Which are?"

"They know who she is," he said, eyeing the mobile like it was a bomb. "And Eb? They will be coming for you."

Galactic Star Key: Zozes Karbroe
Astral Nav-Coordinates: EAS-APL-4
Data Sequence: 13.0

The Link-Trone broke the silence, its precise speech alerting Zozes to activate his cyber-optics to prepare for a subspace freq-com call from the Major. "Scanning NAV site coordinates now, Sir."

While the system loaded a digital overlay, he took a quick scan around the immediate area to see nobody was around. Kaze had pulled into an Earth energy station, claiming he knew how to refuel the vessel. Something Zozes had grave doubts about.

Satisfied with the scan, he turned over his left hand, activating his subdermal clasp-activator within the centre of his palm, generating a small cyber control pad. Ring pointers appeared over his right fingers, allowing him to manually operate it. Observing his cyber-optic display hud, Zozes minimised the primary operative menu into micro-tabs. Focusing on the site-map, he enlarged this to reveal a surveillance view of Freestone.

At a second alert from the Trone, Zozes ordered, "LT open and bridge a freq-com line to the Major's Star-Key."

His site-map zoomed in further, the Link-Trone uploaded Rajek's exact location. It was near a large, heavily fortified facility that was restricted to military and government personnel outside Freestone Valley.

"ID verification set," reported the Link-Trone. "Uplinking SS freq-com. Channel open."

"Understood." Zozes glanced around the vessel, briefly eyeing his brother near the rear. "Major, Sir, what's the situation?"

"Alpha Green," responded Rajek. "Examinations have found the Kadra's bio-status to be of a high-risk state, though its condition is viewed as stable."

"Are you calling us in, Sir?"

"I am," said the Major. "Astral Guard has given you clearance to initiate operation 'open-wound'."

"Sir," Zozes turned the vessel's reflective mirror to watch his brother, "what took place at the crash zone has affected my brother. This may cause complications—"

"Understood," interrupted Rajek brusquely. "However, no more time can be allocated, Blade. There has been a development with the Kadra prisoner gaining us a small opening to begin extrapolating a viable intelligence profile."

"Understood, Sir. Alpha Green out." Deactivating the cyberscreen, he straightened, adjusting the vessel's reflective device to see what his brother was up to.

Something metallic tapped at the rear of vessel. Twisting in his seat, Zozes watched Kaze wrestling with a long hose, trying to get its nozzle into a hole at the rear. It looked to be anything but easy.

So, this was how humans injected liquid energy into their engines, thought Zozes. Something called petrol.

When the vessel started rocking, Zozes shoved open the door in alarm, climbing out.

From the rear, Kaze grinned at him. "What'd the Major say?"

With a bad-tempered push, Zozes closed his door, wondering if the rocking had been done purposely. Since there was no one nearby, he shoved his hands in his pockets, deciding to let it go. "The Kadra's bio-status states it's in a high-risk, but stable condition."

Kaze watched the fuel box as he pulled the trigger. "What'd I tell you? It's one tough vokker."

There was no arguing with that. "Clearly we shouldn't underestimate their genetic manipulation. It's made them incredibly resilient."

"They're powerful, but not unstoppable." Kaze jutted his chin forward arrogantly. "We've ran the simulations. Take away its weapon, that zaphna rod, and it's game over."

"If it was only that simple." Zozes huffed a breath looking around.

"I'll tell you what surprises me," said Kaze. "That our combat rating with LT only recommends engaging Kadra targets up to a level two. What's that about?"

"There's something you need to understand." Zozes stepped closer to see what his brother was doing. "Our upgraded status to Alpha doesn't increase our abilities' output, not until our spawn-net with LT matures, and that takes training and most of all experience." Perplexed, he pointed at the nozzle. "You don't seem to be accomplishing much with that."

Frustrated, Kaze kicked at the hose. "The information I got was very specific. All I need to do is pull on this trigger to activate that fuel box." Giving the line a tug, he jerked the trigger.

"Well it doesn't appear to be working."

"Of course not. That'd just make things too easy now, wouldn't it?"

"Wouldn't it be easier to ask LT?" Zozes noted several vessels departing. "It's obvious you're doing something wrong."

"You rely on that thing too much," Kaze nodded toward the ute. "Soon it'll be thinking for you."

"I see." Zozes peered at his brother's nose. "Don't like the nose bleeds?"

Face screwed in concentration, Kaze pulled at the trigger. "Hilarious! After the crash-zone, my spawn-net went through its paces ..." Face reddening, he caught onto his brother's dig. "I'm handling LT just fine if I monitor the length and expenditure while I'm paired into the spawn-net."

Zozes made a non-committal noise letting his brother's outburst run its course.

"Maybe it's a type of pump and release extractor?" he suggested mildly. "You need to prime the device ..."

"Humans are far more backward then I gave them credit for," muttered Kaze, jerking repeatedly at the trigger.

Zozes could see Kaze was close to exploding, the redness of his face a strong giveaway.

"I think it's working ..." Kaze wrenched it again and again before pulling it out to observe the nozzle. "Nope, not a drop, so it's obviously not a release extractor." Noticing his brother's grin, Kaze's eyes narrowed. "Having fun there, Chuckles?"

"I just wanted to see if you would actually do it."

"I'll get LT to power the ute," Kaze spat, "nosebleed or not."

"Wait a moment." Zozes looked across the street, noting a group of women talking in a food shop, and only a few humans passing by on the footpath.

Everyone seemed busy with their own affairs, the service station's customers hurrying back to their vessels before driving off. Activating his spawn-net, he waited for the cyber-optics' overlay to drop before his vision, outlining the issue. "I see ..."

A loud thumping on the fuel station screen had both brothers turning.

"I believe," Zozes angled his head to look across, "she is signalling you?"

After a glance, Kaze shrugged. "I am the handsome one out of the two of us."

With a harsh movement, the woman ripped the screen back on her booth to stick out her head.

"Are you blind?" she screeched, pointing at their fuel box. "It's out of order, read the sign!" Slamming the screen closed, she continued to glare, clearly disgruntled.

"Out of order?" Kaze looked around in bewilderment. "What's that mean?"

Humans were looking at them, clearly laughing at their incompetence. For once, Zozes was not the butt of one of his brother's jests. Maybe it was time for a little revenge.

"Perhaps we're meant to line up in some form of order?" he suggested, glancing at the side of the fuel box. "Here, that's an Earth numeral ... number five. You've skipped the first four positions."

"You mean that number sequence is literal?" Kaze looked around goggle-eyed.

"Obviously," Zozes nodded sagely. "They must activate only in the right sequence pattern."

"Then we need to move, find numeral one, right?"

"You could always stay here, suffer a repeat performance."

By the time he had finished, Kaze was back in the black transport, firing the engine. The throbbing noise drew additional looks as he began idling around the station's fuel pumps.

The moment he parked, Kaze stepped out grabbing a handle, waving its nozzle in the air. Looking at Zozes with a smirk, he placed it into the vessel's fuelling outlet.

The strong smell of liquid fuel reached Zozes as he approached. Leaning against his brother's transport, he crossed his arms. "What did I tell you?"

"Humans are clearly slaves to structure," grumbled Kaze. The moment the trigger clicked, he hung it up eyeing the grumpy woman in the booth. "Time to pay the piper."

The two made their way to the station's shop, Zozes trying to read the woman's expression.

"You fellas have trouble reading the written word?" she asked sourly.

For a moment Kaze scratched his head, obviously not expecting a direct question. "The right sequence order needed to fuel the vehicle. A simple misunderstanding."

"Sequence?" The woman's mouth dropped open. "Are you for real, son?"

As she placed the machine before him, Kaze tapped his currency ID card on it. "As real as they come." At the automatic door, he swung back. "You really need to replace the indicator sheet on the fuel box, it's a little confusing."

"Indicator sheet?" The woman's eyebrows climbed toward her hairline. "The signs are pretty self-explanatory, my boy."

"Sign!" Kaze stopped short of slapping his head. "That's the word! If I was you, I'd throw in a brief description for good measure."

"Or," Zozes thought on it, "construct a bigger sign and move it to a more prominent position, explaining all this along with the sequence line-up."

"Yes." Kaze nodded in vigorous agreement. "Service to the community, as they say, bigger is better."

Mouth still open, the woman stood to watch them leave.

His brother's swagger as they crossed the station's platform almost cracked Zozes' control, and by the time they got to the vessel, he could tell Kaze was suspicious.

"Problem?" Zozes queried as he fastened the vessel's restraint.

"Just checking something."

He waited, already knowing Kaze was pairing with his spawn-net, obviously scanning what the sign actually represented.

"Nose burning yet?"

"Alright." Kaze ran a finger beneath it. "What just happened here?"

"I believe," Zozes said as he straightened his jacket, making himself comfortable, "I successfully — how do humans say it? — pulled the wool over your eyes. So much for your acclimatisation into the humans' culture."

"Really?" Kaze grinned broadly, surprising Zozes. "I can take a hit, but I believe something greater has taken place."

"What do you mean?"

"Well, it's only taken twenty-five cycles, but you seem to have finally grown a sense of humour."

Zozes pointed to the numbers on the fuel boxes. "Or you're an easier target than I originally thought."

"Careful now." Kaze drove off slowly, engine throbbing. "Just remember who started this."

Once they were driving along an Earth track-lane among many transports, Kaze shifted the conversation. "Why haven't we been granted clearance for LT to make an overview of that Kadra's body?"

In search of fresh air, Zozes wound down his window. "Could be due to a security precaution, making certain the Kadra poses no threat."

"Want to know my take?" Kaze tapped fingers on the steering wheel. "This has more to do with the Inspector sticking it to us because she thinks we've been stepping out of line."

"Sticking it to us?" Round-eyed, Zozes mulled that one over for a moment as his brother turned left, Freestone River running alongside the track-lane. Traffic was thick here, near the town centre, but Kaze appeared to be handling it with ease. "What did you expect would happen?"

"Oh, I don't know. Maybe a little gratitude for rescuing a vital asset that could change this entire investigation? They'd have nothing if it wasn't for us!"

"We're Blades, we don't seek gratitude, or need it."

"Oh, come on! Roccna's had us retracing old leads for days over town. Still trying to wrap my head around that last one."

"It was quick."

"Inspecting the grave site? Like an end to a really bad joke."

"The body," reminded Zozes, "was missing from the holding casket."

"So?"

"Every detail, brother, means something."

"It's called keeping us out of the way. Not an opinion, that's a vokken fact."

"If she is," Zozes muttered darkly, "it's a ploy that will only work short-term. The Major's stepped in now. He's reported our situation to the station's Astral Guard Command."

Kaze digested this before exploding. "So, I'm supposed to drop it, just like that? She was out of line, not us!"

"We're back in, that's proof of our worth. So don't make an issue out of this."

Kaze stared out the side-shield, clearly grinding his teeth.

"Or do you need me to hold your hand?" Zozes demanded.

"Fine." Kaze thumped the car's steering wheel. "The matter's dropped."

When they reached the edge of town, Zozes used his cyber-optic to understand an upcoming sign reading, *Welcome to Ridge Falls Base*.

"Alright," said Kaze, rubbing at his neck. "Something must have happened between Roccna and the Chief. Whatever it was, the blame's clearly shifted onto us."

Zozes let him have his say while eyeing the large fortified defence wall which spanned both directions, disappearing from view. He counted several communication towers within the perimeter, some that were still under construction. Military personnel were posted at the gate, a line of Earth transports waiting for entry. A female officer spoke to the driver in the car ahead before letting it through. Slowly, the large double gates retracted, allowing access.

As they closed, Kaze edged forward, pulling up next to the security booth. An unmarked vehicle, sleek and black, cruised past on its way out. The screen shields on it were very dark, impossible to see through without the use of his optics.

Zozes eyed the male and female inside, the contained air they displayed. This base was far more than it appeared.

When the security officer approached, Zozes and Kaze each held up their identification at her request and the gates opened again, sharp spikes retracting into the tarmac.

The atmosphere felt different, Zozes noticed as soon as they entered. Obviously, security was much tighter than it appeared, the entrance heavily fortified even if it displayed an ease of air.

"This track-lane is smooth as skin, not a bump or indent. Big funds spent on this place," Kaze said, running a hand over the steering wheel.

"Yes," Zozes agreed, eyeing the buildings. "Looks like a whole other world in here."

Since this was to be one of the primary Global Capital Bases, Zozes had been briefed on what the humans were currently constructing. Even so, seeing it, viewing its size and grandeur, caught him a little off-guard. Obviously these humans understood architecture and could design to a standard far superior to what he had seen outside the walls.

"They must have been working on this for a long time," Kaze said, following the location marker the Link-Trone had uploaded to his cyber-optic overlay.

"No doubt." Glancing at the Trone, Zozes asked, "LT, give us a brief rundown of this Base."

LT chirped to life, lights flashing. "The Australian Government was granted permission by the United Nations to open the first Global Capital Base of this country for planetary relations with primary factions across Earth."

"What was this Base's previous function?" asked Kaze.

"Overview states it was a militarised training facility for human flight pilots."

"Makes sense," Kaze said. "The layout, and it's a good distance from Freestone Valley."

Zozes assessed the many buildings lining the smooth track-run. Humans were moving busily about, some in uniform, others in civilian attire.

"Aerodrome," he said. "That's what I believe humans call a place where their flight planes take off and land. I'd say there's more to choosing this location than its convenient outlay assembly."

Ahead was a large building, oval in design. It had multiple levels, and for some reason he got the feeling that a lot of the base was constructed around it. "LT, upload the archives on this Global Base, accessing any relevant data. Why was this location chosen?"

"The information you requested is in a restricted archive."

"Restricted?" Kaze stared at Zozes. "What level?"

"Class five ID, status to Star-Key is required."

"I see." Zozes digested this for a moment. "The Astral Guard would have had influence on that decision, I'm certain."

"There's a pattern forming," Kaze said, "of questions that don't have answers."

A group of military officers ran across the road before them, jogging in formation. "The military have a well-established presence here."

Kaze pulled up at a docking zone in front of the large building. "Looks like this is our destination." For a moment, he sat and stared. "Is it me, or does this Global Complex remind you of something back home?"

The two climbed out, Zozes studying the assembly of Earth transports. "You're thinking of the Astral State Command Centre."

Elbows resting on the roof, Kaze nodded. "There's more going on here, brother, than forming a facility for diplomatic relations."

The two made their way to the building's main entrance, the high wide doors inscribed with the Global Reach emblem sliding open. Security waited inside, and again their badges were requested.

The atrium was large and airy with multiple levels rising above. All personnel wore the insignia and uniform of Global Reach, and there were a lot of them.

"Come on," Zozes said, moving off, his brother and the Link-Trone in tow passing through the crowd.

"Karbroes!"

"Is that ..." Kaze turned. "Clarkov?"

Through the sea of personnel, Zozes spotted Ensign Clarkov. Arm waving, he jogged toward them dressed like everyone else, in an Earth Global Reach uniform, sporting a crest high on each arm and on his chest, his black hair short and tidily combed.

Before he was in earshot, Kaze mused quietly, "If Commodore Vae'gon's duty-arm is here, then so is he."

Slightly out of breath, Clarkov pulled to a halt, his yellow eyes altered to brown, via a cyber-optic overlay.

"I heard what happened at the crash zone. You've certainly got a lot of people talking." Leaning in, he added, "The Astral Guard placed the Galactic Force Fleet on high alert, and they've increased Combat Space Patrol around this solar system."

"CSP's a waste of time," Kaze said in disgust. Zozes privately agreed.

"What if this is a prelude to an all-out Kadra attack?" Clarkov argued. "We have to protect Earth."

"Of course we must." Zozes held up a hand to quiet his brother. "But Kaze's right. Whatever's taking place here stands apart from Kadra Prime."

"You mean a Kadra Outcast Sect?" Clarkov was clearly enthralled by the possibility.

"Most likely allying itself with the Assultra Rebels," finished Kaze.

"I don't think Commodore Vae'gon will agree, but it's an interesting theory."

"Why doesn't that surprise me?" Kaze eyeballed the duty-arm.

Before his brother could stir further trouble, Zozes stepped in, "Where is the Commodore?"

Still watching Kaze, Clarkov answered slowly. "Detention level facilities, the holding chambers. I believe he's reviewing the Kadra's bio-status personally. I'm on my way there now actually. Is your Link-Trone going to conduct an overview?"

Zozes could not hold back a sigh. "I believe the Major has other ideas. He wants us to stand witness to one of the victim's statements in advance."

"Really? Which victim?"

"Ebony Casteel," Kaze said. "You know her?"

"Ah." Clarkov nodded, smiling. "Yes, I saw Major Rajek and Lieutenant Thaytis escorting her to the investigation ward." The duty-arm indicated a set of doors behind him. "I can take you to detention level, show you the observation lobby which overlooks the hold and investigation ward."

Kaze waited for Zozes to nod, then held out an arm. "Lead on, kid."

"Oh, no problem," stammered the ensign, making Kaze laugh.

When the three reached a powered stairway, the ensign stepped on, motioning for them to follow. After flashing his ID, he spoke a command to start the stairs moving in the direction of the underground level.

Arriving at yet another security station Clarkov again flashed his ID.

"You have above-standard clearance?" Zozes asked.

"I can bypass most checking stations." On the right was a sign that read: *Global Personnel Only.*

"Feeling welcome?" Kaze asked, elbowing his brother.

Clarkov held out a hand. "If you give me your ID cards, I'll add you. I realise your Link-Trone could hack into the network, but for now I suggest you respect diplomatic relations with Earth officials. We're trying to abide by their customs."

"Of course," Zozes said, watching Clarkov input a series of commands.

"I'm properly instating you as Global Reach members," he said. "That will grant you access throughout much of the base's facilities."

"You can do that?" Kaze looked at the duty-arm with new eyes.

While he was adding the information, Clarkov spoke absently. "I've been stationed on Earth for three years now, grown quite used to their way of life. Also, I was part of the Headman Program, which was set up to train humans that are to become representatives of the Earth Global Council."

"Wait," exclaimed Kaze. "We're training humans?"

"Of course. That's how Global Leaders help bridge relations between us and the humans." Clarkov closed the panel. "Right, everything should be in order." He passed back their IDs. "If there's trouble, or someone questions your access, I've attached my own Star-Key. Get them to contact me, I'll be your Global Guarantor."

The security checkout line was full of personnel. One thing Kaze loathed was waiting in queues. "I'd say you're more help than we're worth. I think we owe you a few drinks for avoiding all that."

Zozes cringed, already guessing what his brother would say.

"We should go out!"

"Go out? That's an expression for what exactly?" Zozes sensed trouble.

"Socialising? With me, Sir?" stammered Clarkov.

"Cut the Sir, kid. What's this world's custom?" Kaze ran a hand over his hair. "The beverage they serve? Err ... bee ..."

"Beef?" Zozes cast the duty-arm a subtle 'stay quiet' look.

"Umm." Clarkov had no idea how to respond.

"I can see it now." Kaze tapped Clarkov's shoulder, waving a hand like he was conjuring an image. "The first taste of that beef touching your lips, moments before it slides smoothly down your throat. Kid, you'll be gagging for more."

"Gagging, Sir? Trust me, that's something I ..." He looked at Zozes. "... don't want to miss."

As the ensign walked ahead, Zozes watched his brother frown. "Something wrong?"

"The ensign looks a little flushed. I'll go easy on him in the first round, takes some practice, and this is coming from a pro."

"Oh, you're a pro alright." Over the Blades' freq-com, an incoming signal alerted through Zozes' optic overlay.

"Message uploading," he told Kaze. "Looks like the Major's about to start."

Clarkov signalled from up ahead. "This way, Blades."

The three moved quickly past Global personnel, accessing the final checkpoints with ease. Upon entering the Control Centre of detention level, the brothers found themselves amongst numerous Galactic Inspectors. These were either working at terminals or gathered in groups talking while going over evidence.

The place felt alive with energy and enthusiasm.

There were human police officers present, touring the facility with looks of awe on their faces. A guide was in the lead, speaking confidently, answering numerous questions.

"This is the Ward's Information Centre. You are now in the base of operations which conducts all major investigations that includes all states."

Zozes paused, watching how they took in what they were seeing and hearing. He had a feeling some were making the leap into the new world with more apprehension than others.

"Freestone Valley Police Station," continued the woman, indicating a nearby monitor, "will function as it has but with some significant changes."

At the next door, Clarkov flashed his card. "It's this way, Sir."

Zozes stepped into the adjacent corridor to see Major Rajek leading a female with long black hair into the end interview room.

She glanced toward them briefly, her dark eyes anxious. Zozes gauged she was around twenty, twenty-one in Earth years, and very uneasy about being here.

Clarkov led them on, up a flight of stairs to an observation deck where the three could witness interviews being undertaken.

The first thing Zozes noticed was Thaytis standing at the slanted surveillance screen. Her hair was different, not plaited but twisted into some type of roll that showed the length of her neck.

The rest of the bay was taken up with Astral Guard Inspectors working on terminals, human computers. Obviously, these had been upgraded, enhanced with technology that was recording everything happening below.

Ebony Casteel was in the first room, taking a seat. From where their observation post was situated he could see numerous interview rooms, all able to be observed.

"Contact me if you need anything," Clarkov said before moving off.

Before he was aware, Zozes was standing beside Thaytis. She smiled at him, though he managed to keep his focus mostly on Major Rajek, who was handing the Casteel girl a drink of water. She immediately gulped at it, staring into the glass.

"Crowded room," Kaze murmured, leaning against the screen's edge, crossing his arms. "Especially for someone so young and fresh-faced."

"Really?" Zozes glanced at his brother, rolling his eyes. "Even now?"

"Mmm."

Roccna entered, wearing a nondescript suit, her dark hair twisted in a low bun, followed by Senior Sergeant Perkins and one of her detectives. Over the communication speaker, Zozes heard the Inspector pull out her seat, its grating legs making Ebony jump.

"Thank you for your time, Miss Casteel."

"How old is she?" Kaze asked.

Thaytis answered, not bothering to turn. "Just turned twenty-one cycles of age. Conservative by nature, and has no convictions. She's clean. I'd say ordinary."

Head tilted, Kaze grinned. "Experience tells me it's the conservative ones who appear clean, who are usually quite the opposite, Doc."

Open-mouthed, Thaytis looked at Zozes. "Does he take anything seriously?"

Kaze spoke before his brother could even open his mouth. "I leave that to Chuckles here, then at least one of us has fun."

"For some reason," said Zozes loudly, "he's made it an objective to experiment with various species on different worlds. Even maintains," he sighed, "a list of conquests."

"When I finalise the Astral Twelve Interspecies Index," grinned Kaze, "you'll know I've conquered them all."

"Hmm, so you've taken it upon yourself to entertain every Astral State." Thaytis' gaze roamed him from head to feet. "Sounds like overcompensating for lack of worth below the belt."

At the sight of his brother puffing up, Zozes thought his sides would split from restrained laughter.

Challenged, Kaze leaned forward. "You getting personal with me, Doc?"

Hand up in surrender, Thaytis laughed softly. "Clearly you aren't oversensitive on the matter."

"I believe humans call that particular emotion ego," said Zozes.

"Okay, okay, I see what's happening ... got the old tag-teams going." Kaze stepped back. "Just let me say, what lies below this belt satisfies completely. I've been known to weaken their stride, if you get my drift. And the rest of this?" He tapped his chest. "They don't look for loving elsewhere, not for a very long time."

Finger on chin, Thaytis eyed Kaze. "So, you're open to anyone, anywhere? I guess that explains a few things."

Zozes was surprised to see his brother pause, belatedly catching Thaytis' meaning. "Maybe I'm a little more particular then taking on just anyone, I do have standards."

"Oh, I'm sure you do." Thaytis eyed Zozes. "Ever heard of the human expression chalk and cheese?"

Zozes shrugged, looking sideways at Kaze.

"It applies to you two, in so many ways."

"You know, Doc," Kaze's glare cut the short distance, "you've got some go in you, and I like that. How about this human saying, winning the battle, only to lose the war?"

Thaytis laughed in delight. "My, haven't I ruffled you. Shame on me when I was aiming at another target." Her gaze flickered cheekily over Zozes. "Calm yourself, young Alpha, it doesn't look good getting flustered over being proven wrong."

Before the situation could escalate, Zozes stepped between the two.

"Let's call it a point to each." Grabbing his brother's shoulder, Zozes urged him along. "Dropping in was a formality for the Major. The entire squad isn't needed for this, so let's not keep the Commodore waiting."

"Already?" Kaze tried to look back. "Come on, why?"

Zozes pointed at himself, then his brother. "Because Green outranks Blue. We'll pick this up later."

"We just got here."

"Kaze!"

"Alright." Disgruntled, he trudged along, but could not resist throwing a parting comment at Thaytis. "Enjoy the view. I know I was."

On an eyeroll, Zozes followed his brother from the Observation Deck into the lobby, then across into the holding ward where the Commodore was observing high-risk detainees.

"Most of these are empty," Kaze noted, glancing through the slanted windows.

"Hmm." Zozes nodded toward the end of the room. "There's Clarkov with the Commodore."

The two eyed the small group gathered around the Commodore, then looked back out the window. The end Holding Room was dramatically altered, appearing more like a human medical chamber in Zozes' opinion.

Nose almost touching the view screen, Kaze leaned close as Clarkov joined them. "That thing's in there?"

Clearly unnerved, Clarkov nodded. "It's suspended within a reinforced holding enclosure. The walls in that room are reinforced. There's no getting through them."

The Kadra prisoner was virtually unrecognisable, its entire body wrapped in white medical-gel bands to protect wounds sustained during the crash. Only the mouth was visible.

"Is it secure?" Zozes jerked closer, joining his brother. The Kadra's arms and legs were pulling up and in. It was testing its bonds.

Noremar entered the room below with two Astral Guard Enforcers. A nod to the staff cleared the room of all medical personnel but one who was activating a hi-cap glove, moving it over the Kadra's body in slow deliberate movements that started at the feet, every now and again checking its vitals on a porta-tool's generated screen.

"They're taking a risk," Kaze said. "I thought it was reported the Kadra's bio-status was in the high-risk condition?"

Zozes looked over at the Commodore. "Come on." Covering the short distance, the two waited for a break in the conversation, then saluted Vae'gon.

"That thing's healing fast, Sir," Kaze said.

Vae'gon turned to face the brothers but was interrupted by an electric current that wavered in the air before materialising into a tele-warp rim. Levitating in place, it began to spin, generating a warp window that widened to include a teleporter-beam, streaming glowing orbs that formed into several personnel.

As soon as this was complete, they moved, granting room for the lead warp-entry, the Actrix High Priestess and her personal Disciples. Dressed in deep red robes, the High Priestess unwrapped the veil covering the lower half of her face, stepping to the view screen.

The tele-warp rim continued rotating, telling Zozes their gathering was about to grow much larger.

"This Kadra's pulling some interest," Kaze remarked quietly.

"Maybe it's no ordinary Kadra," Zozes muttered, moving back to the observation view screen.

Kaze joined him, arms crossed. "Wasted resources, if you ask me. Give me some time with that Kadra, and I'll have it shed its silence,"

"With this much interest," Zozes said, glancing around, "you'll be standing in line."

Warp-orbs spiralled to form a number of Galactic Force officers, then finally their superior.

Zozes and Kaze immediately took at-stance. Commander Vome stepped from the beam, her black hair cut to chin length, one side secured behind her ear. She looked as energetic and forceful as ever, though she must be twice his birth cycle.

Hand to chest, Vome saluted the brothers. "Take easement, Blades."

One of her officers used their porta-tool to deactivate the teleport-rim, reforming it to a disc, the device crossing before the brothers, mag-locking to an officer's forearm control unit.

About to move off, Vome's sharp gaze caught sight of the hovering Link-Trone. Almost instantly, her expression softened. "I see you've both acquired an unofficial field advancement?"

Kaze opened his mouth, but Zozes beat him, clearing his throat. "Details of which best spoken in private, Sir."

"Indeed." Vome looked over Kaze quietly. "My respects for your former Alpha Chief. She was a fine officer whose status will not be easy to uphold."

With that, she joined the Priestess at the view screen. "So this is the Kadra that has the entire sector talking."

The atmosphere, already stiff, jumped to formal, all standing at attention. Vae'gon signalled an officer to activate freq-com so the assembly could converse with the Holding Room.

"We have been attempting to establish a dialogue," Vae'gon said, "but received no response yet."

"Perhaps it's mute," supplied the Actrix Priestess.

Zozes could hear Noremar asking a series of questions below, all to no avail. It was either choosing not to respond or was too ill to.

The medical officer finished her examination, deactivating the hi-cap glove. Looking across at Noremar, she said, "No change in condition that I can tell, Sir."

"Is the Astral Guard in need of assistance?" Vome asked bluntly.

The officer held her composure while looking up. "None of our scans can effectively establish this Kadra's condition, let alone read its internal makeup. The bio-signature pulse it's amplifying is very powerful, a charged energy field, one that's interfering with our equipment."

Clearly challenged, Vae'gon eyed Vome. "Astral Guard's jurisdiction in this matter cannot be questioned. Keep in mind, Commander, the Kadra was apprehended upon this world—"

"By Blade officers that are in service to the Galactic Force," cut in Vome. "Not Astral Guard. You were not even aware of its presence until they recovered it."

Vae'gon chewed on this before spewing his usual rhetoric. "The Overwatch Initiative protects Earth and grants me every right to hold that Kadra."

"That directive is controlled in accordance with Primordial technologies that endanger developing civilisations. You cannot hold this Kadra without proper validation of its crimes, Commodore. The state of special investigation's role is to determine ..."

Vae'gon laughed, the sound gravelly, arrogant. "You underestimate my authority within the Overwatch Initiative. A joint operation is already underway, led by Superintendent Roccna. She will confer with your division, relaying all findings."

Jaw clenched, Zozes listened to the exchange. The Galactic Force and Astral Guard were once again at odds. The same conflicts rumbled away, as they had since the Second Galactic War. Neither gave ground, each constantly questioning the other.

Vome did not back down, if anything she looked electrified. "This Kadra Outcast must stand trial for illegally entering the galaxy, breaking the Oath-Creed taken after the war. Pledges drawn up by the Kadra themselves. That is the law."

"Enough." The Actrix Priestess stepped between the two on a loud sigh. "All of us stand as an integral arm under the banner of the Planetary Allegiance." She nodded at Vae'gon then Vome.

"What these Blades discover will ultimately decide this Kadra's fate and whose responsibility it is to become."

There was no mistaking the heavy atmosphere, a step beyond social tension. Vome and Vae'gon did little to disguise their dislike, the only thing keeping the discussion civil appeared to be the Priestess.

Whatever task-duty she wanted performed would no doubt prove challenging, and was most likely the reason his brother stayed as silent as himself. Thinking back on the meeting with the Priestess, Zozes remembered her words, still not liking the idea of her trying to turn them into some version of her own champions.

Finally, Vome accepted her ruling. "Of course, your Eminence."

"Agreed," stated Vae'gon, flatly.

By the look on the Commodore's face, this was not in line with his personal beliefs, thought Zozes. Vome's expression was more difficult to read.

"So we are here at your request, Eminence." Zozes nodded at the Priestess.

"I see the Commodore has not underestimated your strategic mind," she observed with a smile.

"Believe you me," interrupted Kaze, "that particular power comes with lots of strings." At her sharp look, he added a hasty, "Ma'am."

One of her Disciples stepped forward. "You may only address—"

She cut him off, holding up a hand for silence. "No offence was intended and none has been taken. The young Alpha needs time to adapt and understand proper decorum."

On a deep swallow, Zozes looked to Vae'gon when he spoke again. "Yes, Blade, you have been summoned by the Priestess of the Actrix Covenant, and as you know, their influence travels far."

"The Actrix Gods cast their light upon all. Blades, the Covenant is here seeking your help," the Priestess said.

"Light or no light." Kaze's gaze fell on the mutilated Kadra form. "Dealing with those things is our specialty."

The Priestess eyed the brothers' Link-Trone as it disengaged multi-cloak, hovering between them. "There's no conventional means of identifying this Kadra's identity."

"Your Eminence." Zozes searched her face. "What do you require of us?"

"Something suited to your unique talents," she replied mysteriously. "The two of you are to establish a spawn-drift with your Link-Trone, which will give you the ability to access the Kadra's weapon."

"Its zaphna rod?" Kaze looked at his brother. "Is that even possible?"

"Yes," the Priestess answered. "They are linked, the zaphna and the one who wields it. Through the drift, you will discover this Kadra's identity."

The High Priestess moved before the view screen, studying the Kadra. When she turned her eyes fell on Vome.

"Commander?" she asked calmly.

"Identifying the Kadra is only the first step. Assessing its crimes will ultimately determine if it must be transported by the Galactic Force to its native Astral-State to face trial upon a High-Throne world."

Vae'gon made no comment, appearing to ignore the statement.

"I assume this Kadra has rejected all med-agents that it has been given?" asked the Priestess.

"It has," confirmed Vae'gon. "Not even a physical genetic identifier can be established from tissue we have extracted."

"Let me guess," Vome said. "Cellular breakdown begins instantly, anything taken becoming useless. That's a rare ability, even amongst their own kind."

"Looks like you're right, brother," Kaze murmured. "We're dealing with no ordinary Kadra."

Lips pursed, the Priestess looked to Vae'gon. "Which brings us to my earlier suggestion. There's only one way to determine that information, and as I stated, it involves the Blades' Link-Trone."

Vae'gon glanced at his duty-arm, giving him a weary nod. "Ensign, release what was discovered with the Kadra."

Clarkov indicated for the containment case to be set on a circular control station behind them. After inputting a series of codes, the portable device's reinforced grid-shield was awakened. A wave of his hand before a panel deactivated the shield, opening it. Inside was a fixed ISO-Tube in which the Kadra's weapon was levitating, held within a grav-beam.

The discomfort level of the room rose sharply at the sight of the deadly zaphna rod.

"My Disciples," began the Priestess, "explained that it took a great deal of time to extract the weapon from the Kadra without inflicting permanent injury."

"Contact with its zaphna rod," Vae'gon swallowed on the name like it was something distasteful, "dramatically bolsters their augmented enhancements. In the end, we decided to leave it with the Kadra to aid its regenerative factor for a short duration."

"You left the weapon with it?" Kaze exclaimed, clearly astonished.

All eyes shifted to him. Seeking to calm the atmosphere, Zozes spoke quickly. "LT, prepare to initialise spawn-drift cycler to connect to the Kadra's zaphna rod."

"Excellent." Straightening her robe, the Priestess looked around. "Now that the weapon has been removed, all the Kadra's abilities have been dramatically suppressed. However, in several planetary rotations, I estimate it will reach full recovery."

He was listening with only half an ear, most of Zozes' concentration centred on the Link-Trone. It looked like it was back to its cooperative self, undertaking the preliminary analysis scans as instructed. If for one moment Vae'gon believed they had lost control …

"LT," he ordered, "activate and upload analysis scans. Review your findings upon rundown mode."

Frustrated, Kaze drew alongside his brother. "I thought initiating a spawn-drift was a bad thing."

"Just follow my lead," Zozes murmured quietly.

"Something about my spawn-net overloading?" Kaze reminded him.

"You want to argue in front of them?"

Instantly his brother's chin jutted forth.

"Fine. Excuse us," Zozes announced. Pulling his brother to one side, Zozes spoke his mind. "Your spawn-net needs to be as balanced as possible."

Shocked, Kaze demanded, "You knew they wanted us to try this?"

"Partly," he said, "but not in such detail."

"So, the run around town for the last couple of days?"

"Was much needed time so your spawn-net had a chance to rebalance itself while aligning with your nervous system. The crash zone affected you more than you care to admit, and you know it."

"So dropping this on me now, and lying about Roccna was a better plan? Remember what I told you earlier. None of this will work if you don't trust me!"

"I'm trying to protect you!" Zozes growled. "If you knew about this earlier, your recovery would have taken twice as long. Time we simply don't have, and to be honest, I'm considering doing this one on my own. Knowing what happened to you during the crash of our ship, falling into the drift unprepared? It's lucky you didn't sustain permanent damage."

"It's called dual-pairing. Us, working together," Kaze hissed. "Not you going it alone."

"You can't even initiate it," Zozes exploded. "What you did was impossible."

"It was instinct. I can't explain what happened." He threw up his hands. "Now I'm paying the price and you're heading off, going solo. This'll end badly, I know it."

"Kaze, you talk about trust. What you did saved my life, I know that. Now you have to trust me in doing this."

"Seems I don't have a choice."

When the two approached, Vome lifted an eyebrow. "Do we have a problem?"

"No, Sir. We're ready." Zozes let out a breath of relief seeing that the Link-Trone's base structure plate was retracted and its cybernetic rim loaded, displaying a series of screens. These were taking internal scans of the weapon.

"Alright." Zozes viewed several screens before ordering, "LT, activate the spawn-drift."

As the Link-Trone complied, a corresponding pull centred in his mind. Almost like a drawing in of everything that was happening in the room. What took Zozes by surprise was the upping of the link between him and his brother, highlighting the dual-pairing of emotion and action, one where he felt all.

When he had a semblance of control, he focused on the zaphna rod. A radial energy field surrounded it to the point it was almost blinding, something that had not been visible until the spawn-drift had been triggered.

From that moment on, Zozes was operating on instinct, every movement and thought merged to become one. The zaphna rod drew him, almost like he could align with its energy. After a wave of his hand, the Link-Trone began uploading further data, depicting a wireframe template of the weapon's composition.

Vome leaned close to that cyber-screen, clearly satisfied. "Ah, it's beginning to form."

Though he heard the Commodore replying, his voice seemed distant, far away. The Kadra's weapon had a pulsation like a human's bio-pulse, but it was erratic, verging on unstable. There was also energy flowing seamlessly through the centre of the weapon, feeding out to an external component.

The Commodore's voice penetrated his reverie, each word coming from a distance. "Can you verify the weapon's frequency signature?"

He focused, attempting to do as asked.

"It will take focus," the Priestess said, "as the weapon's natural defence shield generates a false signature. You must calm your mind, Blade, clear the deceptions to reveal its true frequency."

Zozes narrowed his focus, looking deeper into the weapon. As he did, the spawn-drift revealed a new level of awareness. Already open, his psyche became hyper-receptive to all that was happening. Every breath a body took, each movement made. All this was altered to a vibration and texture. Even the equipment around him was generating a radial energy he could now read.

The Priestess moved close, her tone lilting, each word delivered in slow motion. "The Link-Trone can only do so much. You must open yourself to all, see through its natural defences to what is beyond."

For an instant, he believed he saw what she spoke of, could feel its shape, the tone it generated. Then his brother's presence emerged, a lead weight disrupting the connection between himself and the Link-Trone.

Intense pain shot from the back of his head, abruptly severing all, bringing him back to the room, dragging in breath.

"It won't work with you dragging me in behind." Kaze stood at his side. "This is too complex, even for you."

The Priestess nodded in agreement, turning them both to face the weapon.

"I will guide you both. Through the drift your minds will meld, knowledge and emotion will become connected. Listen to my words. Move beyond the physical, see what lies between. Breathe in, for in that is life, and in life there is knowledge. Now exhale, leave all that surrounds. Your Link-Trone is a doorway, your mind is the key. Bring the two together, open your instincts so that through the spawn-drift you can see what lies beyond."

Her words distorted, faded, disappearing in the darkness, and from that darkness came his brother's sharp thoughts and strong feelings. The linkage within the spawn-net was strong and powerful. Zozes had never felt anything like it.

He could hear Kaze now. *Let's take this vokker together.*

As one, their focus centred solely on the zaphna rod. Like before, Zozes not only heard but felt energy vibrating, surrounding him. Pattern and sequence, an almost rhythmic melody he could remember hearing somewhere a very long time ago. Ageless, its continuous flow of viber-wave beats spoke to him, all mingling into one form, the zaphna rod's frequency pulse.

Upon hearing it, Zozes' eyes sprang open. His brother stared back, just as amazed and stunned.

"Well." Kaze swallowed visibly. "Well, that wasn't ... weird at all."

Zozes could feel the room's eyes on them. The Priestess and Vome looked over at the Link-Trone's cyber-screen which was now displaying the Kadra weapon's true frequency pulse.

"Amazing." Clarkov leaned close, examining the readout.

Since the spawn-drift's effects were slowly subsiding, Zozes could view the room as he always had. For the first time, it made him feel empty, alone, and that bothered him more than he cared to admit.

Kaze wiped at his nose, coming away with only a small amount of blood. "I'll ask the obvious question: what now?"

"Your lack of command training puts you at a disadvantage." Vae'gon stood alongside the Priestess, not turning from the uploaded data. "Simply put, your part in this is now concluded, Blade."

Vome spared the Commodore a dark look before eyeing the frequency, the Link-Trone hovering near her. "After the Second Galactic War, an anti-zaphna code was enforced. All Kadra who operate these weapons were instructed to surrender their weapon's frequency signature. These have been stored with the Kadra Registry Archive, giving us the ability to track any augment who enters our galaxy without clearance."

Almost on cue, the Link-Trone spoke. "Uploading registry. Scanning all zaphna frequency patterns." More lights flashed. "Locating base linage signature. Connecting to profile."

Everyone appeared to hold their breath, waiting for the Trone's final confirmation.

"Registry indicates this zaphna rod is a class three, and belongs within a Kadra Bearer-ship Linage."

"Ah," murmured the High Priestess. "That explains its enhanced abilities."

"Kadra Outcast," added the Trone, "banished from their Order. Known by the name Cedos, son of Sonan, to the clan of Garrold."

Kaze made an angry noise, but it was Zozes who spoke. "Impossible!"

Though their spawn-net was almost reset, Zozes felt a swell of fury and shock, but it was not his own. When the wave of energy hit, he was unprepared.

At his side, his brother stood in full Blade armour.

"Kaze!" he yelled, but it was too late.

His brother was leaping, crashing through the view screen, shattering it before landing on the deck below, side-arm already drawn.

On the point of apprehending him, Enforcer Noremar was knocked into the rear wall when his brother upended a table. Next breath, his weapon was pointed at the Kadra's bandaged skull.

Zozes saw all this as he jumped, activating his armour mid-air, to land beside his brother, fighting to control his own fury.

"Kaze!"

On the floor, Enforcer Noremar took aim with her plasma rifle. "Holster your weapon Alpha Blue. That's an order!"

In warning, Zozes held up a hand. Rage ran like fuel through the spawn-net, colouring his thinking, all of it coming from his brother.

The only way he could stay clear and focused was to fully block Kaze, centre his mind on the job at hand.

"Listen to me," Zozes spoke cautiously, calmly, hoping it would penetrate, stay the finger tensing on that trigger. "This isn't our way, brother. We can use him to draw out his father. Make Sonan Garrold answer for the crimes he has committed against our family. If you do this, we lose any hope of that happening."

The change came slowly, the feel of his brother calming. When that impotent rage finally drove his brother to his knees, a terrifying scream ripping out of him, Zozes made his move, placing himself between his brother and Enforcer Noremar, eliminating his brother as a target.

Insides vibrating, Zozes waited for Kaze's fury to temper, though he shared that desperate need for justice.

The moment Kaze deactivated his armour and weapon, Zozes did the same, helping him stand. Together, the two left the medical holding room side by side. When they were alone, Zozes turned to his brother.

"I promise you Kaze, it will pay. It will answer for what the Garrolds have done to our family. We are at the beginning. In there lies the answer for us all."

Galactic Star Key: Bendon Clarkov
Astral Nav-Coordinates: EAS-APL-4
Data Sequence: 14.0

It was hard to believe something like that could happen. Stepping gingerly into the medical holding room, Bendon stuck to the edge, trying to avoid chunks of broken glass.

Commadore Vae'gon was already there speaking with Enforcer Noremar, who was suffering through a medical treatment. The gash on her cheek looked deep, but the hi-cap glove's tissue welder beam was regenerating the wound, an experienced medical officer controlling it.

"I should have shot first," Noremar ground out. "Worried over questions later."

Vae'gon merely grunted in response, his gaze fixed on the Kadra across the room.

The door opened, admitting the High Priestess. She marched straight across the room, glass crunching, to halt before the Kadra.

She was there to oversee her Disciples and Astral Guard Enforcers as they were about to begin the process of transferring the Kadra, Cedos Garrold, to another holding facility.

The Priestess looked satisfied, especially when she glanced up, taking in the gaping hole in the view screen where Commander Vome was conversing with Galactic Officers.

"Impressive," she murmured. "Despite all that happened, their state consciousness stayed intact and their Link-Trone in control. What took place here is 'proof of trial'. We now understand the Blades' true resolve."

Vae'gon moved to her side, also glancing up. "Perhaps, but I believe more testing will be needed to prove that. The Blades may succeed where their previous Alpha Chief could not."

"You wish to place them through the Alpha Trials and bestow on them a more permanent status upon Earth?"

"Those are Commands orders, though I have reservations."

Reflective the Priestess crossed her arms. "Despite all the challenges that lay before us Commodore, even you must realise that those Blades may be our final hope."

Galactic Star Key: Baden Casteel
Astral Nav-Coordinates: EAS-APL-4
Data Sequence: 15.0

As the school bus pulled up, Baden jumped clear. Wandering down the gravel drive, he scrolled through his iPhone playlist while shoving in earphones. Choosing a song, he hoisted his backpack, looking up the long drive toward the cream farmhouse, trimmed in blue.

The heady scent of wattle flowers in bloom filled his senses, their yellow flowers full of bees. The main farmhouse, his Uncle Rickard's and Aunt Grace's, looked quiet, not one car in sight. Shielding his eyes, Baden peered down the track, noting the rotary dairy was deserted, only a small group of cattle in a holding pen. This time of day it should have been in full swing.

Something was up. Kicking at the gravel, he started shuffling through his playlist wondering if he should chase down his uncle or start on the homework assignment from history that was bound to twist his mind into a million shapes.

The sound of a car skidding into the drive penetrated his earphones. Turning, he eyed the dust cloud, which was already billowing across the front yard into the paddock.

The beaten-up red ute and radical driver were instantly recognisable. Stepping well clear, Baden pulled out his earbuds, watching it fishtail toward him, rolling his eyes. His uncle was not going to appreciate running the mower over the driveway's lawn now that it was covered in stones.

Window down, Jevon stuck his head out, sporting his usual lopsided grin. "C man, how's it hanging?"

Baden continued walking. "One day you're going to overcorrect and end up through the front fence in the bull paddock." Baden pointed. "Old Tyson's always up for a bit of a spoil."

Jevon eyed the Hereford and its horns. "That old roid-fest's exhausted from shagging all day."

"Dunno." Baden jerked irritably at his backpack. "He looks fresh enough to me, loves making the ladies his bitch. You'd fit right in, Starrik."

Arm out the window, Jevon tapped at the door of his ute. "I always play the odds, mate. Only way to live."

"You heard of the law of averages? One day they're going to stick it to you hard." A snigger came from inside the ute. Leaning down, Baden saw Jevon had company. "You've got James in the car? Starrik, you must've been deprived of oxygen at birth."

"Who's a little bitch now, eh?" Jevon glanced at his young passenger, then back. "My brain cells are more than accounted for, mate. Aunt Grace messaged me at work, asked me to stop by the café and grab this man of steel here, plus some other stuff. Necessities, she called them."

"Necessities?"

"Eb's welcome home ... the beast feast, mate!" Rubbing his hands together, Jevon grinned at James. "Perks is dropping Ebony off after she gives her statement with the detectives."

"So, it's tonight?" Baden halted, Jevon shoving the ute in neutral. Giving his backpack a shake, he thought fleetingly of his homework ... looked like a late night. Leaning down, he eyed Ebony's little brother who was once again playing on his mobile phone. "Sup, Jammer!"

"Hey Cass." James, glanced up briefly, his thumbs flicking over the phone's keypad.

"He's like a silent little ninja," said Jevon. "Didn't even flinch when I swung in. He knows how to have some fun, unlike Captain Straight Shooter over here who hates stepping off the road of life to see what's waiting around the corner."

"Called natural selection."

"Natural selection?" Jevon rubbed his chin. "Sounds made up, yet familiar."

"Go home and research it. With a little luck, you might make it to twenty-one."

"Mate, I'm there in a couple of months, already planned the menu." Leaning back, he eyed Baden. "That what's this about? You hating on me because I'm over tonight, gonna eat all the food?"

"You are a food whore." Baden eyed James squirming. "What's up?"

"I gotta go," he finally admitted.

"Go baptise the land's little one," laughed Jevon. "Like your forefathers before you."

"Alright, but wait for me." James hopped out, heading for a dense bush.

"Better be quick," he added. "I think the milk tanker's heading this way. Don't want the driver catching sight of that little pecker." Fingers tapping lightly on the door, Jevon looked at Baden. "I can do you a solid for later tonight, cutting back on the chow intake that is."

"A solid?" Baden laughed at Jevon's pained expression. "What's your angle?"

"Just a casual, simple favour."

"Casual, simple, huh?" Baden immediately smelt trouble. "That doesn't sound creepy at all."

"Nah." Jevon leaned forward, sticking his head a little out the open window. "But you have to shut up and keep it quiet … way clear from Eb."

"So far it's sounding anything but casual, simple."

After checking where James was, Jevon brushed that aside. "Long story short, it's something important about someone we both know."

Baden hated when Jevon attempted what he called code talk. "You mean Ebony."

"Didn't say that specifically."

Frustrated, Baden kicked at the grass along the gravel edge. "Starrik, I'm fast losing interest in this back and forth."

"All I need is Kevo's number."

Surprised, Baden's eyes narrowed. "Why?"

"Unlocking a phone, nothing he can't handle."

On a snigger, Baden ribbed, "Forget your pin again?"

"Something like that."

"Just restore it from your home computer."

"Well, aren't we Mr Solve It. Nah, mate, I need Kevo."

"I can't figure if you're incompetent with life or just plain lazy."

"Trust me, being lazy as opposed to being incompetent at life are entirely different." Jevon yawned, scratching his head, adding grease to the shaggy mess. "Though you make them sound the same."

"Something tells me," Baden scrutinised Jevon's relaxed posture, "you're still learning the difference."

"Fine, you need the deets." Jevon rolled his eyes. "The last backup on the mobile was questionable. Almost a year ago, so I need this done. Can't afford to lose all the info mate, especially the current stuff."

Baden thought of Kevin and Jevon together. "I dunno. Kevo's kinda private, he lives off the radar. If you saw his room you'd understand."

"Come on, mate, I'll be there and gone. It's just a quick unlock. Besides, playing hermit's no way to go through life."

"Kevo's got this circle of trust thing. If you give out his number freely, let's just say you're out for good."

"If he asks," Jevon brushed that aside, "I'll cover for ya. All good."

Baden raised an eyebrow, shaking his head. The movement had Jevon tapping on the steering wheel, clearly thinking hard.

"Fine." Regrouping, he looked up. "How about you be the go-between ..."

"Nope." Baden stepped back. "Not getting involved."

"I was going to say," continued Jevon stoically, "all you gotta do is tell him to meet me out front of his school tomorrow, shouldn't take long and I'll have the mobile with me."

A wicked thought brought spark to Baden's eyes. "Bring cash, none of this IOU crap and he may be interested. That's all I can promise."

"No IOUs? Where's the love, mate?" Jevon glanced around the cab like he expected dollars to appear. "Err, sure. Just remember, keep this on the QT, especially around you know who."

James reappeared, yanking open the ute door.

"Incoming," Jevon yelled. Placing it back in gear, he started off. "I don't see any blatter explosion. Wind direction good I take it?"

Baden laughed, eyeing James's sheepish look. "Starrik, the fact this kid actually understands what's coming out your mouth is scary."

"He's gotta learn from someone." Jevon tapped the wheel. "Besides, Jammer here reckons I'm a joy to be around."

"Joy's when you leave," Baden assured.

As the two came to the central roundabout, Baden headed left, aiming for the second home past the farm shed, a small two-storey cottage built for share-farmers. He and his mother had lived in it most of his life.

Jevon headed right, pouring on speed aiming for the main farmhouse. As soon as he pulled up, Baden saw James jump out, fighting with the catch on the back gate before disappearing around the corner.

About to enter his yard, Baden paused, glancing toward the silent dairy down the track. He was so engrossed he did not even hear Jevon pull in next to him.

"The old man's finished milking before four?" exclaimed Jevon, climbing out to join him at the gate. "That's unheard of, he operates this place like clockwork."

"I know." Baden climbed onto the fence eyeing the close paddocks but could not see anything. Jumping down, he took another look around, for the first time noting the angle of red diesel ute parked at the machinery shed. The tandem trailer was hitched, his uncle's long-bar chainsaw resting on the mudguard. "Something's up."

"He can't be cutting firewood, the man's got his seasons mixed up." Jevon looked at Baden dubiously. "It's spring."

"No way he's getting a load of wood," assured Baden.

As if summoned, Rickard appeared moving fast from the shed toward his ute. Spotting the two, he signalled them over with an aggressive wave.

Jevon's head shot up, reminding Baden of an animal scenting danger. "My keen long-sightedness suggests our uncle's pretty pissed. What've you done?"

For an instant Baden wracked his brain, but came up empty. "Ever since the Festival and Ebony's return, he's been wound pretty tight."

"You bloody coming or what?!" Rickard roared from the ute.

"Yup, he's pissed. Dick-shrivelling time fellas." Jevon jumped back in his ute and took off, creating a cloud of dust as he tore around the roundabout to the machinery shed.

Baden hightailed it across the roundabout, trying to avoid being snagged by his aunt's roses in their curved beds, while circling the central oak tree. A cagily placed wheelbarrow almost sent him sprawling, secreted behind a shrub she had been trimming that morning.

When he reached the shed, his uncle was moving quickly, dropping the chainsaw on the tray, the screeching sound of metal against metal jarring in the tense atmosphere as he shoved it along. Jevon was trailing him, throwing in fencing equipment.

Baden was surprised to see his grandmother May carrying out a battery drill together with its chargers, a worried frown marring her round face.

"Rick, you're going to need all the help you can get." Baden quickly caught on that this argument had been going awhile. "So I'm coming too."

"Bay's home." Rickard nodded in his direction. Looking over to Jevon, he added. "And Jev can at least hold the tools."

"Hey, I ain't anyone's coathanger!"

Irked, Rickard glared in his direction clearly demanding silence.

"But today I'll make an exception," grumbled Jevon.

Rickard moved past May. "You need to look after Eve, and get the rest of that cooking done for tonight. Grace will be home around five."

"Nina texted me," interrupted Jevon, pulling a large set of pliers from his uncle's toolkit. "Eb's interview was cancelled with the authorities. I reckon she'll be home earlier now."

May was the first to respond. "Cancelled?"

"Yeah." Jevon opened and closed the jaws, smiling at their strength. "Nina didn't think they'd be long, her text was thin on the deets. Something about them evacuating the building."

"The Freestone Police Station was evacuated?"

"No, no!" Jevon laughed heartily. "The location for Eb's interview was changed. You didn't hear? She's been taken to the old RAAF base by two suits now."

Rickard snatched the pliers from his nephew's hands. "What do you mean two suits?"

"You know," Jevon swallowed noticeably. "Kinda like government officials. They were escorting Eb to the base out at Ridge Falls. You guys didn't know?"

Rickard looked at his mother. "No, we didn't."

"Nina's with Ebony now?" May asked. "You certain of that, young Starrik?"

Jevon nodded urgently. "She only texted ten minutes ago, literally."

"Right." May ran a hand over her hair, the scatter of grey threads shinning in the afternoon sun. "If anything like this happens again let us know immediately."

Clearly confused, Jevon agreed. "Sure thing, boss."

"Call Mara," said Rickard, dumping the pliers in his toolkit. "Find out what's happened and why we weren't told."

If the level of tension had been high before, Baden had no idea what it was now. Rickard made to move, but Jevon stepped in the same direction, the two colliding. At the end of his tether, Rickard shoved by him. "Find a bloody place to stand where I can't bowl you over!"

Baden had never seen Jevon react so fast in his life, leaping onto the back of the trailer from standing position. Not a bad effort, he thought.

From there, Jevon perched, watching his uncle sheepishly. Rickard grabbed a file from his toolkit to begin sharpening his chain with slow, even strokes. Baden could see a sheen of sweat on his brow, knew by his look he was worked up.

"Rick, this'll take hours," said May. "Leave it until morning, go call the station now."

"There's already eight cattle dead." He ran the file rhythmically over the teeth of the chain. "Now half my yearling herd is missing. We can't afford another loss, you know that."

"You're right." May looked toward the hills. "First the farm, now this with Ebony. When it rains, it pours."

"It's us," grunted Rickard, dry humour appearing. "Just heard over the ABC radio that this morning's earthquake measured four point two."

"Yeah, we felt it in town." Jevon stood in the trailer, bouncing lightly. "Didn't have much in it, more like Mother Earth having a grumble."

May raised an eyebrow in his direction, then turned back to her son. "We've had several quakes over the years. I can't understand why the cattle scattered this way, when they never have before."

"I think," Rickard checked the chainsaw's fuel, "this was more to do with the aftershocks. That's when they bolted."

"Aftershocks can go for days," said May worriedly.

"Why I milked early, changed the main herd's paddock. Got them where I can keep an eye on them. When I was tracking where the yearlings ran off earlier they were heading for the bush block up the back."

"The uncleared land?" Baden was starting to catch on to what his uncle was up to.

"Yes," Rickard nodded. "They're moving east, looking for high ground, crossing gullies. Already tore through a dozen fences."

"You ever seen them act like this before?"

"Nope, this one's brand new even for me." Finished, Rickard shoved the chainsaw up the tray, toward the cab. "Cattle usually stay close to fresh water, good pasture. This lot have spooked."

"They're yearlings," reminded May, looking at the boys. "Like minding a group of teenagers hunting for fun."

Rickard pushed the toolbox up to secure the chainsaw, in the process slicing his finger on its teeth. Grumbling, he rubbed it against his flannelette shirt, glaring at his mother. "It's a good thing I've got you around to point out the blatantly obvious."

May grabbed a tissue from her pocket, unperturbed. "Anger won't help the situation. Clear your head before you do more than cut a finger."

"If I swore like I wanted those ears of yours would be dripping blood instead of my finger." Fighting to calm himself, Rickard looked apologetically at his mother. "I'll be right, go mind Eve and get ready for tonight. Baden," his gaze cut to his nephew, "change into work clothes, and Jev ..."

"Yes!" Jevon jumped from the trailer, slapping his hands. "What do you need Uncle C?"

"Shut up, and knock off the grab arse." Rickard sucked at finger, eyeing the cut. "Let's find these yearlings, get them secured before dark."

Jevon's failed attempt to lighten the mood left Baden grinning.

Especially when he slumped against the tray, muttering, "Great. All work and no food is gonna make me a dull fella."

May waved Baden toward the house. "Come on, the quicker this is all done the better."

Baden jogged back to the gate, then down the path toward the two-storey cottage. He could see his mum had been out weeding, probably seen Aunt Grace at it in the roundabout.

She never used a wheelbarrow, liked to pile the grass next to the beds. Slowing, he eyed the great chunks of earth attached to the roots, the few half torn-out plants. He knew those piles would rot where they sat, be there the next time he mowed, he thought in frustration.

"I was just getting to them." His grandmother called, coming through the yard gate. "Evie enjoys it out in the sun."

"Yeah," he grumbled, heading down the path, nose tickling at the scent of food. Looking toward the house, he eyed the open front door. "She alright cooking alone?"

"Nothing too complicated left." May grabbed a couple of handfuls of weeds, ignoring the soil on her way to the fence. "You get on."

On the veranda, he made his way around to the back, opening the sliding door. Kicking off his shoes, he stepped inside spotting his mother at the stove.

"Hey, I could smell that all the way from the Valley." No laugh greeted his words. She remained stiff, staring at the sizzling fry pan. Closing the door, he walked around the table.

The chicken pieces looked well sealed on their way to overdone. Wooden spoon in hand, his mother was staring vacantly into space, her mind anywhere but in the kitchen cooking.

"Mum?" Baden lay a hand on her shoulder, trying to ignore how slight her frame felt beneath his touch. "You good?"

Still she did not move. Turning down the stove, Baden eased the spoon from her hand, in the process rousing her from wherever she was mentally. Snapping back with a ferocious twist, Eve knocked the frypan sideways, scattering chicken over the stove and bench.

"Mum!" Jerking clear, Baden pulled her against him, for the first time noticing her expression, like she was in a fight for her life. "Hey, it's me, it's me!"

"Bay?" She froze.

"Yeah, you alright?"

"Of course, I am! What'd I tell you about sneaking up on me?" Eve pulled free, righting the pan with a jerk, grabbing pieces of meat with tongs, returning them to the pan.

"I called your name twice," he said slowly. "You zoned out again. You shouldn't be cooking this on your own."

"Just because I'm not allowed to work anymore doesn't mean I'm incapable around here. This is my home." The last was said vehemently, like she was reminding herself.

Baden eyed the overcooked food, which his mother was stirring agitatedly.

Gran May came through the back door, moving straight to wash her hands at the sink. "I heard you two from outside. What happened, Bay? You do something?"

"Hold up, me?" Baden stepped back as his grandmother began wiping down the bench and over the stove. "Just commenting on the food, she didn't hear." He thought about adding this wasn't the first time, but held back.

"You can't startle your mother in her condition."

"Mum, please." Eve turned off the stove with a jerk. "This isn't Baden's fault, and I'm fine."

May eyed the state of the stove. "Another blackout?"

At that Eve deflated, sagging from soul to skin. "They're getting worse." She looked at her mother. "Aren't they?"

"Honey, it's just a minor setback. We've been through worse, we'll get through this. Now let me clean up here while you sit."

"No!" Before May could move, Eve straightened. "I'm not letting you brush this aside. I'm starting to lose more than just memories." Gripping her own hand, she stared at them for moment, then turned to her mother. "My fingers are numbing, parts of my body, it's ..."

That was when Baden spotted the burn on his mother's hand, a large welt that sent his mind momentarily blank. Distressed, but still reactive, May grabbed her daughter, shoving her hand beneath the cold water of the faucet.

Glassy eyed, Eve stared out the window like she was somewhere else. "I-I can't feel it, Mum."

Baden felt as hollow as his mother looked. He was losing her a little every moment of every day. Clenching his fists, he tried to think past that knowledge.

"Bay," May looked over her shoulder. "You've somewhere to be, don't you? I'll take care of this."

Still he hesitated, terrified to leave, but just as scared to stay.

"Go!" his grandmother urged. "Your uncle's waiting."

He tore up the stairs, slamming the door to his bedroom before hurling his backpack at his bed. Tearing off his school clothes, he began rifling drawers, dumping half their contents on the floor in a mad search for shorts and a tank top like it was the most important thing in his life.

Don't think. That's the way through this ... just keep moving, doing what comes next.

By the time he was dressed, Baden was breathing hard. Grasping sunglasses, he crossed the room, wiping cold perspiration from his face. Hand on the doorknob, the state of his room hit him. Clothes scattered everywhere, even on the desk. His backpack had slipped off the bed, vomiting its contents onto the floor, books strewn around like litter.

He couldn't let his mother see this, he thought. What if it triggered something worse? Sprinting back, he grabbed at clothes, began stuffing them into drawers, but nothing seemed to fit. Fighting temper, he kicked at a couple, barely feeling pain.

Then the irony of the task hit. These drawers were him, overstuffed, leaking around the edges, fighting to cope. Slumping to his knees, he fought for control, belatedly aware of his throbbing foot. Leaning back against the drawers, Baden stared across the room at the mirror stuck to his bedroom door.

Red-rimmed grey eyes, dark hair sticking to his sweaty face. There was no avoiding it anymore. No skirting the fact why his Gran May had moved in six months ago.

His mother was getting worse, but today was still a shock. Things he fought to suppress began crowding his mind, creating an ache in his stomach as he thought of what had happened the night she had disappeared.

No word, no phonecall, no nothing. Just gone.

For hours, his aunt and uncle had searched with a group of friends and family after Baden had alerted them. When they could not find her, his grandmother had placed a call for help.

"You called Dallas Noble?" bellowed Rickard. "I made it clear it's too dangerous to have him involved."

Dallas's ex-wife had been off-duty at the time. When Mara Perkins arrived at the farm it had surprised everyone. Ever since her divorce from Dallas, she had distanced herself, vowing never to be drawn in with any of the Founding Families again, until now. Rickard standing apart from the Fellowship seemed to have challenged that resolve. The search continued all night into the next morning.

When they met at sunrise in the kitchen, all empty handed, Mara had been on the point of calling the station to report Eve Casteel as a missing person.

Then Dallas, her ex-husband, had clambered onto the back veranda, an arm supporting Eve. The relief Baden felt at seeing her alive was quickly subdued when she stumbled in, dreamlike, soaking wet, clothes filthy. Her lips had been pale, tinged with blue, hands white, fingers blue.

She was babbling strange words, disjointed sentences that made no sense. Baden thought she was just stuttering with cold, but quickly realised it was more to do with her state of mind. She was also uncharacteristically angry, could not understand why no one understood her.

Dallas seemed to be the only who could calm her, make any sense of her incoherent state. Every moment of that day Baden could recall vividly, especially the way his uncle had looked at Dallas Noble when he left, an almost silent communication in that final exchange.

While his grandmother helped Eve upstairs, Rickard had sat him down, the scarred kitchen table between them.

"Your mother's been through a great ordeal," he began. "What happened here tonight cannot be known by anyone. Understand?"

Baden nodded silently.

"Evie carries wounds from the past. I know you're too young to remember the way she used to be, and that's a shame. She had such spirit, was an adventurer, much more so than me."

"You're twins," Baden had pointed out.

"We were born into this world equal by blood, but Evie's drive gave her a unique purpose in the Fellowship, something I didn't have. But I understood her and grew to accept what she wanted and believed it was my job to protect her the best way I knew how. When she met your father, Evie's world was complete."

A bolt of lightning coming through the ceiling would not have surprised Baden more. "No one talks about him. I've learnt to not ask—"

"I know," Rickard interrupted, visibly uncomfortable, rubbing his hands briskly. "We've buried it, along with the past. But after this, you need to know … something."

"What?" Baden demanded.

"That they loved each other." Rickard paused, grimacing like each word was a struggle. "And it wasn't a swift thing, they were together for years."

"Years! Before her abduction?"

Rickard's jaw clamped, his eyes roving Baden's face, noticeably searching it. "There's reasons for every action, Bay, but the primary one was the safety of this family."

"Safety?" Baden eyes rounded. "So he wasn't a drifter? That was a lie?"

Rickard shrugged, looking back at his hands. "It was Evie's decision to protect you with a lie, and for right or wrong it has kept you safe. The irony is, with her condition stripping her memory she can't even recall it, let alone your father."

"Did you know him well? You must have a picture? Something?"

Rickard shook his head. "All that is left of your father is memories, Baden."

Fingers scrunched, Baden scrubbed at his face, recalling his uncle's bleak expression. It was rare anyone spoke of his parentage, of the mysterious figure Baden so desperately wanted to ask about. That night his uncle had, and it had been raw, like those wounds had never stopped weeping.

"When she lost him," Rickard shook his head, "it changed her. It changed us all."

Suddenly Baden snapped back, realising his mobile was ringing. By the time he pulled it from his pocket the call had gone to voice message.

He had to get moving, they'd be waiting. Clambering to his feet, he rubbed at his eyes, detesting that they were moist. He needed to shrug this off, just like he had the last six months. That was something he had learnt during their talk. Bury it, seal the pain inside. There was no changing what was happening to his mother. His uncle knew that, and it was how he coped.

At the head of the stairs, Baden paused watching his grandmother gently walk his mother to the bathroom, both engrossed in the task. Jogging down the stairs, he jumped the last few racing to the back door.

Outside, he breathed deep while pulling on his Blundstone boots. Moving fast through the backyard he avoided the gate, placing a hand on the top rail of the fence to vault it. A quick look told him the ute was still at the machinery shed, a four-wheel motorbike loaded and tied down on the trailer. Seeing the driver's door was open, he jogged over.

As he got closer, he saw two feet resting against the dash. Jevon glanced up from his mobile as Baden looked in from the passenger door.

"Damn, I know that look."

"Huh?" Baden resisted the urge to scrub at his face.

"The look of an unsatisfied fella that's been fooling around with himself achieving only a short-lived happy ending."

"Rushing always ruins the fun." For once Jevon's banter was welcome. "Surprised Ebony and Nina haven't trained you better."

Now it was Jevon's turn to look confused. "A fine specimen needs no training."

"Either that or retune the filter. People around here don't think like you."

"Pfft to what society wants, such a bore." Jevon stuck up his middle finger grinning. "I live outta the box mate, proud too."

"Until you're lying in one six feet down ..."

"What was that?" Jevon frowned straightening in his seat.

"Nothing." Baden looked around. "Where's our uncle?"

"He's got a head start, taken James with him."

"Cool, I'll grab my bike, you head off."

As he slammed the door, Jevon fired the diesel engine. Running into the shed, Baden held his breath as the ute's fumes filled the air pulling away. Grabbing his helmet from the work bench, he tugged it on, straddling his dirt bike. Already his adrenaline was spiking, dispelling the last of what he had seen.

Kickstarting the engine, he built up its revs before dropping the choke. In gear, Baden idled out of the shed, pausing briefly to connect the chin strap of his helmet.

Jevon had left the gate open and was almost at the dairy. Leaning most of his weight on his right leg, Baden angled the bike, released the clutch, turning the throttle hard to peel out the back wheel. Spinning in an arc he sent gravel and dust in the air before launching off at the last minute. As he sailed through the gate, the last of his dark mood vanished in the thrill of the ride.

At the milking shed, Baden hit the brake, locking the back wheel. Ahead, Starrik was playing around with the gate latch as only a town boy seemed to.

"Come on! Stop pussyfooting around, man!"

Jevon shook the metal chain in clear frustration, making Baden smile. On their right was a paddock fondly referred to by the family as the 'maternity ward.' Casting an eye over the herd, he made certain none of the pregnant cattle had gone into stress labour until he heard Jevon start cursing.

"Lift the gate!" called Baden, taking pity. "It's pulling on the chain."

As soon as he did this the chain slipped off with no effort. Kicking the gate, Jevon watched it vibrate open. "Premium fencing, mate. That gate's as level as a cliff face!"

Fresh tractor tyre marks led toward the back of the property, the bush block. Baden began revving the bike's engine. "Guess who's closing it!"

"Cass!" Jevon bellowed, already heading back to the ute.

"You need the practice," he laughed, throttling past, popping the front wheel as he sailed into the paddock. "See ya on the flip side, bitch!"

From there Baden flew across the paddock past the large tree line. Jumping an embankment, he skidded around a corner to finally spot his uncle on the tractor, circling the farm's recycle dam.

The back tyre bit as Baden hit the brake, skidding to a halt. Looking ahead he saw the boundary fence that divided the cleared farmland to the family's bush block. Downed gum trees had levelled the fence in places, making an easy escape route for the yearlings.

The further he rode the softer the pasture became until water began spraying from the tyres, hissing as it splattered the exhaust. Half the paddock was torn up, turned to mud, mangled holes showing cattle had sunk deep, sharp hooves boring the ground.

An irrigation pipe used for transferring water must have burst. His uncle had obviously plugged the dam at the outlet, but the damage was done. This paddock would need serious restoration.

As he drove further, Baden spotted the dead cattle. Halting, he switched off the bike, quickly yanking off his helmet. Ruffling his hair, he saw where his uncle had shifted them from the fence line to the side of the dam. He could see their wounds, the sight thoroughly disheartening.

Jevon pulled up, unusually serious. "This place looks a war zone."

Together the two began walking the embankment, toward the boundary fence. Some of the wire had been cut and bundled by his uncle where he had freed cattle. The rest was on the ground, insulators scattered, even posts broken off.

"Red box strainer post snapped clean in half?" Jevon whistled. "Not a bad effort."

Baden kicked at it. "We re-fenced this boundary line only a few years ago."

At the roar of the tractor the two spun. Shielding his eyes against the afternoon sun, Baden watched his uncle manoeuvre the tractor, angling the bucket to shove and push the downed trees and timber that had killed the cattle, making room for their vehicles to begin the climb into the bush block.

When he was finished, Rickard started driving back, heading for the ute.

"Come on," said Baden, turning around.

He and Jevon got there to find his uncle unstrapping a four-wheel bike off the trailer. James was on another four-wheeler, his expression pensive.

"How many yearlings are missing?" Baden asked as he climbed onto the trailer to straddle the bike.

"Eighty-six." Rickard tossed the last tie down back in the trailer.

The rasp of metal filled the air as Jev pulled out a set of ramps. Starting the bike, Baden backed it down, grunting as the front wheels found pasture. His uncle's urgency was mixing with his own, creating a potent brew.

"We need to get moving," Baden muttered, eyeing the sun.

"Locate as many of the herd as you can," instructed Rickard, unhitching the trailer. "Drive them back this way. I've already set up a strip fence further down the paddock, we'll lock them in there." He glanced at Jevon. "You remember how to ride one of these things?"

"I can handle anything that's got an engine."

Obviously doubting his nephew's boast, Rickard pulled a spare helmet from behind the seat and hurled it at him. "Here."

Jevon grunted, curling as he caught it. "Not a bad arm for an old dairy cocky."

Whether his uncle ignored the remark, or did not hear it, Baden had no idea, since he did not pause heading for the driver's door.

"Let's get this done before dark," he yelled, firing the engine.

As he jogged back to his bike, Baden noticed Jevon try to secure a helmet that was obviously a size too big.

The group moved into bushland following hoof prints which had formed a rough track. The deeper they got, the harder it became, torn-up scrub and a lot of freshly fallen trees making the going difficult. Casting a glance up, Baden searched ahead for branches caught in trees.

Obviously his uncle was thinking the same thing. "Keep your eyes sharp boys, watch out for widow-maker branches overhead!"

Everyone indicated they would and the group moved again. Noticing his uncle talking on loudspeaker on his mobile, Baden tried to catch up, until Jevon called out from the back. "Any word how far this earthquake travelled?"

Rickard looked back. "It's more like it travelled down."

On his four-wheeler, James skirted the group, riding ahead. Pointing to a rough track on the left, he looked back. Rickard nodded, giving his son the go ahead.

That track led to a rocky creek that flowed from the mountains. Surrounding it was lush pasture, but still no cattle in sight. Baden rode into the creek, looking up the stream eyeing the steady flow of water. On the opposite bank hoof prints were evident, leading even higher up.

Rickard came to a stop at an old, gnarled red gum that had lost enough limbs to block their way. Grabbing the chainsaw from the tray, he knelt taking hold of the cord, giving it a swift pull.

It was sweaty, tough work clearing a path for the bikes and ute, especially in such dense scrub where there was not even a hint of breeze.

Baden could not remember one other time when something like this had happened. One or two cattle had gotten out, there was always a broken fence to mend, but they tended to hang close to the farm.

"Safest track to move the herd is down through here," called Rickard, slowing the chainsaw, "back across the water ..." Catching the sound of familiar music, he switched off the chainsaw.

Over the ute's radio came the voice of the local news reporter. "At a little after twelve this afternoon an earthquake registering four point two on the Richter Scale shook the East Greenland area of Lake Rock down to Freestone Valley. Several aftershocks have already been reported with more expected to follow ..."

Obviously fed up, Rickard pulled the cord, restarting the chainsaw. When enough of the track was cleared, he returned the saw to the tray.

Still thinking about the news report, Baden wiped sweat from his face. "Lake Rock's gotta be an hour's drive from here."

"More than that mate," said Jevon, drinking water from a flask. "Lake's on the other side of Skyfall Mountain."

Rickard pulled a tarp over the chainsaw. "This could take some time, looks like they've travelled well up. You two scout ahead on the bikes. Turn back if you reach Stone River, I doubt the herd would cross currents that strong."

"Government property, too," agreed Jevon. "Don't need authorities up our arse today."

"They will be if they've got in there. It'll be a much bigger job."

"If we find them, we'll just push them back this way." Baden looked at the creek.

"Keep your eyes peeled, we don't need any accidents, just some common sense." His eyes focused on Jevon. "Which I know is lost on some."

The remark seemed to confuse Jevon, who pointed at himself. "Me?"

Rickard climbed back into the ute. "If you can safely move any of the stragglers, do it. If you can't, come back and grab me. Simple as that."

"Got it."

The three got on their bikes, moving much faster than the ute up the terrain. Riding through brush and scrub, the group skirted fallen limbs and muddy bogs. When they came to Stone River, the bush got even thicker. There Jevon headed upstream, turning off.

Baden and James hit the brakes calling, "You bailing already?"

"Hunter's instinct mate, trust me on this."

The two followed until they came to a large clearing.

Here the dense grass was knocked over, showing the direction of the herd. Over the next rise they came across the yearlings, standing in the shadow of a bluff. None of the girls were eating, nor looked relaxed. Bunched together, they looked agitated, tails flicking while moving around before a thunderstorm.

Cautious, the three pulled up halfway across the clearing, not wanting to spook them any more than they were. Jumping up on his four-wheeler, Jevon stood on the metal rack at the back.

Face brimming with excitement, he glanced briefly at Baden pointing ahead. "Uncle C's always claiming the Casteels are born with an overdose of common sense. Wanna explain that?"

Baden kicked the stand on his bike, walking around to have a look. Ahead was a line of brown soil that seemed to curve and disappear. Frowning, he eyed it trying to decide what it was before clambering up on the four-wheeler beside Jevon.

"The grass's been burned?" The soil appeared dry and fine-grained. The diameter looked to be about thirty feet, he estimated.

Jevon leapt off the bike. Walking over, he knelt beside the stripped pasture.

"What did this?" Baden walked along the edge, realising the area was probably bigger than he had first thought. "It looks like a ring."

Without hesitation, Jevon buried his hands in the soil, picking it up. Dry, fine powder ran through his fingers. Sniffing at it he pulled back.

"Okay, that's got some kick to it." He coughed, shaking his head. "Wouldn't recommend doing that, unless you do it for a lifestyle." Clearing the dust from his hands, he stood, eyes roaming the land. "Check that, there's other lines inside, finer ones."

Baden nodded, noting the way they arrowed toward the centre. "Looks like they form some sort of pattern."

From across the clearing came James's voice. "Hey! There's more over here."

Baden and Jevon jogged across, both stopping openmouthed. James was standing between two rings marking the ground side by side. Smaller in diameter, there was no mistaking that they were all somehow linked.

"You seeing what I'm seeing?" asked Jevon, then dropped his hands to knees breathing deeply. "Is it me or is anyone else feeling a little lightheaded?"

On a pained look, Baden shook his head. "After that snorting session, you're surprised?" Looking across, he realised James was about to touch it. "Leave it, Jammer!"

Immediately James jerked to his feet shoving his hands in his pant pockets. Baden signalled for him to come back, then looked at the cattle. Not one had moved during the exchange.

"Let's finish what we came here to do ..." Baden trailed off mid-sentence when Jevon started jogging across the clearing, heading for the bluff.

Great, Starrick was either tripping or he had spotted something else. Feeling like he was herding a child, Baden followed, signalling for James to follow.

It took him a moment to realise what Jevon had seen. The shadowy mouth of a cave, half hidden by a bunch of scrub. How he had spotted it, Baden had no idea.

"Starrik!" Baden bellowed, already guessing his intent. "Don't even think about it."

James was hanging back now, much to Baden's relief. He had obviously inherited the Casteel common sense.

"Hold up here for minute?" he asked James, who nodded, mouth a straight line of nerves.

Resigned, Baden doubled his pace, finally reaching the ridge to see Jevon at the cave mouth, pulling at the scrub, while looking inside.

"Does the ground feel like it's still moving to you?" he called.

It was only then Baden noticed the odd movement, like a vibrating rumble moving through the dirt beneath his feet. Almost like the earth itself was speaking in code.

"Jevon!" Baden hollered, throwing as much authority as he could into the word. "That entrance could collapse and I'm not gonna drag your arse outta there!"

The closer he got to the entrance, the more pronounced the vibrating became. It was the most eerie feeling he had ever experienced. Determined to save Jevon from himself, Baden climbed faster.

Almost there, he spotted a second group of young cattle on the right of the bluff. This lot was smaller, and clearly just as spooked. Animals, he knew, sense things humans could not.

The hairs began to prickle on the back of his neck. Something strange was definitely going on. On impulse, Baden approached one of the yearlings. It was clearly too terrified to move. Running a hand over its hide, down its rump, he felt the quiver of fear.

From the mouth of the cave, Jevon watched. "In my experience touching a female's rump usually gains one of two strong reactions."

"Guess I know why you're still single."

Jevon frowned, abruptly serious. "They're terrified."

The animals snorted, seeming confused. It was almost like they had no idea what to do. From the deep in the cave came a sound, like something had been dropped and was rolling across solid ground echoing back out to them.

Instantly Jevon ducked inside, walking a little way. "Can you hear that?"

"Hear what?!" Baden lunged up the hill, through the grass and shrubs. At the mouth of the cave he spotted something black protruding through the dirt, a strange polished rock.

"You've ever been here before?" Jevon called back.

Baden shook his head. "There's over two thousand acres of bushland up here."

Like he was not surprised, Jevon edged further in. "It's pitch-black, I'm gonna need some light." Activating the torch on his phone, he kept moving. "Seriously, can't you hear that? We've gotta check it out."

"You go in there you're on your own!"

Nothing.

Baden felt like his head was about to explode. If he yelled like he wanted would the whole thing collapse? Not game enough to find out, he watched the light and Jevon's silhouette disappear inside the cave.

With only one choice, Baden stepped out waving to James. "Go grab Uncle Rickard, get him up here now!"

James took off instantly, then skidded to a halt glancing back. "What're you going to do?"

On a sigh of resignation Baden glanced back. "Make sure the fool doesn't get himself buried alive. Go!"

On a deep breath, he clambered back up, ducking inside. Turning on the torch of his mobile, he moved deeper, trying not to think what he was doing. It was hot inside, the air heavy and thick. A strange vibration kept rolling through the rock, standing the hair on his body to attention.

There was no sign of Jevon or his torchlight, but since his own was reflecting off the walls it would be hard to tell another light source. Pausing next to the wall, he studied the rock, trying to decide if it was coated in the material or had become solid black over a long period of time.

At a noise up ahead, he switched his phone, risking a shout. "Jevon?!"

Only the echo of his own voice bouncing around came back. How damn deep had he gone?

Furious, Baden stumbled onward, keeping a close eye on the battery of his phone. The last thing he wanted was to end up lost in a pitch-black cave.

A massive vibration shook the rock, halting him mid-step. It seemed to thicken the air and heighten the humidity. Sweat was now pouring down his face, dampening his tank. Head reeling, Baden fought an unexpected bout of vertigo.

Jevon had been feeling dizzy before going in, he remembered. What if he was passed out? Gripped with urgency, he stumbled forward shining his torch into corners, covering as much of the cave floor as he could. He even checked to see if there was any kind of mobile phone reception, but of course that was ridiculous. Besides, he was having trouble focusing.

Another shake came almost on top of the last, this one producing a high-pitched sound that resembled a swarm of cicadas converging on a field. Covering his ears, scrunching his eyes, Baden fell to his knees, fighting the assault on his senses.

"Jevon!" he yelled.

Hands slippery with sweat, Baden gasped as his mobile slipped, skidding across the cave floor ... then everything went black.

"Come on!" Dropping forward, he instantly began scrounging in that horrible dark. Fighting to think past panic, he cursed, barking his knuckles, bashing his head, desperately ignoring the shrill noise that was on the point of making his ears bleed.

When his hand knocked the mobile sideways, the torch flared. Grabbing it in relief, Baden hugged it hard, pointing it instantly around, desperate to get his bearings.

This was serious, he had to go back, get his uncle, before both he and Jevon were lost permanently.

"Cass? Cass is that you?"

"Jev?" Baden swung to the right, aiming his torch. The noise seemed to be easing, or he was getting used to it.

Jevon appeared, thick hair plastered against his head. "You got more hairs on those balls then I gave you credit for."

Baden shook his head, fighting to see straight. "Okay, this has been an experience, now let's get out of here. This place isn't normal."

"Mate, relax, that noise was kinda my fault."

"What?"

"Follow me." Jevon pulled him to his feet. "I'll show you."

Angry, Baden jerked back. "Dude are you kidding me?"

"You're going to want to see this." Jevon kept walking. "There's a large open cavern ahead …"

With the sound finally subsiding, Baden followed, trying to calm his nerves. When his torch flickered, he halted, swallowing until it steadied. The cavern Jevon entered was creating a faint blue-white glow, which was comforting as well as strange.

A large system of tunnels connected to it, making him realise it was enormous.

Jevon nudged Baden. "Looks like the Solomons aren't the only ones with all the wealth."

Mouth open, Baden stumbled forward. All around him were black crystals but these looked different, almost fully transparent. Baden could see that within each was a series of internal blue-white veins. It was these that were giving off the strange luminescent glow.

"I can't believe this," he muttered. "What is this place?"

"Looks like the answer to the Casteel money problems if you ask me. Uncle C won't lose the farm with this here."

"Jevon, we don't even know what it is."

"Dollar signs for you at the very least."

For some reason, Baden felt his uncle's opinion would be different.

"And check this out!" Jevon walked to a wall, touching the black crystallised surface with his hand. Instantly it flared, drawing in light tinged with what looked like blue energy. From the centre, it shot off like a lightning strike, bouncing around the walls, a strange hum accompanying it. Shielding his eyes, Baden watched the strange phenomenon as it moved faster and faster throughout the cavern.

As it eased, Baden cautiously stepped closer viewing what looked like micro veins beneath the black crystal. "They're pulsating blue."

"Mate, explain that to me."

The energy in the veins began to slowly fade. "It's like it drew in something from you, then sent it out."

Again, the rumbling in the cave intensified. Covering his ears, he waited for it to fade away.

"That sound?" Jevon pointed to the crystals. "Is coming from them."

Warning bells began going off inside Baden. "Okay, the tour's over. We really need to get out here."

"Don't you get it?" Jevon threw an arm wide. "What's in here may be responsible for the earthquakes around Freestone."

"I don't care, enough dicking around." Grabbing his arm, he started dragging Jevon toward the tunnel they had come from.

"Wait ..." Jevon shrugged Baden's hold off, turning back. Unprepared, Baden fell sideways, throwing out a hand to stop himself falling.

The instant his palm came in direct contact with the black crystal surface it felt like an electric shock bit into his skin, yellow energy flaring from the point of contact. Warmth, the heat of his body seemed to centre in his hand, disappearing into the crystal. Though he tried, he was unable to jerk back. Energy splintered around the cavern, green energy that he felt was drawn from his body.

That brief contact, where the flash flared was enough to drop him to the cave floor, his heart pounding in reaction.

"Baden!"

He could hear Jevon shout his name, but it felt like it came from a long way off. Head buzzing, he tried to focus and stand at the same time. Streaks of green lightning lit the cave, but these were slowly settling. Looking again at the crystal, he blinked, spotting a reflection.

But it was not his own. "Err, what the ...?"

Jevon blinked, walking toward the black surface. "How'd you do that?"

On a step back, Baden stared openmouthed at the black crystal. There was now a group of people moving about in the image.

Jevon glanced behind them, clearly checking there was no one standing there. Three men who Baden had never seen and a girl. She was standing in between them and they looked to be having an argument.

"No way," whispered Jevon suddenly. "Hey! I know those guys."

"What're you talking about?" His palm was tingling, the sensation spreading up his wrist into his arm.

"I was talking about them at the festival last week. Those are the guys that came to my father's mechanic shop. I drove them out to the farm, out to see your uncle and aunt. And look who's with them!"

The girl was arguing with the tall, blonde man. When she spun around, he felt like his stomach rolled over.

"That's ..." he could not believe what he was seeing, "Ebony?"

Both heard the footsteps, knew who was coming.

"Right on cue, Uncle Rick," muttered Jevon nervously. "This isn't going to be easy to explain."

"Who'll believe us?" muttered Baden.

"Mate, anyone with a pair of legs could've wandered down here."

"You're missing the point," growled Baden. "We don't know the side effects being exposed to this. Could be RA for all we know."

"Maybe what happened to you and me was a one-off?" Jevon slapped his hands like he was trying to rid them of tingling. "What's RA code for?"

"Radioactive dick-weed. What if someone dies from this?"

"Well ..." Jevon sighed. "That would be a tragic thing."

"Let's just shut up and leave this weird energy thing between us for now."

Struck, Jevon laughed softly, staring at Baden. "You know what, you and Ebony may actually be related."

"What?"

"Forget it," Jevon shook his head. "Let's just say sweeping things under the rug seems to be a trait found in most Casteels. Blood-born or not."

Not needing another headache, Baden let it go. "I'll talk to our uncle. He'll be the one to decide what happens next."

"He's more a realist than you. No way he's gonna believe anything we say we saw. Not without eyeballing it for himself."

The two made their way from the large chamber into the tunnel. Turning back on the threshold of the cavern, Baden took one last look. The images were slowly fading from the black crystallised wall.

It was almost like they had experienced a vivid, joint hallucination.

"What about the Ebony angle?" asked Jevon.

"What about it?"

Without saying anything, Jevon's look said a lot.

Baden's eyes narrowed. "She's been through enough, man."

"Ebony has a right to know, mate. It can't be coincidence that she's somehow connected to all this."

"For all we know telling her could do more damage than good. You saw her at the festival!"

Thoughtful, Jevon looked back at the cavern. "The last eight months of her life have been questionable. This right here could be the answer to some weird-arse play at work."

Frustrated and angry, Baden pushed past. "You have next to zero control over any of this, and no idea what she's involved in."

Not in the least put off, Jevon followed. "Never underestimate a Starrik. You'd be surprised what I know. This cave could redefine the Casteel name, and the fact that Eb is somehow connected? *Seems* like the next move's ours, mate."

"Ours?" Still battling to digest what had happened, Baden jerked back to stare at Jevon. "How've you got a say in this?"

Jevon's fingers made air quotes around two words. "The *weird* and *unexplained* is my world."

"Maybe we should just shut up, what if someone is killed through this?" argued Baden, wondering how Jevon could somehow sound convincing after what they had just been through.

The straight and narrow road felt like it was crumbling around Baden, leaving a new path, one that was anything but comfortable.

"This kind of thing can't be buried forever, someone needs to step up," said Jevon, obviously still mulling. "Only question is, who's it gonna be?"

Galactic Star Key: Bendon Clarkov
Astral Nav-Coordinates: EAS-APL-4
Data Sequence: 16.0

Storage case in hand, Bendon moved quickly down the track-run toward the Station Personnel Elevator. Flashing his card, he juggled it in the crook of his arm, waiting for the computer to verify his ID. As soon as it opened he was in, quickly hitting D-3, lower Detention Level.

"Hold the elevator!"

Before he could respond a hand appeared, solving the problem. Bendon held his breath, waiting for security to alert, but the two Enforcers flashed their IDs on entry.

"Enforcer Level Five," confirmed the computer. "Access verified."

Instantly the elevator was moving, leaving the three occupants in an uncomfortable silence. Both Enforcers were wearing helmets, something Bendon knew was a clear violation of procedure when entering Detention Level.

"New here, are you?"

The tallest Enforcer answered. "Recent transfers to assist with the Kadra's security detail."

"Interesting." Bendon tilted his head, eyeing the smaller of the two. "There are certain restrictions when enlisting in Astral Guard for Enforcers, size being one. What division did you say you're a part of?"

The smaller of the two began fidgeting, forcing the larger to answer. "The forty-fifth, Ensign." The larger officer nudged the smaller aggressively.

Wide-eyed, Bendon took in their actions. Activating his porta-pad, he held up a map displaying the Southverse Astral State.

"I thought the Forty-Fifth Division was part of the Integration Task force working on bringing in the planet Vorsa." He indicated the astral map. "Right here, see?"

The larger officer glanced at this then looked away leaving the leaner to respond.

"Our work is classified, Ensign, though I am curious over your interest."

"Don't mean to pry." Bendon immediately closed his porta-pad. "I loathe silent elevator rides. Just passing time."

"Passing time?" The leaner tilted his head. "Embracing the human culture?"

"A little," exclaimed Bendon. "You've caught on quick for a recent transfer. I know most of the Enforcers with Level Five clearance and above since senior operatives answer directly to State Commodore Vae'gon."

"How would an Ensign of your rank know this?" queried the tall Enforcer.

Ruffled, Bendon straightened. "I'm personal duty-arm to the Commodore."

"Duty-arm." Immediately the Enforcers looked at each other, but before either could respond the doors opened. Stepping out, all saluted to the waiting Enforcer Noremar.

Bendon handed her the case with a nod.

"Thank you, Ensign." Accepting it, she turned to the doctor at her side. "You may begin immediately, Doctor Venlara."

"Is that the reformer-interface?" Thaytis looked at the case sourly.

"You know it is," snapped Noremar, shoving it into her hands.

"I want to see the Commodore," Thaytis demanded.

"Doctor," Noremar's eyes narrowed dangerously, "that device stands between us and that thing's ability to enter our minds, not to mention …"

"I'm well aware of their capabilities," assured Thaytis loudly. "I don't have the facilities to properly calibrate this type of neural device. If I cannot isolate the exact electrical impulse signature, I'll do more harm than good."

Noremar's eyes narrowed dangerously. "You care for its welfare?"

"I am a Medical Officer to the Galactic Force," snapped Thaytis.

"On service detachment to the Astral Guard while assigned to this system," reminded Noremar. "A reassignment of your own choosing, might I remind you. Best you understand that our division is not restricted by unnecessary practices when dealing with Kadra."

"Unnecessary? My first allegiance is to the preservation of life. Ethical conduct in this matter is in question. This type of neural programming is permanent."

"These things are a product of advanced genetic augmentation," spat the Enforcer, taking a step closer. "You speak as if Kadra have some form of rights? Nothing about them is natural."

"There's a flaw to your assessment," warned Thaytis. "Overwatch cannot be used to hold the Kadra indefinitely. The Galactic Force is to transfer that Kadra back to the High-Throne planet New Hasna, for trial."

"The Eastverse Astral States' lack of leadership was proven the moment they signed a State-Armistice within their own quadrant."

"That Armistice was the first step in ending the Galactic War as well you know. All states then followed."

"The act that crippled us," said Noremar, leaning close. "Signing it led to the amendments that absolved many Kadra Clans of their war crimes. Hasnirians are a species that lack the ability to rule or dispense justice against the Planetary Allegiance's true enemies."

"That is a living, breathing lifeform," spat Thaytis, visibly revving up. "And what's being proposed is wrong, regardless of how we define sentient proof of life. We're no better than the enemy in doing this."

"Proof of …? Ah, I see your dilemma." Noremar ran a hand beneath her chin. "You have two choices, to either follow my orders and perform the task-duty in which the Kadra will most likely survive due to your instinctive abilities as a physician. Or I will have the responsibility passed to another of your staff, someone less qualified but still able."

"And if the Kadra dies?"

"Then it's one less."

Floored, Thaytis swore heartily. "The Galactic Force will launch an investigation upon immoral acts of incarceration, enemy or not."

Noremar did not blink at the warning. "Your ethics may feel shaken, Doctor, but you need to make a choice. Which of these will compromise your code of morality the most?"

"Clearly the Astral Guard is not offering a choice, Enforcer."

Noremar's lips twitched as she nodded, clearly satisfied. "I'm glad we have an understanding. You're dismissed."

Bendon watched Thaytis spin on her heel, moving off stiffly. As he had not been dismissed, he waited.

Still angry, Noremar's glare cut to the two new recruits. "It's regulation for all officers to not have helmets active within Level Five security zones unless authorised."

The taller accepted the reprimand with a nod. "We are aware of that protocol."

"I'm still waiting."

Immediately both activated their helmets, retracting each to their neck braces. Bendon eyed the Lakorians, taking in their wide, fleshy necks, sparse blue-white hair.

"Good, see that you follow procedure." She looked across at Bendon. "Protocol seems to be a problem around here, something I have been coming up against frequently today."

The two Enforcers stood at attention. "Understood, Ma'am."

"Sir will suffice, or Enforcer." Her critical eye travelled to the short Enforcer. "Seems to me Astral Guard's standards have dropped somewhat by the look of your size. Am I correct in assuming you're my missing Lakorian Enforcers for Outcast's security detail?"

"We are, Sir. Processing took time."

"Fine, and since there's been no alert from security, everything must be in order."

The taller Lakorian glanced at his partner, a smile haunting his mouth.

Bendon led the group to the information centre. Astral Guard Inspectors filled the area, the majority at workstations, others processing information on view screens or meeting in clusters. Single file, he led them through, passing before a massive reflective wall at the end, where he halted.

"Sir," he turned to the Enforcer, locking his porta-pad to his belt. "A moment if you please. In regard to the reformer-interface, the use of such technology does breach Neural Control Acts without a proper judgement trial. If Kadra Prime gains knowledge of this, they could see this as an unquestionable violation."

Noremar glanced at her Enforcers. "Wait at the entrance, I require a moment with the Ensign." As soon as they cleared earshot, she spoke brusquely. "You and I both know this Kadra will be dead before anything can go to trial."

Silence dominated for several moments. "Dead, Sir? What of its transfer back to the High-Throne world and the Galactic Force?"

"Commodore Vae'gon places a great deal of trust in you, Ensign."

"Of course, Sir. He changed the course of my life." Tightening his lips, Bendon tried to gauge her meaning. "The Commodore will always have my support to serve."

"I've looked over your Star-Key. I understand we can't choose where we are born and to whom. The Commodore has placed trust in you, made you one of his own by giving you a life, prestige working as his duty-arm."

"Why are you saying this, Sir?"

"He needs your support, all our support, now more than ever. What we face cannot be solved through conventional means, it will take more. Once the extraction of information is done, the Kadra must be disposed of."

"He is the eldest born to the clan of Garrold. Outcast or not, if word gets out ..." Bendon chewed his lip.

"This planet, Earth, what we're trying to accomplish is one of the most important Integration efforts in the galaxy. Securing Earth to sign the Pre-Warp Amendment, advancing it to a warp-capable civilisation, it will lead us to finally locating all twelve Origin worlds."

"The humans," he asked slowly, "are they ready for this? For what is to come, Sir?"

"Our job, Ensign, is to protect them and prepare them. If the Kadra needs to die in order to accomplish this then so be it. Do we have an understanding?"

"Yes, Enforcer." Bendon nodded sternly. "I understand."

After a reassuring nod, Noremar walked ahead. Bendon ran a quick hand over his uniform before following. Nodding to a squad of heavily armed Astral Guard officers, he saw they were clearing each passage, and all detention cells of remaining Global Reach personnel.

When the two came to the Kadra's holding cell, Noremar paused. "Where's the Lakorian Enforcers?"

Bendon followed her into the cell where they were found standing either side of the reinforced enclosure holding the Kadra.

Doctor Venlara was carefully placing the Reformer Interface over the bio-bands on the Kadra's head. When she activated the side panel, Bendon winced, hating the idea but understanding the need.

She continued programming it, each move delicate and precise, linking the unit into the Kadra's state consciousness. Time moved slowly as she made adjustments upon each neural point activator, cyber-screens flashing up and down as she worked.

Commodore Vae'gon entered, Major Rajek at his side, the two watching the intricate procedure.

"Major." Vae'gon glanced briefly at Rajek. "I understand you support the Blades and believe they should be here, but after their last incident, I do not care to recur that performance."

"Understood, Commodore," Rajek inclined his head. "It was simply a recommendation."

"Doctor," called Vae'gon advancing several steps, "whenever you are ready, you may begin to question the Kadra."

Thaytis looked up briefly from another adjustment, giving him a nod. Returning to her work, she activated her hi-cap glove, connecting it with the cyber-visor covering her eyes.

Carefully, she began loading another set of digital screens, controlling each interface separately. "I'm attempting to lock onto the brain's higher functions. The device is almost calibrated, Sir. The only issue I'm experiencing is securing the final lock, somehow the Kadra's—"

Without warning, it began thrashing violently against its bonds, knocking the doctor back. Instantly, the larger Lakorian Enforcer stepped forward, bracing the Kadra's shoulders.

Vae'gon moved to the edge of the cell. "Doctor?"

"I'm ... fine." Rubbing her shoulder, Thaytis prepared to step forward. "It's the neural activators. They're affecting the frontal lobe and need realigning. I'll just need a moment."

Annoyed, she waved at the Lakorian to step back.

Eyes narrowed, Noremar moved closer. "What's on the Kadra's shoulder?" she demanded. "It wasn't there earlier."

Thaytis went still. "I ... I didn't place that device. It looks like a tele-warp badge." Reaching forward, she tried to knock it off, then yelped, "Electric defence charge!"

Instantly the Enforcer drew her weapon, pointing it directly at the Lakorian officer. "What is that?"

Obviously a silent alarm had been triggered, security officers entering the cell to stand beside Vae'gon and Rajek. Each was pointing weapons at the two Lakorian Enforcers.

Before anyone could move, the smaller Lakorian grabbed Bendon, attaching a similar device to his shoulder. Pulling him along, the two backed up.

The taller Lakorian finally broke his silence. "Professor, I think we've overstayed our welcome."

The moment Bendon felt the Lakorian's grip slacken, he headbutted him in the face, struggling to slip his grip.

The face of the Lakorian began to distort, closing in on itself.

"It's a cyber-halo mask," Noremar realised. "He's Moncovian."

"Welcome back, Professor Marzden." Vae'gon recognised the face instantly. "You choose poor allies, I see." His gaze flickered to the larger Lakorian. "And who might you be?"

Magel moved closer to the Lakorian Enforcer. "I learnt long ago to never fully commit to a side. Such acquaintances are of my own choosing."

"Professor," the Lakorian warned. "Get us out of here now!"

Magel eyed Vae'gon while edging closer to the Kadra.

"Stay where you are!" yelled Noremar.

"My dear!" Magel held up a hand. "Calm yourself."

"Marzden!" she warned.

A deadlock ensued, saturating the room with the scent of nerves and adrenalin as each pointed their weapon at a target.

"You'll recall, Commodore," Magel said, holding his position, "that trivial conversation has never been my forte."

"You aren't going anywhere," Noremar vowed. "Return to us the Positronic Drive you stole."

"Stole?" Magel straightened, clearly offended. "What is mine you will never lay eyes on again."

Before anyone could move, the Professor jerked a circular device from his belt, activating and throwing it in the air in one move. Within a breath, it had expanded revealing a portable tele-warp disc. Magel swiped his forearm's porta-unit, and instantly all bodies tagged began to fluctuate.

"Don't shoot!" yelled Vae'gon. "You'll set the room alight with warp-flash!"

Moments later, Magel was drawn and transported through the device, followed by the taller Lakorian Enforcer, and the Kadra.

"Commodore!" Bendon grabbed at his shoulder in desperation. The device was now alight on his shoulder. Major Rajek attempted to pull it free, but his arm was thrown clear, electrified.

Warp-fibres streamed over Bendon's body. There was a flash then a pull. He was struck blind until he materialised in another section of the complex.

Before he could catch himself, Bendon was thrown to his knees and hands, the sheer surprise of the tele-warp taking its toll.

Weapons' fire sounded ahead, and he saw security officers lying face down on the floor. He also saw a plasmic-rifle which was just out of reach. Rolling forward, he attempted to grab it, but was brought up short by a rough hand lifting him upright.

"The less you do, the more likely you'll survive this."

Clarkov gulped as the holo-mask wavered on the large Enforcer, dissolving to reveal his real features, wavy brown hair and ultra-bright blue eyes. "You're Hasnirian?"

"Everyone's from somewhere."

Professor Marzden stuck his head through the circular doorway. "Keldon, I need the duty-arm at least conscious."

"Me?"

"You." Keldon grabbed him by the shoulder. "You're going to release the manual override."

Before he could object, Bendon was shoved down a long corridor, past more unconscious Astral Guard security officers. Ahead was Professor Marzden standing with ... the Kadra.

Instantly Clarkov's legs turned to water. It was still heavily bandaged, though no less intimidating, standing before the Armament Chamber's Seal-Gate.

He knew exactly why they were here. Eyes wide, Clarkov hit panic mode, attempting to pull back, but the one called Keldon's grip was firm. "You're after the Kadra's zaphna rod?"

Keldon shoved him forward. "You catch on quick."

The Professor activated his portal-tool, accessing several layers of cyber-screens, lighting them up around the central control screen that sealed the door. He then began turning screens, moving them back and forth, loading more cyber-tabs, shifting them into place. The process only took several moments.

"Captain," Magel barely glanced up while clucking in disapproval. "You display foolish confidence deactivating your holo-mask."

"Wasn't voluntary," Keldon snapped back. "Vokken thing's defective. Closed off the moment I came through our tele-warp window."

"Interesting." Magel paused in the process of shifting a cyber-tab. "That tells me two things. The Astral Guard security net must have readapted the EM static pulse countermeasures running within this sector, rendering the device inoperable."

"The other?"

"We've far less time than I initially projected carrying out this extraction."

"I could've told you that!" snarled Keldon.

"Bypassing my adaptive counter frequency would've been no easy feat, I assure you!" snapped Magel. "My evaluation, Captain Ryko, you're a victim of chance. Nothing more."

"Want my evaluation?"

"No—"

"You passing failure off on chance, to justify poor performance!"

From his position, Bendon tried to analyse the data stream moving within screens, while ignoring the haunting presence of the Kadra on his right. It was pacing.

"You can't break an automatic screening sequence," he said desperately, trying to think of a way to stall them. "It's an AG-encrypted defence system."

Thoroughly engrossed, Magel ignored him, working intently at the screens, relocating them as required.

"Ah," he sighed. "There we go."

A large circular cyber-window lit up. Bendon goggled, hardly daring to look across. When he did, he saw the panel was now active, ready for input.

The computer's static voice spoke. "Manual screening mode unlocked."

Another click and a second cyber-window generated displaying how to operate the device. Magel looked at Bendon smugly.

"Who said anything about using the automated system?" He stood up, pointed to the door. "Off you go like a good ensign, and place your hand on the screen."

From behind, the one called Keldon gave him an encouraging push. "If you don't mind, we've a taut window here."

Though Bendon struggled, he was no match. Keldon grabbed his arm, placed pressure above the wrist to forcibly splay his clenched hand, laying it against the screen.

Immediately the computer woke up. "Activating bio-map screening."

Magel kept working on the cyber-screen, filing through volumes of streaming data. "The security system is uploading and processing registry ID codes."

"Take your time, Professor," snapped Keldon, rechecking the corridor. "Not like anyone knows we're here."

"Sarcastic wit is of no use here, Captain."

The panel suddenly flashed, signalling it was powering down. Clarkov noticed he had downloaded something. Immediately the Kadra moved forward, thoroughly unnerving him.

"Access denied," announced the computer. "Error AG-147–32. Please observe display instructions."

On a dramatic sigh, Magel stretched his fingers. "Almost there!" Deactivating the screen, he added another. "I have it. Uploading identification screen of the Commodore's bio-map."

The panel continued to flash red for several moments, then the door deactivated opening, and everything shut down.

"Bio-map accepted," stated the computer. "Level Five clearance verified to lethal grade chamber five. Welcome Commodore Vae'gon."

"You used me to gain access to system's registry codes?" spat Bendon, suddenly catching on.

"Yes, Ensign." Magel eyed him critically. "You are but a step in the equation."

The Kadra paced silently up to the door, and both Keldon and Magel stepped aside allowing it to enter first.

Clarkov was truly horrified.

"After you, Ensign?" Keldon gave him another shove into the long chamber.

As soon as he entered, the Professor reset the seal of the door, locking it closed.

"That should hold them for a while," he muttered, then turned to inspect the crowded surrounds, musing, "Astral Guard issue, Armoury Bunker, lethal grade weapons ..." His gaze passed over the diverse weaponry held there.

Clarkov followed his gaze, eyeing the Primordial weapons which had been located only days ago during a deep-sea exploratory mission. They had discovered a submerged research facility, which was currently being studied.

Magel turned to him suddenly. "I don't suppose humans have access to what's in here?"

"It's for their own protection!" Clarkov made a face. "The lockdown of weapons as powerful as these are ..."

Magel held up a hand. "A simple no will suffice."

"The Installation of a lethal grade chamber is clearly the embodiment of trust." Keldon eyed the vast array of Primordial weaponry.

Incensed and scared, Clarkov fired. "You speak of trust? You're the ones who abandoned the Planetary Allegiance, siding against your own kind." His eyes flicked briefly to the Kadra who was moving ahead. "And for what? You don't understand—"

Clearly angry, Keldon shoved Bendon to follow. "Don't spout that Astral Guard propaganda of Vae'gon's to me. You both sound like their puppets."

On a frightened shrug, Clarkov turned back. "You have no idea who he is, and what we stand for. After the Kadra Exodus from the Galaxy, the Planetary Allegiance has adopted and saved more worlds through the Integration Effort than Kadra Prime had ever done in a millennium. We are a galaxy united!"

On an eye-roll, Keldon held up two hands. "Wow, I'm converted!" He then shook his head, expression pitying. "You speak like a true Planetary Allegiance citizen. What you call saving, I call profiteering."

The group moved deeper into the crowded bunker, coming to a balcony that overlooked a lower level. The Kadra was already down the stairs, standing on a large circular platform. In front of him was a spherical-shaped grid-shield that was constantly cycling its settings, protecting the most lethal-grade weapons held in the armoury.

Bendon found himself shoved down the stairs in its wake, to stand on the same platform, next to Magel. The Professor activated his porta-tool, then started reading through the telemetry on a cyber-screen. Nervously, Bendon eyed the Kadra when it started pacing, its movements reminding him of a predator.

As he shifted things around, Magel mumbled to himself. "The connecting grid layer beam is generating a very powerful repulse field ..."

"Can it be dropped?" interrupted Keldon. "Don't make all this for nothing, Professor."

The graviton generator at the base of the platform released strobes of grav-beams.

"You forget!" Magel eyed Keldon. "You're now looking at the acting Commodore of this entire Integration Effort. This chamber belongs to me."

The cycling grid-shield dropped and the group walked through. It was there, just ahead, what they were here for.

Bendon's eyes fell on the zaphna rod hovering within one of the many gravity containment fields, along with several other high-grade weapons of varying, alien design. From back down the corridor came the sound of a large explosion.

"That didn't take long," spat Keldon. "Everyone take cover!"

The moment Astral Guard security officers crested the overlook, they began firing, energy bolts exploding on walls and columns.

Bendon grunted as he was shoved behind a pile of equipment, Keldon covering them both as he drew his side-arm to start firing, the noise of the combined weapons an assault on the senses.

Magel jammed himself beside Keldon. "The grid-shields are initialising a start-up sequence. Once it's fully active—"

"We're vokked!" snarled Keldon.

"Crude but accurate. The security update cycle's locked me out of this chamber's network."

"Already?" Keldon let off a shot, nodding to the right. "Cedos, draw the rod!"

The Kadra did not hesitate, dodging energy bolts in a way that did not seem possible before halting at the grav-beam. Reaching through the gravity wake turned its bandages to tatters, but the hand that gripped the zaphna rod was sound.

The instant the two made contact, the polished black rod's configuration began to alter. Mesmerised, Bendon held his breath as the device transformed in its hand, like it was coming alive, charge reformer ports opening to run its length. An eerie blue-white smoke began pouring like oily, liquid fire, streaming through the air as it turned.

It was like the Kadra and the weapon became one.

Another energy bolt hit close, almost grazing the Kadra's shoulder. Turning, it spun the rod, in the process shifting and expanding its length, striking towards energy bolts on the staff. The instant they made contact, white sparks lit the armoury, the zaphna dispersing them to particles.

Keldon lay down cover fire as the Kadra slid to cover on the opposite guard rail, irritatedly pulling at bandages that had come loose.

"Marzden!" Keldon bellowed. "Where's our exit?"

"Working on it!" Back hunched, the Professor punched away at an advanced looking porta-tool, cringing as bolts continued to explode around him. "We can't tele-warp while inside this armoury. This structure is comprised of duzanium."

"What?!" roared Keldon. "Now you tell me?"

He gave the Kadra a signal and, to Bendon's utter astonishment, it charged forward advancing to the second level as energy bolts struck around it. Kicking off the stairway's guard rail, the Kadra used its elevation to launch over the remaining flight of steps.

In its hands, the zaphna lit up, blue smoke a fierce burn as the Kadra manoeuvred the weapon around its body, deflecting and rupturing a wave of energy bolts on impact. Cowering behind his barricade, Bendon covered his ears against the deafening noise.

On his feet, Magel moved in behind it while Bendon cringed until Keldon grabbed his arm, pulling him along at a fast pace up the stairs, straight into the fire fight.

Hunched, Bendon stumbled forward, briefly noting defensive grid-beams reforming behind. At least there was no way any Assultra Rebels would have the time to extract the remaining Primordial weapons.

The Kadra showed no fear, charging forward, breaking all incoming bolts, vaporising the atmosphere as it moved. The stench of weapons' fire almost choked Clarkov, but he could not take his stinging eyes off that whirling weapon or the Kadra, who was eliminating all bolts before its path, the zaphna truly lethal in its hands.

Many of its bandages had come loose, revealing olive skin. Unexpectedly, it feinted to the right, altering the weapon's configuration to a loose charge cable, whipping it forward doubling the zaphna's length to touch a security officer with a loud crack.

Bendon's eyes goggled. Its body became pure energy, shifting forward in the blink of an eye to materialise mid-air before the officer, ploughing a foot into his chest. The action sent him flying, collecting two of his comrades before all hit wall.

The Kadra was now in the archway amidst Astral Guard security, its zaphna rod reconfigured back into a single-form staff. Sweeping the weapon in an arc, it sent two more officers airborne while rotating its weapon up and across to spear another's plasmic-rifle, causing its power chamber to explode.

Keldon never stopped firing his pistol, working on a group of officers guarding the exit door. Bendon stuck close, not wanting to take a stray bolt. As the two huddled near a rail he recoiled, noticing where the zaphna weapon had impacted. The material was still smouldering, melted where the two met.

Though he resisted, Keldon moved him through another chamber's entrance. Bendon grunted as he was thrown from his feet, skidding across the deck, something heavy and mobile collecting him. It took him a moment to realise what had impacted his captor, throwing him into a nearby wall.

"Major Rajek!"

In full hybrid Blade armour, the Major grabbed Clarkov, shoving him behind. Speaking through a digitally enhanced vocal processor, he ordered, "Stay behind me."

Rajek then faced the Kadra, who had managed to clear the room of all remaining security officers and was turning to face its final opponent.

A tense standoff took place, Bendon holding his breath, eyeing the bandaged Kadra. He could see more of its skin, even part of its mouth, which was held tight with tension.

Shoulders back, Rajek met its stare, segments of his silver and grey armour glinting in the low light. Eyes narrowed, he measured the Kadra, neither advancing nor retreating, almost like he was goading it by not moving.

Bendon knew additional officers would not be far behind, but until then it was just Rajek and the Kadra … with its weapon.

The moment he spotted a dropped side-arm, Bendon slid down the wall, wiggled sideways grabbing it, thinking maybe he could help the Major. Hands shaking, he lifted the gun, aiming at the enemy …

"Professor!" yelled Keldon.

"We're clear!" Magel threw a tele-warp rim high in the air which activated on point, powering up.

The Major instantly activated his phaser-blade from his weapon gauntlet, plasma energy racing to form an energised cutting edge, but warp streams were already surrounding the Professor, taking him first, then Keldon.

Bendon cringed, watching them begin to flow around him. With no other choice, he pointed the side-arm at the device on his arm, closing his eyes he grit his teeth, pulling the trigger.

The bolt took a chunk of flesh, left him screaming in agony on the floor, weapon dropped as Astral Guard Enforcers poured into the room followed by Lieutenant Noremar and Commodore Vae'gon, all taking aim at the Kadra who was now surrounded by warp streams.

The last left standing was the protector of those that had come to its rescue. Unable to halt the Assultra Rebels' dematerialisation protocol, Bendon caught a glimplse of radiating particles phase-shifting from the zaphna rod to coalesce over its body. This generated the beginnings of an energised armoured exo-suit before full reintegration.

Moments later it was gone, body absorbed into the tele-warp rim, the device vanishing, engulfed in warp-orbs, leaving only traces of energised fibres dissipating in the atmosphere.

The room was abruptly silent, Enforcers standing and staring at the empty space in shock at what had just transpired. Rajek spun to Bendon, kneeling beside him.

"Fast thinking," he said, inspecting the wound. "Surface wound, doesn't look too serious. Calling in an MO."

"Just feels serious, Sir."

The Major pulled him upright to stand on his feet as the Commodore walked up. Bendon forced himself to at-stance despite the plasma-burn gripping his shoulder and arm.

"At ease, Ensign. You alright?"

"Sir." Clarkov looked around, shaking his head. "What of Global Reach? How can it be launched in such a short amount of cycles? The Kadra ..."

Vae'gon stepped forward, eyeing the final warp-particles evaporating in the atmosphere.

"We go ahead," vowed Vae'gon. "Postponing the launch date is not an option. Not while I'm in command." Looking up, his hard gaze included the Enforcers and all others present. "That Kadra Outcast has illegally entered our Galaxy and will be treated to the full force of Astral Guard." He glanced back at Bendon. "You ask what is to be done, Ensign? We do what we must. Like all Kadra who violate our laws, it will be hunted down and brought to justice."

Galactic Star Key: Baden Casteel
Astral Nav-Coordinates: EAS-APL-4
Data Sequence: 17.0

When his phone vibrated again, Baden snuck a look, trying to keep it out of view of Mrs Gault. Since there was a controversial documentary playing about the Second World War, he had pretty good cover behind Adam Joyce's sturdy frame.

The text was from Jevon, the third one in ten minutes. He was now waiting out the front of school.

Baden jammed his own back in his pocket, trying to focus on the video playing. Written across a whiteboard up the front were the words: *Impact of the First and Second World Wars. Did they change the planet for good or for bad?*

Baden slumped back in his seat, picking up his tablet computer to eye the two columns of pros and cons. Swiping a finger across the screen, he began scrolling through the notes he had taken during the video.

Like she could sniff out disinterest, his history teacher straightened in her seat, pausing the video from her laptop.

"I can see wandering eyes," Mrs Gault warned. "I suggest you all use this time wisely, or tonight you will be watching this again looking for the information you need to gather for the assignment."

As she continued the video, Baden tried to get comfortable in his seat, fighting thoughts about the caves and what had happened the day before.

"Psst! Bay?"

He knew that voice, but ignored it, hunching over his desk, continuing to type notes onto his tablet computer.

Small paper balls began hitting him from behind. Gritting his teeth, he eyed the ones that bounced onto his desk. Sweeping them off, Baden glanced up to see if old Gaulty had noticed, but she appeared engrossed in the documentary.

Another hit the back of his head, rolling into his shirt collar. Agitated, he swung around slowly, trying not to draw attention.

Alexa Noble glared at him, leaning on her elbows. "I need to talk to you after class!"

Furious, Baden whispered harshly. "You know the rule! Text me. Good luck if I reply."

Alexa rolled her eyes. "I have! You've been ignoring my texts and ducking calls."

"You should probably stop wasting your credit."

"Look, I backed off after what happened at the Festival last week." Alexa leaned in, tucking her short, blonde hair behind an ear. "What I have to say can't be put off any longer."

The scrape of a chair told him Mrs Gault was on her feet. "Baden, turn around!"

"Roger that." Baden turned back to see her peering sternly over her glasses.

He knew Alexa, knew she wasn't the type to let a matter drop. No doubt she'd bail him up after class, try and involve him in some weird venture. One thing the past had taught him was to stay clear of the Nobles.

There was just one problem. Kevin. Could this be tied to his entry at the Youth Inventors contest at the Festival? Fuming, Baden sat through the rest of the video not taking in a thing.

When the credits started rolling, he sighed in relief. Turning off the video Mrs Gault stood up to address the class.

"For those who were paying attention, it's easy to see these two global events impacted and altered our world in a fundamental way. It has even been theorised we could have restarted our calendar at the end of World War Two. Mr Casteel?" Looking over her glasses once again, she pointed in his direction. "Do you agree?"

She was pissed now. The teacher with tuckshop arms that wobbled whenever she moved seemed to always have it in for him.

A smart-arse remark would land him in detention, and he didn't feel capable of anything smarter, the result a mute silence.

"Baden, focus!" She snapped her fingers, clearly frustrated. "I've been lenient over the last couple of weeks due to your family situation, but you need to get your head back in the game and move on. You need to pay attention!"

A bright flash of anger filled him, bringing with it bitter words that wanted to rush from his mouth. Biting down hard, Baden forced them back. The only place that would land him was in detention.

"I'm waiting," she said.

An unexpected voice charged to his rescue, one he could have done without.

"To be honest," began Alexa Noble, "I think this whole assignment is way off base."

"Off base?" Baffled, Mrs Gault appeared to gather herself. "I don't believe I asked for your input Ms Noble. "From what I can see you don't agree with any of this school's curriculum, and that's a pattern that vexes me greatly."

"Don't get me started on that." Alexa sat back fiddling with a pen, obviously happy to have the floor. "I just think this assignment should be focusing on the next global event that will change the world we live in. We should take our history, what we've learnt, to evolve us as a race to become a better civilisation."

Baden heard students muttering and slumped further in his seat. She was at again.

"Many would not agree with you Ms Noble," Mrs Gault snapped. "Wars are not the answer to resolve our world's problems."

"Oh, I'm not talking about war. I'm talking of events on a global scale that impact the majority of people on our planet. Events that change us and we know from that day forward we will never live again as we used to."

At her wits' end, Mrs Gault turned away. "This subject is the study of history, not philosophy, Ms Noble. Your father's homeschooling is not welcome in my class. I have warned you on several occasions, as have other teachers, to not bring up his ideals at this school."

"You sound very defensive. I'm curious why a lot of people react to change like this. Or even a different way of thinking."

"The only different way of thinking you need to worry on is if you will be sitting in detention at the end of today."

"But I haven't finished answering your question."

Mrs Gault took off her glasses, rubbed her forehead. "Ms Noble, I won't indulge you anymore. I will see you after class."

Baden heard Alexa heave a huge sigh while throwing her pen on the desk. He had seen this play out so many times in the two years since she'd left behind homeschooling to come here. Alexa had just never learnt when to shut up.

The moment the bell rang for the end of class, Mrs Gault called, "Don't forget these assignments are due next Tuesday. This is a major assessment, people, so I suggest you apply yourselves."

Baden closed down his tablet computer, grabbing his few belongings while kicking in his seat.

"This won't take long," Alexa grumped. "I'll see you outside in five."

Baden shrugged. "Good luck with that." About to turn, he felt rather than saw Mrs Gault walking up behind him.

"Goodbye, Baden."

He took her hint, moving after the last students into the hall then down to the lockers.

"Incoming, bitch!"

Baden had a moment to brace himself before a body used his shoulders as a ramp to launch itself into the air. His head hit the locker, but his bigger concern was the juggle to try to save his tablet computer.

"He flies in catching a screamer!" Lance landed, mobile in hand, having snapped himself in the air. "Damn Cass, did you catch the height? Twelve foot in the air, easy!"

On an inward groan, Baden stretched his back. "You've the blood of an AFL star."

"I call it as I see it, Cass. Your shoulders are a wide load like your uncle's, you can take a hit." He then patted Baden's head soothingly. "Too bad you didn't inherit any of his other genetic advantages."

"He kept growing after eighteen, so suck it. I ain't done."

"Face it." Lance burst out laughing, flashing the screen of his mobile before Baden. "You've peaked, man. That neck of yours must get a daily workout looking up at me."

"We'll see in a couple of years." He eyed the pic which saw him scrabbling to save his stuff, Lance in mid-air. "How the hell did you manage to score that photo?"

"I got skills, man. Anyhow, the look on your face alone was worth it." Lance swiped the screen. "I'm heading this one up as my DP on Facey! For sure it'll grab some likes."

"Don't you get tired of posting your entire life on that thing?"

"Everyone who's anyone's on Facebook, bro."

"Sure, stalking it with the best of them."

Lance laughed. "You're in the minority here. I'm as normal as a fart surprise."

"Right." Baden unlocked his locker, hauling out his backpack. "Life always makes sense when someone's comparing themselves to a lump of crap."

Face screwed, Lance looked up from his mobile. "What?"

"Fart surprise? Get it?" Baden eyed the blank face. "It's more than your casual passing of wind."

At his wits' end, Baden demonstrated with a hand something shooting from his arse.

The instant Lance cottoned on, his eyes flared. "As in product of Uranus? Flunk a dunk? Give birth to a food baby?"

"Sank in finally!" Baden slapped Lance on the shoulder. "'Bout time, only took you half a year, you're improving!"

"I've been throwing that term around thinking it was one of those unexpected farts." Lance laughed at himself good naturedly. "You know, the one that can't be tamed."

"I know." Chucking books into his backpack, Baden sighed. "It used to piss me off, then it just got funny." When Lance's mobile rang the two glanced at it, Baden spotting the words *my bitch*. "How do you get away with calling Cathy that?"

"You've got your assets." Lance cancelled the call, sliding it in his back pocket. "The size of my dick's mine. You wanna hear the triple combo I got her doing now? It's the order that'll get ya."

Horrified, Baden held up a hand. "Nope! Your twisted sex adventures will land you with the most creative kinds of STDs. I'm surprised the thing hasn't fallen off."

"Normal has strings attached. Cath knows I'm not," he paused, obviously trying to get the word right, "monogamous. Gotta keep things interesting, trick it up yah know, unlike your straightforward platonic conquests."

"I dunno how you do it." Baden leaned his backpack against the locker. "Just dealing with one chick is a mind funk."

Lance offered a suggestive eyebrow wiggle. "Threesomes make it easier!"

"Okay," Baden slammed his locker, threw his backpack over his shoulder. "Now I'm wondering if you're full of it."

Lance's phone rang again, which he ignored as the two moved off.

"Aren't you going to answer? She'll be pissed."

"Nah, she can wait." Lance shrugged his shoulders as they moved through the students. "Treat 'em mean keep 'em keen, bro."

Ahead, he spotted Kevin as the hall started to clear. His backpack looked twice as full, but then again he was a straight-A student.

"Chinksta man!" Lance bounded forward happily, rubbed Kevin's head.

"Donkey Kong!" Kevin yelled in return, shoving him off, grinning.

"You're both idiots," Baden laughed.

"How's the liver?" Lance quipped. "Your skin's looking a little yellower than usual."

"Sorry, I missed what you said." Kevin stared hard at Lance's hand. "Couldn't hear you over those dragging, bleeding knuckles."

Baden sighed, dumping his backpack, seeing this would take a while. "You two spend half the day trying to one-up each other."

"Ethnic slurs are what keeps this bro-ship afloat, yah wanksta." Lance tapped Kevin's head. "And this mind sharp. Come to think of it, I'm the reason he's a genius."

After slamming his locker, Kevin hefted his backpack, signalling he was ready. "Nice try, but that won't get you any dollars when I make it big."

"Kevo, man, would I ever ask?" Lance's mobile started ringing, cutting him off as he glanced at it.

"For the love of god, answer your woman," Baden growled, shoving Lance against a locker, one of the doors catching the edge of his shirt.

"Hey, man!" As Lance pulled free, he ripped a hole, revealing something nasty. "Easy on the merchandise."

"What is the go with that?" Kevin asked, pulling a face.

Annoyed, Lance pulled up his shirt, eyeing the weeping cut. "Nothin'. It's healing, if Mr McShovin' over here doesn't break it open."

Doesn't look that way, thought Baden. It was the same wound he had seen on Lance earlier in the week. "I told you to get that … whatever the hell it is, checked. It looks infected."

"Time heals all wounds, or something to that effect." Lance pulled his shirt back down. "Give it another week. Gotta lay off the gym, let the immune system kick in."

"Immune system?" Kevin winced.

"Dude." Baden shook his head. "Your immune system ain't gonna do squat. You need antibiotics along with a skin graft."

"That's bitch talk." Lance pulled his phone from his pocket when it started ringing again. "Suppose she's been dangling long enough. Catch you on the flip side, men." He grinned, turning to walk in the opposite direction. "Yo, baby, you missing me? Nah, nah, just rolling with the crew … what? The reception in the school's archaic …"

"He better not do anything with that chick." Baden shook his head. "He's probably contagious."

"Guess we'll find out how bad she can be," agreed Kevin.

As the two headed down the hall, Baden felt a kernel of guilt wind through his stomach. "Thanks for doing this. Jev's been on my case since yesterday, texting me hourly."

"Hey, I heard money, so lay it on me. Nothing more demoralising than being a start-up inventor trying to land a break."

Baden had a good idea what Kevin was getting at. "How much of your savings did you blow on that invention?"

"The whole nine yards."

"Serious?" Baden paused. "Tell me you didn't invest your inheritance? That was over twenty grand!"

"You gotta believe." Kevin kept right on walking. "I was really riding on at least getting third place."

"Bye bye uni fund." Baden pulled a face. "When they cancelled all events at the Festival, it must have been like taking a bullet."

"A year's work down the drain and zero dollars." Kevin sighed heavily. "I'll get a scholarship; the money was really for living expenses. Now I'll have to work and study."

"Does your dad know?"

"I'm still breathing, so no. Hopefully I can get some funds back in the account before the bank closes it."

"Good luck when he sees your next bank statement."

"If only things had played out differently. All I needed was to showcase my work with the right people. That was truly one of the worst nights of my life, period."

"You're preaching to the choir man, just ask my cuz."

"Oh wow." Kevin froze, clearly remorseful. "Okay you win. Your problems are a lot bigger than what I got going on."

"It's not a competition, man."

"No form of justification will save me now. I just wanted to impress the right people. It would've been good to be recognised."

"I'm more interested in why that idea took every cent you have."

Realigning his thoughts, Kevin answered without concentrating. "Well, we had to do preliminary trials before we got a stable prototype—"

"We?" Baden pulled him up. "I thought this was just you."

"Oh." Kevin laughed nervously, obviously caught. Shuffling his feet, he tried again, "We, as in me and the additional voices running around my head."

"Nice try but your poker face is literally non-existent. And whenever you're lying your pitch goes way up, chick-like, not to mention your left eye starts twitching repeatedly."

"Eye twitching?" Kevin poked at it curiously.

"There it goes again."

"Hey ... I've got allergies!"

"Allergies, my arse. This better not have anything to do with Alexa." Baden swore angrily as Kevin dodged his stare. "Don't tell me you two have been working together on this?"

"Alright then I won't."

Baden walked out the entrance, pushing the door so hard it bounced off the stopper on the wall.

"Testing the door's durability?" Kevin jested weakly.

"The only sure way is ramming your head into it. How could you let her suck you in?"

As the door closed behind, a droll voice called out, "Howdy boys."

Baden turned to see Alexa sitting on one of the concrete bollards lining the entry to the school. Pushing off with her hands, she joined the two.

Baden glanced across the car park to see Jevon's red ute. "Dude, head over to Jev, this won't take long."

"Wait." Alexa grabbed Kevin's arm. "This involves him, too."

"Haven't you done enough to him? Kevin's giving me the crystal, I'll give it back to you. Then you and he can go your separate ways."

"What've you told him?" Alexa turned on Kevin.

"I know all about the growth crystal," Baden interrupted. "That Kevin spent every cent of his inheritance trying to win at the Festival."

For a moment, Alexa chewed on a nail. "Some mistakes were made, I know, but in the end …" She shook her head. "Bay, it's not from a growth vein crystal. Hard to explain."

"You're so cracked out!" She was trying to snow him like she had Kevin. Baden could see it in her eyes. "They're the only known type that hold condition out of the rivers and caves."

"Apparently not." On that, she smiled widely. "There's so much more to this Bay. We really need to talk."

Every instinct he possessed told him he was on the doorstep of another bizarre situation, that he should just keep walking. Looking at Kevin, he eyed the other's sheepish expression.

"Well." Kevin shrugged. "You wanted to know where all my money went."

"I can't believe I'm still standing here." He glared at Alexa. "Why does this sound like something the both of you shouldn't be getting involved in?"

Kevin stepped forward, frowning. "We haven't broken any laws. At least, not really. Just some broken dreams along with my deceased bank account."

"Bay," Alexa touched his arm, "I know your family and mine aren't crazy about one another, but they've worked together when larger concerns are at play. This is one of them."

"Stop calling me Bay," he grumbled, having a good idea what she was about to bring up.

"My dad was there," she reminded. "The night your mum disappeared. He was the one who found her."

"So he found her." Baden did not want to be reminded of that again, not after reliving it not so long ago. "What's that got to do with anything?"

"It's how he found her, Bay, and where."

The three spun at the blast of a horn, which then began rhythmically beeping from the car park. Glancing over, Baden spotted Jevon's waving arm and was uncomfortably reminded of his surrounds and the other students looking at them curiously.

"We'll deal with this tomorrow. Jev's waiting." Baden slung his backpack over his shoulder. "We're heading over to Kevo's. He needs a favour."

On a broad grin, Alexa grabbed hold of Kevin's arm. "Perfect, that's where we need to go. We'll meet you there in ten. Come on, handsome." She started dragging him after her.

"What?" Baden stood blinking as the two raced down the steps until another beep from Jevon's ute drew his attention. Jogging down after them, he eyed the ute's lights, how they were flashing and attracting the attention of every student in range.

"Where's he going?" Jevon burst out as Baden opened the passenger door. "I thought you made good on this arrangement?"

Baden threw his backpack into the tray. "I did, it's still on. We'll meet them at his joint, looks like I'm coming along."

"Come off it?" Jevon laughed. "You're catching a ride with me?"

Baden peered into the rubbish, dust and grime coating the cabin of the ute. "I've had my shots, and it's only a five-minute drive. How bad could it be?"

After climbing in gingerly, Baden slammed the door, cringing as Jevon roared the engine to life.

"Aren't you still on your P plates?" he asked. "I never see them up."

Jevon laughed, backing out. "Their life expectancy is always short-lived in here. The last pair eroded."

Baden fought not to touch anything. "Probably because this thing's bacteria central. Has it ever been cleaned?"

"Cleaning's is for people with too much time on their hands." Jevon grinned impudently. "Besides, a place like this toughens the immune system. That's a scientific fact, mate."

"If that's a fact then I'm a germaphobe. A divider between me and everything in here'd be great."

"Right-e-o Captain Perfection. Life lessons from a sixteen-year-old." Jevon laughed good-naturedly, his elbow resting on the window ledge. "Boy, do I remember those days when I had all the answers ... what a trip that was."

"Did you hit your head or something?"

Jevon glanced across, shrugging. "You've got a smart mouth. Let's just say life doesn't always go to plan, or the way you think it will."

This was a first for Baden, noticing that beneath Jevon's carefree attitude lurked more. He had layers ... even his eyes had narrowed. "What do you mean?"

"Like getting out of this place."

"You mean Freestone?"

Expression reflective, Jevon turned a corner, following Baden's instruction. "You know, real stuff ... there's gotta be something more out there." He gestured wide. "The real world."

"This isn't real enough for ya?" Baden looked around. "Why haven't you left? You seem like the kinda guy that needs to cut loose, get out for good."

"That's not what I mean." Jevon slowed, letting a couple of kids cross the street. "The way most of us live, not many get to make a difference, or even have a choice in the matter."

"You gearing up to be some kind of activist?" Baden pointed to a turn up ahead. "Make a right."

"Activist?" Jevon laughed. "Hardly. I'm talking about that subconscious voice that sneaks in when your mind starts to wander. Questioning the future, what you're supposed to do."

Baden goggled for moment, wondering if Jevon was serious, or just playing with him.

"Don't look at me like that." Jevon laughed even harder. "I just don't like feeling boxed in, like we're conditioned to accept the way things are, the way the world is. Go to school, get the job, attract a woman, add some kids."

"It's how the human race keeps on keeping on."

"Yeah, maybe. I don't know." Jevon looked out the side window. "Which house is it?"

"The yellow one on the right down the end of the street." Baden glanced sideways, pondering what Jevon had said, having no idea if he was being sarcastic or serious. "This is exactly what I mean." Jevon eyed the houses lining the street, shoving back his hair when the breeze ruffled it. "We live in such a monotonous world, like a hidden curse, programming us to such a degree we can't even identify it. The world doesn't accept free thinkers, so people like me gotta learn to change to exist, like wearing a mask."

"Mask?" Baden found the idea sickening. "I dunno where you're going with this. The meaning of life stuff on a Friday afternoon is a little heavy-handed for me."

"Forget I mentioned it." Jevon grinned, but it looked forced. "Just thinking out loud, mate."

"Has this got something to do with what happened at the cave yesterday?"

"Don't worry." Jevon's hands gripped the steering wheel. "Uncle Rick put the fear of the Almighty into me, cue in his usual shut-up-and-don't-talk-about-it speech."

"Should be used to that one by now, huh?"

"A total pro."

"You agreed not to talk about it." Baden wanted to make certain.

"I haven't." Jevon slanted a look sideways. "You checking up?"

"Maybe. We don't need any more trouble."

"Don't you wonder how big this all is? Where it could lead?"

"Nope. He completely shut us down, didn't want a bar of what we saw."

"Government seizing his land sounds a little extreme," said Jevon, thoroughly frustrated. "The damn rings were right in front of the man when he let loose with that spiel. Playing the ignorant card won't get the Casteel name far."

"He's under a tonne of pressure, stuff we don't know about. Until he tells us otherwise, we do as he says, so let it go." Baden pointed to the yellow house. "It's right there."

Jevon turned on an indicator, pulled his ute onto the nature strip before Kevin's house. "One thing I really don't get, Bay. That cave is clearly worth a mint, more than you or I can process. All of your family's money issues, and I know you've got lots, would be gone." He snapped his fingers. "Just like that, that's the true spin he seems to be missing."

Baden had a feeling where Jevon was heading with this. "Don't you bring up Ebony."

On an eyeroll, Jevon leaned across to slam a fist against the glove box, opening it. Baden recognised Ebony's mobile as Jevon snatched it out, pocketing it equally fast.

"She seems to be right in the middle of this," Jevon muttered before climbing out.

"You said," Baden slammed the ute door, "that this had nothing to do with Ebony. Why've you got her phone?"

"Mate, I know what you're going to say but something happened at her apartment yesterday. What's on this phone could be important. Ground-breaking."

"Then why isn't Ebony with you?"

"There's reasons ... nothing I want to go into right now. Just know I've got her back in this. All the bases covered."

Mouth a flat line, Baden narrowed his eyes. "In other words, you stole it."

"Stole is such an incriminating word. Loaned, borrowed, that's much more my territory."

"Fine." Baden yanked his mobile from his pocket. "I'll message Nina. She can word up Ebony then they can deal with it and you."

Before he sent the text, Alexa pulled into the drive on her bike, dumping it on the lawn. Kevin came in after her on his skateboard.

Kicking it into his hand, he headed up the path, giving everyone gathered a head nod to follow.

When Alexa bound ahead, letting herself in the back gate, Baden grit his teeth. She obviously knew her way around, and was comfortable enough to just barge in. Kevin looked over his shoulder, holding the gate for the other two.

Baden paused, phone in hand. "If you keep pushing this, Starrik, the answers might not be good. Why keep forcing it? What do you get?"

For a moment Jevon fidgeted, obviously pinned. "I dunno. I'm flying blind, working off a gut feeling, but something tells me if I don't push now, none of us will know the truth."

Baden watched Jevon stalk through the gate, into the backyard. For a moment, he and Kevin eyed each other, his friend clearly at a loss as to what this was about.

"I'll just be a sec. Go in." Baden re-read the message he was sending to Nina and, after a moment's hesitation, he pressed send before slipping his mobile back into his pocket.

Boba, the Zhengs' Golden Chow Chow, greeted him exuberantly in the backyard. Running around madly, he picked up his toy duck, ready for a play.

"Not now bud. Got things to do."

Alexa shoved open the back door. "You coming or what?"

"You know your way around here," he commented, climbing the short ramp. Walking through the laundry, he did not even glance at the piles of washing waiting to be done.

"Kevo's parents consider me part of the family, if you must know." Alexa charged down the hall after Kevin. "I babysit now and then, too. So we're cool."

At his door, Kevin entered a code in the handle, then turned it. By the time Baden got there, Jevon was standing in the centre, the only free space.

"It's like NASA in here," he muttered. "The electricity needed to supply this room alone must up the dollar on your folk's power bill."

His awe was understandable. Kevin's room resembled a miniature tech lab, complete with a custom-built workstation. The main monitor to his computer was surrounded by two more either side, currently powered down, shelves of spare parts, or what Baden assumed were computer parts. Above Kevin's bed was what he classed defunct equipment, or 'just in case'. Alongside this was a series of tablet computers which he always seemed to be stripping for parts.

With a sheepish smile, Kevin looked at Alexa. "I've recently found a source of power that's pretty favourable."

"Solar? I didn't see any panels installed on your roof."

"Nah, it's like an alternative source. Let's just say I'm trialling something cutting edge, and leave it there."

At that moment, Baden's mobile vibrated, and he knew before looking it would be Nina, could almost feel her wrath. Pulling it from his pocket, he sighed. She was picking up Ebony from the farm then coming to Kevin's. There were lots of exclamation marks on the end.

Jevon obviously sensed the urgency because he quickly shoved Ebony's phone under Kevin's nose while he was booting his computer via some sort of custom-modified touchscreen pad.

Bored, Alexa lounged against the doorframe. Baden briefly eyed Kevin's half-open closet filled with an array of either forgotten or failed experiments. Some even he had not seen.

Jevon leaned across Kevin's desk to run a hand over the wall. "Why've you lined this with something metallic?"

Before Kevin could answer, Baden jumped in. "Don't get him started, it'll take forever and you won't understand half of it. Short answer is it keeps him off their radar."

A huge sigh came from Alexa at the doorway. "This looks like it's going to take some time. Bay, come on, let's go."

Eyes already glazing into his world of science, Kevin glanced up. "Yeah Cass, prepping this will take some time for sure."

It felt wrong. Baden's gut told him to stay put, not get involved, but there was no fighting his curiosity. Following Alexa out of the room, the two moved down the hall to the door that led to the Zhengs' basement.

The first thing Baden noticed was the cold. Every breath he took released condensation in the air. "What's with the low-riding temperature back here?"

Alexa touched the door handle, then jerked back. "I'm not really sure."

"Is it locked?"

"No," she said, rubbing her hands together, shivering. "It's just freezing. But the knob was turning."

She tried again, pulling her sleeve over her fist to turn the handle. "It's stuck," she grunted.

Annoyed, Baden tried to push her aside. "Let me have a look."

"No!" Alexa kept turning the handle, fighting him and the door. "This's beyond ridiculous."

Despite his misgivings, Baden got in position, aiming his shoulder at the door. "Alright, let's give this bastard a go on three. You turn it, I'll give it some encouragement."

When he rested his shoulder against the wood, he almost pulled back. It was freezing to the point it made his arm tingle.

"Okay," Alexa began, "One, two, and be ready, three!"

Together they shouldered the door. Baden felt it give, heard a strange cracking, like a seal breaking, followed by an eerie scraping of something sharp over the cement floor. About to step in, the two jumped back as shards of ice showered from the doorframe above. Baden could hear it scattering in the darkness, tumbling down the barely visible staircase.

A shiver tracked down his back, and it wasn't just from the cold. "Okay," he muttered, "this isn't at all creepy."

Alexa frowned, leaning forward. "There's a light switch on the right, just near you."

Gingerly, he peered into the darkness, then felt with his hand until he had it. It was wet, slick with ice. About to try and flick it, he pulled back, cursing.

"Did it shock you?"

"Nah." Baden blew at his fingers. "More like a cold burn. It's covered in ice." He began backing up. "Let's just—"

"No!" Alexa moved to the edge of the first step. "Can you see that?"

Hesitant, Baden looked down. He could just see the floor, and speckles of light reflecting off what appeared to be a large mound of ice.

"Judging by the look on your face," he said, "that isn't supposed to be there."

"Come on." Alexa cautiously took the first few steps. "I was literally in here this morning, dropping by to meet up with—"

Both halted at the halfway point when the basement floor lit up, a pale luminescing glow coming from what appeared to be a thin sheet of ice covering it. The glow was strong enough to cast numerous long shadows that seemed to stretch across the floor like they were searching for something.

"Alexa ..." Baden finally managed.

"This hasn't happened before." Again, she started down.

Baden followed, cursing his own curiosity. At the bottom of the narrow staircase he took a moment, barely believing what he was seeing. The entire basement was engulfed in frozen ice mounds, some small, others up to his knees. Even though he had never been in there, it was obviously not the norm. It looked more like a frozen cave than a basement.

"Alexa?" he hissed, fighting to see her as she became little more than a slowly moving shadow. She was walking toward one of the ice mounds with a distinctive glow. He could hear the ice cracking with every step she took. Taking the plunge, he stepped onto the ice, following the instinct to stand beside her.

She was staring at a large portable containment case set in the centre of the basement. Looking through the transparent material, he instantly recognised a growth vein crystal. It seemed to be connected to a series of wires. Crouching, he thought he could even see energy trickling inside.

"Hey." Baden pointed to one of the larger cables at the base of the unit which was frozen in ice, appearing to be connected to a makeshift power box. "What's this?"

Instead of answering, Alexa reached out a hand toward an icy screen.

Alarmed, Baden shoved her back. "What's going on here?" When she did not respond, he gave her a shake, not liking the slack expression on her face. "Come on, what's up with you?"

The last seemed to snap her back, her glazed eyes clearing. "I ... I don't know. What just happened?" she stuttered.

"You just took a trip, and not a good one." A strange prickle crawled the back of his neck. "Start at the beginning. Where did you even get hold of a growth crystal?"

"Umm." She looked groggy to Baden, much like he was starting to feel, as she moved around the case. "If you're thinking I stole it from the Solomons you're wrong."

"Then where?"

"The Solomons aren't the only ones who have access to Skyfall Mountain. There are three main caves that lead deep into the mountain's caverns. These are all enriched with crystals, and there's many growth vein deposits."

"Okay." Baden thought back to what had happened only yesterday with Jevon, and for the first time wondered if coincidence was even possible. There seemed no escaping the caves and what was in them.

"The three Founding Frontier brothers were entrusted with the ownership to protect the caves," Alexa said. "That includes our families. They were first to form the Fellowship here in Freestone."

One word caught Baden. "Protect?"

"Yes, a protection that spans generations." Alexa eyed the ice mound. "This growth vein crystal is from my family's northern cave, Bay. The Solomons were entrusted to the southern, and your family have the eastern."

For a long moment, Baden digested this, thinking of his uncle's hard face. Was this the reason he reacted to the caves that way? Lost his head over anything to do with them?

If it was, that seemed good enough reason for Baden to not get caught up in this, and to choose what he said to Alexa wisely. Especially after what had happened with him and Jevon yesterday.

"Hello?" Alexa waved a hand in his face. "Are you tripping like I was?"

"How do I know if any of this is true? Why hasn't my mum or my uncle spoken about any of this?"

"Because of the abductions," Alexa said. "After that, everything changed. From what I can gather, some kind of agreement was made to keep it from us, the next generation."

"Listen to yourself, none of this makes sense. Why drag me into this now?"

"You've made your position clear, believe me." Alexa leaned forward, bracing her hands on her knees to examine the ice mound. "I'm here because of what happened to Ebony."

The cold of the basement was penetrating, but it was nothing to the ball of ice her words produced in his stomach. "Her abduction, you mean?"

"No, not that. This began a long time before that. It connects to her adoption, Bay, and whoever made contact with her eight months ago. Somehow, they've changed everything in the Fellowship, and even though I know you want to stay out, you really can't."

"What do you mean?"

"Because they'll be coming for us next."

"They?" Baden almost laughed, crossing his arms, rocking back on his heels. "Who are *they*?"

"You wouldn't believe me if I told you."

Baden glanced at the containment case. "Is this why you and Kevo have been experimenting on crystals?"

"Kevin's been helping me to artificially recreate the cave's natural environment to make them grow so we can study them. There are so many grades of crystal, Bay. This particular type draws in all forms of energy."

"Yeah, Kevin drained my mobile at school," he remembered uneasily.

"That was a spore crystal grown from here. It does far more then draw in energy, Bay. Kevin doesn't fully understand, but it's almost like it's alive, a form of organism you could say. He's been testing with what is called attuned vibrations, trying to communicate with it."

"Talking crystals?"

"I'm serious. You can deny everything as much as you want but this morning, this basement looked nothing like this. No ice, just the containment case."

Baden looked around. "What did Kevin bring to school then?"

"He was never meant to use it at the Festival. I didn't agree to that."

There was a pain building in Baden's head, one he was fighting to ignore. "You two are clearly out of your league with this. That containment case isn't containing anything. You need to pull the plug on all of this."

Alexa shook her head, then stumbled, forcing Baden to grab her.

"Your eyes look weird," he said, watching them close, noticing the green seemed to be trembling. "A lot weirder than normal."

"Feels like a drill is boring into my skull," she began, shaking her head. "I think you're right. Kevin installed a manual kill switch under the unit."

"It's covered in ice," he remembered. "We'll need something to chip through it."

"Pull the latch that unclips the cable. That should disconnect it."

Baden forced a nearby work drawer open, grabbing two long screwdrivers. He passed one over to Alexa. Together, they moved to chip at the ice, but before either could even begin, it began to pulsate more intensely.

Baden jerked up, feeling something land in his hair. "Alexa!"

"It … is that snow?" Alexa held out her hand to see illuminated speckles of snow drifting through the air. "This's really weird."

"It's coming from the ice!"

As more and more landed on him, he felt weakness take hold, his muscles feeling leaden. Even his sight was affected. "Shut it off! We have to shut if off."

On her hands and knees, Alexa fought with Baden to get to the kill switch.

"What's that noise?" Alexa halted, listening. "Is it coming from the ice or the crystal?"

"I don't care if it's singing a symphony," Baden growled. "We've got to shut this thing down."

The vibrational pitch was growing in intensity, to the point he could barely think. Covering his ears, he sat back. It hadn't been like this at the cave, he thought. This sound was different, almost threatening.

"I've chipped through, but can't …" She was panting hard, having trouble speaking. "The cable's completely frozen solid. There's no way from here to stop it drawing energy—"

Suddenly, she slumped on the floor, her hands sliding and she tried to get back up.

"Alexa!"

"Bay … my head … I can't …"

He quickly moved her aside then started pulling at the cable and the latch, trying to ignore the fact his entire body now felt numb. Eyesight blurred, he was starting to see double.

The latch was red, at least he thought it was. Alexa had managed to release it partway. Pulling on the lever was a challenge, and no matter how much energy he put into it, there was no release. Ripping off part of his shirt, he wrapped it around his hand to get a good grip, then leaned back with all his body weight, pulling as hard as he could.

When it released, he fell back, tripping over Alexa, the freed cable tangling around his legs.

They needed to get out of here. Looking up the stairs, Baden saw three doorways to the hall dancing before his eyes. Opening his mouth, he tried to call out, but the raspy squeak he managed was barely audible.

Body almost completely numb, his mind began to slow as the basement spun around him uncontrollably. He was now frozen stiff, a strange tingling invading his limbs, almost like pins and needles, but not. He could barely even roll his eyes.

Fighting through shallow breaths, the last thing he saw was the growth vein crystal's illumination starting to fade before all fell to darkness.

Galactic Star Key: Zozes Karbroe
Astral Nav-Coordinates: EAS-APL-4
Data Sequence: 18.0

Accustomed to his brother's moods, Zozes ignored Kaze's pacing and took a seat in one of the straight-back chairs offered at Global Base's Medical Centre.

"How long are we supposed to wait?" Kaze exploded, staring angrily at the personnel on the opposite side of the window.

Zozes sighed and leaned back, crossing an ankle over a knee, looking for something to occupy his time. This waiting room seemed even sparser than the police station's, not a single piece of reading material on display.

"I know how you feel, brother, but that Kadra isn't going anywhere, so stop with the pacing. You're making me apprehensive."

"Apprehensive? You?" Kaze laughed, shaking his head. "It was both of us who jumped from that observation platform. You followed me, remember?"

"And look where it's got us. The more you step out of line, the tighter their hold's going to be. Our duty service is of a temporary status remember."

"You're right." Kaze ran a hand over his face, then ruffled his hair. "The guilt's choking me up." Grinning, he held out his arms. "Hold me?"

"Joke all you like." Zozes rolled his neck, easing its tension. "We've finally made progress, then you risk it all on a personal vendetta."

"In other words, leave this alone?" Incredulous, Kaze stared at his brother like he was a stranger. "The Garrold clan and what they did to our family are the reason we enlisted in the Blades." Jabbing a finger at the medical bay, he snarled, "It's our job, no, our *responsibility*, to make certain their kind becomes extinct."

"I haven't forgotten, not for a moment." Zozes held up a hand, trying to head off a full-on confrontation. "We need to prioritise. There's a lot going on, you know that. Burning sorge-rounds into its chest won't produce anything lasting."

"Blasting that thing on principle alone would've been enough to help take the edge off." Kaze's hand grazed the side of his hip, an action Zozes had seen many times. "What the Garrolds took from us cannot be forgotten."

"Treating it less than ourselves would be a mistake. We're supposed to be better than Kadra. I suggest you sit down and shut up so we can prove it."

For a long moment Kaze seemed to weigh his brother's words before finally taking a seat. Leaning back, he groaned stretching out his legs. "We'll try it your way. For now."

On a silent breath of relief, Zozes activated his porta-tool, generating a cyber-screen from his palm, initiating it to connect via cyber-explorer with the subspace channel. While the newsfeed loaded, he cast a sideways glance. Kaze appeared to have fallen asleep, mouth slightly open. Laughing softly, he began scanning the first few news-scripts from AstraCom before selecting something current.

Halfway through a rather lengthy article, Kaze stirred, grunting something unintelligible before cracking an eye. "Don't you get tired of looking over the Alpha's Entry Posts? You probably know them word for word."

"I'm not reading those reports. This is a current news-script from AstraCom."

"We can now uplink into its subspace service from Earth?" Kaze sat up. "How come I didn't know?"

"Maybe you missed the update during one of your vehicle-driving, window-jumping, slang-learning exploits." Settling back, Zozes made himself comfortable. "Hard enough to keep up with you, if I cared to pay attention."

"My fun bar's set way up here," laughed Kaze. "Care to play?"

Zozes left that one alone. Bored, his brother started to fidget, obviously having taken the edge off his fatigue.

"So ... whatcha reading?"

"Information."

"Space stuff?"

"Close enough."

"Hmm," Kaze tapped the side of his seat. "What space stuff could that be? So many topics to choose from. Maybe further insight into the Chief's prior mission, and why Astral Guard gave her above duty-status privileges?"

"You already know the answer to the question, why persist?"

"Because you've never answered the question." Kaze stretched looking around. "Lots of personnel around today. Perhaps I could ask them if it was because of the Link-Trone?"

"You're reaching and will end up embarrassing yourself."

"You're the one with the image to uphold."

Zozes hunched to the side while Kaze attempted to antagonise him with a series of taunts that had him biting his tongue. When he finally fell silent, pulling out a chair to shove his feet on and lie back, Zozes breathed a sigh of relief, maximising his cyber-screen, loading additional news-scripts.

The heading of the next article caught his attention: "Spawn Concord". Opening it, he began reading. "Astral Guard's State General has finally passed down the ruling titles of Spawn Rights to the Grand Minister of the Civil Federation. An agreement has been signed between both parties to launch a Galactic Program for implementation, replacing bio-regulators with spawn-TECHS. The four base advancements within spawn-types will target many and varying defects in ..."

A nearby screen-door slid open, interrupting his concentration. Deactivating the screen, he glanced up to see Thaytis entering, Global Reach pants and shirt hugging her trim figure.

On his feet, Zozes nodded. "Doctor."

"Sorry it took so long." She rubbed at her head tiredly, knocking hair free from her braid. "We had some issues opening the Link-Trone's construct-dish for its diagnostic."

"Complications?"

"In a way." Thaytis sighed, rolling her shoulders. "It appears your Link-Trone has become rather temperamental."

"Really?" Zozes glanced at Kaze slumped across two seats. "I've a few ideas why that could be."

"Is he asleep?" Thaytis leaned over.

"Just enjoy the moment." Then Zozes spotted what caught her attention. Kaze was drooling from the corner of his mouth. "He tends to exert more energy than his body can maintain. Leave him, Doctor. Call it a detox."

"Listening to you explains some of what's happening with the Link-Trone," she murmured thoughtfully. "Even your turn-of-phrase is somewhat Earth-like now."

"Mine?" Zozes straightened instantly. "Unlikely." Then he noticed the amount of Global personnel looking in their direction. "Maybe we should wake him before he starts talking in his sleep."

"He does that?"

Zozes gave her a pained look. "He does everything, Doctor."

"As much as I'd like to have fun with this, his condition worries me." Thaytis pushed a strand of hair behind her ear. "His compatibility into the spawn-net, how has this progressed?"

"Virtually no nosebleeds."

"Well, that's a good sign."

"No head strain from the unibind dual-pairing."

Puzzled, Thaytis frowned. "The neural load within your pairing should still be establishing itself. It works as a push-pull interaction on both your spawn-nets' pathways to balance your connection to the Link-Trone. Maybe you should wake him so we can begin testing sweeps."

As Thaytis moved back through the door, Zozes aimed a hard kick, knocking Kaze's legs from the chair. Balance questionable, Kaze came up fighting. Half asleep his hand grazed his side, drawing an invisible weapon, even pulling at its trigger. When he realised where he was, he shook his head, glancing at Zozes.

"That," he said, wiping saliva from mouth, "was some trip."

"Welcome back." Zozes angled his head, enquiring sarcastically. "Need a moment?"

"Moment's over." Kaze slapped his brother's shoulder, starting for the wrong door.

Zozes grabbed his arm, swinging him toward the med-lab. "There we go."

Sullen, Kaze flashed his ID card and the two entered.

The medical facility was set up to human standards, very different to what either was used to. As he passed a tray, Kaze picked up a piece of the medical equipment, eyeing the spike on the end.

"One of the drawbacks of living on a pre-warp world. The treatments look worse than the disease."

Zozes cast a side look at the pointy tool. "Energy-based technologies definitely have their place."

"Much needed upgrade," added Kaze.

"We used these in practice during training, remember?" Zozes said, picking up something that looked like pincers. "You haven't forgotten training module 'Fall Back'?"

"On Dexta Nine's moon." Kaze's eyebrows rose at the memory.

"Before the spawn-tech's implantation into our nervous system."

Kaze thought back. "The opposition activated that EM pulse field over the entire moon and it destabilised all energy-based training equipment."

"Won't forget that anytime soon." Zozes well recalled the shock to his system. "And for an entire moon cycle we had to defend our position relying solely on emergency hard-surface tech and armaments."

"Shooting solid-based ammunition." Kaze shook his head. "Changes the rules of combat engagement."

On the last, Thaytis joined them. "Dexta Nine, the training moon? Only the best enlisted Blades are chosen to go there."

Pleased, Kaze puffed out his chest. "We were the only trainees in our squadron to not be physically affected by the destabilised bio-regulators."

"Really." Thaytis ran an eye up and down Zozes. "Neither of you needed your subdermal devices to help optimise your body's natural immune responses against common illnesses?"

"That's right." Kaze's smile broadened. "I still remember the other trainees suffering from reversion syndrome. The throwback sicknesses are like what Earth suffers regularly — common colds, stomach viruses ..."

"And much worse," Zozes said with a slight shudder.

"Would've been an education," Thaytis remarked. "As the Earthlings like to put it."

"Still, I think we were more than lucky," Zozes said. "It's next time I'd be concerned about."

"Luck?" Kaze pretended to dust himself off. "This body here has some well-tuned genetics that took generations to perfect. No surprise endings for this fine form." He winked at Thaytis. "It's a rare thing indeed."

Thaytis edged toward Zozes. "Too bad if it became extinct, huh?"

"You wanna try speaking up, Doc?" Kaze looked over.

"Just mentioning that the Planetary Allegiance are phasing bio-regulators out, replacing them with spawn-techs."

"You mean?" Kaze spun around, looking at her, incredulous. "You're saying civvies will be operating spawn technology? But Blades go through extensive training!"

"It won't be military-grade," assured Zozes. "I was reading a news-script earlier, and all civilians will be taught properly how to handle the changeover."

"That's way too dangerous." Playful mood abandoned, Kaze frowned. "They seem to be taking this reversion syndrome seriously, but moving civilians in that direction ..."

"There really is no choice, and no halting progress," said Thaytis. "Not with the growing concern. Research on the biolen-spawn type has seen a major breakthrough. They're now able to target and repair various defects in genome types."

"You're talking genetic augmentation?" Mouth a flat line, Kaze glared at Zozes. "And just who does that sound like?"

"We aren't the Kadra."

"No, we aren't," agreed Thaytis. "Spawn technology will operate similar to the Link-Trone, locking off functions to prevent manipulation. It will be there to treat defects, nothing more."

"So we're going to be one big spawn family," said Kaze. "I suppose natural is really a thing of the past."

"You've a better idea?" Zozes snapped.

"Space love."

"Here we go." Zozes pushed past his brother, warning Thaytis. "That's his answer for everything, especially when he's losing."

"Not my fault that it surrounds and binds us." Kaze smirked. "Not to mention penetrates us in a most satisfactory way."

"I do believe this conversation just collapsed in on itself," Thaytis said as she shoved Kaze forward. "Blades, we're moving on. Follow me."

She led them into a private room, one that looked to have been outfitted with a M1-class porta-station, their Link-Trone held in grav-beam. Thaytis moved beside this, numerous digital screens surrounding her mobile workstation.

At her side, Zozes eyed the schematic breakdowns of the Link-Trone, each revealing the AI's internal and external telemetry.

Zozes leaned closer. With its top, outer plating hatch retracted, he could see the positronic mass drive's internal components lighting up randomly. Either side of it, scanning discs moved in random patterns, finalising tests.

Thaytis generated one of her diagnostic implements using her personal porta-tool, operating the entire system from this while standing before the main screen of her cyber-controller.

A stream of light from the second level caught Zozes' eye. Glancing up, he spotted the Major watching them from an observation deck.

"Good work, Doctor," he said, speaking over a voice communicator. "I've just completed relaying the Link-Trone's diagnostics. Commodore Vae'gon has given authorisation to conduct the overview on the Blades' spawn-nets when ready. Once you've cleared them, bring them to Stasis Morgue so we can continue our assignment."

"Understood, Sir." Thaytis glanced back at her porta-station. "Right Blades, let's begin." Looking at the brothers, she indicated two scanning pads for them to stand on. "Alpha Blue step on to the right pad. Alpha Green, you're on the left."

As each took their position, the circular pad lit up, releasing three scanning arcs that rose to take sensor sweeps of their bodies.

While generating two more cyber-screens, Thaytis explained, "The biomech crew have compiled a Positronic Drive overview of your Trone. Now I'm gathering telemetry data on each of you. Every sweep the scan arc performs, I get an in-depth map of your physiology."

When it was finished, Thaytis nodded. "Done, you can step free Blades."

Zozes and Kaze joined her, studying the bio-maps. Both were quite different from when they were on the station.

His brother was the first to question this. "What am I looking at this time, Doc?"

"Just let me ..." Thaytis worked fast, uploading each of the brother's spawn-nets onto their bio-map. Initiating a trigger pointer, she began highlighting certain areas on their nervous systems.

"Right." Thaytis took a breath. "Alpha Green's bio-map is still stable. However, I have some concerns over these indicated areas in your spawn-net. Yours are primarily localised in your cerebral cortex. It appears from these scans you have established yourself as primary controller over the bridged unibind's dual-pairing."

"He has a controlling complex, Doc," Kaze grinned.

She glanced from one to the other. "So you're both aware of this?"

Before Zozes could say a word, his brother jumped in. "Of course. Boss man over there thinks he can more than single-handedly go it alone."

The moment Kaze drew breath, Zozes spoke, "You said it yourself, Doctor. LT is changing and not for the better. On occasion, it is undisciplined and can't be controlled. And that's more than dangerous."

Frustrated, Kaze ran a hand over his hair. "I told you this was a trust thing."

The fact his brother knew exactly which buttons to press was no surprise. "You haven't had command training. It's illogical to believe you can handle any of this on your own."

"And here it comes."

Angered, Zozes slammed a hand on the bench, vibrating several of the sensitive tools, making Thaytis step back in surprise. "I completed several moon cycles of training to handle the spawn command program. And if you remember correctly, I tried to get you to come with me."

"If I had, you'd be dead now," Kaze reminded him hotly. "Gaining sub-command status would've had me transferred to another squad. Leaving you to die landing on that station like some sacrificial hero."

"You can't always be around to save me."

Teeth bared, Kaze puffed out his chest. "Try and vokken stop me."

At that, Thaytis slapped a hand on the bench, not rattling one of the instruments, however it was enough to remind the two she was present and listening. "Well, cry me a galaxy of stars. Looks to me like you're both in your own deluded minds trying to protect one another."

Zozes and Kaze stared at her, stunned.

"Not many go to the extremes of you two, but at least I know what's going on now." Thaytis eyed the screen. "It's strengthened you both, compensating for the other's lacking abilities."

Face puckered, Kaze glanced at Zozes. "Lack? Did she say lack?"

"A co-dependent relationship is not a conventional practice. But in this particular situation, it can be used to bolster your connection to your Link-Trone."

For a moment Zozes chewed on this. "What of the mental component to controlling LT?"

"I understand your hesitation and the need to protect your brother, but let me further explain the underlying issues in suspending his spawn-net." Bringing up a fresh diagram, this time of Kaze, Thaytis moved her trigger pointer over his bio-map. "Solo-operative control has reinitialised itself overriding command-operative control. If this is ongoing, it could undo all the progress Kaze has made in his connection to the Trone. Reversion protocol has already set in."

He listened to each word, already guessing her remedy. "I know what you want me to do."

"Teach him, Zozes. That's what I want you to do. He needs to learn to command the Trone."

Jaw tight, he said nothing while looking at his brother, trying to imagine Kaze in charge of something as powerful and deadly as the Link-Trone.

This time when his teeth flashed, Kaze was grinning. "Like a pro."

After running through a series of screens, Thaytis shut down the station that held the Link-Trone, watching its outer plate close.

Automatically, Zozes activated his unibind bridge to their dual-pairing, then on a large breath decrypted the lockout sequence. "It's done."

At the abrupt connection to it, Kaze's eyes flared. "Must've blocked out how much this hurt."

"Good." Thaytis watched him carefully. "This will activate all his dormant command spawns. My suggestion now is to guide him through, teach him what it is to be an Alpha."

Grim, Zozes looked at his brother, noting the fine sheen of sweat already coating his face. "Second thoughts?"

"Minimal problems here." Kaze dragged in a deep breath. "See what I just did? The key is to breathe and at the same time try and not vomit all over my boots."

"Good." Thaytis stepped back. "Because what happened earlier during the Kadra's interrogation can never happen again." She looked at Zozes intently.

"It won't," Zozes assured.

After a moment's hesitation, Thaytis added, "If your brother attempts to mark a lethal firing target without the Link-Trone's confirmation, it can be very damaging to his mind. The AI system will do whatever is necessary to stop him from engaging."

For a moment, Kaze looked thoughtful but distinctly unhappy. "If we're done here, Doc, best we head up to speak with the Major."

"We're done, Blade."

But as Kaze moved out the door, heading for the steps, Thaytis caught Zozes' arm.

"There's something else," she added. "You need to understand the rebound effect, Zozes. It could damage the unibind's bridging control to your dual-pairing permanently."

"Then it looks like we'll all have to learn to trust my brother, won't we?"

"Excuse me?" Thaytis frowned, crossing her arms.

"Thaytis." Zozes shook his head, watching his brother, now on the second-storey observation deck. "LT's override protocol wasn't what stopped Kaze."

"You mean …" Thaytis's face lit with realisation.

"My brother is many things, but he would never kill an unarmed captive in cold blood. He'll tear down a room to make a point, but when it comes down to it, he'd never have pulled that trigger."

"I see," Thaytis weighed the words. "So, if that Kadra wasn't apprehended or unarmed?"

"Then it's fair game," Zozes looked away, his mouth a flat line. "Probably would still be back there now, sorting this out."

"Right then." Thaytis slowly deactivated her porta-tool, waiting for the cyber-screens to collapse. "I see your past story with the Garrold clan has varying complexities."

That was one way to put it, thought Zozes, rolling his shoulders, looking again at the second level. "Perhaps we should join them."

"Of course." Thaytis moved ahead of him, out the door and up the stairs, hesitating a couple from the top. "If you should ever need to speak with someone, you can always find me."

Her soft words made him freeze, for the first time Zozes perceiving how many layers Thaytis possessed. It was like seeing the essence of the woman behind the quick tongue and fast mind.

Unsettled, he climbed the last of the stairs past her. "I appreciate the offer, Doctor."

The Major was nowhere to be seen, and Kaze had moved to the next room. Zozes could see him through the sliding glass door, leaning over the rail observing another med-ward. Beside him was a young blonde medical officer.

"Well there's a surprise." Thaytis's eyebrows shot toward her hairline. "He certainly likes that type of distraction."

"You've no idea what an understatement that is."

As the two entered, Thaytis nodded, but kept moving. Zozes paused, a pointed look telling his brother this was neither the time or place.

"… for diplomatic reasons, of course. Call it an in-depth exchange of cultural differences." Kaze grinned cheekily, eyes flashing in invitation.

"Really?" The nurse reached up, tucking a stray dark-blonde curl back in her bun. "You don't seem the diplomatic type."

Kaze's eyes admired her physical form. "Sweetheart, I'm any type you need me to be. Only a handful of humans brought in to work here know of our alliance. That grants you special privileges over most humans on this planet." Leaning closer, he assured, "Privileges you won't forget."

At that the nurse laughed softly, glancing briefly at Zozes. "You're pretty sure of yourself. Let's see what happens at the Global Reach launching ceremony."

"I'll keep an eye out for you." Kaze tapped her name tag. "Carlee? That's how it's pronounced?"

She looked down as personnel entered the first-floor med-ward, led by an Astral Guard Medical Officer. "I better go. Oh, and its pronounced Carly. Just so you know."

His brother's gaze never left the young woman, following every step she took. Rolling his eyes, Zozes leaned against the rail. "Not even spawn reversion can stop you."

"What can I say, the way she's built could be just the distraction I'm looking for." Gripping the rail before him, he breathed deeply. "Whether I can do anything besides talk is another matter entirely."

"Head spins?"

"Along with stomach rolls, muscle cramps. You name it, I feel it."

A large group of medical personnel, all human, entered the bay below led by an Astral Guard Medical Officer. Going to the head of the room, she began an induction telling them the advances medicine was about to take after Global Reach. These people would be the first to learn how their world was about to change.

Zozes spotted Carly moving to join the group, as well as the smile she shot his brother. "What's with you and inter-species relations?"

Kaze straightened. "Maybe I like a challenge. If you need, think of it as an open-minded experiment."

They left the viewing area, moving into another long hall. Ahead, Zozes spotted the door to Stasis Morgue, several Astral Guard Enforcers standing guard.

"It's the anatomy part that I have trouble with," Zozes mused. "Knowing how each has its own personal attributes and that they need to be understood beforehand."

"You think too much." Kaze flashed his ID card after Zozes and the door slid open. "Half the fun is discovery and once you start, it's kinda hard to stop."

Zozes ignored the guard's odd look following his brother, who of course caught it. "Eyes forward, solider."

"I really thought you'd grow out of that form of experimentation," grumbled Zozes, moving past him. "Or at least slow down."

"Maybe I'm the equaliser for your lack of interest," Kaze said. "You know, since you don't seem to like experimentation full stop."

Exasperated, Zozes swung back. "Don't pretend this has anything to do with me."

"Okay," Kaze returned the look with one of his own. "Take Thaytis for example."

"Oh, nice lead-in."

"You opened the subject, brother, I'm merely seeing where it takes us. Just answer me this and I'll walk down these stairs, Blade authority in check, salutes and all." Kaze tacked on a final word, unusually serious. "Respectable."

"For that last reason alone, I'll indulge you." Zozes waited, raising an eyebrow. "Well?"

"Alright, take Doctor Sassy Pants. She's been sending out a copious amount of signals," Kaze's eyes widened noticeably, "that even the sensory-deprived could not miss."

From the head of the stairs, Zozes surveyed the large, gently lit morgue, taking in the multiple stasis-tables preserving deceased bodies, countless rows throughout the holding area. Like she had been cued, Thaytis entered through a side door with the Major, her blonde hair a beacon in the otherwise sombre room.

"In the interests of saving time," he answered slowly. "Yes, I've noticed the signals, and no, I won't act on them."

"Ah, well at least you've noticed and have the ability to actually generate a sexualised thought process," Kaze said with faux enthusiasm.

Momentarily lost for words, Zozes eyed his brother's smug face, trying not to counter that remark with his fist rather than words. Anything to stop that jaw flapping.

"Seriously, good for you for noticing." Kaze's chuckle turned into a full-bodied laugh, one that had him holding his stomach.

"So, drop the sham already and park that diminutive ship of yours in her hanger bay before it closes for good."

"Think again, brother." Zozes shove past, using his body weight to shunt Kaze into the stairs' guardrails, ignoring the fact he was still laughing.

Zozes jogged down the stairs, struggling to block the image of his brother's head meeting the wall. Spotting Inspector Roccna cooled these images, her brusque march and stiff features taking her directly to stand beside Thaytis and Major Rajek.

As he passed the first platforms, Zozes paused, noticing many of the deceased victims on the open stasis-tables had undergone what looked to be a type of unnatural mutation. Some disfigurements were so severe he could not identify the species.

"LT," Zozes waited for the Link-Trone to move alongside. "Run a bio-map of the deceased bodies, verify species and report cause."

Through his cyber-optics, he eyed the Trone's preliminary scans. The victims were all the same species.

Curious, Kaze walked up, leaning close to the stasis shield, eyeing the bodies. "Humans?"

Inspector Roccna drew alongside, the Major and Doctor with her.

"They certainly are, though you would never know it," she said. "Each has had their physiology completely altered."

Rajek nodded toward their AI. "Would you have your Link-Trone please do the honours, overlay selected bodies with a cyber-screen so we can view the results?"

Once LT had done as instructed, marking each with a cast of ray energy, the Trone generated a series of screens. From there it added the data collected from the bio-maps, uploading injuries and projected causes of death.

For a moment, Inspector Roccna read through the information. "Your Trone has now been cleared to have full access to Earth's identification database as that's the next part of your assignment. The Trone should be able to correlate between these bio-maps and the identification database to generate an ID profile on each of these humans."

It took several more moments for the cyber-screens to begin filling with the victims' ID cards. Zozes went over the information being loaded, viewing each profile, recognising locations from his previous Alpha's mission reports.

Kaze eyed the closest one. "They look bigger than the average human."

Grey, thickened skin, facial features sunken, eyes hollowed to look like pits. All were hairless.

"We should have been shown this sooner," Zozes said, thinking back to the evidence presented at the police station, suspecting there was a connection.

"Each stage is a necessity," countered Roccna. "We need to protect the sensitivity of this assignment. However," she glanced at the Major, "the situation has escalated beyond our initial projections and as you know," she eyed their dark expressions, "the Kadra Outcast managed to escape."

"The thing what?" growled Kaze.

Zozes placed a hand on his brother's shoulder, understanding his anger. "I was just updated before we were ordered—"

"Vok withholding this from me!" Kaze shrugged it off, glaring at Roccna. "And you can include Astral Guard in that for not assigning us to its security detail sooner."

"The blame should be cast upon yourself, Blade," snapped Roccna. "Your display whilst identiflying the Kadra earned you your penance."

"I should've shot that thing ..."

Zozes turned his back on Roccna looking directly into Kaze's eyes, subtly shaking his head. Kaze let out a long breath clenching a fist.

His brother was attempting to calm himself, that much was clear to Zozes. Anymore acts of defiance would have them both permanently stripped of this assignment.

"Inspector," Zozes turned back, once again formal. "It sounds like you are aware of its mission."

"That mission is lying before us."

Confused, the two looked around at the deformed bodies.

"The Kadra," Rajek added, "is not working alone. A group has been targeting specific locations across the planet. Twelve, to be exact."

"You're saying it's experimenting on human physiology?" Kaze cleared his throat and moved next to Zozes. "To what end?"

"Global Reach," said the Major.

A looming silence coated the med-ward.

"Genetic Augmentation," Thaytis said. "Its kind are attempting to drastically mutate the human's genome, attempting to enhance and control them."

"Control them?" Zozes was starting to get the idea. "The Kadra are responsible for all the abduction cases that span across the planet?"

Roccna frowned. "It's still unknown if Kadra Prime are involved or if this is the work of an Outcast Sect."

"My guess would be an Outcast Sect," Zozes said slowly. "Most likely they're working in conjunction with the Assultra Rebels."

"How do we know if this isn't bigger than that?" Kaze looked around. "If Kadra Prime is responsible, this could be a prelude to all-out war. A war this planet isn't ready for."

"Careful, Blade," warned the Major. "Accusing the wrong party could lead us to that fate. Best we discover the true enemy before directing cause and blame."

"Toeing around all this won't gain us points." Kaze shook his head. "You all know who's inbound for Earth for the signing of the Galactic Civilisation ship if Global Reach Launch is successful. And this is no regular planet, so they're coming in force."

"That's why we are following this to the directive," Zozes said. "Honour the treaty, do our duty. So the pre-warp development scheme can get underway."

"I agree to disagree," Kaze argued. "Something more is happening here. The Alpha spoke of a truth, maybe this is it."

"Kaze!" Zozes barely controlled his shock.

"She wouldn't have given her life for anything less! You know that."

Roccna had been listening intently. "What is he speaking of?"

"Nothing of relevance, Inspector, I assure you." Infuriated at his brother's slip, Zozes could see Roccna was anything but convinced.

Her next words proved it. "You seem quite absolute in your opinion, Blade."

Nostrils flaring, Kaze looked at Zozes, finally heeding the warning. "What can I say? Sometimes I think out loud."

In an attempt to shake off the slip, Zozes refocused. Global Reach was the objective, seeing that succeed and not allowing politics to interfere with the Integration effort.

"I think," began Rajek, "we all agree this assignment needs to be handled with sensitivity and," he looked at each in turn, "that it may prove to become far greater than just the elimination of one renegade Kadra or its Sect."

"Right," Kaze ploughed in, ignoring the minefield his brother was tiptoeing around. "Since we're all hugging and agreeing here. That crashed recon ship, the one we pulled the Kadra from. Was he targeting Ebony Casteel?"

Surprised, Zozes looked around the group. This was a fast, valid pick-up by his brother.

"You're thinking a failed abduction?" He thought back to the police station briefing they had attended. "She's most likely to be tied to the original survivors, the Casteels, Nobles and Solomons. Each of those families had someone escape over twenty star cycles ago."

Roccna ran a hand over her head tiredly. "A coincidence that can't be overlooked."

"But why target these families?" Kaze asked. "What makes them unique?"

"Just add that to the list of mysteries we're yet to unravel."

"And how did she escape?" Kaze demanded irritably, his manner falling just short of grilling the Inspector. "I'm not buying the fact she got out on her own, there had to have been help."

"Or did she?" Zozes stepped between the two, halting their back and forth. "Did the Kadra simply let her go? Transport her off that Warront Craft?"

"You mean," Roccna eyed the bodies, following Zoze's gaze, "has she been genetically altered?"

Rajek whistled appreciatively. "I told you he was good."

"A set-up?" Kaze looked confused. "I guess getting shot down wasn't a part of the Kadra's plan."

"Was it one of our own?" Zozes looked at the Inspector. "Who took that ship down?"

"That is still classified," the Inspector said.

Kaze shook his head, looking from the mutilated body back to his brother. "You're saying she could be one of these things? That she never even escaped, she was let go?"

Looking thoroughly sickened, Roccna spoke slowly. "And that for now, her mutation remains dormant. We have been monitoring her involvement ever since her landing at the Freestone Festival."

"You mean you knew?" exclaimed Kaze. "Why hasn't she been quarantined?"

"An issue," chimed in Thaytis, "I have clearly addressed in my reports."

Roccna straightened her uniform, jutting her chin. "The mutation is non-transferrable. It is the result of genetic augmentation, not contagion."

"I would have thought that her safety and that of her family and friends would have been of more concern," Thaytis said. "Once the mutation triggers, Inspector, what then?"

"An acceptable risk, Doctor, and something we have been over countless times. You can't fight me on this. I have the full support of the Astral Guard Overwatch Directive."

Thaytis' response was one of silent disagreement, but Zozes knew what she wanted to say, so he said it for her. "You're using this girl to draw out the other humans?"

"Let's go over this using your Link-Trone," Rajek said, indicating the victim's ID profile cards. "Ebony Casteel is now part of an Instinctual Collective group. Before long, she'll be seeking out others. As you can see from the ID profiles, these humans were abducted from different corners of the globe, and have all been genetically altered to serve the Kadra's purpose."

"Maybe a star cycle ago," Roccna said, "I led a series of interviews speaking with the victims' families. All of them told a similar story."

"Which was?" Zozes asked.

"They were going about their daily routine, everyone present and accounted for. Some walked out the door to never be seen again. Others disappeared from work, vanished without leaving their office. Many were at their residence having walked from one room to another. There is simply no discernible pattern and no sign of departure."

"Your conclusion?"

Roccna brought up a map on her porta-tool's generated screen, showing the twelve locations where the humans had been taken. "They appeared to be targeting specific zones around this world. Your Alpha and her previous commando squad formed a joint operation with Astral Enforcer combat company, charged with hunting them down."

"And mutated humans were all located near Global Reach bases," Zozes observed.

"Correct."

"I take it," Kaze said, inspecting one of the bodies, "they aren't the talkative type once the mutation manifests?" He pointed to a gaping wound on one corpse from a charged plasma-round.

Arms crossed, Roccna looked at the doctor. "I'll leave that deduction to you."

"The gestation period of the mutation is virtually impossible to detect or screen with current practices at disposal. Only once it has fully manifested are we able to verify any form of genetic manipulation."

"So, you're saying that anyone in Freestone could be a mutation carrier? Talk about easy!" Kaze exclaimed.

"We call them sleepers." Roccna ran an eye over the room. "And once activated, they become just as formidable as any one of these was. I've lost several of my best Inspectors and entire Enforcer Fire squads hunting these humans down."

"And with the launching of Global Reach," Rajek said, "the Global Capital Base will be their primary target."

"With Garrold now free, it and the Assultra Rebels will finish what they started." Kaze shook his head, thoroughly disgusted. "Triggering the sleepers' mutation cycle to sabotage the launch of Global Reach."

"I can see you now realise the steps we have had to take to ensure that does not happen. Global Reach must succeed."

For the first time, Zozes understood the Inspector's dilemma. She had been forced to make some very difficult decisions.

"And knowing all this you'll still let the girl attend?" Kaze asked, incredulous.

"Kaze," Zozes cautioned, "we'll find a way to save her, but it clearly isn't going to be accomplished with a straight-line approach."

"Thank you, Blade." Roccna eyed Kaze. "Some choices are not easy, and we believe this girl holds the key. We must protect planet Earth and the partnership that has been built. Global Reach is the culmination of that foundation, and protecting that can only be done," she looked at each brother making sure they understood, "through her."

Galactic Star Key: Major Rajek
Astral Nav-Coordinates: EAS-APL-4
Data Sequence: 19.0

The moment Rajek was waved through the Global Base checking station, he began moving swiftly down the Detention Level's main corridor. Here there was none of promenade's chaos, security keeping a tight rein on who entered and left.

He found the Information Centre busier than usual, most of the human terminals all in use. Security patrol officers combed the area before moving off down the corridor that led to the holding wards. General duty personnel took enquiries at the long counter separating the main area from the corridor.

A company of Astral Inspectors exited an Investigation Lobby, where a human detainee was being questioned by Enforcers. By the looks of it, they were finishing up, the Enforcers moving him out, guiding the man down the hall.

Lieutenant Noremar was among the group, her eyes meeting his. There was no mistaking the heat of temper in her gaze, something she usually kept contained, as she paused.

Not deterred, Rajek left the desk, shortening the distance between them, not about to make every officer present privy to something that was obviously going to be intense.

"Major ... Sir!"

At the call of his name, Rajek turned. "Doctor?"

"Sir!" Flush faced, Thaytis jogged the last of the distance to reach him. "I cannot agree to this! The Blades are simply not ready ..."

"Doctor Venlara!" Enforcer Normar closed the last of the distance, clearly angry. "I suggest you remember your place. The Major adheres to Command's orders, not yours."

Lips pursed, Thaytis took a bold step forward. "We aren't dealing with Devron law here, Enforcer Noremar. Perhaps it's you that's out of step. My medical authority stands, and I and my department will have a voice in this decision."

"Best you take a step back, Doctor." Noremar's slit pupils flared, overtaking all colour in her eyes. The two were so close her breath ruffled Thaytis' hair on exhale. "Intent of challenge to a Devronian isn't wise."

"Enough!" snapped Rajek, finally finding a break in her cold words. "I need answers, not division. What's this in relation to?"

On a swallow, Thaytis pulled her gaze, facing him. "Command hasn't contacted you, Sir?"

"The Commodore's duty-arm contacted me through freq-com earlier, requesting to suspend our meeting due to a state of legal quandary."

Eyes narrowed, Thaytis swung back to the Enforcer. "You lied?"

"I said what was needed, Doctor, to have you submit."

"You told me he agreed! Devron morality is truly equal to that of a common Nova Trade agent."

"You persist in insulting my race when having lost cause for refute. My Devron morality needs no justification."

"Many other races would disagree, Lieutenant," snapped Thaytis.

"This ruling requires compliance, not unwarranted interference," snarled Noremar, then redirected the conversation. "The timing of the assessment will not be altered."

"Even though the Blades are not ready," Thaytis said flatly. "Lack of training places them in a dangerous position, one where assessment results will be unquestionable."

Rajek sighed inwardly, seeing how deeply Command's decision to bring forward the Alpha Trials was dividing his squad, knowing no way to counter it.

Further up the corridor a set of twin doors opened, Ensign Clarkov appearing, waiting at the sector block's Investigation Lobby. The haunted look on his face was almost a replica of the doctor's.

Rajek could see that Thaytis' medical code of conduct was being challenged, while Lieutenant Normar believed all action was just. Command was not about to be talked out of these trials, which would challenge his unit's viability, as each believed they were on the side of right.

A deeper look at the doctor's flushed face gave him further insight. She appeared to be more than ethically challenged, perhaps emotionally attached. A dangerous development that could someday be used against her.

In an uncharacteristic move, he placed a hand lightly on her shoulder. "We all understood this was an inevitability from the moment the Blades were placed in our squad. Each must prove their title as an Alpha in battle. The Trials is how this is achieved."

"Sir ..." Thaytis shook her head. "Alpha Green's Command Training may not be enough. You know the consequences if they fail."

"Stay strong, Doctor Venlara, this is far from over." Rajek did not miss Enforcer Noremar's look of disgust toward Thaytis. There was something brewing there, something he would need to keep an eye on. "With me, squad."

Ensign Clarkov moved to at-stance as the three approached. "Commodore Vae'gon is waiting for you inside, Sir. Apologies for withholding your attendance."

"Understood, Ensign." Rajek approached the doors which retracted automatically, the sound of weapons fire and detonation blasts instantly detectable.

The duty-arm held out a hand. "Enter please."

The moment they stepped inside, Rajek took the room in while moving down a flight of steps, then along the central aisle. Numerous chairs on either side faced the central briefing platform, a chest-high podium centre-stage. Behind that was a curved table and several chairs for senior officers during conducted proceedings.

Commodore Vae'gon rested against the table, arms crossed. A mobile cyber-router hovered next to him, generating multiple cyber-screens. Each screen was cycling surveillance records of the Blade brothers as they demonstrated their abilities, some on the blast range, others at the crash zone of the Warront Craft.

The top two cyber-screens were reserved for their spawn-nets' Star-Key profiles.

The moment he reached the platform, Rajek drew to at-stance, the screens constantly shifting images on his right. Enforcer Noremar and Doctor Thaytis followed suit, eyes forward.

The moment the feed came to an end, several cyber-screens collapsed, silence settling over the room, one that was almost as deafening as the sounds relayed through the cyber-router. Neither the Major nor his squad said anything, the Commodore still eyeing the screens displaying the Blades' Star-Key profiles, like he was contemplating the next action to be taken.

The moment he shifted to his feet, Rajek braced. Vae'gon was not the type to call for this kind of meeting without cause. He wanted something.

"Enforcer Noremar, Doctor Venlara," he nodded to each. "I will speak with the Major in private. You're dismissed."

The two left without a word, Vae'gon watching silently until the twin doors were closed, and the two were alone.

Comfortable in his surrounds, the Commodore reactivated the cyber-screens remotely through his porta-tool, replaying the Blades, this time disabling the audio.

"At-easement, Major."

Rajek placed both hands behind his back, his relaxed stance at odds with how he was feeling. Casting a glance at the images, he looked back at Vae'gon impassively.

"So much overshadows us at this time," began the Commodore, then seemed to stall.

Rajek frowned, wondering if this was a statement or question. "Commodore?"

"These Blades stand to intrigue a host of influential minds." Vae'gon faced him. "What they are sets them apart, grants them dangerous privileges that could very well poison our way of life."

It took Rajek a moment to sift through these words, find the meaning. "You speak of the Actrix Covenant."

"Competently deduced." Vae'gon inclined his head. "The Priestess would crown them her chosen champions. Are you familiar with this divine title?"

Rajek said, "Champions are foretold to be gifted the lifeblood of the Star Gods, consecrated at birth with the purpose of serving them without equivocation."

Clearly appalled, Vae'gon looked back at the screen. "What I see is something far more insidious, a use of ancient practices to manipulate the weak-minded."

Watchful, Rajek held his silence, waiting for the critical strike. Vae'gon was not the type to hold back.

"Such an act questions the chosen faith, that a High Priestess would bestow this on a Blade." The Commodore glanced at Rajek. "Wouldn't you agree?"

Uncomfortable, Rajek kept his expression schooled. "I learnt long ago to leave the mysteries and the words of Star Gods to those who study them."

"Hmm, a faith realist, are we? Someone who believes in a higher cause." The Commodore's mouth formed a hard line of thought. "Yet I also perceive a practical mind that can be spoken to, reasoned with."

"Sir." Rajek would rather fly through a plasma storm than have this discussion. "Those words are spoken far easier than practised. Faith and duty often contradict one another."

"Still." Vae'gon lingered for a moment, silently watching the Blades battle. "Here is where we stand, contradiction or not. If these officers are perceived as more than what they truly are, that needs to change."

"Sir, your concern," began the Major cautiously, "appears more directed with the Actrix Covenant rather than the Blades themselves?"

"The Blades," Vae'gon spat the name, "are a convenience, Major, and they suit a deeper agenda for the Covenant to regain its position, its power ..."

"Power, Sir?"

"Status, foothold, whatever you wish to term it. Star Gods." He spat the title. "For me, they represent all that is impious, a past that should remain buried, forgotten. No, I won't stand idly by while this ancient way of thinking is resurrected, damaging what we've achieved. The last time this faith was armed with power, we almost lost this entire Galaxy."

The Major stared straight ahead. "You believe the Actrix Covenant seeks to integrate Blades?"

"And more." The Commodore's lip curled. "These philosophies, beliefs, they run deep in certain parts of our culture, and they endanger all we have achieved, all we fought for during the Second Galactic War." He advanced to stand before Rajek. "Right now, Major, duty must be placed before faith."

Silent, Rajek let these words wash over him.

"The Global Reach Launch needs no more complications," continued Vae'gon, "so none will arise. Is that understood?"

"There will be none."

"See there isn't." Tone condescending, Vae'gon added viciously, "If the hand of the Star Gods truly befalls these Blades to inevitably face the Kadra, we must know their connection to their Link-Trone cannot be broken … right until the end."

Rajek's gaze met the Commodore's for the first time. "I understand the Blades are to be placed through the Alpha Trials."

"They are." Vae'gon paused, like he was expecting the Major to argue. When none came, he added, "And you have been selected to test their control and abilities when performing as an Alpha."

"Sir?"

"You may speak your mind, Major."

"Alpha Green's command training holds strong, however the youngest Karbroe will complicate the testing. Gauging a factual assessment as they stand now, I believe, they will …"

"Fail?"

Rajek left the word alone, neither confirming nor denying. He felt either would inflame the other's prejudice.

"Perhaps you'd best concern yourself with how these Blades fail," suggested Vae'gon.

"Pushing them to control a spawn-drift is dangerous. You realise what you are asking of me?"

"If the Trials claim their lives, so be it." The Commodore stated this flatly. "I've indulged the Priestess and her beliefs, but not anymore. This issue is to be silenced once and for all."

Fighting to keep his expression neutral, Rajek's tone became clipped. "And if the brothers succeed in controlling the drift? What then?"

Vae'gon immediately stepped closer, intent on ramming home his point. "Well, Major, that's why I've chosen you along with a set of contingency measures to combat all eventualities."

"I see."

"Do you?" Vae'gon fully closed the distance. "If those Blades walk out of that arena, it will only strengthen their position within the Actrix Covenant, something I won't tolerate. The title of the champions," he hissed, "will finally come to a close."

Rajek looked from the narrowed eyes of the Commodore to the cyber-screen which appeared to have static gaps every now and then during the feed. Needing a diversion, he indicated this with a nod of his head.

"Is the Trone's surveillance compiler malfunctioning? I have noticed breaks within the recordings used to monitor the Blades' movements, Sir?"

The Commodore glanced back, eyeing the feed where the brothers were operating the Link-Trone on the firing range. A portion of the sensor recordings froze, fried, became static, then went dead.

"Occurrences such as this," murmured Vae'gon, "are what make me uneasy."

"And the Alpha Chief's unauthorised dual-pairing with a Link-Trone makes them unique, Sir," surmised the Major.

"It makes them dangerous." Vae'gon deactivated the hovering cyber-router, triggering its storage function. It flew into his hand, reforming into a rectangular disc to attach to his belt. "The list of unknowns surrounding the Blades grows far beyond coincidence. Once these Trials are undertaken, all will be as it should." Striding down the aisle to the exit, he glanced back to deliver a final, cold warning. "Consider yourself called upon, Major. Silence this threat."

Vae'gon continued up the stairs, exiting into the main hallway, the twin doors closing behind him.

Rajek had not been dismissed, but then wasn't that the point, he thought, drawing long, slow breaths, seeking to dissipate his anger. Stepping onto the platform, he walked to the table. Running a finger over the polished metallic surface, he eyed his reflection, an impotent rage filling his mind, his body, one that drove down his fist, warping the metal table.

Loose strands of blond hair fell around his face, a red haze momentarily clouding his vision. Straightening, he turned and walked down the aisle, the doors opening as he approached.

Doctor Venlara looked toward the platform, past the Major, while Enforcer Noremar waited in the hall. Striding past them both, he managed a brief sentence only.

"It is done. There's no turning back."

Galactic Index Key: Ebony Casteel
Astral Nav-Coordinates: EAS-APL-4
Data Sequence: 20.0

As Nina's car pulled to the curb outside Kevin's house, Ebony tried tempering her thoughts. Jevon's ute was parked on the nature strip, the driver's window down. Spotting it, she sneered, instantly jerking open the passenger door.

"Well, he's still here," Nina said, turning off the car to follow suit.

The Zhengs' house looked quiet, but the way Ebony was feeling it would not stay that way. "He'll wish he wasn't when the fool sees me."

"Relax," Nina said, pressing lock on her key remote. "You're getting worked up, and it's not a good look for you."

"He stole my phone!" Ebony still could not believe it. "I told him to leave this alone but no! He never listens."

The two began walking to the front of the house. "Please don't make me regret telling you, let alone bringing you," begged Nina.

"I know you hate confrontation, but Nina, he's brought this on himself. I just want my mobile back."

"That's fine but let's do it calmly."

Ebony halted, pulling Nina up. "You mean like, 'Let's all sit down, hold hands and talk this out like besties'?" She bared her teeth. "I don't think so. He's earned this one."

"FYI ..." Nina instantly got her back up. "I've heard myself on video and I sound nothing like that."

"Ever the cheerleader for diplomacy," mumbled Ebony.

"Excuse me?"

"Nothing," she sang, marching up the drive onto the front veranda.

Nina followed, worriedly. "Last time you two fought it took months to get over. I haven't the energy for this today, remember my PT gym session later—"

"Wait, when was the fight? I don't remember that."

"During winter. Major disagreement over something big, don't ask me what, but it took ages for you guys to even be in the same room with each other."

While Ebony chewed over this revelation, Nina sighed in relief, knuckles tapping the door. "Good. I'll knock."

"Guess my amnesia's good for something."

"You have a strange sense of good."

"Well, I don't remember, so it doesn't count," she decided. "Call it a do-over."

"What?" Nina's head looked like it was about to pop off. "That doesn't make any sense. Just because you don't remember doesn't mean he doesn't."

"No one's going to hear that girl knock." Patience at an end, Ebony rapped on the door using the rhythmic tune her father did to grab people's attention.

"And using amnesia as a defence doesn't work," Nina decided, crossing her arms.

"No way, it's my right." Ebony circled a finger over her ear. "Perks for the mentally impaired."

"I hate when you get in these moods because clearly all logic escapes you."

"Maybe I'm speaking on a level beyond logic." Ebony prepared to knock again, but Nina knocked her hand away. "Dissect that one, if you can."

"Well, with you and Jev, someone has to play lion tamer. Sometimes I wonder if you'd even be friends if I wasn't around."

Ebony threw back her head. "Who's being overly dramatic now? Cousins fight. Sheesh, relax, Mum." She loathed it when Nina started treating her like a five-year-old child. "You can't control everything."

"You know I hate being called that!"

Ebony tried peering through the flyscreen door. "Come on, Kevo!" she called. "Don't make me start yelling."

"You've already started," Nina hissed. "We need your outside voice to become inside! You're not on the farm now."

Ebony poked out her tongue, raising her fist to bang on the door. Nina grabbed it, this time not letting go. While the two struggled, Jevon appeared.

"Hey, don't stop on my account." He leaned against the frame, smirking. "Got wind of a new politically-correct term for lesbians the other day ... vagetarians."

"Ha ha." Nina rolled her eyes. "I was saving your skin. She needs to relax, remember?"

"Stop saying that!" Ebony pulled free, rubbing at her wrist. "Look how red it is!" she said angrily. "When'd you get freakishly strong?"

Jevon laughed. "Gym life paying off, along with some sneaky doped-up peptides?"

"So I lift. It's better than having spaghetti arms like Gumby in there. Now," Nina gripped the flyscreen's handle, "are you two going to talk sensibly?"

Ebony glared at her friend's hand. "Sure, so much for us acting conventional."

Nina waited, while Jevon leaned against the doorframe, munching on a sandwich. "It's locked, Perky. Not born stupid."

Furious, Ebony yanked at the handle the moment Nina released it. "Give me my mobile!"

"I would but ..." Jevon scratched at himself, contemplating his sandwich, "no dice. The guy's a genius, Eb. Kevo's close, real close."

"Close to what?"

Jevon took a huge bite and chewed for a minute. "He's backing up your phone's data, of course. And get this, it has a ridiculous memory capacity for a smartphone. Kevo's already used up four of his external drives and it's still going."

Furious, Ebony shoved at the flyscreen door, barely resisting the urge to kick it. "I can't believe you've involved other people in this!"

"I can see you're angry."

"Ya think?"

"I know taking it was wrong, but—"

"Then give it back!"

"I will." Jevon glanced at his watch. "Come back in say ... an hour? This'll all be done." He held up a finger before she could yell some more. "It'll also give me a headstart to leave town until you cool your heels."

"Cool my heels?" Ebony could have sworn steam came out her ears. "Kevo!" she yelled, trying to peer down the hall. "Hey, Kevo!"

Jevon hissed a breath when Kevin came out his room. "Oh, Ebony! I thought you were still in the hospital."

"Really?" Ebony spared Jevon a withering look.

"Nope." Nina rubbed at her temple. "That's where Jevon's going."

"I've just stopped by to pick up my phone," Ebony snapped.

"Right," Kevin looked between the two. "Alright then, check out what I'm on to." Glancing at the door, he leaned forward, releasing the latch. "Why's this locked?"

"Thanks Kevin," Ebony said as she sailed in. "Jevon's just playing the dick."

Nina followed, shoving past Jevon. "Teach him to be a gentleman."

"Kiss-arses." Jevon took another bite of his sandwich.

The moment she walked into Kevin's room, Ebony was distracted by the brightly lit equipment. "How do you sleep at night with all this?"

"My guess is he doesn't," Jevon said, shoving clothes to the side of the bed and slumping on it while grinning at Nina's speechless reaction to the mess. "That's why he's so wired. Hey Perks, take a seat!" He patted the bed.

After delivering a blistering look, Nina stood beside a one-armed chair. "I'm fine here."

Ebony shared a reluctant grin with Jevon. Nina looked like her skin was crawling. The fact she was staying proved how much she wanted to save their relationship.

Deep in concentration, Kevin picked up his rewired tablet computer to start scrolling. "Sorry about the mess, maid's year off. I can grab another seat from the kitchen though."

"Don't, I can just stand. It's fine." Nina crossed her arms. "Better for my back anyway."

Kevin looked at her strangely, finally noticing her stilted posture.

Jevon laughed. "Don't sweat it, mate. All her phobic disorders are probably kicking in right about now." Stuffing the rest of his sandwich in his mouth, he chewed vigorously, spitting breadcrumbs everywhere when he spoke. "How bad do you want to clean this room?" he mumbled, wiping at his full mouth.

Horrified, Nina looked at him. "I don't know what you're talking about, you giant talking germ!" Noticing Kevin's sideways glance, she laughed weakly, fighting to make it sound natural. "He's kidding, of course. Cleaning a stranger's room." She swallowed, looking around weakly. "That's just bizarre ... not to mention a violation of privacy. Although ..." She scratched at her arm. "If you wanted a hand, you know, if we're going to be here a while, I could organise here or there, maybe vacuum the floor ..."

"Err ..." Bewildered, Kevin jumped when his computer alerted. "The encryption program's done!"

"What's that mean?" Ebony leaned over his shoulder trying to make sense of the code on the screen. It looked like another language, either hieroglyphic or some kind of symbols?

"I've got access to your phone."

"You unlocked it?" Ebony chewed at her lip, rolling her eyes at Jevon who was staring at her, eyes pleading. "It took a while."

"That was the easy part." Kevin turned the phone over and pointed. "This thing here, it's got me intrigued."

Ebony leaned closer seeing that he had removed the back cover. "What am I looking at?"

"See this?"

"The battery?"

Kevin shook his head. "It's not a battery, it's something else. Somehow, it's replacing your processor, though I've never seen a design like this on the market."

Lost, she scratched her head. "And that's important because?"

Like he had just won the grand prize, Jevon jumped up, throwing his hands in the air. "Ladies and gents, Ebony Casteel!"

Irritated, Nina kicked at him lightly. "Behave! I knew the moment he pointed at the inside of the phone he'd lose her."

Kevin began to laugh, then realised Nina wasn't joking. "Really? She's serious?"

"It's no secret that I fail with this kind of thing," Ebony admitted.

"Right. Well, what do you want to know?"

Ebony straightened, for a moment scrunching her eyes. What *did* she want to know? Did she have a choice, now that Jevon had dragged her this far? Leaning down, she glared into her phone's innards.

"I get that you've unlocked the phone," she began, "and somehow I have a battery that's gone super or something, controlling the entire thing?"

The bewildered look on Kevin's face told her she was not even close.

"Nina, help me?" Ebony pleaded.

"I got this." Jevon jumped to his feet. "Translation for the mentally impaired. Your new little friend in there," he pointed inside the phone, "isn't a battery, so forget that."

"Right, no battery. Gone." Ebony looked at the square device puzzled. "So what is it?"

"Someone's removed your battery," Kevin said, "tricked your phone up and added this high-tech device."

"Question is, who put that there?" Jevon asked ominously.

"Well." Ebony chewed at her lip. "I was at least half right. It's running my phone."

Eyebrows puckered, Nina joined them. "Strange how something so small can do all that."

"From what I can tell, the rest of the phone's components are there but inactive," added Kevin, peering inside. "It can still receive and make calls, texts, but everything else is defunct. Probably has been ever since this device was installed."

"Must be for show," Jevon said. "To keep it looking the part."

"That'd be my guess."

"So you're both saying someone's messed with my phone? But why?"

"Why?" Kevin shrugged, pulling a face. "The model's at least four years old, odd choice with what's out on the market these days."

"I hate learning new phones, the software updates." Ebony laughed at herself. "Was thinking of trading it in though. I saw the other day that my plan expired ages ago."

Eyes wide, Kevin shook his head. "I'd hold off on that if I were you."

"You haven't heard the best part yet," Jevon intoned mysteriously.

"I think I've seen enough crazy over the last week to hold me for years. Let's call it quits here."

"Quit now?" Jevon looked truly appalled. "Kevo's been at this for a couple of hours, slaving to give you answers."

"You're trying to draw Ebony into this under false pretences." Nina wagged a finger at him. "She never asked for answers, Jev. This is all you and you know it."

Now Kevin was looking at her the same way.

"Alright," she relented, ignoring Nina's eyeroll. "Five minutes, then Nina and I are gone, and the phone comes with me."

Kevin spun on his chair, loading up three screens, pointing to the middle one. "Watch here, it'll be easiest for you to understand. I'll work your mobile primarily through my main screen."

The screen lit with a picture and icons. "Look! That's my home screen!" Despite herself, Ebony was intrigued.

"Nothing more relieving than sighting the familiarity." Kevin began moving through her apps then paused at her Utilities folder, enlarging it. Clicking through to a second screen, he paused. "What's that app?" He pointed to one with a badge. The title above read *Fellowship*.

"No idea. I can't even remember downloading it."

Kevin clicked on it and a security box appeared. "This's where you need to pay attention, it's password protected."

"Password?" Ebony stared at the box. "Good luck with that. I wouldn't have a clue."

"Already done. I've had an encryption program running for the last couple of hours, along with back-up for the phone."

As soon as he entered the code, the Fellowship Badge splashed across the screen, and a program began loading.

Moments later, it was still sitting on five percent. "Forgot how long this took to load the first time. I'm gonna go check on Cass," Kevin said, about to stand up.

Jevon pounced like a predator onto prey. "Don't even think about moving from that chair!"

"Right." Kevin leaned back in his seat as everyone in the room seemed to be holding their breath, watching the line grow.

Clearly beside himself, Jevon grabbed Ebony's arm, a stupid grin on his face. "All about the build-up, Eb!"

Ebony rolled her eyes, looking again at the line which was now at thirty percent. Even Nina was drumming her fingers where her arms were crossed. Into that collective silence came a sharp knock at the front door.

Everyone jumped.

"Expecting someone?" Nina asked, looking around.

"Err, no." Like he was mesmerised, Kevin watched the line on the screen. "But maybe I should ..."

The doorbell rang several times in a row.

"Don't sweat it," Jevon said. "Nina can get rid of them."

"Oh, can she now?" Nina jammed her hands on her hips. "Why don't you go?

"Because I'm not the phobic who needs an excuse to evacuate the area before they undergo a psychotic break."

"Jev, I'm fine so give the quips a rest and bite your tongue." Nina scratched an arm. "When you start tasting blood, don't stop."

Another bang on the door, this one sounding like a fist. "I think I'll just ..." began Kevin.

"I'll get the door." Jevon backed up immediately. "You stay put, mate. Show Eb what you've got."

"Oh, alright!" Nina shoved past him. "I've seen your unconventional meet-and-greet at Starrick Motors. I'll get the door."

"Hey Nina," Kevin called before she left, "if they don't look related, don't let them in."

"Of course."

"That's the great thing about reverse psychology." Jevon grinned at Ebony. "You never know who it'll work on."

"We're there," Kevin announced. "One hundred percent."

Nothing happened.

Thoroughly disappointed, Jevon huffed a breath. "Well, that's a little underwhelming. Is it frozen or something?"

"No, the programs running ... but ..." Kevin clicked on the screen.

"Okay guys," Ebony picked up her phone, turning it over, "I think your five minutes is over."

Suddenly the badge on the mobile's screen flashed, began to alter and expand, loading as obviously an entirely new program.

"Wh-what's it doing?" She dumped the phone back on the desk, unnerved.

"It didn't load all this before." Kevin began moving through the new program, obviously still figuring his way around. "It looks like some sort of system reboot has taken place to load an entirely new user interface." Turning to his second screen, he loaded the data. "It looks ... Okay, so that's happening."

"What is?" Jevon demanded.

Kevin sat back. "I think this phone is connecting to a private satellite network."

"A what?" Ebony felt like her brain had frozen. "Why would my phone do that?"

"My guess?" Kevin kept moving through the data. "I'd say it's to—"

"—stay off the map," finished Jevon.

"Exactly." Kevin narrowed his eyes, clicking his way in. "Satellite phones are much harder to track. Having your own private network has many advantages."

"And you know who would have to have their own satellite network?" Jevon was practically on top of Kevin, his eyes glued to the screen. "The Fellowship. Obviously, they're bigger players than I thought. What're all those symbols?" he pointed. "Can you click on them?"

"Most seem non-responsive." Kevin hovered over several that were locked, darkened. "See."

"Eb, see if you can open it from the phone," Jevon said.

"Me? What difference will that make?"

"Humour me."

"Oh right, another one of your hunches." Annoyed, Ebony picked up her phone and instantly it became active.

Like something had just clicked for him, Kevin smiled. "Okay, it seems to only respond through the phone."

"Or maybe," said Jevon, "the mobile can only be worked through Ebony."

"Like a security precaution." Kevin nodded, impressed. "The how on that intrigues me greatly."

Ebony stared at the device. "I'm sure there's a more logical explanation." Picking one of the darkened symbols at random, she pressed it.

The symbol lit, forming three points that connected into a triangular shape. The phone began to vibrate, releasing tones that everyone heard before an image shot from the screen to hover in mid-air above it.

Written in English, rotating beneath that symbol were four words: *The Law of Three.*

"Eb," Jevon whispered. "How'd you do that?"

"I …" She felt strange, like there was a warm pull toward what she saw. The sensation was so foreign, it freaked her out. Dropping the phone back on the desk, she backed up, knocking over the chair, breaking its other arm.

Kevin jerked to his feet, hitting Jevon under the chin, giving him an instant bloody nose.

"Ow, mate!"

"Err, sorry, man." Kevin shoved a box of tissues at him, looking at Ebony. "Did it hurt you? The phone?"

She stared at her hand, fingers spread. "No …" She made a fist, glaring at Jevon whose eyes were streaming along with his nose. "I told you nothing good would come of this."

Without warning, the phone re-lit on the desk, displaying a rotating triangle. Tissues stuffed up his nose, Jevon leaned forward.

"The triangle," he mumbled. "It's actually a symbol. And look," he pointed, "I think it's translating them into English. The Law of Three: Centre, Control, Commitment."

"Looks like some type of teaching aid," Kevin said.

"Maybe." Jevon stretched a hand toward the image.

"Don't touch it!" Ebony hissed.

"It's …" Jevon's fingers danced over the symbols. "I can feel energy pushing my hand back. It's almost solid."

Without warning the energy screen retracted, taking the image with it. The room was abruptly silent, the phone dark.

Jevon's jaw dropped in astonishment. "What just happened?"

Like he was reaching for a bomb, Kevin carefully picked up the phone, turning it over. "I don't know … apart from the fact I just experienced a major nerdgasm."

Scared, barely able to think straight, Ebony watched her cousin and his friend study her mobile. Kevin was even daring enough to prod at the innards.

"Eb!" Jevon turned to her. "Here, touch it."

As she extended a hand to touch the screen, Ebony came to a decision. Before either of the boys knew what she was up to, she had pulled Kevin's cord from her phone and pocketed it.

Jevon shoved past Kevin. "No way, we have to try that again!"

"Until what, Jev? When's it enough?"

"Until we get this right! It only responds to you."

Ebony eyed the bruising beneath her cousin's eyes, the tissues stuffed up his nose. "Clean yourself up Jev, you're losing it. And Kevin," she gave him an apologetic look, "I'm sorry, he got you involved in this."

"Are you kidding?" Kevin shook his head. "Whatever this is, I'm in."

"None of this can leave the room. Not even Baden can know." She eyed Kevin in warning. "This is dangerous. It somehow connects to my abduction, and I don't want anyone else getting hurt, or involved. You get that don't you?"

Kevin nodded, his gaze moving between her and Jevon.

As she marched from the room, her cousin dogged her heels. Nina was nowhere to be seen and the front door was wide open, creaking back and forth in the cooling early evening air.

"Where's Nina?"

"I don't know, probably with Bay or something. Look, you're not thinking this through."

Ebony swung away from the front door, and as she did her gaze fell on the living room to see Nina sitting on the Zhengs' couch, staring blankly ahead. "Nina?"

The moment she entered the living room, she became aware of the men in dark suits, three of them. There was also a woman, kneeling before Nina, saying something Ebony could not hear. Nina looked out of it, like she was in some kind of trance.

"Hey!" Ebony shoved past Jevon. "What've you done to her?"

"Ebony?" Kevin called her name, halting mid-stride. He was standing behind Jevon, white-faced and scared, an older, bald man pushing him into the living room.

"What's going on?" Ebony demanded, recognising him from the hospital. Axel? He worked for Xavier Solomon.

"What's necessary, Miss Casteel, to protect you." Axel then signalled his men by giving them a nod.

Ebony's world spun as two of the men drew strange-looking guns and fired at her cousin and Kevin. She screamed, body hunching in reaction, until she realised they were caught before hitting the carpet, then taken to the couch to sit beside Nina, in a similar catatonic state.

Axel spoke to a tall black man. "Wipe the computers completely and leave no trail." He then looked at Ebony. "You're scared, and you should be. But not of me. Your friends aren't hurt. I'm protecting them too."

"Protecting?" Gripping her head, she felt a strange buzzing at the back of it, a feeling of losing control.

Axel sighed, looking at the three on the couch, his calm a strange anchor. "Yes, Miss Casteel. I'm here to quarantine this outbreak. Your friends have learnt too much, and now they're in danger. I need to stop them from learning more."

"You work for the Solomons. I remember, you were at the hospital."

"It's more complicated than that. I work for the Fellowship as the lead agent to the Solomon family. I've been charged with protecting you, so consider me a friend."

"Protecting me? You said that before." Hugging her arms around her middle, she fought to control her roiling stomach. "From what? What do I need protecting from?"

"Ever since your very public return to Freestone, you've made my job difficult. The loss of your memory has," his face briefly twisted, "let's say, complicated things."

"My father left the Fellowship before he adopted me. He hates them. Why would they send you to protect me?"

"Don't believe everything you hear. It is true Rickard has stepped down, but the Casteel name still has an active presence within the Fellowship. He is still bound to us by two things that are precious to him."

When Axel paused, she stared at him defiantly. "They are?"

"His land," he finally answered. "The other, Miss Casteel, is you."

More agents walked into the lounge room frightening her silent. There had to be at least six of them now, everyone looking out of place amongst the Zhengs' family photos, kids' toys and old couch and recliners. An agent whispered to Axel, his expression so hard her knees locked in reaction.

"Are they alive?" he asked, clearly surprised.

"Are who alive?" she demanded, thinking they must be talking about someone from the Zheng family.

The agent whispered something else.

"They were attempting to grow *what*?" Axel looked furious, his face hardening even more. "Inform Doctor Walker, she'll need to examine the pair." He trailed off, shaking his head in disbelief. "If they come off clean, transport them back to their homes. Clearly, we've underestimated the children's resolve. We can't afford to have this happen again. Understood?"

"Yes, Sir."

Axel turned back to Ebony. "Whether you want answers or not is no longer relevant. You are to be transported to White Pier. Xavier Solomon is waiting there for you with someone who can help."

"Help me with what?"

"Your treatment. Let's call him a specialist."

"I don't care how special they are, Doctor Walker's treating me. I'm happy with her." Ebony looked at the catatonic states of her friends' white faces. "None of this can be legal. What if I call the authorities?"

"The police?" Axel chuckled, sliding a hand into a pocket. "I suppose to the uneducated that would seem the right course of action. If you go to the authorities, reveal what's taken place here, you and your family will never see the light of day or breathe free air again."

"And I'm to believe that? Believe your every word?" Lifting her chin, Ebony dug deep, hands making fists. "You're trying to frighten me to get me to do what you want."

"Yes, I am. You need to be scared, Ebony. You've already been critically wounded once. Do you want the same for them?" He indicated her friends. "For your family?"

"No." Ebony shook her head, remembering the pain, recalling the terror of forgotten memories. "I just want to go home and for this to all just go away."

"The true words of a Casteel. You're really one of them, aren't you?" Axel grabbed her shoulder turning her toward the front door. "My suggestion is to unlearn such habits. One day it could save your life."

"No!" Ebony, grabbed for the couch. "I won't leave my friends with you. You'll have to drag me out here screaming! That'll draw attention," she threatened, pulling away angrily.

"Actually," Axel nodded to one of his silent agents, "that won't be necessary."

Ebony's mouth opened as the weapon fired, the bolt striking her chest, instantly cramping muscles, locking them in place. Paralysed, she felt the room spin sickeningly, her body falling a moment before she was caught and carried outside.

She could detect voices, but they were muffled and distant, like they came from another room. Her eyes would not stop blurring with tears, so much so that they began running into her hair.

Panic flared when Axel leaned close to deliver a message while placing her on the back seat of a car. "I'm sorry, Miss Casteel, but this meeting at White Pier cannot be undone."

Galactic Star Key: Kaze Karbroe
Astral Nav-Coordinates: EAS-APL-4
Data Sequence: 21.0

Aboard a Warront Craft, Kaze walked to an energy-window, scrutinising Global Base's subterranean flight hangar. The moment their craft began to rise from the platform, he got a better view of all Planetary Allegiance vessels below. Divided into service-zones, a number of ships were placed in engineering-dock for serious overhaul, while others were undergoing routine maintenance.

On the far side, he noticed many newly constructed sub-light Earth vessels, human crews working alongside flight-engineers.

Dust and debris swirled as a large circular door opened above, bright rays of sunlight streaming in. The moment the bulky Warront cleared ground level, Kaze looked across Global Base, eyeing the copious amount of Earth vessels entering the base.

The launch was now only a few cycles away.

"Attention all," announced a voice over the Warront's freq-com PA. "Pre-flight systems complete, hover-launchers engaging in five, four, three, two, one ... initiating."

With hover engines powered, the Warront began to rise to an optimal launching altitude level where the main magna-drive engines would take over. Employing masking technology during this manoeuvre made certain the craft remained unseen before clearing Global Base's Terrain-cloak.

Kaze watched the base shrink to include Freestone Valley and its tree-covered hills as their vessel speeded quickly to pass through a thick layer of cloud.

Freq-com opened again, their captain warning, "Brace for sub-light thrusters."

A deep rumble shook the ship before it was propelled forward, pushing free of Earth's gravity to achieve space-flight velocity, bright red and yellow plasma flames igniting sparks which scattered across the energy-window, ionised gases contacting the ship's shields.

The moment their vessel broke orbit, its thrusters powered down, their ride smoothing out. Straightening, Kaze looked around the bay, noting the calm of the two working Astral Guard officers seated at their private stations.

No fun there, he thought. Glancing back, he frowned as a reflector mask came online. Disgruntled, he stepped closer to the energy-window, having only caught a brief view of darkened space before it was replaced by a dynamic digitised pattern that reflected his surroundings.

What was this about? Tapping the energy-window's controller on his right, he tried entering his Star-Key to shift the view back to its original state only to discover he was locked out.

Kaze turned to his brother, seated before a cyber-screen, his furrowed brow hinting he was engrossed in the task, the hue of the screen intensifying his eye colour.

"Why the reflector mask?" Kaze asked loud enough to attract his brother's attention, but not that of the officers. "This Warront runs like a cheap ride compared to a Galactic Class vessel."

The criticism received no response, further fuelling Kaze's exasperation.

Zozes shifted his weight, leaning against the ship's tactical-base terminal, used for strategic planning of battle operations. Behind him rotated a virtual schematic of the Warront on the centre table, the cyber image's light blue hue casting his frame in shadow.

"Mind stepping into the light, brother?" Kaze lifted his chin. "That shady display's giving you a baleful air."

Still nothing. Rising to the challenge, Kaze activated his porta-tool, opening the Blades' personal freq-com channel, increasing the audio cap to maximum.

"Look alive, space-wrangler!"

Zozes jolted as if struck by a surge bolt. Glaring at his brother, he came to his feet, rubbing at his ears. "Vok it, Kaze! You trying to burn out my audial implants?"

"Better than wasting words on deaf ears. Or a boot at the head." Shrugging, he glanced at his feet. "Didn't fancy going about barefoot."

"At least you knew the consequences," Zozes muttered, tucking back his hair. Then he noticed the energy-screen's digitalised reflector masks. "Warp screen's active?"

"Why yes, it is!" Kaze swung back, thoughtfully crossing his arms. "Strange, huh?" Stepping forward, he flicked the cyber mesh, distorting its reflection, like a stone dropped in water. "Got any theories why it would be kicking in when we aren't at warp?"

On a frown, Zozes came alongside. "They're usually generated for those who suffer warp-gyre sickness while in a temporal slip-tunnel."

"Don't look at me! My stomach's got the stamina to keep its hatch sealed — even while performing an orbital space jump," smirking, he mouthed the last word, "naked."

Zozes rolled his eyes. "Nothing but your skin holding back the vacuum of space. You're a new kind of special."

"No BS, brother."

"I've no idea if what comes out your mouth is true, or is something to throw me off my stride."

"Maybe a little of both." Kaze bumped Zozes' shoulder with his own. "Helps break up the uniformity we've had to endure since arriving on this planet."

Zozes glanced at the two working officers. "Perhaps dealing with Primordial technology brings that type of complication."

"It's a theory," Kaze said, though he chewed on this with difficulty. "Doesn't explain the forcefeeding us Origin theory, or that TECH-jawed garble that keeps most a step behind on that Primordial Station." Kaze eyed his brother's smug grin. "Don't tell me you're enjoying learning that stuff, because there's no way."

"Understanding how the galaxy works is such an inconvenience to you. Not my fault we're ... what's that human expression? Polar-opposites."

"Well, I've a more simplified approach to coming up with those answers."

"Meaning harassing me until I give you the answers."

"A system that you cannot deny works." Scrubbing a hand over his face, Kaze wished he could clear irritation as easily. "Because it's not the norm for the rest of us to process, and neither are the convoluted answers we're being given."

Zozes did not even try to deny that.

"The difference between you and me," Kaze concluded, "is that it just makes me want to hit something, while you ..."

"While I do what?" Zozes demanded, eyebrows drawn together.

"Make adoring eyes at a cyber-screen while reading." Kaze wiggled his eyebrows. "The only way I'd do that is if a naked constellation model was displaying her universe."

On a coughed laugh, Zozes eyed his brother's expression, a battle between disgruntled and boldness. "So, you don't want to know what I found about this Galaxy Class ship?"

"If that's what you've been doing," Kaze jabbed a thumb over his shoulder at the energy-window. "I'm listening."

"Hassling me for the answers again, Kaze?"

"You got some?"

"There's an explanation for everything." Thoughtful, Zozes ran a hand over the cyber reflector mask's netting mesh, eyeing the swirling mask rippling beneath his hand. "Even this minor inconvenience."

"So even eyeballing Earth from outer orbit is classified?" Kaze pondered his brother's words, something clicking into place. "That's got to be next level paranoia."

"Sound reasoning to me." Zozes stepped closer to his brother. "Interconnecting inconveniences, brother. They point us in the true direction, you just have to follow their lead."

"To more questions that won't be answered." Kaze glanced at his brother's profile, realising Zozes was guiding him to answers, and he had been completely unaware.

Something that irritated Kaze, no end. "Fair play, puppet master. I suppose it explains why this Warront's security network is prejudiced against Blade ID authorisation, the cyber-controller has already locked me out."

Before Zozes could answer, Major Rajek entered the bay. His fast stride took him around the tactical operations base, past the few comp-stations.

"Sir." Both Kaze and Zozes straightened while addressing him.

"Alphas." He must have caught the last of Kaze's words, because he nodded to the energy-window. "Standard protocol when dealing with a Primordial World. The ship's sensors have locked out your Star-Keys, they're below clearance level."

"I see." Zozes frowned while enquiring, "Does that include yours, Sir?"

Rajek looked back at the screen, his open expression telling both he could see past the reflector mask to view the planet. "No, I see Earth's true state. Its existence clearly reveals reclamation to what it once used to be." The Major touched the cyber-controller, the same one Kaze had tried to access, triggering a blast shield to cover the energy window. "You can thank your cyber-optics' adaptation to Astral Guard's security censorship, the onboard pairing signal detects Star-Keys to mask off a view-screen."

"Technology can be a real tragedy sometimes," Kaze grumbled, looking from Rajek to his brother. "What's so dangerous with taking in a space view of Earth?"

Rajek looked from Kaze to Zozes, before turning to stand at the round tactical operations computer, indicating for them to join him. "Alpha Blue, you wouldn't believe me even if I told you."

Mouth tight, Kaze joined him, one question floating to the surface. "Now that we're spaceborne, either one of you care to explain why we were pulled off Earth only a few days before the launch?"

Rajek and Zozes eyed each other across the tactical computer, a virtual image of the Warront continuing to rotate before the three. Neither answered.

"You know something?" he demanded of his brother.

The Major turned to the two officers present. "You're both dismissed," he ordered, then watched as they left before turning back, nodding to Zozes. "It's time he knows, Alpha Green."

"What we're about to say, Kaze, will come as problematic, and in your case not well received. Remember we're a team and whatever happens, we'll work through this."

The words instantly set Kaze's teeth on edge. "If this connects to LT being sealed back in its stasis-holder, I know I won't be keen on the reasons."

"We're being called on to undertake the Alpha Trials to solidify a permanent duty service upon Earth," Zozes finally admitted.

Blindsided, Kaze stared at this brother, noting that Rajek did not move to correct him. Shock turned to anger, an emotion he felt comfortable expressing.

"Well, aren't we just warping through the ranks. Throw aside all preliminaries and finals. No, the Karbroe brothers are powering straight to the grand final, like we're—"

"Careful, Kaze," interrupted Zozes quietly.

The Major raised an eyebrow. "You forget what you've accomplished with Alpha Green. Your control has been progressive."

"Yeah." Kaze fought to keep his tone even a little respectful. "Because a couple of weeks' field experience with a Trone makes every Alpha in the galaxy worth something."

"You also have a strong advantage," Rajek said, looking at Zozes. "Your brother and his control over the unibind bridge of the dual-pairing."

"We're evaluated together," Zozes said. "As one. I'll pull you through, Kaze."

"Well doesn't that fix everything! It's a good feeling to be declared dead weight. I still haven't a clue how to operate LT's most basic command orders." Kaze glanced at the hovering image, wondering if he was of sound mind. "Wouldn't want to make this any easier on us."

"I know we can do this," Zozes said, clearly concerned. "Remember back to the Blade ship, when we were first paired with the Trone? You trusted what the Chief said then, how certain she was. Trust her now."

Kaze looked from the Major to his brother. "The Alpha Trials are for Blade elites, after countless solar cycles of command conditioning with their Trone."

Zozes fronted his brother, searching his eyes. "Where's that overblown confidence you throw around, spoiling for reaction? You've been looking for a way to prove you're in control since we stepped onto that planet."

Mouth a stubborn line, Kaze stared at his brother, barely understanding the turmoil of his own feelings.

"This is a bad idea. Clearly Astral Guard want our duty-service revoked so they can ship us out of this system," was all he could manage.

"I'm afraid there's no turning back," Rajek said. "Alpha Green has been working toward this for a number of service terms, and his Star-Key states he is indeed ready. Trust that, Alpha Blue, and you'll pull through."

But could Zozes do that, dragging him like a grav-anchor? "The probability for me surpassing, let alone matching, your command experience, brother, is not high. Not even a Nova Trade Agent would gamble on those odds. They're setting us up."

Zozes was still watching his brother, expression thoughtful. "Then let's go out there and prove them wrong. You won't fail yourself, Kaze," Zozes leaned closer, "or me. We hold together."

On a deep swallow, Kaze stared back, knowing exactly what his brother was saying. "Well now, aren't we feeling all emotional?" he replied, searching for his bravado. "Best I agree before you both start growing lady parts. Hard enough to take you both seriously."

"Then let's move on," Rajek urged. "The Blades and Astral Guard are specialist-arms within the Galactic Force. General practice is that no division alone can completely influence the Trials without Command's full involvement. However, these Alpha Trials stand to be unique. Astral Guard will be taking complete authority over your evaluation through the Overwatch Initiative."

"I see." Kaze shook off the last of his emotion, finding greater understanding. "Overwatch Initiative's being used and abused around this planet."

"Galactic Force officials would openly oppose this," Zozes said, homing in on certain words. "How has Command responded?"

"Not well," Rajek admitted. "Commander Vome has been sent to renegotiate with the Astral Guard on the way these field assessments have been authorised, not to mention taken off site."

"Off site?" Kaze glanced at the shield before the energy-window. "Where exactly is the testing taking place?"

"Aboard a Galaxy Ship," the Major replied. "One that's been positioned near the centre of Earth's solar system."

Nauseous, Kaze swallowed into a bellyful of resentment. "Clearly, Astral Guard wants us to fail, everything points to that." He glared at his brother. "Why else bring forward the testing?"

"They want us out of reach of the launch," Zozes agreed. "Issuing Overwatch upon Earth grants the Astral Guard with emergency authority. The power to order and protect the planet and its inhabitants from all influences regarding Primordial technology."

"Can someone then explain to me," Kaze demanded, "how the Alpha Trials fall under the same jurisdiction that governs Primordial technology?" He looked at the Major. "There's something you're not telling us."

The brothers waited, watching the Major wage an internal war, one that was clearly keeping him silent.

"Sir—" Kaze began.

Rajek held up a hand, standing to his full height. "We are Blades, sworn to abide by the orders of our superiors who are in authority. Is that understood?"

Kaze fought back a sneer, remaining silent.

"Is that understood, Alpha Blue?"

"Yes, Sir!"

Zozes nodded once. "It is, Sir."

"You will enter these Trials," Rajek leaned forward, fists on the table, staring each in the eye, "and you will prevail. Have I made myself clear, Blades?"

Eyes now locked on the Major, both brothers received his message answering as one. "Understood, Sir."

"Good. Then let's get to the details." Rajek moved around the table. "Your strength and fortitude needs to be centred on controlling Trone spawn. If either of you come into that arena with any degree of emotional impairment, it will doom you both."

"I've been going over the strategic analysis," Zozes said. "Looking at how best to combat each testing phase."

"Let me guess." Kaze rolled his eyes. "You want to take command charge of LT while grav-towing me behind?" A standard Zozes call he knew well.

"Because I know what's coming," Zozes argued. "How to defend against each of the Trial's objectives."

"You think this'll be standard? That Astral Guard will play nice?"

"Play nice?" Zozes shook his head, shoving back his hair. "Drop the human vernacular, Kaze, I think we've enough to deal with."

"Attention all hands," announced an officer over the Warront's freq-com. "Galaxy Ship D11-*Trollo* inbound for manual landing to hangar bay four, due to the graviton-runway's automated system's offline status."

Surprised, Zozes looked to the Major. "The Galaxy Ship's grav-runs are out?"

Automatically, Kaze looked to the energy-window, gritting his teeth at the blast shield covering the view. "The Alpha Trials are being held on a vessel lacking the basics in space flight operations? Not a good start, Sir."

"There's a Traverse Fleet space-yard secured in this system controlled by the Galactic Force," the Major said. "Production of a new series of vessels designed to protect Earth has been underway for some time. The D11-*Trollo* is a part of a new defence force, but most are still at space-dock undergoing service-flight construction."

"Wouldn't it be more resourceful," Zozes said, "to set up a Galactic Force shipyard on the Primordial Station rather than establishing another command base?"

The room fell silent, Rajek appearing to deliberate over the answer. "Initially that was the case, but due to certain station sensitivities, the Astral Guard found it necessary to evacuate them."

"Sensitivities?" Kaze goggled at that one.

"Let me guess," Zozes ground out, "they used the Overwatch Directive to have it moved."

Kaze took a step back from his brother, finally understanding just how angry he was. Even the Major appeared to collect himself. "Alpha Green—"

Zozes shook his head. "There's no point in defending the Astral Guard, Major. They are using the Overwatch Directive as a means to an end. They're not here to protect a developing civilisation, but using it as a tool to gain power."

"Suppose that explains why we saw mainly Astral Guard personnel aboard that Space Station," Kaze said with a spark of realisation.

"Tell me I'm wrong, Sir," Zozes said.

The Major's silence was answer enough.

Kaze looked at the two in turn. "It seems internal politics are spinning in Astral Guard's favour right now."

Clearly thinking hard, Rajek finally answered. "There's been a different approach from either side when dealing with the countermeasures the Kadra left on the Primordial Station."

"Countermeasures?" Kaze noted his brother had calmed only marginally, and could not help giving him a nudge. "You're saying Astral Guard cleared them off due to a set-up of Kadra booby-traps?"

"Booby?" Rajek's eyes flared at the word. "I fail to see how a human's breast comes into this situation."

Kaze laughed softly. "So much for being a tin man." He glanced at Zozes, adding, "Can't fight nature, Major. It's the carnal words in language that keeps us ... stimulated."

One eyebrow rose. "I believe you'd be surprised what stimulates me."

"Ignore the sub-verse word connotation," Zozes advised, glaring at his brother. "More often than not it's a word trap of questionable diversion. The Galactic Force makes up most of the Planetary Allegiance's fleet. Astral Guard understand this, they need them to successfully combat against any large threat."

"I'm certain they do," the Major replied. "The Actrix Covenant leaders were called in to mediate the dispute."

"A waste of time," Kaze said.

"Yes, the outcome was an unavoidable setback, resulting in the shipyard being relocated off station, something I need you to look beyond. What is the real reason the Kadra left these countermeasures in place?"

His brother's chin lifted in response, puzzling Kaze into theorising, "To sabotage the Station?"

"I'd guess more," Zozes said slowly. "The Kadra's countermeasures are twofold. One, to slow us in unravelling the Station's mysteries."

"And two?" asked Kaze.

"To divide us," Zozes said. "Fracture Planetary Allegiance's hold in this system."

"Exactly," Rajek said. "Those that stand apart, stand alone. The Overwatch Initiative grants the Astral Guard the power to authorise who can step onto that station and Earth."

"What good is knowing all this?" Kaze grumbled.

"Because times change, and now we know more." Zozes smiled thinly at his brother. "The Blades are clearly not the only division bound to Overwatch Directive in the Planetary Allegiance."

"You are not alone in this segregation," assured Rajek. "Astral Guard operates the Overwatch Initiative and casts it over any relation that may endanger or influence Primordial discoveries."

"Not sure if knowing all this makes me feel worse or better," Kaze complained. "Astral Guard's grasp for power seems to have limitless reach, to the point that scratching an itch in this system means going through them?"

"Right now," Zozes shook his head, "I'd say we'd be lucky to even use our own hand."

"Crude, but maybe right," Rajek said. "All Galactic Forces that have been granted authorisation on the Station first had to gain clearance, every directive outlined, right down to the smallest detail. Both of you noticed the lack of Galactic personnel. That's because their assignments have taken them off Primordial sites."

"What I want to know," Zozes snapped, "is why weren't we briefed about the shipyard and Overwatch? That dispute should have been brought to our attention the moment we arrived on that Station."

"That," Kaze said with a thin smile, "I can answer. They didn't want any information about 'discord' or 'disharmony' or whatever other political term they like to throw around, getting back to the Planetary Allegiance's lead planets. It's all about appearances."

The sub-light engines began powering down at the same moment the reinforced blast cover retracted on the energy-window, deactivating the masking screen and dissolving the cyber reflections.

Through the energy-window, Kaze caught sight of the Galaxy Ship D11-*Trollo* as they moved along its port side. Multiple decks visible, the outer hull was still under construction, large portions of its assembly-armour not yet plated down.

The curve of Earth's sun was just visible as they crested the ship, heading for docking bay four, passing by the *Trollo*'s three large magna-nacelles which rode high at the stern, each releasing a translucent energy vapour that wisped into space.

There was something else he could see also.

"You certain this ship's spaceworthy, Major? Because that looks like an exposed engine-bay, complete with a magnatronic core-drive. A well-placed phaser-point warhead would light up this space rig in less time than it takes to explain it—" Kaze moved closer to window, breaking off mid-sentence as he spotted several vessels.

Tan and desert-sand in colour, their underside dark grey, he would recognise them anywhere. Weaponry wings retracted, the triangular shaped vessels flew in formation followed by a curved, circular based Astral Guard cruiser, its twin flight nose extended forward, extended wings swept back.

Before they finished passing, Zozes was standing beside Kaze, their noses almost touching the energy-window.

"The convoy's heading for hangar bay four." Kaze swung to the Major. "Sir, last we understood all ship movements from the Station had been placed on stand down. Traversing through subspace layers was too dangerous."

"Unless," Zozes held up a hand, "another Blade ship finalised the mapping of the subspace layers around the Station?"

"Your Blade ship's original scouting of the subspace telemetry was utilised to recreate the map. There have been setbacks in creating a viable model, similar to Professor Marzden. Restrictions apply on ship deployment from the Station as only an AI Link-Trone powered vessel can navigate the subspace layers."

"When did this revelation happen?" Kaze demanded, itching to know if phase jumping may now be an option.

"Very recently. Magel's staff was instructed to go over all available data, use what they could of the Professor's."

Kaze looked at his brother, eyes narrowed. "It seems Magel's earlier warning on restricting all active ship launches from the Station was a little exaggerated."

"All of Professor Marzden's findings have been placed under extensive evaluation," the Major said. "His staff are being questioned to separate truth from the lies."

"Major." Zozes pointed at a slick-looking vessel outside the energy-window. "That vessel's markings are that of an Overwatch Command Cruiser?"

"They are." Rajek seemed to eye the ship warily. "It's Commodore Vae'gon's personal flight vessel, *The Carowa*."

Kaze blinked as a new warp slip-tunnel window lit up in open space, a Galactic Force Warbird taking position next to the Astral Guard cruiser. Beneath the curve of the Warbird's wing, a small vessel was deployed at the same moment *The Carowa* launched a shuttle.

Each was bound for the *Trollo*.

Silent, the three watched as each of the Blade vessels began entering hanger bay four one after another.

With the *Trollo*'s primary power offline, the hangar bay's interior looked much darker than normal, each vessel powering a forward ray lighting-emitter.

Their ship was one of the last to enter, the Galaxy Ship's vacuum shield lighting up as they passed through into overshadowing darkness lit randomly by emergency illumination beams, the sun's light a memory.

"Why is the *Trollo* running on emergency power?" Kaze asked, feeling distinctly uneasy.

Before Rajek could answer, their Warront touched down, manual landing struts finding the deck. Zozes was again staring out the energy-window, his expression anything but easy to read, almost like he was on guard. A movement beyond the screen caught Kaze's eye, a Lead Alpha Commando together with Optives walking down the landing ramps of their Blade Ship. Various races began assembling, all coming from different Astral States over the Galaxy.

Guard Enforcers were tasked with the duty of guiding stasis-carts holding the Link-Trones of each squad. Kaze lost count at twenty.

"I can see you both want answers," the Major said, standing between the two. "Those answers are out there." Moving off, he motioned for the brothers to follow. "Gear up Alphas. It's time for you to break through your limits."

Galactic Star Key: Zozes Karbroe
Astral Nav-Coordinates: EAS-APL-4
Data Sequence: 22.0

Zozes walked ahead of his brother down a short corridor into the Warront's evac-bay, noting its ramp had yet to be deployed. Enforcer Noremar stood at the centre, finalising diagnostics upon the grav-cart holding their Link-Trone.

Zozes heard his brother's groan, and could see she heard it too, glancing up from the porta-tool she was working on.

"So," Kaze cast fuel on the fire, "enjoying that we've been reduced to this again, Lieutenant?" He looked pointedly at the grav-cart.

"As they say," Noremar's teeth flashed in an uncharacteristic smile, "no trouble can be found in stasis, Blade."

"Is the only time those asinine fangs of hers surface, at someone's expense?" Kaze glanced at his brother. "Or is it just at ours?"

Jenvar triggered the mag-clip on her belt, disconnecting an LT-7 bolt overrider used to control the Trone. "Enjoy the rarity while it lasts Blade, I know I'll be savouring every last moment of this."

"Devronians embrace anti-humour," reminded Zozes, trying to diffuse his brother's ire.

The Enforcer bared them again in his direction "Let's see if all falls into place during the Trials, Blades." Rather than appease, Zozes' words appeared to ignite. "Of one thing I am certain, it will be unforgettable."

"You playing the line between a bad joke and a threat?" snarled Kaze.

362

She believed they would fail the Trials, thought Zozes, his cavalier response not touching on the realisation. "Perhaps a converging of the two."

Noremar powered the grav-cart's stasis-loader via its interface loading the storage units inventory. A virtual wireframe schematic generated above, displaying the contents inside that currently held the brothers' Link-Trone.

"I suppose, Lieutenant," Zozes spoke into the silence, "we'll just have to prove you wrong, and those that doubt us. Then," he looked her in the eye, "that smile of yours, will be ours."

Since his tone was even, Noremar had no option but to bite down on a retort, returning her attention to teleporting the LT-7 restraining bolt into the grav-cart's stasis-loader.

"I'll remember those words." Thorough by nature, she activated cyber triggers around her hand, checking the schematic of where to place the bolt. "Then we'll see who's left smiling at the end of these Trials, Blade."

Satisfied, Zozes accepted the challenge, considering the debate over.

Kaze had never been one to back down, digging in. "Becoming a little phobic, aren't we, Lieutenant? Attaching the restraining bolt via the stasis assembly teleporter?"

Regard fixed on the grav-cart's interface, Noremar answered tightly. "Orders are orders, Blade."

"Still ..."

"Kaze." Zozes eyed his brother who was rocking back on his heels. "That's enough."

"No." Noremar straightened slowly. "Allow him to finish."

"Fear's made you somewhat allergic to our Trone." He regarded her through hooded eyes. "And you call yourself a Devronian of tradition."

In a burst of speed, Noremar shifted her full weight to front him, her cold gaze boring into his.

"You're standing in my light." Kaze did not back down.

Pupils double in size, Noremar breathed deeply, adrenalin visibly pumping up her muscles. "Then move me, Blade."

One fast move and Zozes shoved between the two, making certain his brother stayed behind, ignoring his hot-tempered expletive. "Enough, Lieutenant."

"That Blade will show respect." Predatory, Noremar loosened her stance, muscle mass increasing with each shift of leg and arm, roll of her spine. On the hunt, Devronians were known to be stronger and faster, lethal when challenged. "Southverse Astral State will show him what it is to be of Devron."

"Let her try," Kaze laughed coldly. "I'll have her braced facedown, kissing the deck, venting useless rage ..."

Zozes interrupted the threats in a clipped, even tone. "Regain control, Enforcer! Take a step back."

"Move aside, Blade." Noremar's gaze was locked over his shoulder, onto his brother. "Or shall I go through you?"

He had to do something fast. Knowing the risk, he grasped her uniform at the throat, pulling her close, speaking forcefully.

"What are your orders?" Throwing authority into each word, he drew her gaze to his. For a moment, Zozes believed he was too late, the hand covering his severe enough to bruise. Then she blinked, seemed to break back, seeing him standing before her.

"Secure ... to secure the Link-Trone."

Noremar unclenched her fist while shoving his hand from her jacket. With each breath, her muscle mass began to return to normal, pupils retracting.

He inclined his head. "Then let it be done, Lieutenant."

For a long moment, Noremar eyed him, completely ignoring his brother. Straightening her uniform, she turned away, moving back to the grav-cart, to load a second virtual wireframe, this time of the LT-Bolt overrider within the grav-cart's stasis-loader. She repositioned that cyber image next to the Link-Trone's schematic.

Thoughtful, Zozes looked over the grav-cart, noting the increased measures the Enforcer was taking in securing their Link-Trone. Orders she claimed to have been given.

A sneer curling his lip, Kaze pushed his brother's shoulder. "You enjoy stopping things right before they're fun."

"You want to go into the Trials with no arms?"

"Who said I'd get injured?"

"The hunt-state of a Devronian fuelled with adrenalin." Zozes lifted his eyebrows. "They only understand the kill."

"So you're saying I should poke a little more, maybe pull some hair?"

"Brother ..." Zozes stretched his bruised hand, looking back at the grav-cart. "One day your mouth's going to put us into trouble that can't be mended by words."

"You make that sound like it's a bad thing." Gaze turning speculative, Kaze glanced at the grav-cart. "Got any idea why LT has been sealed inside this thing again?"

Zozes tilted his head, obviously weighing his words. "The heavy security measures and Noremar's reaction with that slip of temper were indicators she's under pressure. Leaves me wondering what—"

"Astral Guard is afraid of," finished Kaze wide-eyed.

Zozes frowned, glancing at his brother. "Blunt as always, but correct."

The door behind Zozes opened on the Major, who paused at the grav-cart to check the positioning of the Trone's restraining bolt. "At your convenience, Lieutenant, we are ready to depart."

"Understood, Major."

The tension in her voice was obvious, and not missed by Rajek, nor was the heated look she threw Kaze.

"Is there something I need to know?" he enquired.

"No, Sir." Kaze stepped forward. "Everything's always copacetic around me."

Zozes watched Noremar pull at her uniform, straightening where he had gripped it.

"Just a misunderstanding, Sir. Squad correlation is still finding its place."

Rajek's hand rested briefly on Zozes' shoulder as he stepped to the ramp. It seemed nothing escaped the Major's scrutiny, something he deeply respected.

Noremar finished locking in new distribution coordinates on the interface of the grav-cart for when the Link-Trone was to materialise, restraining bolt attached.

After clearing her throat, the Enforcer stood at-stance. "Teleporting load-out schematics have been locked in, Sir. The Link-Trone is ready for materialisation upon your order."

"Then let's get underway." The Major's hand waved over the cyber panel beside the ramp.

The holding seals instantly began depressurising, repulsing magnetic fields and releasing the locked mag-clamps. Metal shifted, echoing throughout the evac-bay, hydraulic rods extending to settle it upon the deck.

"Fall in." Taking the lead, Major Rajek stepped forward, Noremar in his wake, the grav-cart tethered to follow her via her porta-tool.

Side by side the two descended, stepping through an expulsion of vapour spewing from the Warront's exhaust vents positioned on the underside of the ship's aft nacelle. Peering through this, Zozes eyed the closest Blade Ship as they moved around, trying to gauge their gathered comrades' mood while finding their squad's position. A company of Astral Guard personnel drew alongside, blocking his view, Rajek leading them closer to Vae'gon's Warront Craft.

That was when Zozes noticed that each of the squads' Enforcers had been placed at the head of their teams, stasis-loader grav-carts out front, secured Link-Trones inside.

"Nothing more beautiful than a Blade reunion," enthused Kaze, saying this loud enough to earn a stern look from a nearby Astral Guard officer. "For a while there it felt like we were the only Blades in the Galaxy."

"Worried you'll get lost in the crowd now?"

"With a face like this?" Kaze grinned cockily. "I should kiss the sky I'm so pretty."

Fast losing interest in the subject, Zozes watched the ramp begin to lower on Vae'gon's ship. "Like I said, lost in the crowd."

"Sounds like you think ..." Kaze fell silent, clearly taking in the comment. "You've got the look on, more than me?"

"Prettier, brawnier, smarter ..." Zozes scratched for Earth slang while watching Noremar position the grav-cart at the head of their squad. "Manlier. You beat me at self-love classing, brother. That's yours alone."

"Manlier?" Kaze almost fell out of stance. "With styled hair like yours? I'd have to kick my own arse—"

"I'm sure you would," interrupted Zozes, avidly watching a heavily armed group of Enforcers coming down Vae'gon's ramp, each dressed in full combat gear, helmets engaged. Behind them came a strangely modified Blade pod that looked to be being transferred on a grav-cart. "That's heavy duty for a spawn-pod."

More Enforcers brought up the rear, situated in guard formation. The pod's design was unique, its outer hatch security screen fitted with a cyber reflector-mask concealing the occupant.

"Care to place a wager on who's inside?" asked Kaze.

Halfway down the ramp the pod jerked, obviously struck from the inside. The closest Enforcers drew their plasma rifles, aiming them at the capsule, all halting.

For a long moment silence reigned, then the pod jerked again, this time violently from side to side, something within emitting abnormal, muffled noises, the occupant appearing to be striking the inner screen repeatedly.

No other sound could be heard throughout the landing bay, all held captive by a distorted vocal processor clearly transmitting the animalist noises and behaviour coming from the capsule. Again and again the hatch was struck, harder each time until the grav-cart's stabilisers kicked in to compensate for the excessive rocking.

"Forget about who," muttered Zozes, an uncomfortable sensation scoring his spine, "I'd be asking *what.*"

The lead Enforcer bent over the pod, activating the cyber-controller interface, speaking into it urgently. "Aggressive behavioural spike, soporific protocol initiated. Flooding capsule with nerve agent grade-five, along with electrical immobilisation charge set to maximum, Standby in three ..."

Another strike to the screen, this one shattering the mask, briefly revealing a large, dark figure before reforming.

"Two!"

"Prime arms!" urged another Enforcer, now leaning directly over the pod, the nose of their rifle aimed point-blank at the screen. As if the occupant knew this, the next strike buckled the capsule's reinforced side plating, warping the metal near the base.

"Whatever that is, it wants out," growled Kaze, breaking at-stance, hand moving to his hip.

"No ..." cautioned Zozes only moments before the Enforcer called out.

"One, administering nerve agent and immobilisation charge ... now!"

The pod jerked once again, a final move of rebellion before absolute silence. The Enforcers kept their weapons drawn, not moving a muscle for a full count of ten. Then, as one they stepped back, each retaking guard formation.

"Well, that was a comedown," muttered Kaze, this time loud enough for the Major to hear. "Let me guess, that pod's content is classified."

"Curiosity isn't a vice, Alpha Blue." The Major's head turned, his gaze following the company of Enforcers as they crossed the bay, their pace now doubled.

"You'll tell us?" asked Kaze.

"However, stupidity is."

Zozes barely restrained a laugh. "Should've seen that one coming."

"Yes," agreed the Major, moving off, "he should."

Zozes glanced toward the rear of the bay noting that many of the Enforcers were keeping a generous distance between themselves and the deathly still capsule. The gateway rolled upwards as they approached, the heavily armed group disappearing the moment it sealed behind.

Another ship drew the squad's attention, the Major pulling up beside a group of Blades to face it silently. Zozes fell in behind, Kaze at his side. He had a feeling the Major knew who it was, something in the way his eyes were narrowed, expression turned thoughtful.

It looked to Zozes like a Galactic Force Warront, but the shudder of the landing bay's vacuum shield hid the vessel's identity. As it flew overhead, Zozes got a good look at the markings and finally understood the Major's interest. This was a Command Class Vessel.

The ship flew overhead, releasing its landing struts, slowly descending to land on the deck not far from the assembled squads.

"These Alpha Trials are certainly gaining attention." Kaze whistled softly. "Looks like this wrangle's just warming up."

Zozes watched the vessel drop its ramp lower to reveal a Galactic Force Fleet Commander, standing beside a full ranking

Colonel. The two descended at a swift pace followed by a company of armed troopers.

"Commander Vome," murmured Kaze, clearly shocked. "Who's she with?"

"Colonel Baydro," said Zozes. "It was he who briefed us about the mission to map out the subspace layers to the Primordial Station."

"Memory's still foggy on all the specifics," grumbled Kaze, obviously angry over the fact. "Come to think of it, I don't even remember what our previous assignment was?"

"Magnify your awareness," suggested Zozes. "Baydro's one of the last surviving pilots to have flown in the Pentar Gold-Wing squadron during the Second Galactic War."

At this, Major Rajek turned. "Making him one of our finest pilots."

"And he's only made the rank of Colonel since?" Kaze eyes narrowed in. "All Gold-Wing pilots were classed as war heroes."

"Those who fought in the war were of a different time." Rajek looked back at Baydro. "He, like many other officers, was moulded to become a devastating weapon. Once the Galactic State-Accords had been established with the Kadra's Oath-Creeds, Command restricted the ranks of many officers that were to serve in what was termed 'the new, civilised era.'"

Vome and Baydro, both from the world New Hasna, appeared to hold a comfortable air between them. Something Zozes knew was forged only over time.

"You're saying Command restricted his promotional rights?" he queried.

"Vok, that's a cold deal," growled Kaze. "Fight for your galaxy through war and blood only to be overlooked on the return."

"Almost like coming out the other side only to find yourself an outcast." Zozes' mouth twisted, the words sour on his tongue. "Especially within your own ranks."

"It was difficult for many," agreed Rajek. "One of the first measures handed down by Astral Guard almost sparked a civil war."

Zozes glanced at the Major, for the first time questioning his rank, wondering if Rajek had been restricted by those same orders. By his reckoning, the other should have held a much higher position.

"Well," Kaze redirected the conversation, "so much for the Galactic Force not having any involvement in this."

The Colonel was much older than Vome, dark skinned, bald. A trimmed, pure white beard seemed to highlight the blue of his Hasnirian eyes, while Vome's black hair popped hers. A partially hidden battle scar on Baydro's right cheek hinted he had seen his fair share of on-ground combat, not simply the cockpit of a Pentar.

It was quite something to see them stride so confidently across the deck, ranks and commendations from past battles clearly displayed.

"They're certainly making a statement," muttered Zozes. "No one wears full dress unless they have to. Think they're here to challenge the Trials?"

Kaze shrugged. "Doesn't look like they're here to hand-hold."

Eyes narrowed, Vae'gon waited at the base of his ship's ramp, his narrow-eyed gaze taking in Vome and the military contingent following in her wake. Before she was halfway across, he began ordering Astral Guard personnel to move the closest Blades out of the bay.

"It looks to me," observed Kaze, "like the Commander and her second-in-command were not on the guest list." A subtle shift of his head indicated the gathered Blades from different Astral States on his right.

A heavily muscled Covon Blade Commander on the other side of Kaze seemed to be observing all through narrowed eyes. Their raw tempers were well known, as was their lust for battle, just two of the traits that made them a lethal adversary.

"Imagine," muttered Kaze softly, "waking up next to that face in the morning."

Zozes' lips twitched, fighting a grin while eyeing the dark-skinned warrior. The ridged skin around each eye met at the bridge of his nose. "Wouldn't say that too loud."

Vae'gon nodded to the head of the Astral Guard, indicating for him to pick up pace, moving the squads out of the bay. Noticing this, Vome quickened her pace to head the officer off, throwing out a terse order to hold.

Infuriated, Vae'gon crossed to confront her, barely acknowledging Colonel Baydro now at her side. Baydro did not seem to care, Zozes noticed, as his interest was focused on the Blades, looking over each squad carefully, settling for a long moment on Kaze, and himself.

Vae'gon wasted no time, not even pausing to address her formally. "Your orders were clear, Commander. This ship is now under Astral Guard control. We are fully within our right to conduct the Alpha Trials, as you well know."

Not daunted, the Commander stood her ground. "Commodore, it isn't the Trials that concern the Colonel and I. What you intend after is another matter entirely, and far too dangerous a ploy, especially if you lose control."

Obviously caught off guard, Vae'gon still lifted his chin when asking, "The Actrix Covenant has contacted you?"

Vome crossed her arms. "I am here at the personal request of the High Priestess."

As if listening to something distasteful, Vae'gon puffed up, indicating the Astral Guard and the ship. "The *Trollo*'s specifications are able to counter any unwarranted objection. All," he leaned forward, "is in order."

"You're forgetting one very important fact." Vome smiled coldly. "You believe, no, you act, as if the Overwatch Initiative grants a type of immunity to 'rule of order.' That every officer in the Planetary Allegiance is governed by these." She looked over the Blades, shaking her head. "Overwatch is not an absolute, its reach ends here. With me."

"You're a bold one, Commander." Vae'gon huffed a laugh, "I knew your father well during the Galactic War, we were comrades. I believe he shared a similar conviction." Leaning close, he snarled, "One that led to his ultimate end."

Vome's eyes narrowed dangerously. "Is that a threat, Commodore?"

"It's a truth." Vae'gon looked to Baydro. "To know that you need only ask your second, here. Been a long time, Colonel." His eyes settled on the scar. "I see time has marked you with age beyond your years."

Baydro looked anything but intimidated. If he was to guess, Zozes would have said he was amused.

"Just like that same smarmy smile and smooth tongue has elevated you to power." Baydro's voice rose, the closest Astral

Guards clearly hearing all. "An unfortunate happenstance for those beneath you, Erise."

Stung, Vae'gon lip curled. "Reminiscing past glory? Best you leave that behind along with our friend and her father. It's a shame that after his death your talents never quite extended beyond the cockpit of a fighter, or the bridge of a ship."

"War changes many things. I know it changed me."

A true hunter, Vae'gon zeroed in on a perceived weakness. "Is that regret, Colonel?"

"There's many things I regret during my time in service." Baydro leaned closer to Vae'gon. "Remaining loyal to the Galactic Force has never been one of them."

"An idealist to the last." Vae'gon laughed in disgust. "Joining Astral Guard could have nurtured those wounds, advanced your duty-status. You could have been—"

"Standing beside you?" interrupted Baydro loudly. "I'd rather be vented out an airlock."

"Whereas now," Vae'gon said, his lip curling, "you serve the child, one who clings to the past ideals of a long-dead father. Sooner you both realise that, the sooner you will be free."

Neither Vome nor Baydro responded, the Commodore's assuredness halting them midstride. Zozes eyed each expression, realising there was a deep past here, something Vae'gon was not above exploiting or manipulating to suit his agenda. These Trials were personal to him, something he desperately wanted to go ahead. It was why, that Zozes wanted to know.

Vome was the first to break silence. "The Planetary Allegiance has taken a pivotal role in the lessons of our past to form a shield, one that defends our future."

"Has it?" growled Vae'gon.

"I'm by no means a philosopher," responded Baydro, "but the lessons learnt have given us tools that maintain peace, but we must acknowledge our limitations."

Disgusted, Vae'gon shook his head. "You fear we walk the same path as the Kadra?"

"Even the blind can see the growing commonalities, Erise." Baydro sighed, obviously trying to reach him. "Earth will become a staging ground where a new threat can rise. Don't become the seed that brings down all."

"Threat?" Vae'gon frowned over this. "Would you care to enlighten me on who we are to fear?"

"Us," started Vome.

"The Kadra," growled Baydro, becoming worked up, "were the founders to the Planetary Allegiance long ago. They too once shared Astral Guard ideals ..."

Vae'gon appeared to have had enough. "They turned their backs on us the moment they proclaimed themselves beyond the Star Gods. Those that never fell victim to their theology understood what needed to be done to protect our way of life."

"That idolism led to war," stated Baydro flatly.

"Where duty must come before faith," recited Vome. "That Astral Guard precept holds more danger then you know."

"The words of Astral Guard have never failed me," declared Vae'gon. "Even now they guide my hand on the right course of action."

"I see." Vome glanced Baydro's way before asking Vae'gon, "Is this why you've blocked the Actrix Covenant's involvement? Why the Priestess came to us?"

"No more delays," declared Vae'gon. "The Blades play an important role in protecting us against all threats of this Galaxy. Particularly those that are growing as we speak."

"There'll be repercussions to this, Erise," warned Baydro. "Don't cross the line so far there will be no restoring the damage."

"The Actrix Covenant will know their place," Vae'gon declared.

Vome glanced back her men, then at Baydro who nodded.

"If you are here to relieve me of duty, be done with it, Commander, for I will not yield." Vae'gon signalled his Enforcers, each immediately priming their weapons. "Mutiny is something Astral Guard does not take lightly."

Instantly, the Galactic Troopers followed suit, to which Baydro held up a hand, neither side taking aim, both parties appearing to offer intimidation rather than theat.

"Think carefully, Erise," he warned.

"Zozes," whispered Kaze, "what the vok is this about?"

The Blades standing beside his brother and behind were falling into combat position, obviously preparing for whatever consequence. Though silent, the bay was heavy with intent, each group measuring the other's tenacity.

"What is it to be, Commander? Test each other's resolve? Or will you abide by your original orders, and allow Astral Guard to commence the Blade Trials without further delay. Think carefully, for one of these ways will have a lasting effect."

Mouth a firm line, Vome looked around, seeming to take her time. Her eyes scanned the Blades. Zozes felt them pass over he and his brother carefully, before looking to the end of the bay where the heavily fortified Blade pod had disappeared.

Finally, she broke her silence. "Colonel, recall our troopers back to the ship."

"Sir?"

"Those are my orders," stated Vome. "Get our officers off this hangar deck now."

"Yes, Commander." With obvious difficulty Baydro turned on his heel, indicating for the Galactic Troopers to disengage and fall back.

Vae'gon indicated the Enforcers to do the same. Looking over the bay, he watched them climb the ramp and board their ship.

"Congratulations, Commander." He smiled at Vome sweetly. "Your Command remains solidified. Now get out of my sight."

About to move off, Vae'gon paused, hearing Vome's soft laugh.

Three steps brought her toe to toe with the Commodore. "Generally, I can be reasoned with when reason is on offer. I will give no latitude to threats, the Astral Guard, or least of all, you."

Vae'gon looked at her narrowed eyes, not saying a word.

"My orders are to contain any threat that endangers Earth." Vome's voice took on a dark edge. "If Astral Guard is in violation to those orders, I will take all necessary action, whatever that may be." Leaning closer, she snarled, "Heed the warning, Commodore, for our next encounter may not be an exchange of words."

When Vome strode away, Vae'gon watched her go through narrowed eyes, then turned to his officers. "Get these Blades moving!"

Zozes' gaze never left Vome as she climbed the ramp of her ship where Colonel Baydro stood waiting, allowing her to board the Warront Craft first.

"She looks anything but defeated," observed Kaze. "Think it's safe to say I'm going to like that one."

"She's direct," said Zozes thoughtfully. "I'd say Vome was here to measure Vae'gon's resolution."

The Warront's engines fired, the craft lifting off almost immediately.

"Blades!" called the Major. "Fall in."

The brothers took up position, following the Major across the deck to join Lieutenant Noremar.

"For a moment back there," Kaze added, "I thought it was going to get a little hot."

Obviously listening, the Major answered, "Never initiate a battle if you don't achieve anything by winning, Blade. Only when language fails is when force must be called upon."

Kaze chewed on this, clearly not certain if he agreed. "I'd say all other diplomatic channels must have been exhausted to have Vome make an unofficial visit."

Noremar glanced back, catching Zozes' eye. Obviously she was taking an interest in their discussion, before moving off with the Major.

"It appears," Zozes held Kaze back momentarily, "this face-off may be all but inevitable. We need to be ready for this, brother."

Unusually serious, Kaze nodded. "Remember the Chief's words? She spoke of a truth ... do you think that could somehow be connected to the Astral Guard?"

Surprised at the question, Zozes thought before answering. "Unclear, much conflict surrounds Earth. First we must pass the Alpha Trails, for what comes after may very well throw us into civil war."

Galactic Star Key: Kaze Karbroe
Astral Nav-Coordinates: EAS-APL-4
Data Sequence: 23.0

Before falling into line behind Zozes, Kaze deactivated night-sight upon his cyber-optics' overlay to energise his porta-tool, activating his placement generator to form a lighting unit-clip that ran along his temple, curving behind an ear.

Major Rajek and Enforcer Noremar took the lead, each having done the same. Glancing behind, Kaze caught sight of the Covon Blade Commander's scowl, completely understanding his distrust of this process.

Commodore Vae'gon called the teams to attention before guiding them out of the landing bay. Kaze cast a quick glance back to see Vome's vessel passing through the vacuum shield, her ship's nacelles glowing bright against the darkness of space.

Out of the landing bay, the squad moved into the ship's main track-run, the wide corridor leading down the spine of the ship. Many of the *Trollo*'s systems were offline, cyber-outlets and internal electrical components left exposed, bulkheads and ceiling plates still in the process of development.

No one spoke during this walk, the blunt silence grinding on Kaze's nerves to the point he began whistling softly, desperate to shift the energy.

"Don't start," Zozes snapped.

"To march a Blade force this superlative," Kaze rolled his shoulders irritably, "requires a trekking tune."

Mouth clamped, his brother looked straight ahead.

"Come on," Kaze nodded toward Vae'gon. "Think the Commodore's got a personal request?"

"After that near blow-out in the hangar bay, I'd say Vae'gon's more likely to blow you out an airlock."

"You're such a critic of enjoyment." Kaze rolled his eyes, halting in time with the rest of the squads, craning his neck to see if they had reached the Training Bay. "I'll break you down one day, no matter how much push-back I get."

"For now, adapt to the droning sound of our boots echoing in the darkness," Zozes suggested, shuffling forward as the main Gateway in the bay rolled open.

"Like you've adapted to the absence of our go-getting doctor?" enquired Kaze, following his brother inside.

Zozes cleared his throat, throwing Kaze his usual silent frown.

Like this meant nothing, Kaze ran an eye over the darkened Blast Range which was as quiet as the corridors. By design, it was nearly identical to the one he and his brother had undergone preliminary testing in before landing on Earth.

The Commodore did not pause, leading the squads on to circumnavigate this via a bridge.

"It wasn't me she set trembling with her barefaced interest," mused Kaze mildly.

"Since Thaytis is half a solar system away, I'll try to contain myself," snapped Zozes.

"Which just leaves the hangdog expression you've carted here," griped Kaze. "It's droopy at best, brother."

"Hangdog?" Zozes was clearly scrambling to decipher the word.

Kaze grinned wickedly. "To be honest, I was getting over the tag-team thing you two had going ... ganging up, hunting me like good game."

"Repercussion for those with no verbal filter." Zozes smirked. "If you eased off occasionally, that red target on your back may finally lose a little colour."

A long silence fell, the only sound that of the Blades' footfalls marching over deck plate as the squads approached the next Gateway at the end of the observation bridge.

Without the sound of blast-fire, Kaze found the constant silence gnawing, his thoughts too loud, somehow amplified by the multiple grav-carts being guided by Enforcers, their anti-grav ports vibrating softly.

Zozes lit the unit-clip along his ear, unexpectedly cutting through the dim light, flaring it into his brother's eyes. "You miss her."

"What? The doctor?" Kaze chewed on this, finding the assumption bitter. Shoving his brother around, he kept him moving. "Let's not leap out of an airlock here. I do admit she carries a strong feminine power, one I may like to test." There was no missing his brother's eyeroll. "Besides, you only bite at half my remarks, the doc loves a good spoil with words."

"She's won more with you than lost," goaded Zozes, then seemed to be lost in thought.

Uncomfortable and not understanding why, Kaze blurted, "You miss her more."

Zozes did not deny it. "There's no point in belabouring this, brother. The way our situation is forming up, having her grounded planet-side is for the best."

"Right you are, a true flag-bearing romantic."

Zozes shook his head, eyeing the darkened Blast Range. "Considering current events, I see no other option."

"So now we're looking out for the doc's wellbeing?"

The Blades paused when the Commodore bellowed an order to halt. Behind, Kaze noticed the main Gateway to the Blast Range being sealed. A large contingent of Astral Guard personnel was operating a nearby control station where several Enforcers stood watch. Beside them was a team of engineers, observing as they let through a small unit of medical officers.

"Kaze," Zozes drew his attention, "I don't want to discuss the doctor. It would never work, her and I."

"Fine, but it appears she has made some moves herself."

"What do you mean?"

"Somehow she has gone and got herself reassigned to the medical detail below." Kaze indicated several officers congregated at the Training Bay entrance. "Must have transported over here via another ship."

"Reassigned?" Zozes stepped to the side, gripping the rail while scanning the crew. "On whose orders?"

Kaze leaned close to his brother, indicating a team of Reptoids as they stepped from the Control Station. "Err, my mistake. There's no way her fine features could be mixed up with one of those lizard-looking Reptoids."

Caught, Zozes glared at his brother. "You think this is funny?"

"Nice reaction on your part." Kaze grunted as his brother shouldered him when turning from the rail to move back into line. "For a moment there, I thought you were about to charge off. Clearly you've got the hunt of her scent."

Disgusted, Zozes fumed in silence.

"Evidence is stacking against you, brother," Kaze said with a smirk. "The verdict, if not obvious by now, reveals an unmistakable truth."

"That my life would be so much easier without you in it."

"If I weren't around, your body would have already given out long ago," Kaze warned, "living an asexual lifestyle of monotony."

"I'd give it go," Zozes swore. "Dual-pairing or not, it couldn't hurt to try."

The main Gateway was almost sealed, Kaze noticed. Reptoids were moving past the medical officers to join the engineers in finishing the shutdown process which activated the grid-shield, multiple beams forming a net over the surface. These shimmered once before disappearing. Freq-com alerted, helm established contact. "All hands stand aware. Emergency power overriding protocols have been initiated: Training Bay's distribution relays are now online, direct channel-line has been linked into the Combat Arena. All remaining sectors throughout the training area are now operating on minimal power."

The moment the freq-com closed the bridge, Blast Range lit with scarlet light, Commodore Vae'gon waiting for the next Gateway to roll open.

Emergency emitters lit the corridor, but these grew fewer the further along the group traversed, until they were passing through long pockets of darkness. Glancing up, Kaze eyed a series of exposed outlets, cables swaying gently as they filed past leaving him with an uneasy feeling.

Moving past these guardedly, Kaze entered into a wide, deep corridor, a series of doors on the right side. Blood-red light lit the track-run, revealing a series of comp-terminals that looked to be only partly fitted, electra-cables hanging loose, cover panels resting against a wall, system components spread like foam on a sea ready for instillation. Lining the rear wall were several grav-carts holding a number of large storage compartments that were deactivated, officers moving around the powered-down equipment.

Kaze stepped over a stasis tool-kit sitting beside an exposed maintenance hatch lock-outlet. A thick cable ran from this, obviously powered down. "Looks as if everyone's literally upped and abandoned their posts."

"Form up!" called Commodore Vae'gon, halting before a wide door.

Squads assembled behind their team leaders, each Enforcer manoeuvring their grav-cart to the head of the line.

Kaze eyed a slimly built O'Garcian Captain leading her squad beside the Covon Commander. She carried a different air to the Major, as they were renowned throughout neighbouring Astral State races for being fast and nimble. Balance for them was second nature, able to climb any terrain or surface without aid.

Her long white hair was tied back, something customary with her race's culture when preparing for battle. Her eyes caught his showing only determination. She was here to advance.

A head engineer joined them, materialising a cyber-controller around her hand. Moving into a large control station, her officers fell in behind. The area was built with numerous terminals, engineers able to pair their forearms' control units to power the devices remotely. A steady pale white light suffused the main cyber-controller which generated a large cyber-screen over the wall.

"Coordinating power flow with energy distribution map, Commodore. The arena's system is coming online."

"Understood." Commodore Vae'gon eyed the large cyber-screen's schematics. "Uplink all Astral Senior Officers' Star-Keys to grant them full access."

"At once, Sir."

Kaze shifted to get a better view of the engineer's power distribution map. There looked to be multiple zones with restricted emergency sections highlighted red, while fully operational zones were designated pale white fluctuating to green. This seemed to indicate the systems were still coming online.

As soon as all zones were stabilised, an insignia lit on the large twin doors before the Blades, then the doors retracted. White light flowed from the bay, strong enough for Kaze to shield his eyes until they adjusted.

Vae'gon moved off, guiding the teams into the arena.

The Major led their team through last, following the O'Garcian squad, all officers deactivating their lighting units. Enforcer Noremar's grav-cart hummed softly when they drew to a halt, all moving to at-stance.

The arena was fully operational, all combat areas powered and lit. Cylindrical in shape, there appeared to be numerous interchanging levels proving the space was designed for a variety of combat scenarios, including small and large-scale skirmishes.

The command engineer moved back to the door, speaking quietly over her personal freq-com with maintenance technicians that were stationed throughout the facility. Two remained at her side, watching a specialist team work at mag-locking the twin-doors. Once this was completed, a grid-shield net shimmered briefly before disappearing.

"Get the feeling we'll be here for a while?" Kaze murmured.

Zozes' mouth twisted, the only indication he was hearing and analysing all that was going on. Vae'gon signalled for the command engineer to begin materialising a series of mobile tele-warp disc pins from the utility stasis dispenser connected to her belt, then walked with her as she handed them to Astral Guard personnel.

When she generated two more to give to Major Rajek and Enforcer Noremar, Kaze glanced at the Covon Commander and the O'Garcian, noting that neither were handed a transport unit.

Rajek was looking at the disc pin, seeming to study its configuration before warping it into his utility belt's stasis-loader.

"Enforcers." Commodore Vae'gon drew attention to the Astral Guard personnel around him, moving to the head of the assembled Blade squads, hands behind his back. "Release the Link-Trones!"

Noremar leaned over the grav-cart, working the stasis-cart's cyber-controller, reconfiguring the magnetically sealed latches surrounding the access port. The circular compartment's energy shield deactivated, releasing a wide ISO-tube and dispersing a thick burst of vapour, other grav-carts going through the same procedure.

Moments later, through the ISO-tube's outer screen Kaze could see warp-orb patterns emerge, tele-warping their Link-Trone from the stasis-unit into physical form.

An internal grav-beam containment field held the Link-Trone momentarily suspended until its own anti-gravity nacelles lit up taking control of the flight. Lieutenant Noremar deactivated the ISO-tube's outer hatch, the containment device retracting back into the grav-cart's stasis compartment.

The instant the Link-Trone came fully online, Kaze felt its sync-pulse moving through his spawn-net, then the dual-pairing with Zozes. Configuring its combat armour, their AI unit hovered before them, spinning on its axis, as if saying hello.

Then it was gone in a burst of speed, joining the other Trones who were being released, to become the centre of attention.

Kaze was not the only Blade watching this. "I think our Trone's in love."

On and on their AI moved, mixing with the Link-Trones, optronic emitters flashing in a vibrant manner. Many of the emerging Trones were still reforming their exterior bodies' structural designs.

Throughout the Astral State regions within the Galaxy, the Blades were of numerous species, which resulted in various Trone designs. The Covons' Trone was a wide triangular shape, plated down with D-50 duzanium armour. What it lacked in mobility, it made up for in durability.

The O'Garcian Trone was, in one word, elegant, Kaze thought, its armour etched in an ancient native script that glowed pale white. A set of anti-gravity injector-wings gave it the ability to move through the air at a slick pace, and change direction just as fast. Beside it flew a Devronian Trone, its external ribbed form rounded off sharply in a series of inner ridges converging into forward weaponry. A nearby Reptoid Trone displayed a layer of virgule-scales running across its outer plating, on emergence extending into stark ridges above and below. These slowly retracted, each scale flattening while unthreatened. Active, each scale was lethal to touch.

Kaze eyed the Reptoids standing alongside the Devronians. The heavily scaled race seemed to wear a perpetual frown which made them difficult to read. Pleated skin edged with spurs surrounded their faces, something they used during battle when skull-striking an opponent.

Their AI was now centre of the Link-Trones, moving in sync with a Moncovian Trone, the smallest of all. Mirrored, lightweight armour was installed with minimal offensive armaments. This AI was fitted with a unique techno system built for covert operations and surveillance.

When the Link-Trones began communicating through a freq-com channel via cyber-digit coding, Kaze employed his cyber-optic vision, finding an endless stream of numbers and codes filling his data-feed. They seemed to be exchanging information.

"You ever make sense of their cyber-digit communication?" Kaze asked, noting that the other Blades were also watching the Trones.

"No." Zozes shook his head. "That communication exchange is a little too concentrated for me, though it's an efficient means for the AIs to converse."

"Multiple sets of mathematical values?" Kaze eyed the incoming freq-com data through his own cyber-optics. "Cause and effect. In other words, overthinking this in my case will leave brain matter bleeding through the nose."

"It's a clean form of communication that cannot be readily tarnished by sub-verse rephrase."

Annoyed, Kaze became immediately defensive. "Sub-verse rephrase is life, brother. Without it there would be no verbal diversity which would leave a galaxy full of Zozeses, artificially programmed to run ..." Kaze gestured a human expression with quotation marks used, "efficiently."

"So, cyber-digit coding of language somehow escalates into reprogramming our inner minds?" Zozes rolled his eyes. "Your skill in theatrics during wait periods is never off pace, brother."

"There's laws against mental reconditioning. We all know a galaxy of no choice would be, well, vokked—" Kaze broke off when his brother's hand shot up. "What?"

"The Trones ... what's LT up to?"

Distracted, Kaze glanced across, his eyes widening at the sight of their Trone drifting in in a strange manner, emitting soft tones. Other AIs were revolving around it, like they were performing some type of collective practice.

"Nothing normal," he muttered, noting that more were joining as they were released, rushing too. The longer it went on, he noticed a pattern starting to form, the Trones movements almost mesmerising, rhythmic, difficult to look away from. "Is that LT, in the centre?"

"Of course it is," Zozes said through gritted teeth, glancing at the assembled Blades.

"Maybe it's just being friendly," Kaze hazarded, then laughed. "It's a little robo-slut lapping up the attention."

"They're forming a rotational pattern," Zozes mused, pointing out the movements. "It's a spiral."

Zozes was right. The Link-Trones had formed a type of rotating spiral and were now revolving in perfect sync. Each began expelling an anti-gravity wake, a strange visual effect that seemed to be warping space, leaving behind particles that sparkled.

"It's a ..." Kaze's throat closed unexpectedly.

"Galaxy," supplied Zozes. "A representation of our galaxy."

"You're certain?"

"Look." Zozes began uploading information, sending it via their cyber-optic link, marking various points of the Link-Trones' flight sequence. He then layered the galaxy schematic over it, leaving Kaze in no doubt.

"Well, their aerial flight formation is clean." Kaze felt a shift within himself he could not explain. "Visual accuracy alone deserves applause."

Zozes seemed to barely hear. "I've never seen Link-Trones interact like this before."

Neither had the Commodore, Kaze noticed. His eyebrows were drawn together, and the Astral Guard Enforcers that had released them from their stasis compartments were looking just as concerned.

A deep shiver moved through Kaze, one generating from the centre of his being, pushing up, pushing out.

"Karbroe ..." The voice was soft, a vibration travelling the air, bridging now with them. *"Step into the light ..."*

Unsettled, Kaze turned, but could find no one close, only his brother. When he looked back, his gaze was drawn to the revolving Trones and the way the particles moved and bled together, seeming to conjure a lone, shadowy figure.

"Zozes?"

His brother did not move, remained frozen in place like he was unable to acknowledge anything around. It was at this moment Kaze realised everyone appeared caught in the same phenomenon, gripped by some unknown trance.

Stepping around the Major and Enforcer, the shadowy figure suddenly disappeared. Curious, Kaze moved slowly forward, approaching the revolving Trones cautiously, detecting a shift, a lightening in the atmosphere as he closed the distance.

Somehow the AIs coming together, the releasing of multiple gravity wakes, had reduced time to a crawl for everyone except him. Pausing beside the Commodore, Kaze eyed his gaping mouth, realising he had been in the process of bellowing an order. A close Enforcer was trying to activate an LT bolt overrider.

"Now there's a face hit by the ugly stick." Irritated, he eyed the blank expression, waving a hand before Vae'gon. Nothing. Trying to shove the Commodore's arm aside, Kaze's eyes bulged when his hand passed straight through, leaving a strange glow in its wake.

What was happening? How was he still moving around unaffected? Or was he affected, and everyone else was watching him?

Kaze eyed the Enforcer next to Vae'gon, gingerly running a finger over her arm only to find his passing through. Turning away hurriedly, he thought back to Zozes talking about waking dreams. Maybe his spawn-net had deteriorated to the point his state of consciousness was breaking down, producing this type of vivid hallucination.

Instantly, he glanced across the arena, somehow drawn toward the AIs, his gaze unconsciously searching for the shadowy figure ...

"These Alpha Trials are a fallacy. None of what once was remains. No truth, no honour. Their only intent is to deceive ..."

Breath locked in his chest, Kaze fought to see the shadowy figure, discern whose face it was. As the dark mist slowly faded, the form drew together, finally revealing that of the Alpha Chief.

"Chief?" She looked well, whole, her skin almost luminescent. No scars marred her face, nor did pain dull the bright blue of her eyes. Even her dark hair was curled, resting on her shoulders.

"*Do not become complacent upon victory,*" she warned, raising a hand, reaching it slowly toward his face. "*Darkness gathers, smothering all as it feasts. The true test lies in finding where it dwells ... eclipsing the sun.*" The instant the Chief's hand connected, Kaze felt hit by a plasma bolt. "*There will be no retreating, and I can offer no forewarning, only grant you the light to bring forth revelation.*"

Kaze blinked as his focus distorted, the violence of the move leaving him breathless, vertigo almost knocking him from his feet as a series of fast moving images tore through his mind. Blades firing desperately, darkness, blood, hate, the lash of fire, crushed bone, splayed forms, torn flesh, plasma fire and darkness, glowing eyes. Death.

"*Trust lies in allies, for with their sacrifice you can cut through the darkness to a horizon of light.*"

In a flash, Kaze was floating, completely weightless within a liquefied substance. Vision blurred, he struggled to see ahead. From deep within, figures obscured by shadow walked toward him. The first approached then paused, seeming to study him intently before reaching out a hand. Without fear or doubt, Kaze lifted his own. The point of contact brought forth a bright flash ...

And he was standing beside his brother, and the other Blades, back in the arena. Rajek was ahead of him, the Trones moving in formation. His brother leaned forward to speak with the Major softly.

The Trones were spiralling, but their movement was slowing. Vae'gon stepped forward to yell. "Break them off!"

Charged, Enforcers ran ahead, activating their porta-tools, bridging to their LT bolt overriders, seeking control.

He looked again at the Chief, saw the shadows slowly darkening, distorting her image as they once again took control.

From a deep place, beneath an age of knowledge, came her final words. Ones that he knew his brother could not hear.

"Beyond these Trials you will come to understand the true test of what haunts all. Ancient, prepared. So must be you, for it knows no honour, nor will it yield, not even in death."

Galactic Star Key: Baden Casteel
Astral Nav-Coordinates: EAS-APL-4
Data Sequence: 24.0

Streams of light flashed across his closed lids. Blinking, Baden lifted his head groggily, realising he was in a car and it was now night. Rubbing his eyes, he forced himself upright, in the process knocking junk about in the footwell.

Jevon's ute? Glancing at the driver, he grunted uncomfortably.

"Cass? You coherent?"

Baden rubbed his eyes harder, clearing his throat against the overbearing smell Jevon liked to cart around with him.

"Yeah, I'm just ..." His mind kicked in, a rush of memories pouring into his head, bringing with them the image of Alexa passing out in Kevin's basement. Immediately his throat burnt, and the roiling in his stomach threatened emergence.

Baden grabbed for the door handle, and the seatbelt release. "Out ... gotta get ..."

"Whoa!" Jevon forced him back, shaking his head. "Easy mate, don't push it."

"Don't push what?" Baden grabbed his head trying to stop it spinning. "What the hell happened back there?"

"Bucketloads of crazy."

"Alexa? Is she ...?"

"Fine," assured Jevon. "Same condition as you though, completely out of it. They said you'll both be fine with rest."

"What? Who said?" Before Jevon could answer, Baden started grabbing at his arms and legs, fighting to control the twitching of his muscles. "Why's my body feel all tripped up?" A large knotty lump on the side of his neck froze him solid. "What the hell's this?"

Not waiting for an answer, Baden turned the stiff rear-view mirror to stare at the lump. It looked the size of large white marble and stung like crazy when he pushed at it, leaving the sensation of spiders crawling over his neck. Fighting to see further without panicking, he angled the mirror, accidently snapping its hinge in the process.

"Damnit, mate! I know your freaking, but don't take it out on my ute. It's all I've got and about the only thing that makes sense in this world after today."

Not listening, Baden sat back, using the mirror to study the lump.

"You were injected with something," Jevon finally admitted. "Don't ask me what, because they weren't there to clarify on specifics. Alexa too."

"Injected? You mean a syringe?"

"Mate, you were gone, pure white," he said lamely, running a hand over his already messed up hair. "They brought you back. I think they used something else on your chest."

Baden tore at this shirt, dropping the mirror into the sea of junk. Staring at the centre of his chest, he eyed the round red mark, twice the size of his thumb nail.

"Pull over!" he demanded, fighting with the door handle. "Now!"

"No manners, no say—"

"This isn't a joke!" Baden swallowed woodenly. "Pull the goddamn car over!"

"Alright, alright!" Jevon hit the brakes, yanking at the wheel. "This is gonna piss them off for sure."

Baden stumbled out of the ute, grabbing at the side, fighting to stay upright. He was weak, the muscles of his legs barely able to function. For an awful moment, he wondered if he was paralysed permanently since nothing seemed to respond like it should.

When Jevon appeared at the back of the ute, he shook his head, fighting not to pass out while wiping furiously at the sweat popping all over his face. If he concentrated really hard, maybe, just maybe, he could stay on his feet.

"They're doubling back." Jevon sounded panicked.

"What?" Head between his arms, Baden leaned against the ute, rhythmically filling his lungs. It was helping to calm the contracting of his stomach, since vomiting required energy.

"Them!" Jevon pointed, clearly hysterical. "The ones that saved you and Alexa!"

All Baden could see was Jevon's body in silhouette against the coming headlights. "It's just a car."

Jevon was losing it, he had to be. Shielding his eyes, Baden squinted as the oncoming car pulled up right in front of the ute, nose to nose.

"I told you not to go digging," Baden hissed. "This's all your damn fault. Why the hell can't I stand up?" Feet sliding on the gravel, Baden gripped at the tray.

"My fault?" Jevon looked from Baden to the car, unusually serious. "This isn't about me. I'm just the delivery man, pure and simple." Stepping closer, he added, "And for the record, what happened to you technically wasn't my fault."

Baden heard a door close, a muffled thump that told him it was an expensive vehicle. "You're the technicality that got me involved in the first place." The last reminded Baden of Ebony's phone.

At the sound of feet crunching on the gravel, Jevon pulled Baden upright. "Look mate, these guys used to look past me as if I didn't exist, was no one special. That's changed now and I'm on their radar."

"Radar?" Baden stared at Jevon like he had two heads then at the two men standing in the beam of car lights, talking. "Who are they?"

"Fellowship agents," said Jevon. "These guys have methods that totally redefine the word containment. Whatever was going on in Kevin's basement has got a whole team locking down the area."

"But how could they have possibly known?"

"Err," Jevon coughed, ducking his head guiltily, "accessing Eb's phone may have clued them into something going on."

"Her phone?" Baden sat for moment, trying to join the dots. "They tapped it?"

"Kinda. Her mobile was weird, it somehow connected with a satellite network—"

"Satellite?" Baden blurted. "So this's all your fault? Dammit Starrik, if you weren't blood ... " He bit down hard, swallowing the empty threat. "Why'd they let you go?"

"It's complicated, mate. Had to draw out a wildcard, but doing that brought on repercussions that I really didn't want known. My contact was the one who instructed the agents to let me drive you home."

"Contact? What the hell are you talking about" Baden rubbed at his sweaty face. "Cryptic talk is for the guilty."

"I'm ... " Jevon glanced at the agents, clearly hesitating on answering.

Baden narrowed his eyes, for the first time wondering what his cousin had become involved in. "What's going on, Jevon?"

"I'm doing what's right, mate. Just give me some time. Let me prove it to everyone." Baden heard a gravelly voice speak over the low hum of the engine. "Mr Starrik, we gave you explicit instructions not to detour from your escort."

"I know." Jevon smiled apologetically. "He's awake, along with the Casteel temper fully functioning."

The one speaking was bald and broad shouldered, Baden could just make that out, and somewhere in his late forties. The other was harder to see, since he was dark skinned, and very tall against the night. Both men's features were a mystery, the car headlights throwing them in shadow.

"Doesn't surprise me," continued the bald man. "Simple minds, fast tempers. Canon, get the boy on his feet."

As the dark man approached, Baden fought to stand, then was hauled unceremoniously to his feet with little effort, while being brought forward.

"Do you know who I am?" the bald man asked. Baden glanced at Jevon, thinking he had never seen him this silent.

"No," Baden finally answered. "Should I?"

"Ah, there's that Casteel arrogance, even when ignorant of the facts."

Baden's chin lifted, fighting through the fatigue. "Who are you?"

"Call me Axel, and my partner over there's Agent Canon." For a long moment, he eyed Baden. "Your ignorance is something you can thank your uncle for, as an agreement was made between the Founding Families."

"Agreement?" Mind sluggish, Baden shook his head. "What's my uncle got to do with that?"

"Everything." The gravelly voice spat. "He used to be the head of your house, the head of your family, but more importantly, he is the one responsible for concealing the truth from you."

Again, Baden glanced at Jevon. This was way over their heads.

"I can see the cogs turning in that brain of yours, and it's about time they did." Axel's gaze briefly pierced Jevon. "And now you and your friend here are paying the price, all because of your uncle's indecision to act. All of this could have been prevented, especially if you'd been trained to recognise what you saw."

"Trained?" Baden shook his head, his arm starting to go numb in the dark man's hold since he was relying on it so heavily.

"Yes, training, son. But all that stands before me now is a pitiful excuse of a once noble heritage. That heritage," Axel continued harshly, "would have given you an understanding of how to face an adversary and not hide from it. Mr Starrik," he turned on Jevon, "best we conclude this evening with no more interruptions. Once we've arrived at the Casteel homestead, I will continue to undo all the damage that's been done. Understood?"

Jevon saluted, "Roger, boss."

Like he was assessing something small, the bald man looked Jevon up and down. Taking the hint, Jevon grabbed hold of Baden, nodding to the dark man. Once he was in the ute, Baden watched Jevon race around the bonnet, skidding up gravel.

If only he could think straight, maybe then this would make sense, but he was fighting exhaustion and a sick stomach. Leaning back in his seat he watched the tail-lights of what he now knew was a black sedan, letting his mind go blank.

Jevon had other ideas. "I know what you're thinking."

"Nothing, I'm thinking nothing."

"I'll start listing the possibilities."

"Alright." He guess he had been thinking. "Maybe something along the lines of us being royally boned, and I don't know who you are now."

Jevon chuckled, the sound weird under the circumstances. "You've done well, keeping all the focus on yourself. Little self-centred, but I like the tactic."

Since the seatbelt was pulling at his sore neck, Baden straightened. "Sure. I do everything to keep you in the game."

"You know what I'm thinking? That once this night plays out, you'll get some answers."

"Answers that can be relayed to yours truly?" Jevon glanced at Baden, before turning the wheel, following the sedan down Waters Lane, then into Baden's driveway, the farmhouse coming into view. "Starrick, I don't want answers. Here is where our so-called adventure ends. I don't care what you're involved in."

"You want to bail? When things are just about to get interesting?" Jevon shook his head. "Just give it time, trust me, I know."

"I'm sixteen, man. I have a mother who's losing it and no father. That's enough to deal with along with the fact I just wanna achieve some mid-class grades so I can blow through to year eleven." For the first time, Baden could put into words what rang true. "I want what you don't, a normal life. To work on my uncle's farm, play the field a little until I meet a decent bird."

"Farming?" Jevon eyes went wide. "You wanna be a cow cocky?"

"Nothing wrong with that."

"Farming?" Jevon's eyes rounded. "That's circling the drain, and normal is just another word for lack of imagination. You gotta find a better cause to live for, mate."

"Better cause to live for?" Baden shook his head, watching the black sedan pulling up beside his uncle's home, the two men exiting it in double-quick time, heading for the back door. "Sometimes I wonder if you understand the words coming out of your mouth."

After killing the engine, Jevon watched them enter the house beneath the pale wash of the rear veranda light. "Cass, crazy flew into town last week. You can either stand by, let it happen around you or jump on board, see where it leads."

"You've gotta be smoking something pretty strong to even come up with a sentence like that." Baden shoved open the door, but was too weak to get out.

Critical, Jevon eyed his seatbelt. "You won't get far with that thing still clipped."

On an eyeroll, Baden pressed the release, for the first time catching the sound of an argument from the inside of his uncle's house.

"By the way, my house is that-a-way, on the other side of the roundabout, genius."

But Jevon was not paying attention, his interest centred solely on Rickard's home and the raised voices within it. "Just following instructions, mate. I'm the delivery guy, remember?"

"Fine." He was going to have to go in. On a surge of strength, Baden climbed out, only to lean weakly against the door. "Today, man. You know I'm a cripple."

"Right! I'm on it." Jevon jumped out, moving fast around the ute to support him. "Don't we make a pair? This is how unbreakable friendships are forged."

The porch of his uncle's house looked a mile away to Baden, the two hobbling toward it. "Clearly, you're lacking in that department, because there's no way this is a friendship."

"How about frenemies?" Jevon suggested. "Nina and Eb have a few of those."

"Frenemies?" Baden began the laborious task of climbing the few steps onto the back veranda, his head starting to spin. "You're on your own there."

Grip slackening, Jevon stepped back. "When you put it like that, I may as well park your arse right here, mate."

"Oh, come on!" Sweating profusely, Baden clung on. "We're literally three steps from the door."

"Hey!" Jevon listened intently. "You hear that?"

Like he was switching on his hearing, Baden nodded. "Arguing. Come on, hop to it."

"You gonna say please?"

Wanting to be free of Jevon, Baden pulled open the screen door looking through the backroom, toward the kitchen. "This's getting old. Please."

"Huh!" Jevon laughed. "You realise what just happened here. I just made you my bitch."

The two awkwardly hobbled the short distance to the kitchen door, Jevon pushing it fully open.

The first thing Baden noticed was that Dallas Noble was in a wheelchair. Even through his haze of fatigue, he could not believe how much Alexa's dad had deteriorated in the last six months. Which sent his thoughts instantly to his mother, and the loss of feeling in her hands, how they were going numb. Would she end up the same?

Emotions churning, he almost tripped, barely feeling Jevon catching him as it was taking everything he had to keep himself together.

Axel moved to stand beside Dallas, indicating for Agent Canon to stand by the door.

Like he was guarding the meeting, thought Baden.

"It would be wise to listen to Dallas, Rick. I'm here to help. That's all," Axel said.

Everyone seemed to be talking over each other, clearly no one noticing them. Jevon solved this by walking forward to pull out a chair for Baden to sit on, the screeching of the legs stunning the room silent.

"Err." Jevon dropped Baden on the chair. "Hey, everyone."

Grace immediately circled the table, pushing back Baden's hair like she was testing his temperature. Lifting his chin, she studied his eyes.

"We've been worried sick about you!" she scolded, then glared over her shoulder at Axel. "And Jevon's been dragged into this. Why?"

"These are the complications I was informing you of. He and Kevin Zheng have been exposed to sensitive information upon a Fellowship communicator. We were successful in containing Nina Perkin's exposure, however."

Grace turned back to Baden, giving him an absentminded ruffle of the hair.

He knew immediately her mind was elsewhere, and as she spoke, another piece of the puzzle slotted into place for him. "That must be Ebony's mobile. Where is she? Is she alright?"

"She's safe." Axel chewed slowly on his gum, sliding hands into his pockets. "Protected. Doctor Walker is bringing her before the specialist. I will discuss her involvement once the matter before us is dealt with."

"Specialist?" gasped Grace, looking instantly at Rickard for help.

"And you call this," Rickard waved an arm, "doing your job?"

"Don't lay this one at my door," warned Axel coolly. "Containment protocols have been initiated. None of them will talk, I can assure you of that."

Clearly furious, Rickard swore beneath his breath, the word loud enough to have his aunt spinning around. "Haven't we got enough problems already?"

"My methods," Axel said, "are persuasive. If anything develops, all parties are aware of the repercussions."

"You wouldn't be overstepping your boundaries?" Rickard placed a hand on the dining table, leaning toward Axel threateningly. "If you do, it'll be the last time. That I can promise you."

For the first time, Baden saw how truly angry his uncle was.

"So you finally understand." Eyes narrowed, Axel appeared satisfied. "All that fire Rick, it's been tempered too long. Only now do you realise how truly helpless you are."

"Helpless?" Rickard pushed at the table, straightening. Though still weak, Baden prepared to get up, sensing this was about to get very ugly, maybe turn physical.

Anything but concerned, Axel goaded him further. "Where was this fire twenty years ago Rick? If you commanded with half this passion, even an iota of this authority back then, the past may have turned out quite differently."

"For good or bad," Grace said crisply, "this is where we are now. Rehashing the past does no good, not for any of us." Placing her hands on Baden's shoulders, she patted them. "It can't be undone or changed, not by any of us. I remember what happened to you, Axel." She tilted her head. "What they did. That wasn't Rick. You can't keep blaming him."

"I guess that depends on your point of view," Axel snapped.

"Remember Axel, old scars need tending or they become rigid and cause problems." Satisfied she had made her point, Grace turned to Baden. "Are you feeling sick to your stomach? Or is it just a pain in the head?"

"Neither now. I'm just kinda ..." Baden watched his aunt carefully, wondering how she could know, "weak and tired. I can't stand or walk properly."

"You'll be fine." Grace patted his cheek, looking across the table at her husband. "Eve can't see him like this. It won't be good for her."

"The boy's health was my first concern," Axel said. "The effects he's experiencing will subside with a good night's rest."

Rickard stared hard at Baden, his mind clearly elsewhere. "How are we supposed to explain this to Eve?"

Why were they focusing on his mother? Rubbing at his head, Baden wondered if they had any idea what he had just been through.

"Did you at least explain the situation?" asked Grace. "Because it looks like you've led him about blind."

"Blind? Don't even start with who's responsible for this," Axel said pointedly. "What's taken place is an eventuality of the choices made when Baden was born. Your family made those choices."

"We support Evie and her decision now more than ever," flared Grace, clearly incensed.

Axel smiled, shaking his head. "Eve is no longer part of this, or my concern. Only the boy is. The time for peace is over."

The opening of the door took everyone by surprise, Gran May and Eve adding numbers to the farmhouse kitchen.

"Think we'll need a bigger room," mumbled Jevon.

"What's going on here?" Eve looked around, her troubled gaze locking on Dallas in his wheelchair, then Axel and Canon. When it landed on her son, her eyes flared wide. "Baden Lucas."

She was pissed. Baden knew when she put his names together he was in for it. Sitting back, he fought to muster a cavalier smile. "Um, err, sorry Mum. I kinda got caught up in something."

"Caught up?" Eve's gaze clashed with Grace's worried one. When she turned back to study him, he started fidgeting, could see the anxiety creeping in. "What happened to you?"

"Nothing much." Baden tried to ease back, and found himself almost toppling to the side, Jevon catching him before he lost balance completely.

"Baden." Eve knelt, staring hard into his eyes, all anger vanishing from her face. "What have you done?"

She was paling before him, concern robbing her cheeks of colour. "I'm fine."

"You're not." Straightening, she looked around the silent room. "Well, don't everyone answer me at once."

May stepped to her side. "Evie—"

"No." Eve pulled away, her agitation clearly growing. "No one's going to use my condition as an excuse here. I want to know why he looks like this? He's my son."

"You're right," Dallas wheeled forward in his chair. "Baden was involved in an incident with Alexa today after school, but both of them will be fine with rest."

"Incident?" Eve spun back, grabbing hold of Baden's chin, tilting it up to search his glassy eyes.

"They were crossing the road," Dallas continued. "A car clipped him, knocking him and Alexa to the curb."

"I can't see ..." Eve pulled up his sleeve, searching for injury. "There's not a mark on him."

"Like I said, impact was minimal." Dallas smiled reassuringly. "It was just the direction in which he was struck. His backpack took most of the brunt."

His mother had doubts. Baden could see that even through her haze of panic she was not convinced.

"Paramedics checked them over, and a doctor. Both are fine, Eve. They just need to rest, regain their mobility. It's only a little shock, that's all." Dallas placed a hand on Baden's shoulder, silently communicating a message through a raised eyebrow. "Isn't that right, Bay? You need rest."

"Yeah." Confused, Baden swallowed into the silence. They were protecting his mum, he could see that, he just did not understand the elaborate story. "Of course, I'm alright. Just like when Uncle Phil got hit by a bus."

Horrified, Eve bent back over him. "He ended up in a wheelchair!"

"You ruined my lead-in." Living an uneventful life had left him hopeless at tall tales, Baden realised. "I was going to boast about the Casteel fortitude and such."

"You're cracking a joke?" Eve shook her head. "Baden, are you really alright?"

Rickard broke the back and forth, placing a hand on her shoulder. "If his jokes are that poor Evie, I'd say he's fine. Clearly the experience wasn't enough to knock the Casteel sarcasm out of him."

She seemed to relax, his words and touch soothing a part of her no one else could reach. Maybe it was because they were twins. Whatever the reason, Baden was glad his uncle was there.

As if she just noticed them, Eve shot a glare at Axel and his partner. "Are you responsible for his accident?"

Immediately, Grace stepped forward. "No, that's all been taken care of. They were just on hand at the scene."

"Maybe it's time Baden got some rest," suggested Gran May. "Can't the rest of the details be done in the morning?"

"Couldn't have put it better myself," Rickard said.

May's sharp gaze locked onto Jevon. "You going to keep standing there like a perched galah, young Starrik? Or help our Baden?"

On a mile-wide smile, Jevon jumped to attention. "Why Cass here was just saying how much he appreciates all I've done."

"Hmm." May looked from Baden to Jevon, clearly doubtful.

"For sure." Jevon nudged Baden. "Isn't that right, mate?"

Baden grumbled something unintelligible before realising the abrupt knock had thrown off his centre of gravity. Sweaty hands slipped as he tried to grip the table, and not fall from the chair. Eve gasped reaching out, but Jevon beat her to it, pulling him upright to his feet.

"Set and ready," he declared. "Lead the way."

May crossed the room, urging Agent Canon aside. "Let's get him back to our house," she ordered, holding open the door.

"Yes ma'am." Bracing himself, Jevon hauled Baden forward. "You get heavier in the last ten minutes, mate?"

Exhausted, Baden rubbed a hand over his sweaty face. "Maybe. Fatigue is the only way your body responds to all things physical."

"Still got some fire left in the tank. I'm impressed." Jevon secured his load, grunting at the weight. "Right-e-o, let's move."

Eve took Baden's other arm, sliding a hand around his middle. Together, the two shuffled him across the kitchen, into the back room.

His uncle came abreast, pushing open the screen door onto the veranda, stepping onto it with them. "I'll come over in the morning. We need to have a little chat, mate."

"Yeah," Baden nodded. "Sure thing."

"And if there's anything else, Evie, I'll take care of it. You don't need to worry."

"Thanks Rick." Eve smiled shakily at her brother. "But I'm fine, I can handle this."

"Of course you can." Rickard waved as they moved down the stairs onto the footpath.

May followed, looking back at her son while saying, "Just keep him moving, young Starrik."

As they left, Baden glanced back also, catching the glare his uncle shot Axel, who was standing just inside the screen door watching.

Though his body felt sluggish, Baden's mind was electrified, working furiously. How many people were involved in this? Everywhere he turned, everything he did was met with a wall of secrets, half-truths and even outright lies.

The last realisation triggered something deep inside, a feeling that sat uncomfortably in the pit of his stomach. Resentment.

The crunch of gravel seemed loud as the quiet group traversed the path to his cottage. Determined to spare his frail mother, Baden leaned heavily against Jevon, watching his grandmother pass, saying she was going to turn on the porch light.

From the back of his mind, Alexa Noble's words jumped forward, repeating themselves like a needle stuck on a vinyl record. *After Ebony, we're next.*

If that was true, it was terrifying. Whatever was going on, Baden knew it was something to do with the Freestone Crystals. But what?

As the three entered the small home, his grandmother and Eve saying goodbye to Jevon, Baden's mind continued to worry the question.

It felt as if his life, along with reality, was being twisted and turned into a strange dream that kept shifting the stage. Kevin's experiment with Alexa in the basement, and what had happened in the caves with Jevon. Even Ebony and her mobile phone. Was it all connected, leading him somewhere?

One thing was certain. Damage control was happening at his uncle and aunt's house. For the first time in his life, Baden understood Jevon's insatiable need for answers. What were the Fellowship Founding Families fighting so desperately to keep from their children?

Galactic Star Key: Zozes Karbroe
Astral Nav-Coordinates: EAS-APL-4
Data Sequence: 25.0

"Blades!" Vae'gon's gravelly voice filled the immediate area. "By the order, you are to assemble to the nav-site marked upon your optic map-scouter."

Zozes' cyber-optic overlay updated, showing where he was to reposition himself upon a nearby grav-lift, a thin red glowing wireframe digitised in place, composing its outlines to resemble each squad member.

"Kaze." Zozes sighed, noting his brother's preoccupied expression, nudging him hard. "That's us, you ready?"

"I am." Like he was shaking off a bad dream, Kaze rolled his head, and stretched his neck. "I just need a moment."

More alarmed than he cared to admit, Zozes pulled him around. "Did you receive the uplink?"

"I got it!" Kaze yanked free irritably.

Something was wrong. Zozes could not remember his brother ever looking shaken before an engagement. Glancing down the line, he saw Vae'gon had left the Enforcers who were running final system checks on the Link-Trones, evaluating diagnostic readings through a series of cyber-screens on their porta-tools. His brother was watching the Astral Guard officers following Vae'gon, a definite frown marring his brow.

"Talk to me, Kaze," demanded Zozes.

Kaze jut his chin forth. "Vae'gon's almost here. Fall in."

With little choice, Zozes did, his gaze falling on an additional group of Astral Guard personnel crossing the arena with the reinforced spawn-pod from the landing bay. They halted near the gathered Enforcers, drawing to at-stance.

Vae'gon paused before the assembled Blades, his gaze shifting from Noremar to Major Rajek, before slowly moving on. "Enforcers, I am charging you with the task of supervising how each training quarter is to be operated."

"Yes, Sir!"

There was something in the Commodore's expression, in the look that passed between him and the Enforcers that gave Zozes a sense of foreboding. Like he was aware, Vae'gon met his gaze, before glancing at his brother.

Kaze did not flinch, seeming to look through the Commodore.

Zozes found his brother's utter stillness as uncommon as his silence. The moment Vae'gon walked on, he breathed easier. "Kaze?"

"I'm with you," his brother interrupted, then asked, "Do you think Noremar just gave him some type of Devronian love stare?"

"What?" Thrown, Zozes glanced at the Enforcer.

"You couldn't have missed it. Jenvar giving him a lovelorn look."

His brother's lightning change of mood caught Zozes by surprise, since it was at complete odds with the sweat coating his forehead. Kaze was upset about something, but not prepared to speak of it.

"Forget Noremar's idiosyncrasies. They're no rarer than any of Devron's." Mouth twisting, he leaned closer. "Shutting me out now is dangerous. Is there anything I need to know?"

"More like their entire species is defective." On a heaved breath, Kaze nudged his brother. "Getting cosy with one of them off the battlefield would rate worse odds than even you."

"Fine, we'll speak of this later." Crushed for time, Zozes pushed the button his brother seemed to have constantly charged. "Let's win this thing. Conquering the Trials lands us with a straight shot at hunting down Garrold."

Kaze seemed to like the sound of that. "Bring on the Alpha life of being a bad arse mother—"

"Alphas Green and Blue!" Vae'gon stepped back into Zozes' line of vision. "Care to relay your conversation with the rest of us?"

"No, Sir." Zozes held at-stance. "We are more than acclimatised to all challenges within the Blade Trials."

"Is that so?" Vae'gon's gaze fell on his brother. "Both of you?"

Kaze did not immediately respond. It seemed to Zozes the Commodore was trying to provoke his brother, who was returning the favour by choosing a sustained silence.

"Alpha Blue." Vae'gon's voice rose in challenge. "What say you? Your team stands together?"

"I love to acclimatise, Sir." Kaze stared straight ahead. "Preferably to the weather on duty-leave to Gloveron, but we can't all get what we want."

A couple of Blades fought a smile, several even coughed, garnering a steely glare from the Commodore.

"Gloveron." Vae'gon snarled the name. "The weather will be least of your concerns Blade ... unless ..." he took a step closer, shoving past the Major. "Is this your way of forfeiting the Trials?"

A long silence followed, one heavy with Kaze's dark anger. "You haven't been paying attention, Sir. Blades never fold!"

Zozes could hold his tongue no longer, joining his brother in speaking the Blades' motto. "We hold the line alone — together!" Every Blade joined the final three words: "Till the end!'"

Smiling, Kaze added, "Our duty is to serve and safeguard the Planetary Allegiance."

"Ah, the refrain of the Blades and spoken with such passion." Like he had swallowed something distasteful, Vae'gon wiped his mouth. "Time will be the judge of that, for these Trials will test your true standing."

A drone alarm sounded, numerous yellow flashing lights revealing the depth and height of the arena. Multiple levels started coming online, different combat zones releasing thick-plated training bases, some with walls, others with ceilings and jutting side panels.

Zozes cyber-optics' nav-site signifier lit for a second time, the wireframe representations of their squad flashing red. The wave-path coordinates directed them toward a grav-lift platform.

"Trek your wave-path," ordered Vae'gon. "When every Blade squad has reached their coordinate marker, your map-scouter will transition the wireframe cyber-signifiers from red to green. Once this has taken place, there will be no turning back. The grav-lift platforms will activate, transporting you all to separate training quarters."

Zozes eyed numerous grav-lift transport pathways leading from this platform to different combat courses over the arena.

The arena floor began retracting before the squads, revealing a circular opening. From it rose a submerged six-sided cone structure which Zozes recognised as the primary Ops-Station for the entire arena. The top level's observation bridge formed six ridged faces that sloped down, coming to a flat underside which powered a large anti-gravity port.

After clearing the floor, the structure continued to rise, hovering at the centre of the arena.

A nod from Vae'gon directed the Astral Guard officers to guide the reinforced spawn-pod to a large grav-lift base. Once ready, an anti-gravity slip-beam powered, connecting to a series of relay control rings that led to the Ops-Station bridge.

"We are seeking the most proficient combat officers within the Blades to serve with the Astral Guard while assigned in Earth's system," Vae'gon announced, carefully looking over the Blades, hands clasped behind his back. "Success within the Trials will place officers on service detachment from the Galactic Force. This means you will no longer adhere to their ruling, but that of Astral Guard alone."

A deep silence fell, each Blade taking this in. The Commodore looked carefully over them, his gaze finally settling on the brothers.

"Major Rajek, please step forward." Once he had done so, Vae'gon continued, "Here is a representation of what is required. Texus Rajek is the first Blade officer to officially qualify and serve in the Astral Guard. His success in this role is the sole reason each of you stand before us today."

Zozes remembered back to the meeting on the Warront Craft, how the Major had warned them of what was to come, to be prepared for anything. Was this part of it? A shifting in their loyalties?

"Because of him," continued Vae'gon, "many more Blades have pursued his path, even against my personal grievance." Vae'gon's gaze flicked briefly over Kaze. "Vanguard General Ocun, my predecessor, stood in charge of Earth's Intégration program. She held a firm belief that the Blade program should have been disassembled at the end of the Second Galactic War.

However, I've decided to hold off on summary judgement until my position as Vanguard General is official. Only then will I evaluate if other alternatives need to be implemented, when my ruling will carry strength."

Other alternatives? Drawing a quiet breath, Zozes remembered back to his first meeting with the Commodore, the warning Vae'gon had given regarding Astral Guard and how he and they were reviewing options to replace the Blades. The question was, with what?

Satisfied his message had been delivered, Vae'gon turned to the Enforcers. "They're all yours."

While the Enforcers called for the assembled Blade squads to move off, Zozes watched the Commodore being transported on a grav-lift platform to the Ops-Station, two of his senior officers beside him.

There was a lot more going on here than just the Blade Trials, Zozes mused. The division between Astral Guard and the Galactic Force was a lot deeper than he initially feared.

At a shout from the lead Enforcer, all Blade Squads began moving off, flanked by their hovering Link-Trones. Each followed the coordinates on their map-scouter, the units moving in different directions toward their allocated grav-lifts.

Noremar was the first of their team to walk off, moving to their grav-lift. The Major and Kaze joined her the moment their wireframe signifiers changed from red to green.

The Link-Trone hovered close to Zozes, its lights flashing in sequence. Meeting his brother's gaze, Zozes noted the glint in his eye, one that gave him pause. Jaw clenched, he weighed the risk of what they were about to undertake against his brother's life and the vow they had made together following the death of their father, *to bring all Garrolds to justice.*

Noremar's lip curled, scrutinising the two. "Understand this, Blade. Further delay or hesitation will have you forfeit the Trials and be recalled to Galactic Force for reassignment."

The Link-Trone crossed before her, momentarily blocking Zozes' view. It seemed like the Trone did not care for her opinion. Looking back at his brother, he noted Kaze's smirk, while trying to think of the best way to deal with what they were about to face.

He was going to bring his brother out of this whole, mind and body. Doubt in his own capabilities would only hamper him now, but getting through this by himself would have been a challenge. Guiding another …?

"Alpha Green!" shouted Noremar. "I'm giving you the count of five to get your worthless hide onto this grav-lift, or this ends here and now. One!"

Kaze faced him on the platform as the Enforcer called the second count.

"A recall back to command now?" Kaze shook his head. "Not while Garrold is breathing free air on Earth. I'm not leaving this planet without that Outcast's head."

In answer, she shouted three, but Zozes could see she was taking in his brother's resolve, though her gaze had shifted to eye the grav-lift platforms taking off around them, other Blade squads departing for their Trials.

Kaze looked his brother square in the eye then held out a hand. "Stand with me brother and win this one for us."

"Four! What's it to be, Alpha Green?"

Zozes grabbed the hand, stepping onto the grav-lift to take position as the transporter's circular base lit.

Barely acknowledging the two, Noremar activated her porta-tool, generating a cyber-screen. The moment Rajek nodded, she fired the graviton field, translucent energy shifting through a series of relay rings guiding them up.

The moment the grav-lift's escort base passed through the first relay ring, the platform's gravity thrust increased speed. Using the time to calm his mind, Zozes surveyed the arena.

The higher levels showed various training areas, some still in lockdown, only the platforms to be used for the Trials active.

"Now that we're underway," Kaze said, crossing his arms and turning to the Major, "any last words to prep us, Sir?"

Rajek took so long responding, Zozes wondered if he heard.

"Don't die."

"Very direct, Sir. No hand for tact."

"You require physical ease of stress?" Rajek glanced back, one eyebrow raised.

"A hug, Sir?" Kaze scratched the back of his head. "Best you know I only play off-duty."

"I'll remember that for next time."

Zozes chuckled at his brother's dropped mouth reaction. Since the Major said this deadpan, his words seemed genuine, though Kaze was obviously baffled, uncertain if he was serious.

Their grav-lift moved fast, passing over multiple training quarters. Glancing down, Zozes eyed several circular training quarters from their elevated position, Blade officers stepping off their transport-pads the moment they docked.

Rajek observed a group of Blades gathered in a nearby training quarter. Zozes got the impression he was seeing something else, something from the past.

"Were the Blade Mark One Trials, task assessments, similar to the Mark Twos?" asked Kaze, curious.

As their grav-lift docked, the Major remained silent. Zozes wondered if he would answer, the wind of the anti-gravitation nacelle filling the silence.

Rajek stepped off the platform. "The battleground of war was our Trial, and that spared none that were not worthy."

The Link-Trone momentarily hovered close as Kaze and Zozes disembarked, then charged ahead, its spawn-well flaring white, indicating it was generating a tactical analysis, modulated scanners employed while sweeping the area. Surrounding the squad, an octagonal grid-shield materialised, weaving from the deck's outer rim, upwards forming a laser netting that eventually shaped itself into a dome structure sealing off their training quarter.

The Major indicated for the brothers to follow him, heading for the centre of the training structure, a bare, circular dais, their Link-Trone's scanners now isolated inside the reinforced dome.

Enforcer Noremar stood to one side, positioned not far from the grav-lift, working on her porta-tool. She had a series of active cyber-screens generated, displaying various layout maps for the combat courses.

"Remember," called Noremar, "I will be standing in as an Astral Guard onsite evaluator throughout the entirety of these Alpha Trials. I have absolute authority, Blades, in conducting the testing phase. Beneath this dome, you and your Trone are under my direct control."

Kaze stepped onto the dais, glancing back at her briefly. "Not gearing up for this one, Noremar? Spectator privileges seem a little out of character for a Devronian."

"We all have our orders," the Major said. "The purpose of the Trials is to measure your ability in combating against the Kadra threat."

At these words, Zozes rolled his head and shoulders, striding confidently onto the dais to stand by his brother. They were committed, he thought, to prove their control over the Link-Trone.

Kaze smiled confidently. "We're more than well-versed in that field, Sir."

"You must also be aware," Rajek said. "Your previous service status as a solo-operator paired to an Alpha's Link-Trone is far less complex then taking direct command charge of your own."

"I understand that, Sir." Kaze took the warning seriously.

"Your dual-pairing makes your status unique. You must learn to command the Trone as a unified force, two minds as one. An Alpha's combat prowess alone will not always grant you victory," he counselled. "The Archetype held a core belief that the will of the mind is the most powerful tool in the mastery of spawn technology."

"Will of the mind?" Kaze frowned at this, clearly not convinced. "You speak as if spawn wielding is some form of sacred practice."

Zozes had heard of these ancient teachings during training. Lessons that had long been abandoned at the end of the Galactic War. Clearly what Rajek had initially learnt had been repurposed for the Blade Mark Twos, only a few like the Major knew of the Archetype's true teachings.

"Knowing one's options grants you the advantage." This old knowledge seemed to light the depths of his eyes, while he took several steps back to throw out a bold order. "Stand ready, Blades! Leave armour materialisation on standby while engaging armament load-outs. You are to trigger all weapon types."

At ease with the task, Zozes generated weapons over his body, noting that Kaze was immediately angry, struggling to materialise his weapon load-out in a single set-order. In the end, he was forced to generate each weapon individually.

The Major watched him struggle for several moments then triggered a clasp activator on his hand, generating a reconfigured plasma cannon along his forearm, firing on the stressed Blade.

The plasma blast was strong enough to send Kaze skidding across the dais, smoke evaporating around his body. The only thing that saved his skin was the fact the Major had reduced power output to a non-lethal blast.

"Well?" Rajek moved before him. "Still feeling like you're well-versed in dealing with the Kadra?"

Winded, Kaze rolled over, gaining his feet grimly. "Kinda hard to process anything after taking a throw-blast of plasma at point-blank range."

"You believe that Kadra will give you greater latitude?"

Teeth gritted, Kaze stared at the Major, mouth sealed.

"In the heat of battle, an Alpha's mentality must always be centred," Rajek growled. "Fight any heightened emotional state. It forms ripples through the sync-pulse that fluctuate, creating issues between you and your Trone, blocking your spawn-net."

"You're saying to an Alpha," Kaze said, rubbing his chest, "our goal is to feel nothing?"

"Mastering feeling and thought is the basis of all spawn technology."

"Now you're contradicting yourself for my benefit."

"The Major speaks of control," Zozes snapped, "as you well know."

"Something you lack," added the Major. "This is part of the reason why the Link-Trone does not always obey you. Your state consciousness and emotional control is unbalanced and erratic."

"Talk like this nullifies active instinct," Kaze argued.

"Unfocused control responses weaken not only your connection to the Trone, but also to my own spawn-net." Zozes knew he was pressing another of his brother's emotional buttons, but it had to be done.

"Like frustration in generating a simple load-out?" realised Kaze, glancing at his weapons.

The Major nodded. "Each time this happens, it weakens the Trone's sync-pulse with you. LT cannot fully commit to an issued task when it has to constantly re-adapt frequency to rebalance your spawn-net."

"This seems a little touchy-feely for me." Kaze glanced at his brother, obviously not liking to hear the truth. "The more I hear, the less I regret not undergoing command training."

"A sync-pulse is your heart," said Rajek, "and the only path to becoming a fully-fledged Alpha. You only weaken yourself, and your team, by not abiding by its laws."

Kaze opened his mouth, but Zozes spoke first. He knew exactly what his brother was about to spit out. "You'll what? Punch through it, like always?"

"Close enough." Kaze grabbed his brother's shoulder, pulling him around. "So, stop toeing around, hero. You take the lead, I'll have your back. Trust me."

The last was said so earnestly, Zozes frowned, sensing something grave behind the words. Whatever his brother had on his mind, he had brought it into the Alpha Trials.

The Major nodded to Enforcer Noremar who triggered a schematic map through her porta-tool. The training quarter's configuration immediately began to alter, forming a vast combat course. Numerous platforms began to rise, powered by anti-gravity ports underneath, the layout staggered until more build-constructors fully transformed. Curved walling dividers reconfigured from the deck, separating engagement zones. Long tunnels spiralled to connect each of these areas, all leading back to the centre battle stage. Defence barriers assembled, some generating grid shields.

"Astral Guard have taken into account," called Noremar from her position, "your current service accreditation. This has elevated you beyond first testing phase."

"Looking for amusement with a lie won't end well with me, Lieutenant," Kaze said, clearly suspicious. "I'll take what I can get, but this sounds a little too good."

Noremar nodded at Rajek. "Thank the Major, as he addressed the Commodore and Astral Guard on your behalf. They in turn chose to recognise your prior accomplishments."

Surprised, Zozes looked at Rajek, who offered no explanation. Noremar was another matter. She appeared anything but convinced with Astral Guard's decision, but true to her Devron nature, she followed orders.

But there was something more, thought Zozes, eyeing the tightness of her mouth, something she was holding back.

Rajek noted this also. "The Alpha's success in controlling Blade-Gears during their testing on the Blast Range was key in this assessment. When combining this with the extraction of the Kadra from the crash zone on Earth, it was concluded that you had been adequately tested in base-form operations."

"Ever since the dual-pairing we've been shooting from the hip, playing the odds to land anything critical." Kaze grinned at his brother. "Living in the unknown times isn't so bad, brother. So, we're moving to testing phase two point zero?"

"No." Noremar's flash of teeth was anything but friendly. "Astral Guard has revised the final phases, merging them into a sole module."

"Lieutenant?" The Major immediately stepped to the edge of the dais. "Why was I not notified of this?"

"The Astral Guard does not answer to you, Major."

Not liking the unnerved look on Rajek's face, Zozes joined him at the edge, his brother coming alongside. "What's happening, Sir?"

"The Commodore," Noremar snapped, her eyes never leaving the Major's, "has observed your earlier request for condensing the testing phases. He felt it necessary to incorporate all remaining phases due to the dual-pairing advantage. The Commodore requires an on-field challenger to fully test their capabilities."

"Advantage?" Kaze eyes widened. "Now that's an exaggeration."

"I never agreed to this, Enforcer."

"Your approval was not sought, Major, and the surprise nature of this only enriches the results." Noremar looked the three over. "I thought you would be pleased, as now the Blades and you can focus on delivering exactly what is required. A concentrated effort that will yield the best results."

Another twist to the Alpha Trials? Zozes could see Vae'gon was punishing the Major for intervening on their behalf, and that not even he knew what they were to face now.

Clearly angered, but out of options, Rajek demanded softly, "Then what on-field challenger are the Blades to face?"

"You already know the answer, since the Commodore took the time to speak of you with such glowing language."

"Then let us in on it," Kaze growled. "Who's our challenger?"

Expression radiant, she indicated Rajek. "Your final test stands before you. In order to pass the Alpha Trials, you must have the Major submit. Bring him to his knees."

Galactic Star Key: Rickard Casteel
Astral Nav-Coordinates: EAS-APL-4
Data Sequence: 26.0

For a long moment, Rickard watched the small group disappear down the gravel path, wanting to make certain they were out of earshot. He then brushed past Axel, returning to the kitchen.

"What were they trying to do?" he demanded.

"They've been attempting to manipulate certain properties within growth vein crystal," said Axel, following him like a shadow. "In other words, activate its production cycle."

"Oh." Grace sank into a kitchen chair. "How could this have happened?"

"I think I know," Dallas admitted, hanging up his mobile. "It's Alexa. She was involved."

"Alexa?" Grace turned to him in concern. "Is she alright?"

"Safe at home. Duke is watching her for now, and Charles," he held up his phone, "is joining him."

"Charles? Why is Jevon's father involved?"

"There's been a development in the high-plains," snapped Axel. "His brother, Corbett Starrik *has been hunting*."

All in the room fell silent.

Fist clenched, Rickard looked away fighting to gather himself, barely believing he was in agreement with Axel. There was no denying what was obvious. Peace was at an end.

Grace's eyes glimmered angrily. "What else haven't you been telling us?"

"Enough to say that Global Reach may be soon overshadowed by an even greater event. It was Corbett Starrik who located the latest victim Adele Jones, and that was no accident. How Global Defence got tipped off about his *hunt* is still under investigation by my agents."

"Corbett is the East-Warden to Skyfall," Rickard reminded grimly.

"The Fellowship no longer recognises that title or any of the Rangers under his charge." Axel glared at Rickard. "Something you damn well know."

"Then how'd you come by this information?" growled Rickard.

Clearly caught, Axel shifted on his feet. "Communication hasn't been fully severed."

"Convenient," Rickard sneered, shaking his head in disgust. "Same old Axel … just how many sides are you playing in this?"

"My connections, Rick, are all that stands between those dangers and your twenty year peace."

"There isn't time for all that now," Grace said angrily. "How many Rangers has Corbett called in?"

"All of them." Axels eyes narrowed. "Whatever is drawing the abduction victims to Skyfall Mountain is clearly beyond coincidence."

"You don't say," growled Rickard, glaring across the table.

"I believe," Dallas broke in suddenly, "this discussion is best left for another time."

"How was Alexa involved?" Rickard took the hint, returning to the matter at hand. "Those kids are at worse odds than us. We chose right from the start for them to never be a part of this, using the rift between families to make certain."

"A play that may no longer hold weight, old friend. They've still come together," Dallas said, wheeling his chair to the table. "It's no secret my condition's grown worse, particularly the last six months, reducing me to this damn chair more and more. There's also been lapses in time where I'm losing a half day, sometimes more. Alexa admitted last week she's been talking to me during these states, that I've been speaking of the past."

"Why wasn't this reported?" Axel demanded.

"Reported?" Dallas leaned back in his chair. "Last I looked, I was a Noble, not a damn Solomon. The moment you turned your back on my family, siding with—"

"This isn't about past loyalties," Grace interrupted angrily, looking from Dallas to Axel. "Eve's had no relapse in all this time. One of us would know. May's been living there for over six months."

"If Alexa's found out another way," Rickard said, looking apprehensively at Grace, "we may have an even bigger problem."

"My thoughts exactly," Axel said.

"I guess at this point anything's possible," Dallas said. "And with the new developments and Global Reach, events are changing faster than I can keep up."

Grace looked to Rickard, rubbing her hands in agitation. "And we still haven't heard from Ebony. Maybe—"

Axel huffed a breath, like he was preparing for battle. "She is under the protection of the Fellowship. A meeting has been arranged."

"What?" Grace jerked to her feet, but Rickard held her back.

"What meeting?" he demanded quietly. "I thought I'd made Grace's and my position clear at the hospital."

"We certainly had," Grace snapped. "All decisions the Fellowship make must first go through us. Our right of claim still stands." Like a lioness protecting her young, Grace leaned across the table. "Ebony is our child, our responsibility. You remember that, Agent."

"I'm afraid," Axel said quietly, "that responsibility is now forfeit."

"Forfeit? You can't be serious!" Grace straightened indignantly. "No one in the Fellowship can make that decision."

"I'm afraid it's already been made. She's been called upon by her true heritage."

Stunned silence filled the kitchen, Grace and Rickard staring at one another, then across the table to Axel.

"But that's not possible!" Grace shook her head, starting again. "Is that who Doctor Walker is to meet with? We haven't heard from him in over two weeks, or anyone from his team. We believed everyone …?"

"He made contact with the Solomons last night. It was his recommendation to address the matter personally."

"I don't believe it!" Grace said hotly. "That's a flat-out lie."

"Just a minute." Rickard placed a hand on her arm, still looking at Axel. "Why go to you? Why weren't we told any of this?"

"The Fellowship granted you the position of caretaker, but that title is not absolute. The official representative of your house was contacted."

"Oh." Grace's hand covered her mouth. "May? May was contacted?"

"She was." Axel looked from Grace to Rickard. "Interesting that she hasn't apprised either of you of that development."

"I don't understand any of this." Grace turned away, sinking back into a chair. "Why would she do that?"

Rickard, however, sighed heavily. "I think I have a pretty good idea why."

"Then we'll discuss it in private." Grace appeared to visibly pull herself together while tidying her hair. "You've done your duty. We'll confirm the rest with May ourselves."

Axel laughed softly. "Dismissing me, Grace?" Reaching into his jacket pocket, he pulled out several cards. "There's one last matter that needs to be addressed. I was instructed to give these to May, however she's occupied." Dropping them on the table, he waited.

Rickard picked one up, turning it over. "Global Reach ID?"

"That it is." Axel looked from them to Dallas. "The Fellowship has been invited to attend the official launch at Global Capital Base. I suggest you all be there."

Rickard tossed it back on the table. "Why bring them to us?"

"The Solomons have already agreed to attend. Dallas will stand for the Nobles. These were requested by May."

Grace looked at them with loathing and disgust. "Who are the other IDs for?"

"I'd say for your entire family, with a few requested additional guest passes. Make sure those get to them."

"Requested by who?" Grace picked them up.

"The Fellowship Holding's Grand Librarian put in the request himself."

"The Librarian?" Rickard could see Axel knew more, but was cagily holding it back. "Why's he interested in all of us attending this launch?"

"Unknown. In particular, Jevon Starrik has been requested."

"Jevon?" Rickard looked to Grace whose mouth was now open in surprise.

Dallas brought everyone back to the central topic. "I think with what's coming, we all need to get ourselves prepared."

"Prepared?" questioned Rickard. "What's changed?"

"Everything's changed." Axel leaned forward and tapped a finger on the table. "As you well know."

It only took Rickard a moment to understand. "Skyfall Mountains River Caves."

Axel nodded.

"This is all Solomon's doing!" he exploded. "Marcus going public with the Northern Caverns last year caused all of this!"

"You believe that if you want." Axel stepped back, straightening his jacket. "It's no secret that the Fellowship have ownership over the caves. Contact was made a long time ago, Rick, but these aren't the only caves the Fellowship holds. This is bigger than Freestone. The Founding Families only have claim to one of these sites."

"Skip the history lesson. What're they after?"

"The Global Ambassador has a proposal to make in regards to the caves and what they hold."

"What kind of proposal?"

"I've told you all I know," Axel said. "Those details are only subject to the heads of the three Founding Families. It will be May's decision to tell you if she wants." Walking to the door, Axel paused. "Whatever the outcome, be prepared for change because it's coming for us all."

Galactic Star Key: Zozes Karbroe
Astral Nav-Coordinates: EAS-APL-4
Data Sequence: 27.0

The Major neither challenged nor expressed emotion following Enforcer Noremar's confronting statement. Instead, he walked silently to the centre of the dais, expression shielded.

Zozes watched this just as silently, before turning to his brother. Kaze's expression was the exact opposite of the Major's.

"The Commodore's in-flight run to the *Trollo* must've had decompression issues, because clearly he's suffering a form of hypoxia!" Thoroughly enraged, Kaze leaned close to his brother. "The loss of oxygen in his blood has left him shambolic!"

"Focus, Kaze. Remember the Major's last words," Zozes growled. "We can do this."

"The Major's a vokken Blade war hero!"

Zozes watched the Major energise the clasp activators on his hands, initiating the crawl of his hybrid armour. "None of us have a choice." Triggering the Blade-Gear on his belt, he felt the Link-Trone increase additional spawn feed to his bio-mechanical network, readying for combat operations. "The moment we stepped onto this arena our course was set, the Major's committed. Now, do we stand together?"

"Brother, you're a runner for strategic action." Grim, Kaze activated his own Blade-Gear, "I'm open to suggestions."

"We can't best him in our base-form," muttered Zozes quietly. "Which leaves one edge."

"Spawn-drift."

"They want us to fail," Zozes said. "Forcing us to choose this is their way of seeing we do."

"Yeah." Rather than react with fury, Kaze sifted through the words. "At this point that's kinda hard to miss, applying a level of force to get us to forfeit."

"Whatever Astral Guard's reasons, we'll conquer this test," Zozes snapped, furious but channelling it in the right direction. "It's the only choice we have if we're to defeat Cedos Garrold in open combat."

"Now you're speaking my language." A slow, dark smile curled Kaze's mouth. "Time to bring in the heavy gears."

The two energised their combat suits' reinforced armour, their original set weapon-load-outs compensating for this by breaking down into warp-orb fibres to allow for repositioning. Tele-warp wireframes outlined every component before fully materialising into physical matter.

Reinforced assembly plates formed, sitting comfortably against the body, Zozes sorge multi-rifle appearing then mag-locking to its weapon-dock. Grenade rods began lining his utility belt at the same moment a pistol formed on his hip, magnetically sealed against its docking holder.

The last to form was his helmet, covering his head, the visor coming online, pairing with his cyber-optics to generate a virtual display. Glancing at his brother, Zozes noted that Kaze looked more comfortable in armour than out, rolling his shoulders.

While checking his power armour's ignition status and system operations, Zozes noted the shimmer of his shield covering his body. Beneath all was the steady beat of his sync-pulse, a comfortable vibration, each spawn-net harmonising with the Link-Trone.

On his visor, Zozes noted both his and Kaze's frequency wave-guides, the virtual display highlighting his in green, his brother's in blue.

"Watch your sync-pulse's wavelength," he reminded his brother. "If its retraction and expansion increase outside safety borders, your pulse will fall into rapid dysfunction."

Kaze held up a hand. "Leaving our wave-guide reader active throughout engagement's a distraction."

"That explains how you've been underestimating the stress level applied to your sync-pulse." Containing his anger, Zozes realised he had just got a big answer. "How are you supposed to measure your limitations with your reader inactive?"

"I know you hate me repeating this, but I *feel* the pulse." Fighting for the words, he dived in. "It's a non-intrusive presence along my spine, vibrating through my body."

"You're basing this on a feeling?"

"I know I'm in control," Kaze said. "Maybe if you learnt to recognise this, you'd feel it too, instead of measuring life through every active thought."

"An active wave-guide reader's a tool," Zozes argued, getting worked up despite his best efforts. "And without it we can't measure the stress affecting our spawn-net. That's fact."

"Alright, it stays on." Kaze rolled his eyes. "Like I said earlier, this is your play, hero. Probably a bad thing initiating the drift with two opposing minds anyway."

"There may be hope for you yet." Leaving it at that, he moved before the Major.

When Kaze joined him, he could see he was mulling over the words. Zozes could only hope that his brother would stay true to his word.

The Link-Trone hovered close, initiating SWOT tactical analysis, sweeping the training quarters to extrapolate battle data, while working up the Major's strengths, weaknesses, opportunity and threats, seeking to identify which hybrid mode's load-out he would use during combat. Enforcer Noremar's combat status was identified as non-active, her position marked on the map-scouter.

"Seems LT's scanning sweeps can't break through the Major's shields," Kaze said. "Not without a little encouragement."

"We'll have to track his movements through LT's optic-sight recognition." Zozes grimaced, noticing the Major's bio-marker was absent on the map-scouter. "LT, engage surveillance scanners."

The Trone instantly initiated a new surveillance sweep, opening its optical scan that identified Rajek through visual identification. Star-Key flashing, information followed, listing a general overview of his current combat armour types, weapons and rank.

"Until we bring down his shields," Zozes murmured, "we'll be engaging a masked systemised target."

"Hear, hear!" Kaze threw up an arm.

"Following three alarms," Noremar called from the sideline, "a drone-signaller will sound to commence the Trial of Combat. Prepare battle form!"

Solemn, the brothers demagnetised their sorge-rifles to begin priming their weapons, both watching the Major, who was forming a twin plasma cannon over his forearms, while shifting into combat stance.

The first electronic alarm pierced the air.

"LT," Zozes said, rolling his neck, loosening his arm and back muscles. "Activate multi-cloak, and set an orbital surveillance watch from above."

A second alarm signalled, at which the Link-Trone's shields rippled before it activated and employed cloak.

"And keep your distance while engaged in cloak," Zozes warned, eyeing the Trone's position and noting it was hovering just behind. "The Major's EM countermeasures will render your systems offline."

Kaze nodded once. "No Trone means we're out of the game."

Zozes kept his eyes on Rajek, noting how utterly still he was, looking anything but unnerved. More like fully committed. "We'll begin by laying down a dispersal firing solution ... gauge his firepower during the initial assault."

"Then?"

"We'll use collision blasts to form a smokescreen, pull back to the south side's training quarter using its heavy cover to shield our retreat."

As the third alarm blasted the air, Kaze considered the tactic. "We're going to run?"

"We need LT's SWOT tactical analysis to identify his amour load-out, before engaging head on."

Kaze nodded taking several steps to the left, falling into combat stance. "Setting EM-dispersal rounds to radial burst."

Zozes followed suit, keeping his stance relaxed. Placing a finger over the trigger, he took aim, keeping one eye on the Major, another on the sync-pulse's wave-guide. Armour a comfortable weight, his mobility stabilisers readjusted with each move, a light sheen of sweat beginning to coat his brow.

The instant the final drone sounded, Kaze and Zozes began firing sorge-rounds, meeting the Major's initial assault of incoming plasma fire with fierce intensity at the centre of the battle stage.

The brothers' sorge-bolt's proximity sensors set off an electromagnetic burst upon the Major's own firing assault, each detonation billowing outwards, Rajek's plasma bolts exploding in a series of flash-bangs.

"There's our window," Zozes yelled. "Break off!"

The Link-Trone launched in a burst of speed from behind the brothers, to hover above the training quarter, taking a visual surveillance of the battle, feeding them information.

Grav-thrusters firing, Zozes shot to the left, his brother just ahead, the two entering a short tunnel that led to a flight of stairs. They emerged on a second-level bridge that connected to a circular platform overlooking the deck below.

Once there, the two paused. Zozes kept an eye on his tactical visor's map-scouter where their AI was uploading a visual surveillance. The Major was now standing on the centre of the dais, assembling components from his utility belt.

Kaze leaned over the rail. "Those aren't ...?"

After powering a mechanism, the Major suddenly released four cyber-trone emitters which instantly formed representations of himself, each one scattering in a direction throughout the combat course.

"Trone Replic-bot," Zozes said grimly.

"Clearly, the Major's playing to win."

Zozes pulled his brother behind a barrier. "A Blade Mark One's techno-system is primarily controlled through a neural spawn-tech connected to their brain."

Zozes uploaded the necessary telemetry to his brother's tactical visor. "His Hybrid Trone-net is connected to five main quadrants over his body, funnelling the spawns from his neural implant to his clasp-activators and power-core."

"The way you say it, makes him sound more bad-arse than us."

"Unlike us," Zozes said, "he has perfected controlling Trone spawns, but his power has limitations."

It took Kaze a moment. "His plasma-core?"

"Blade Mark One's spawn infusion was restricted to a single type. Ours is opening the sorge and Trone spawns power within the drift. It'll be our only chance. Come on!"

He moved ahead, continuing past another tunnel entranceway. As he did, he caught movement from the corner of his eyes at the opposite end of the passageway. Holding up a hand, he felt Kaze move in next to him.

"Our goal is to ascertain the Major's armour variant class," Zozes said. "Targeting his clasp-activators is our only shot to immobilise his armour."

"We'll need to bring down his shields to get that far," Kaze said. "That's the only way LT can generate an accurate SWOT analysis to ID his armour type."

"Exactly." Zozes paused to add, "His system can only hold one armour type per load-out. My guess, he'll initialise either heavy-defender, blast-assaulter or masked-surveillance."

"Three class types."

"Each type alters the clasp-activator positions over his body ..." A mag-dart projectile struck the wall over their head, spinning from green to red.

On a grunt, Zozes grabbed his brother and ignited his anti-grav boosters, both narrowly clearing the plasma blast's flashpoint, the aftershock striking the two hard, throwing them off course, ramming into a wall.

Though Zozes' shields took the impact, the blow left a collision crater in the bulkhead. It also left his ears ringing.

Back on his feet, Kaze shook off the blast. "Little heavy on the boost, don't ya think!"

"Eyes up!" Zozes bellowed, spotting a figure dropping from the level above.

It collected Kaze, kicking him mid-air to land flat on his back, while Zozes dropped and rolled, barely avoiding a stream of plasma-fire lighting up the wall, leaving a smouldering trail in its wake.

Sorge-rifle levelled, Zozes fired multiple shots, the assault knocking out their target's energy shields, the shimmer revealing its identity.

"Replic-bot!" Kaze yelled, reforming his rifle's barrel to scatter-shot, jumping back to his feet.

The moment its shields fell, Zozes grimaced, noting his brother's barrage had damaged its emitter, destabilising the Replic-bot's physiology. Seeking retreat, it made double-time across the quarter, looking for a tunnel.

"No way!" One grav-thrust positioned Kaze before the Trone. "Kick this!"

His burst of scatter bolts tore through the Replic-bot's midsection, critically damaging the last of its cyber-Trone emitter. The energised wireframe flared red over its body, the Major's digitalised cyber-form breaking down, the damaged emitter falling at his brother's feet.

"I'd say you're in the zone, enjoying that a little too much," Zozes muttered. "Remember a Replic-bot adapts after every engagement. Next one won't be so easy."

"It relays our tactical data?"

"Learns from every engagement." Zozes grunted as a rain of fire lit the area, one that pushed the brothers into the far tunnel the Replic-bot had been seeking, incoming plasma-bolts leaving collision burns along the wall and deck.

"LT!" Zozes called over the personal freq-com. "Break visual surveillance, form up on our position at a safe distance."

"Understood."

Still cloaked, Zozes eyed his map-scouter as their AI unit began closing in on their position, his brother laying cover fire at the mouth of the tunnel.

"The Major's a dead-eye compared to these pretenders!" Kaze scoffed. "Time to even the odds!"

"Let's do it," Zozes agreed, quickly taking the lead to move deeper into the tunnel.

The next intersection was dark, Zozes adjusting his visor for night-sight, then lowering and rolling onto his stomach to survey the coming tunnel. No shots came his way, and he could identify no current threat as Kaze slid against a low wall, across on his left.

"I need one of the Replic-bot's emitters intact," he advised Kaze over freq-com.

"Understood!" His brother unexpectedly shot at the roof, calling, "Movement!"

At height, Kaze fired an EM-pulse bolt which produced an electric wave, illuminating the ceiling in a brilliant blue hue which expanded throughout the entire area. The unexpected move destabilised the Replic-bot's cyber wireframes, the corridor going from light to dark in a breath, exposing their position as their Link-Trone flew in from behind, marking the enemy's positions for the brothers to begin firing.

Zozes dodged incoming plasma bolts, while altering his rifle's settings from rapid to precision-fire, increasing his accuracy greatly mid-range. He fired numerous times, finally bringing down a Replic-bot's shields.

The moment these destabilised, he prepared to advance, only to see his brother altering his rifle to precision-fire, pulling and holding the trigger on two charged rounds to cut through the Replic-bot's chest plates, damaging their Trone-emitters.

Like a drone lost for power, the Replic-bot's cyber-form wireframes flared, then deactivated, two damaged emitters falling to the deck.

Furious, Zozes bent to examine the devices only to see both were unsalvageable. "When I say intact, I mean operational!"

"Shame on you for holding out on the specifics," Kaze said, gingerly nudging one of the smouldering units with his boot.

"If I—"

A plasma bolt tore between the brothers, each diving for the deck, crossing low to find cover behind a defence guard container. Zozes swiftly activated its cyber-controller, triggering a series of defence shields to come online as blast fire struck it continuously.

"This one's mine," Zozes ground out, then drew several deep breaths, mentally and physically preparing himself. "Cover me!"

On a hard, fast leap he cleared the protective barrier, twisting in mid-air to avoid incoming bolts, his shields detecting the burn of each above and below his body, only his brother's constant firing keeping its aim offset.

The moment he landed, Zozes ignited grav-thrust, sliding out sideways, then dropping to one knee to avoid incoming fire, before regaining his feet to charge forward, seeing his brother's heavy volley of sorge-bolts had forced the Replic-bot to find cover.

"Plasma surge, build-up detected," warned Link-Trone over freq-com.

The moment he employed target-sight, Zozes located the Replic-bot taking cover behind a yellow translucent energy barrier. It was forming twin plasma-cannons that were priming, energy particles radiating above the barrier from the charging weapons.

"It's adapting ..." was all Zozes managed before the Replic-bot jumped from the barrier, firing the twin cannons straight at him.

Zozes calculated the trajectory targets to dodge to the right while firing off a grav-thrust, the detonation of the Replic-bot's weapons rupturing the wall plates behind, debris and metal littering the air amidst smoke and toxic fumes. Using the plasma-vapour, billowing like a blanket, he raced forward knowing it would interfere with the Replic-bot's sensors.

Almost on top of the enemy, he increased speed, aiming at close-quarter combat, until the Replic-bot changed its tactical position, igniting its boosters and unpredictably rushing him.

Taken to the deck, he landed on his back, forcing him on the offensive. Using the enemy's weight and momentum, he thrust the Replic-bot's body over his head. Twisting in mid-air, it landed on its feet, far more agile than he had realised, as he gained his own, only to rush him a second time, its momentum knocking the rifle from his grip amongst the rubble.

As the two wrestled, crashing through a barrier and into a wall, he caught sight of his brother's Star-Key signature breaking position, about to join the battle. Twisting, he tried to free himself, surprised at the Replic-bot's strength and speed in countering this.

Furious, Zozes drew back his arm to elbow its head, forcing its grip to slacken. That opening gave him the opportunity to drive up a fist beneath the under-jaw of the helmet, the unexpected move fracturing its cyber-form.

Bested, the Replic-bot stumbled back, its wireframe flaring red in warning.

On the hunt now, Zozes jumped forward, ploughing a kick into its chest, just above its emitter, feeling immense satisfaction when its body met the rear retaining wall.

For a moment, it looked as if it would rush him again, then its wireframe projector lines began flashing, deactivating the Replic-bot's shields.

"Now who's enjoying themselves a little too much," Kaze laughed, jogging up, kicking his brother's sorge-rifle into his hand, then tossing it to him. Turning to the destabilising Replic-bot, he took aim. "Wanna see it dance?"

"Wait." Zozes eyed the cyber-form's digitised representation, how it flashed between the Major and a wireframe, trapped in a loop.

"You prefer this light show?"

"Give me a moment to think." Glancing at the smoking combat area, he signalled for the Link-Trone to close in while nudging his brother. "Keep us covered."

As Kaze took watch, Zozes looked closer at the Replic-bot. "LT, Trone-slice its emitter's control relay. Sever all ties with its current paired host, then link it to ours."

"Nasty." Kaze whistled, glancing back. "You're going to generate one of our forms through it?"

"Depends how damaged the unit is." Zozes eyed the fluctuating cyber-form, watching as their AI powered a circular Trone-slicer panel, hovering close to the emitter. In no time Link-Trone had overridden the Major's connection. "Whether this new connection's going to be stable is debateable."

"Could be your last kick was a little high-yielded back there." Kaze glanced back, scouting the area. "Doesn't look real salvageable."

A plasma-bolt bowled his brother over, flaring his shields violently. Dodging incoming weapons fire, Zozes cursed, grabbing his brother's arm, dragging him behind a barrier. "Now look who's giving off the light show?"

"Got … the tingles." Kaze blinked groggily, shaking out his arms, flaring his fingers.

"You took that shot to the back of the head," Zozes said, briefly sighting the bot's firing position, making certain they were not rushed. "Lit up your entire system."

"That felt like a Rajek shot!"

"Cover LT." Zozes urged his brother up. "Check your map-scouter, I spotted two more Replic-Bots …"

"Nothing like the thrill of being the centre of attention!" Kaze shook off the shot, surveying the area, clearly smarting over being targeted. "They've up-levelled their game. I'd say the Major is taking scout-charge."

"We don't know that until confirming his ID," Zozes said. "Remember, there's a limit to how many he can replicate at a time."

"Those Trone-emitters' plamsa-cells only hold so much power," Kaze said thoughtfully, planning his own position of attack while checking his map-scouter. "Looks like they're flanking us, the two in the right quarter."

"Hold defence position and mark to deck," ground out Zozes, realising his brother was still having trouble following orders. "Until LT gets this Replic-bot's emitter online."

"You want me to play guard duty?" Kaze blurted, outraged. "Like vok I will!"

"I said hold—"

"If the Major's in sight, it's our job to take him out!"

"Assumptions can't replace authenticating an enemy target!"

"There's more than one way to ID that!" Kaze broke from cover, springing high and twisting, using grav-thrust for momentum to avoid attack. "LT! Assault mode, havoc strike now!"

"Kaze!" bellowed Zozes, laying down cover fire, furious over his brother's lack of forethought. "Break assault mode now!"

Not listening, Kaze charged forward, his sorge-rifle configuring into a triple barrel form. The moment it did, he changed tack, sliding to a halt, shifting all weight to his back leg.

Over his tactical visor, Zozes saw the alert, a havok weapons-lock, only a breath before Kaze released the white-hot havoc beam, the energy seeming to suck up all sound, then came the blast, lighting up the corridor, ripping through barriers, destabilising the Replic-bot's cyber-forms in a brilliant flare of glowing red, vaporising the Trone-emitters, leaving nothing in its wake.

Wary, Zozes eyed the empty blast zone, still covering his depleted brother, a feeling of foreboding growing. On his visor,

Kaze's wave-guide reader fluctuated, the sync-pulse jumping, leaving erratic spikes.

"See?" Kaze said, looking around like he was trying to shake off any weakness.

Disgusted, Zozes shook his head. "You think that's a win?"

"We know it wasn't the Major," Kaze reasoned, his face a sheen of sweat beneath the visor, skin pale. "He clearly can withstand more than that."

"Save our finishing move for the final bout!" Zozes hollered, but more than angry he was unnerved. "I need you more than just semi-coherent if we're to win this!"

"Alright." Kaze held up a hand, one that shook. His systems were still in cool-down mode, fighting to stabilise. Eyeing his sorge-rifle, Kaze triggered for it to reconfigure to base form, the simple move almost bringing forth a groan. "I got a little overexcited."

"Let's get back to LT," Zozes ordered, cutting a glance over the area before heading back to the Trone. With some relief, he noted that his brother's sync-pulse was stabilising much faster than after previous engagements.

"Don't break this defensive position," he said, "until the pairing of the emitter is complete. If our Trone's taken out—"

"we're out of commission," said Kaze. "No one's getting near LT."

"Good." Zozes clapped his brother on the shoulder, before standing.

"If I'm holding defence, what's your play?" Kaze took another glance, scanning the devastated corridor ahead of the two.

"To finish off all remaining bots and flush out the Major."

"All the fun, in other words," Kaze grumbled. "You're a real buzzkill."

"This isn't a game," grunted Zozes, jumping from cover. "Keep watch over your map-scouter. I'll relay the Major's coordinates. The moment our Replic-bot's new cyber-form is established, break defence and find me."

"Understood!"

"Don't come out there alone!" Zozes ground out, while sprinting through the corridor into the open combat course, all the while thinking hard. He needed to redirect the Major's attention from his brother and LT, which meant he needed to make a lot of noise.

Near the entrance, he looked up at a platform held stationary by an anti-gravity port, spotting a guaranteed way of redirecting attention. Reconfiguring his weapon, Zozes charged an EM-dart pulsator recalculating its yield, then took aim through his scope and fired his rifle. The dart made a solid mag-lock under the platform's grav-port's metallic casing.

After finding cover, he triggered the EM-dart pulsator via his porta-tool to release an electromagnetic pulse, tearing through the anti-gravity porter and destabilising its primary levitation mechanism, rendering it offline. Instantly, the platform began to break away from its suspended position, crashing to the deck below, devastating over half of the south side of the training quarter.

Shield-barriers erupted by the impact upon the main level formed a large crater, exposing submerged power relay-lines built underneath the ground level, and causing a cascade of explosions, disrupting the main energy feed, rendering the section dark.

Three Replic-bots emerged from a tunnel to inspect the damage, eliciting the ghost of a smile from Zozes. A Replic-bot's Trone-emitter was severely limited in its tactical programming. Taking advantage, he coordinated with the system to engage immediate level threats.

An encounter such as this was also new and gave him the advantage to end the engagement with the Replic-bots in one final assault before they re-adapted. Breaking cover, he kept low as he ran for a flight of stairs, one that would give him a significant vantage point. There, he positioned himself on the edge, changing his sorge-rifle's configuration to long-barrel sniper. Peering through the scope, he marked the three in survey-mode.

The moment two Replic-bots crossed paths, he primed a sorge-bolt yield, releasing a long, slow breath before firing, knocking out both of their Trone-emitters, their cyber forms destabilising and self-destructing.

The last broke off, running for cover. Widening his scope's range, Zozes used his target indicator to direct him towards the fleeing Replic-bot. Refocusing his sight, he narrowed in, locking onto his target, firing a sorge-bolt that tore through the bot's shields. Its cyber-form wireframe projector flashed red and broke down, Trone-emitter falling to the deck.

"All targets eliminated," he advised over freq-com.

"I heard," Kaze said. "Warm-up's over."

"Yes, he'll be ..." A low grav-hum caught Zozes' ear moments before his rifle's scope went black, a form dropping before it. Jerking back, Zozes immediately powered his grav-thrusters for a speedy retreat, spotting Rajek's powered phaser-blade deliver a critical strike, one that singed his shields, sparks lighting up the deck he impaled.

Zozes skidded back, powering his grav-thrusters to ground his position while mag-locking the sorge-rifle to his back. The Major rose from a knee, slowly drawing his phaser-blade from the deck. Molten metal steamed at the breach, hinting at the weapon's power.

There was no mistaking Rajek for one of his Replic-bots. The power in the O'Garcian's stance, the air of authority he exuded as he came forward was that of a true Blade hybrid.

Readying for battle, Zozes redirected sorge-energy into his forehand's weapon port, igniting his phaser-blade, clear white streams of energy particles forming into a cutting edge.

The Major came in hard, Zozes evading the incoming assault. Igniting grav-thrusters, he slid beneath the phaser-blade, then pushed to his feet. Spinning fast, he kept his balance, bracing for the Major's second attack while guarding his mid-section, until their blades made vicious contact.

Rajek followed through, weaving his blade back around, sweeping it forward with force. The strike drove Zozes back, barely able to deflect the assault.

On a hard breath, he brought up his sorge-blade, falling into combat stance, his blade held horizontally in shield-guard form, ready for Rajek's next strike, only to see him hesitate.

Enforcer Noremar's voice broke the blistering silence, coming over the Major's external receiver, a fact that puzzled Zozes as it was Rajek's personal freq-com with command.

"If you hesitate in your duty to perform as ordered, Major, the Trials will be terminated, the repercussions for the Blades irreversible!"

Still braced for battle, Zozes watched his adversary while his thoughts ran two different courses. Rajek was relaying his own private channel through his armour's exterior audio-com. But what was he attempting to convey? Zozes knew better than to ask, it was obvious they were both being watched and evaluated.

One step back, Rajek broke battle form, stepping to the platform to retake combat stance. Holding his weapon in spear-guard form, he kept the phaser-blade close, beneath his jawline, aiming it directly at Zozes.

The two measured one another, Rajek electing to attack in a hard, swift move that shifted him to the left, spearing his phaser-blade forward. Zozes stepped aside, parrying the attack across his body, dismissing the opening for counter.

The Major spun around, sweeping his phaser-blade back around. Zozes deflected the attack at the last moment, forcing him to step back which Rajek took advantage of by stepping through, clearly testing Zozes' shield-guard form, striking his weapon across.

Zozes ducked the attack, coming up to meet the upper twin strike, blocking the first as the second followed through. Clipping his shoulder, his shields rippled angrily before stabilising.

"Impressive. Your shield-guard's counter-offensive holds strong!" growled the Major, reforming his offensive spear-guard form. "Yet there were openings, you let these slide, Blade. Defence alone will not win you this battle!"

On a lunge, the Major ignited his grav-thrusters, jumping forward to plough a front kick, the move lightning fast. Zozes barely had time to react, sliding sideways to evade the attack, stunned when Rajek changed trajectory, in the process configuring his secondary combat arm to form a plasma cannon, then taking aim and firing.

Zozes caught the edge of the beam with his Blade, managing to deflect it into the ground, the explosion's eruption knocking him backwards. His shield's outer repulse-field drummed viciously, fighting to absorb the detonation blast. Through the billowing toxic flames, the Major appeared, plasma-blade arcing in a downward swing.

Zozes met his attack, the two sliding across the deck, weapons locked.

"The Kadra's martial-forms with a zaphna rod are governed by versatility and adaptation to their opponents," the Major ground out.

"Your fear of the unknown is reflected within battle, crippling your ability to act offensively, something Garrold will see through!"

The deadlock held for a few breaths longer. Rajek twisted his blade while shifting sideways to land a critical strike across Zozes' shield's chest plate, the phaser-burn igniting a stream of sparks.

Still upright, Zozes stumbled, his shield's repulse-field echoing, combat armour fluctuating dangerously. The Major stepped through with a forceful kick that punched Zozes through a guardrail, tearing safety beams from their moorings in the process.

The deck disappeared as he fell over the edge, tumbling backwards onto a sloping wall. Swivelling his body, the slide increased, Zozes about to spear his blade to halt this only to grunt as the incline lit up in a series of flash-burn explosions, energy bolts striking with vicious force.

A head-check showed the Major was giving no ground, firing on him constantly as he leapt from the platform above to begin skidding down the surface in fast pursuit, plasma cannon a non-stop weapon of mass destruction.

Desperate to avoid the bombardment, Zozes triggered his grav-thruster to the right, narrowly evading a near-hit detonation. Firing them again, he battled to circumnavigate the toxic blasts only to see the Major shoot a charged energy beam at the wall's coming ledge.

With little choice, Zozes held course, aiming for the blast zone, firing his boosters to cut through the inferno as fast as possible, his shield attacked by high-grade plasma energy as he slid off the edge.

In freefall, Zozes took control of his descent mid-air, powering down his phaser-blade, drawing his pistol, turning to fire on the Major who was pushing off from the ledge in fast pursuit while exchanging weapons fire.

"Brother!" Kaze's voice broke in over freq-com. "Good and bad news. Preference order on the update?"

About to activate his com-receiver, Zozes took a direct hit to the shoulder that sent his body into free spin, head over feet out of control.

"You better not be eating deck plating!" Kaze warned.

Barely able to breathe, Zozes continued to spiral, his visor's decent-guides moving out of control. Desperate, he managed to fire off a short burst of grav-thrust, level himself and bring his feet forward, the deck coming up fast.

"The battle-chant of holding the line is the only option you leave me with, brother!"

Zozes stumbled on landing, his armour's inertial dampers absorbing the impact, the Major landed solidly only a few feet away, already bringing his plasma cannon to fire again.

Under siege, Zozes rolled and dodged the hail of energy-bolts, focusing his efforts to employ visual locking coordinates on the Major via his tactical-visor, hurriedly relaying his position for Kaze to track while the deck lit up around him.

His brother's voice came over freq-com, the inflection, tone and manner leaving him barely able to comprehend.

"A Blade's resolve is absolute, our force unmeasured and true…"

Metal and debris taxing his shields, Zozes barely managed to dodge these while sliding on one knee across the surface, firing on the Major.

"For we hold the line alone — together! As one … till the end! Till the …"

"Kaze!" Zozes roared. Desperate, he sought shelter, shoving his back up against it. "As long as the emitter is online, enabling to supply cover for LT, it will have to do!"

"Now was that so hard to say?"

His barrier was partially destroyed, but not much around Zozes was still whole. Mag-locking the side-arm to his belt, he demagnetised his sorge-rifle. His suit's respirator indicator was alerting him to control his breathing cycle, as it was struggling to compensate for overexertion.

"Visual target-lock is set from my map-scouter," he advised. "You'll have the advantage to strike, so make your opening count!"

"To maintain your visual-lock you'll—"

Zozes' barrier blew apart, smothering his brother's words. "—have to hold the Major off until you re-enter the engagement!"

About to stand, Zozes was thrown from behind the barrier, rolling through the debris. Using the momentum, he grav-thrusted up on one knee, firing bolt after bolt.

"Moving out!" Kaze called, then freq-com went cold.

Grim, Zozes kept firing, knowing he was running out of time to initiate spawn-drift. Diving for cover behind twisted metal he fired from his position, waiting out his brother.

Like he knew this, the Major began shifting about the engagement zone, firing off shots and plasma-cannon blasts at random intervals while keeping Zozes pinned.

He was hunting their Link-Trone.

From this point on, Rajek's objective was to concentrate all his efforts on disabling their AI before it was able to prime its spawn-well to initiate the drift.

The Major fired a plasma-cannon blast, demolishing Zozes' cover, forcing him to roll into the open and stand before his aggressor.

"Dual combat in base form is a foolish gambit, Alpha Green," Rajek warned. "If you fail now, all fail with you."

"Then we fail," Zozes said, blinking hard to clear sweat from his eyes. "Do as Noremar ordered, grant no special privileges." Head back, Zozes breathed, briefly closing his eyes. "We need to know if we can stand against the Kadra Outcast."

"Till the end, Blade, hold the line." Rajek tipped his helmet.

The Major shifted in a sudden burst of speed, his armour's mobility-gears flaring while firing his plasma cannon as he raced forward. Zozes triggered grav-boosters, leaping clear of the explosion, bellowing as deck plating pelted his shields, his suit's respirator fighting to compensate for the toxic fumes of white hot plasma energy.

The flare of a phaser-blade was all the warning he got, Rajek coming in from above having boosted a jump to move at twice the speed while sweeping his blade, cutting Zozes' sorge-rifle in two and igniting the sorge mag-cell. The resultant explosion threw Zozes onto his back, grav-thrusters engaged to stabilise his position.

Rajek's grav-thrusters fired, charging him downwards, phaser-blade spearing through the air. Zozes triggered his gauntlet's combat-port at the last moment, sorge-energy forming into the bladed tip, catching the attack.

Driven to one knee, he held back the Major, the two weapons locked in a power struggle, Zozes throwing everything into blocking, sparks streaming over his visor.

Rajek employed grav-thrusters with crushing force. There was no room to counter the assault without risking critical damage, the Major's strength and position far superior, finally pushing through Zozes' defence-guard, sweeping the Blade outwards and exposing his chest.

Braced for the end, he saw the Major's blade arcing downward, aiming at a crippling blow, only to be met by a wave of light, the Major's assault held at bay by a second sorge-blade.

"Brother," Kaze gasped. "Little help here ..."

Within moments, Zozes had regained form, stepping to the left, using the momentum to angle his sorge-blade. Bringing it through in a sweeping strike, he forced the Major to break, exposing his flank. Kaze unleashed a series of chaotic offensive-strikes, the three now moving across the deck in an energy clash that vibrated the debris over the devastated deck.

At the appearance of his brother, Zozes redirected his mobility-gear's stabilisers to ground his position. Palming his pistol, Zozes triggered his personal freq-com.

"I'm going to widen the gap, brother. Break on my signal. LT, heavy sorge-cannon, we need to light this place up!"

At the edge of the engagement zone, their Link-Trone briefly uncloaked to perform the operation. "Assault mode three engaging, havoc-strike."

Instantly, Zozes' pistol formed a triple barrel, powering up. "Kaze, evasive RTR!"

The moment his brother rolled to the right, Zozes fired a shot of pure, white-hot energy, the beam so powerful it once again drained all sound.

The Major saw this only a moment before increasing his plasma-blade's output to form a defensive energy barrier, deflecting and rupturing the blast into countless exploding beams around his body.

At an alert on his tactical visor, Zozes glanced right to see his brother powering a second havoc-strike, pistol configured into a triple barrel. The Major caught the second blast, his body sent flying back through numerous walls into the south quadrant of the training platform, a series of explosions erupting.

Spent, Kaze reconfigured his weapon, though kept it locked on target. "That was fun."

Zozes could see the shake of his brother's hand and knew his spawn-net was over-stimulated. "Hate being left out, huh?"

On a weak laugh, Kaze lifted his chin. "Landed a hit by burning in a blast combo, so you're welcome." He paused. "The wave-guide reader's amped up my sync-pulse into a little dance. My command system's going offline!"

"Slow down," Zozes ordered, scanning the Major's impact area, sighting no movement. "Control your breathing."

They had little time, talking here was dangerous, but he needed to keep his brother calm. The wavelength's retraction and expansion flow-line was spiking, though it was still within safety borders.

"Easier said than done," Kaze muttered, though he was trying.

"LT has been forced into initialising cool-down mode," said Zozes, looking up to see the AI's lighting was dimmed, and that it had taken cover near a reinforced shield. "It needs time to prime its spawn-well and calculate correct output yield to execute a chained attack."

"Its offensive and defensive countermeasures are deactivating?"

"To stabilise the sync-pulse with us! You can't keep forcing your way through its control."

"You have your way." Kaze shook his head, obviously feeling better. "I have mine."

Out of patience, Zozes pulled him around. "If you keep overexerting the Trone's systems, it will be forced to lock you out — and right now," Zozes pointed at the Trone, "it's more vulnerable than us!"

"Then let's end this here and now!"

"Should I even ask about the Replic-bot?" growled Zozes looking around for a cyber-form of Kaze.

"Now he wants to know!" Kaze flung up a hand, "If you let me finish telling—"

Zozes cut him off, infuriated his brother was incapable of following the most basic orders. "For LT to initiate the drift at your level, it will have to mark out a hold position that leaves it fully exposed!"

"How simple do you think I am?" Kaze shrugged clear of his brother. "I'm using the Replic-bot to cover LT while we take the drift, bring down the Major!"

From the debris and flame shot a beam clearing a path. Kaze reacted instinctively, kicking Zozes clear while pushing himself backwards as the surge of energy sliced the air between the two.

Zozes came up spitting, having shoulder-rolled to his feet, looking across to see Rajek stepping out from the flames, white phaser-blade powered in his hand.

"Short version." Kaze activated freq-com. "Replic-bot's active and paired to the Trone ... with a slight alteration."

"Alteration?" That sounded ominous.

"It's time to drift this!" Kaze urged, powering his phaser-blade in a brilliant burst of sorge particles streaming into a sharp edge. "Trust me on the rest!"

Zozes momentarily hesitated, knowing they would have but one chance to employ the spawn-drift. Opening freq-com to the Trone and his brother, he ordered, "LT, spin up the drift-cycler. I'll take primary control, set my spawn-net to CAP-2, re-filter secondary output to hold Alpha Blue's sync-pulse within demarcation CAP-1. Don't let him burn out."

"Affirmative," replied the AI. "Setting grounding position coordinates to activate spawn-drift."

A strange visual anomaly appeared on Zozes' map-scouter, relaying Link-Trone's AI-Key's marked coordinates in two separate locations, both signifiers flashing several times before one finally faded, the second one remaining steady.

There was no time to query this. "Kaze, I'll bring the initial assault to drop the Major's shields. LT's SWOT tactical analysis will detect his current armour type, which will locate the clasp-activators positioned over his body."

"Hold on," Kaze argued his previous order, "powering down my spawn-drift CAP's a mistake, you need me peaking at your level."

"Kaze—"

The Major ignited grav-thrusters, landing on a broken pillar, flames and embers sparking behind him, the tenor of his voice filling the area. "Time to end this Blades, one way or another. You have the power. Break through your limits and seize it!"

"Form dual-combat," Zozes ordered over freq-com, powering his phaser-blade. "Protect the Trone until the drift-cycler comes fully online!"

Rajek leapt into the air, firing grav-thrusters and launching himself forward upon the brothers, weapon charged in a devastating attack. Crossing their blades, the two blocked the attack, the force of impact buckling the floor plating around them.

Locked together, the three were rained with sparks, Kaze bellowing as they drove their phaser-blades forward, pushing through the Major's attack, his weapon forced aside opening his combat-form for counterattack.

Kaze swung into action, unleashing a combination of devastating strikes against the Major's shields, which took heavy damage before he could regain position. Following through, he spun to meet Rajek's downward swing, deflecting it with a decisive swipe.

Zozes could see the Major regaining control, powering for a strike which he speared forward, slicing Kaze along the shoulder.

His brother's guttural cry carried into the drift, through the spawn-net, Zozes feeling it on a physical and mental level, his shoulder burning momentarily. Forcing himself in front of Kaze, he redirected the Major's attention, finally understanding his objective. At the edge of the arena was the Link-Trone.

"He's locked onto LT's position!" Kaze grunted, rolling his arm, clearly blocking the pain.

Zozes grunted, taking the heat off his brother, parrying a chain of strikes. Kaze needed a moment for his power-armour shields to stabilise. Using the momentum, Rajek spun, reconfiguring his blade for plasma-cannon, taking aim at the Trone.

Instinct taking over, Zozes grav-thrusted into a slide, his phaser-blade severing the Major's barrel, the other's uncharacteristic roar of rage deeply satisfying, and he knew.

Barely perceptible, it was there, the flow of the drift echoing through his sync-pulse.

Blindingly fast, Rajek powered a phaser-blade, swinging it at Zozes, who caught the attack, managing to parry the strike, take it to the deck, tearing through plating.

When he pressed further, the Major countered, breaking through Zozes' defence-guard to land a critical strike, ripping through Zozes' shields and chest armour, burning the flesh beneath, while lighting up his senses.

Multiple system warnings lit across Zozes' tactical visor. His spawn-drift cycler had almost fully spun up, to be initiated.

Kaze charged between Zozes and Rajek, the Major shifting his stance to agilely duck the sweeping sorge-blade. As he did, he grasped Kaze, single armed around his neck, raising him off the floor, before dumping him amongst the rubble and debris, buckling deck plating, planting a boot on his chest and pinning him in place while sighting the Link-Trone.

Zozes stumbled forward to intercept, fighting damaged systems that needed time to stabilise from the Major's last attack.

"Orders are orders, Blades." Lifting his arm, Rajek reconfigured his secondary weapon port's plasma cannon for an EM pulse, aiming at the Trone. "It is done."

Not knowing what he could do, Zozes stumbled forward, mind scrambling to stop the Major, only to fall to his knees at the sight of the energy surge leaving his weapon, the EM pulse striking the Trone, charged currents rippling outward along its techo-system, destabilising all AI's operative functions.

"No," he whispered, staring at the burn of sorge-blade, feeling helpless, knowing they had failed. The hunt for the Kadra Outcast who had taken all from his family. It ended here.

"What?"

At the Major's voice, Zozes looked up, unsteadily finding his feet. The Link-Trone's external composition had begun flashing like they were on the point of revealing a ... wireframe!

Slack-mouthed, he watched its cyber-form dematerialise, an emitter falling to the deck at the same moment Kaze brought up his right leg, wrapping it around the Major.

On a grunt, he braced against the chest, twisting free of his grip, leaving the Major stumbling for balance while gaining his feet.

"Told you to trust me!" Kaze crowed.

LT's voice broke in via freq-com. "Spawn-cycler primed, initiating core-drift."

A surge of spawns entered Zozes' bio-mechanical network, a steady flow that intensified with each beat of his sync-pulse, energising both brothers' combat suits, while reconfiguring base-form modes into drift-armour variant.

The reinforced plates over his body exposed sorge-thermal ports, each of these bleeding translucent vapour. Trone-sight became fully active, altering his tactical visor to relay every artificial construct within the south quadrant of the training platform, while also revealing the Major's phaser-blade's energy which radiated in a pale white light.

Side by side, the brothers turned on Rajek.

With the sync-pulse's vibration empowering, Zozes felt time begin to slow, the drift giving him a much-needed advantage of anticipation, an almost precognition with every mechanical object in the training quarter sharpening, becoming clearer, emitting a unique radial signature. Only the Major's and his brother's were masked by their shields.

The Major engaged Kaze, not seeing Zozes charge in a burst of speed, phaser-blade ignited. Mind centred, he would not let compromised, emotional responses guide his actions. At this moment, his force-strike must be restricted to intent not desire, speed and strength controlled during attack, or he would sever the Major in two.

Via grav-thrust, Zozes powered, jumping to angle his weapon for a single, decisive strike along the Major's back, rupturing his shields instantly.

The Link-Trone initiated SWOT tactical analysis, breaking down the Major's armour composition, loading its variant type, extrapolating his clasp-activator's locater points over his body.

Before his boots hit the deck, Kaze was grav-thrusting into position, directly behind the Major. The move was so fast, Zozes realised his brother had overwritten his earlier order, and was somehow drifting at his same CAP level.

"Impossible," he muttered, looking through his tactical visor to see Kaze's sync-pulse wavelength, retraction and expansion flow-line breaking through CAP-1 lining at secondary demarcation with his own.

And through the drift, Zozes could feel his brother's control, but also the wave of feelings guiding his brother's actions. His intent was ruled by desire, overwhelming passion.

The Major swung his weapon behind Kaze, who parried the attack, bringing his blade around to arc it downwards, cutting through Rajek's phaser-blade port, rupturing the plasma energy into particles around him.

The Link-Trone transferred the information from gathered SWOT tactical analysis highlighting the Major's clasp-activator locater points over the back of his body.

All sound drained from his surrounds, Zozes felt as if time slowed even further, becoming a crawl, numbing his body, blocking out all but his brother and the Major who was gripping his forearm. Kaze pivoted, swinging his blade through the air, spearing it at the wounded quarry. Like a shrill alarm, Zozes' sync-pulse sensitivity became hyper-responsive, the vibration of his phaser-blade reflected his spawn-net. The Major was defenceless.

Kaze was losing control.

Temporal time-laps stabilised, the uncomfortable shift to the present jolted Zozes into action, stumbling forward, facing off the Major, he bellowed two words.

"Kaze, no!"

Kaze twisted, the move halting behind Rajek to slash his phaser-blade in a chain of strikes targeting all five clasp activators positioned along the back of Rajek's hybrid armour.

The last strike had Kaze leaning into a deep forward stance, phaser-blade held outwards as Rajek fell to his knees.

Zozes could not move, his mind unable to comprehend his worst fears had been realised. Kaze had fatally wounded the Major. The drift had taken him.

Almost immediately, the drift-cycler's CAP level began powering down. Stumbling forward, Zozes automatically disengaged his phaser-blade, ordering the Trone. "LT cut the drift now!"

Zozes retracted his helmet, Trone-sight deactivating, taking with it the enhanced visual representation, returning all to normal while aligning the brothers' temporal phase-motion.

Rajek did not crumble as he approached, he was still holding steady while looking up … smiling?

Never had he felt such relief. The Link-Trone relayed that all the Major's clasp-activator target-points had been effectively destabilised, though not destroyed, no further injuries sustained through his brother's assault.

Kaze had somehow maintained control. *Just*, thought Zozes.

With a decisive shake of his head, Rajek gained his feet, eyeing his compromised phaser-gauntlet. "Impressive, Blades. Both of you held formidable control within the drift."

Zozes watched his brother silently as he retracted his helmet, wiping the blood from beneath his nose. Kaze's fingers were trembling.

How had he managed to increase the drift CAP without issuing a physical or verbal order? Glancing at the telemetry via his optics, not understanding, Zozes began deactivating the statistics, then deleted them, all while watching his brother, and the Trone, which was hovering at Kaze's shoulder.

Could his brother somehow connect with the Link-Trone on an instinctual level? Zozes doubted the notion, but it seemed the only possible answer, meaning the two were ultimately working beyond physical interactions, where mental-mechanics were controlled by very few.

As the thought faded, he noticed the Link-Trone hovering even closer to Kaze, flashing its lights in what seemed an almost cheeky way. Kaze's bond to the Trone was a form of companionship Zozes had never seen before.

The Major broke in on this last thought. "There you are, LT. Not a bad diversion, using my own Trone emitters to generate a cyber-form of your own AI. It appears," Rajek's glance included the three, "I underestimated you all."

At the praise, the Link-Trone spun in exhilaration, firing a series of electrical signals.

"Thank you." Zozes inclined his head, then glanced at the Major's armour. "Sir, your armour type was masked surveillance. If you were equipped with blast-assault load-out—"

"Neither of you would have stood a chance," finished Enforcer Noremar, walking up behind them.

"Regardless." Rajek pinned her with a look. "Astral Guard cannot dismiss this victory, and their success in controlling the spawn-drift."

Before she could respond, the squad's attention was drawn upward. Blade squads appeared to have concluded their own Trials, and were transporting via grav-lift toward a large circular platform connected to the Ops-Station. Other Blades subsequently followed, relocated by gravity lifts from their training quarters to the main combat-platform. It seemed like a mass convergence.

Rajek's and Noremar's porta-tools both sounded, generating cyber-screens. Each silently read the information.

"Congratulations, Alpha Green, Alpha Blue." Enforcer Noremar inclined her head. "It appears Commodore Vae'gon is indeed satisfied with your performance. This now grants you the right to engage in a final joint battle."

"Joint battle?" Zozes glanced at his brother. Kaze said nothing, still breathing heavily. Through their spawn-net, Zozes could feel his brother's fatigue, and the fact he had not set Noremar back in her place with one of his usual rejoinders proved he was in a lot of pain.

Rajek deactivated his porta-tool with decisive moves, clearly angry. "Astral Guard are pushing this well beyond any call of reasoning. You are condemning them all?"

"Astral Guard does not share your reluctance. Choice and time are not ours to command. The dangers we face are real and around us now."

Confused, Zozes decided on tact, hopeful that would gain him answers.

"That spawn-pod in the hangar bay, the one that almost lost containment ..." he paused, seeking the right words. "What it holds somehow connects to this?"

As she deactivated her porta-tool, Noremar glanced at Rajek, who showed her his back in obvious disgust. "Your skill in deduction is finely tuned, Alpha Green. To conquer this final threat will not only test your abilities as a soldier, but every Blade in this arena."

Galactic Star Key: Ebony Casteel
Astral Nav-Coordinates: EAS-APL-4
Data Sequence: 28.0

Ebony could smell the leather of the seat beneath her cheek. The more she struggled, the worse the paralysis, or whatever it was, seemed. Or maybe it was just that she became more aware as she could not move a muscle, let alone wet her dry lips.

As the car picked up speed, she lost track of time, entering a kind of sleep state until a sharp sting on her neck roused her, almost like a burn.

Slowly, the weapon's paralysing effects began to subside, draining from her muscles, leaving them contracting in a strange uncontrolled way. Swallowing dryly, her tongue searched her mouth for moisture, which suddenly flooded, making her gag. The moment she could, Ebony fought to sit up, her numb fingers grabbing at the seat, alarmingly weak.

Watery eyes warped her surroundings. The car was driving along the outskirts of Freestone, a road running alongside the river.

A woman with an English accent began speaking slowly. "Relax Ebony. You'll ... be fine. I'm sorry for what happened ... Axel's methods can be imposing ..."

"Doctor Walker?" Ebony gagged on the two words, her body shaking in reaction.

"Yes ... called in ... containment team ... Zheng house."

Though she fought to focus and narrow her concentration, the ability was beyond Ebony's grasp. Nothing made sense, the doctor's words were disjointed, her image swimming in and out of focus.

There was no way to answer, not when her tongue felt so strange, like it was too big for her mouth. Even blinking was odd. Wiping at her chin awkwardly, her hand came away wet, like she'd been drooling.

Doctor Walker pulled a wipe from the console, gently placing it into her hand. Embarrassed, she rubbed it hard over her cheeks and chin, fighting to not cry.

As the car turned left onto gravel, she looked blearily out the window. They were driving through the entry gates of White Pier car park, its jetty just ahead with a few small boats tied to it. Even though the sun was going down, families were out enjoying the spring evening, walking and jogging along the footpath that led back into town.

The moment the car parked, Dr Walker stepped out, opening the door for her. Hooking a hand under her shoulder, she helped her from the car, supporting her as a black limousine cruised into the car park, circling slowly before pulling alongside.

The windows were blackened so Ebony could not see in, but she had a good idea who it was. A chauffeur stepped out, opening the rear door for Xavier Solomon, dressed in his usual suit and tie.

Gaze speculative, Xavier buttoned his jacket while eyeing Ebony's weakened state. Raising an eyebrow toward Doctor Walker, he enquired, "Did Axel have an explanation?"

"Complications at the Zhengs', a containment breach. Reported that he was forced to improvise as Miss Casteel was uncooperative."

"Uncooperative?" Xavier tilted his head. "And this was his solution?"

Gaze starting to clear, Ebony looked toward the footpath, relieved to see so many people around. When she tried to speak, she ended up coughing, feeling like she was about to swallow her own tongue.

Thoroughly embarrassed, she unsuccessfully tried to pull from Doctor Walker's grasp, the risk of falling on the gravel preferable.

"Axel's improvisations are dangerous," Xavier said, frowning. "He forgets his place. The Librarian will not agree with this type of forced measure, and neither do I."

"The moment she was discharged from hospital," said Doctor Walker, "Ebony should have been placed under lock and key at Wayridge Manor."

"And the authorities?" Xavier shook his head. "They're already suspicious of the Founding Families' involvement. We can't afford to tip our hand any further."

"The Zhengs' house has been placed under quarantine."

"Why hasn't Axel notified me of such a necessity?" snapped Xavier. "The reason?"

Doctor Walker cast a brief look at Ebony. "That's best discussed alone."

Far more alert, Ebony could see the strain on Xavier Solomon, and got the impression there was a wedge between him and Axel, making her wonder who was really in charge.

"Fine. Give me a moment." Xavier took Ebony's hand, helping her walk to the front of the vehicle while Doctor Walker waited near the door.

"What ..." Ebony fought off another coughing fit, leaning against Xavier's car. "What ... do you want with ... me?"

"I apologise for Axel. This was supposed to go much more smoothly, but with the launch of Global Reach, a lot has changed. It doesn't excuse his actions."

Incredulous, Ebony could only stare. "What does Global Reach have to do with me?"

"It affects us all, Ebony. You, in ways you've yet to comprehend."

"Me?" She let that go, focusing on what she could understand. "My friends back at the Zhengs', they're hurt."

"I will take personal responsibility ensuring their welfare." Following this, he seemed to choose his next words with care. "However, that will depend on what they know, or remember. That could complicate matters."

"What's that supposed to mean?"

"I'm speaking in riddles, I know. The way we live, Ebony, can be hard to accept, and for some impossible. Your friends' integration back to their normal lives is a part of what we do."

"You mean the Fellowship?" Ebony shook her head. "This morning they were living normal lives. Now you're saying that's gone?"

"Not gone, nothing is ever gone. Rickard has kept a lot from you, some things I think you've already figured out. However, there have been complications. Your caretakers' positions have been rescinded, their authority passed to another during your illness."

"Caretakers? Do you have any idea how ridiculous that sounds? You're talking about my parents!"

"Adoptive parents," Xavier corrected. "And the claim they had over you has come to an end."

"Claim? End?" Ebony shook her head. "What does that mean?"

"There are formalities that must be adhered to," replied Xavier formally. "Respect the past so that we can prepare for the future ... for what is coming. Because it is coming Ebony, whether you like it or not."

Axel had said something similar, Ebony remembered. He had also mentioned the land the Casteels owned. Her and the farm ... two things that kept her father linked to the Fellowship.

"You're trying to piece this together," Xavier said, obviously pleased. "Well, tonight's meeting will go a long way to answering your questions. I've been given the authority to present you to your new caretaker. He will begin your treatments when you are ready."

"No!" Ebony tried for volume, but just ended up fighting a massive coughing fit. The way Xavier said things sounded like double-talk that just hid his true meaning. "I'm under Doctor Walker's care."

"That will be his decision. The man you're meeting, he's far better equipped to deal with your rare condition."

Ever since she woke up, her choices had been taken away. "What if I say no? What if I just start walking back to Freestone?"

Before she could finish, the word 'no' screamed through her mind, an overwhelming instinct taking hold, a presence that was foreign, but somehow familiar.

"Do you like being kept in the dark? I know I wouldn't. I got to know you quite well during the last eight months. You spent a good amount of time at Fellowship Tower in Melbourne." Xavier glanced toward the pier.

"Fellowship Tower?" Ebony had heard of the place but could not recall stepping foot inside. "Why?"

Xavier glanced toward the pier, indicating it with a nod. "There's a lot of people around. You're perfectly safe. Meet him

Ebony, then decide. I don't want to overburden you, just shine a light here and there. He'll tell you what you need to know. Just head down to the jetty."

Her body was tingling, like it had back at the shop, hands and feet, even her legs, the feeling generating from her spine through to her extremities.

"I … it's dangerous … forcing my memories …"

"Yes, but his unexpected arrival has changed more than you can imagine. Global Reach has forced all our hands. None of us have time anymore, least of all you."

Global Reach again. She was starting to hate those words. Looking toward the water, she eyed the pier, trying to casually shake her arms and legs, rid them of the tingling.

"I know all of this is overwhelming, but you need to trust in the Fellowship. They've been watching over you a long time." Stepping closer, he added weight to his words looking her in the eye. "Can you really move forward and leave all these questions unanswered? You're part of something, Ebony. I believe it's your right to know. This man is where the truth begins."

"Why are you doing this?"

"Because it's the right thing."

The right thing for him, or the right thing for her, she wondered. "Does your specialist have a name?"

Xavier smiled. "He's known by many, but around here we call him Cole."

The moment he said this, she felt peculiar, her body going pliant, almost lightheaded and giddy. A reaction to the needle, or being shot, she thought.

Furtive, she eyed the path back to Freestone only to feel her body tense, prepared to fight even the thought of running.

"You have a stronger backbone than you give yourself credit," Xavier chuckled quietly.

Muscles hard beneath her skin, she looked down at her hand, eyeing the clenched fist, for the first time truly afraid of how she felt.

On a deep breath, she straightened, preparing to decline his offer. Her mind felt like it was electrified, the words she spoke not her own. *"Fine, I'll meet him."*

The moment they were uttered, the force controlling her extremities receded, the tingling nerves easing.

What's wrong with me? Ebony looked again at the footpath, at Freestone in the distance, even took a couple of steps that way until a roar built in her mind, swinging her back forcefully, gravel flying around her feet to face Xavier.

Stunned, she stood completely still, arms outstretched fighting for balance, scared of her body, how it was acting.

"Ebony?"

"I'm … fine." She shook her head, noting the worried look on his face.

"If you're sure …" He glanced at the water's edge. "You should make your way down to the pier. You're quite safe, I assure you."

"Wait! You're not coming?"

"Cole has particular methods on how to approach this. He won't be long."

What did that mean? Her muscles stiffened again, a strange sensation washing from the back of her neck down. Feeling like a passenger trapped inside her own body, she moved across the gravel, stepping onto the footpath that ran beside Freestone River, leading toward the jetty.

A full moon hovered overhead, just visible as the sun dipped to meet with Greenland Hills. Joggers passed her, one looking at her strangely, noticing her haunted expression. Testing, she tried to crack her jaw, only to find it clamped shut. She could not even speak!

At the water's edge, a group of fishermen tossed in lines, unaware what she was going through. Everyone was wrapped in their world, oblivious to each other's worries and concerns. Couldn't they tell she was in trouble?

"Daddy, come on!" Ebony abruptly paused as a young child raced past, her father swiftly following to scoop her up.

"You'll fall," he warned.

"I don't want to miss the start!"

"We won't," he assured her, carrying her immediately to the guardrail.

"Mote lights!" the child squealed, leaning forward. "Look, photo, photo!"

451

Still a passenger, Ebony stepped alongside, glancing at the water, eyeing her reflection to see the right side of her face spasm. The child's father noticed, smiling uneasily before hurrying off to join his wife who was pushing a stroller.

Unable to move, she was forced to stare over the water, her body locked in place. Native organisms that coated Freestone River's rocks began to illuminate the water's depths as dusk approached.

Long wooden boats appeared beneath the wide arch of Freestone River's bridge, lanterns hanging from the bow. A man at the stern guided the narrow vessel along the river, looking at her oddly, as did the two passengers.

The nerves in her face were twitching, she could feel them, knew she must look like she was having some kind of psychotic break. Every instinct told her to run, but her body fought even the thought.

From the back of her mind, Xavier Solomon's words sprang forth. *Do you like being kept in the dark?*

Angry, she faced the pier, eyeing the tall lights illuminating its length and the few boats tied to it. Stepping onto the first wooden plank, she looked around, noting at the end was a group of elderly men fishing.

Maybe one of them ... at the thought, she staggered, feeling horribly lethargic, barely able to stay upright until a rumble in the distance caught her ear.

A black motorbike was entering the car park, moving quickly toward the pier, its headlight slicing through the growing darkness to pull alongside her.

She could see nothing of the rider's face through his reflective visor as he turned the bike off. In a swift movement, he pulled off the helmet revealing blond hair and narrowed, intense blue eyes. Climbing to his feet, he revealed a lot of height while hooking the helmet on the handle bar.

The moment he confronted her, Ebony's neck burnt, her vision instantly distorting as fire lanced her spine, spearing straight into her head, an overwhelming urge to close the gap.

On a gurgle of horror her feet started moving, something she fought with all her might only to realise the battle was useless. Mind burning, her arms lifted of their own volition, her feet tripping over themselves as she fought brutally for control, only to stumble into the rider's arms.

"I'm ... sorry." Looking up, she caught his frown of annoyance while being shifted to her feet.

"I'll live," he muttered, then looked at her again, harder this time. "Ebony?"

"Cole?" This was all wrong, she shouldn't be here. Mind racing, she recognised anxiety stepping aside for a full-blown panic attack, sweat coating her back, prickling her scalp. "This is a mistake, I—"

"Shouldn't have come?"

About to snap yes, she bit her lip, fighting to relax. She had been forced here, forced to face him, but something else was happening. Had her condition escalated, turned into some form of schizophrenia or identity disorder? Looking down, she stared at her hand, flaring her fingers. It was like she had no control.

Something she needed to get back.

"Look, I came here to make this official," she said, then had to look past him at the darkening hills. "I need you and the Fellowship to understand that I ... we, my family and friends are to be left alone. My father never wanted to be part of it, and neither do I."

The silence lengthened, forcing her to look back, to see that he was watching her steadfastly and not in a nurturing kind of way. She needed to finish this, get back to her parents, find out what was going on.

"The time for choice has ended," Cole stated finally.

Ebony thought back to the Zheng house, what she had just lived through, put her friends through. "I won't be part of this, whatever it is."

Cole paused, appearing to run an eye over her before answering. "You're afraid," he took a step closer, "but for the wrong reasons."

"There's right ones?"

"You're standing here." He looked her up and down. "That's progress."

"I ..." Nervous muscles began jumping in her knees eyeing his unnaturally blue eyes. "I can't ..."

"Can't what? Be ordinary, live normal? Normal ended for you eight months ago."

Eight months ago? Those three words dropped an ice cube into her belly. "When I came back to Freestone Valley?"

The way his mouth fused told her he was biting back words, the ones he finally uttered highly tempered, "Yes. For you, that's when this all began."

"You're trying to intimidate me," she realised uneasily. There were people around, something he did not seem to care about. "Why?"

"I'm trying to wake you up!" he growled. "Though I can see that's already started, hasn't it Ebony? And that's frightening you more than the amnesia."

He couldn't know ...

"And if it has, I suggest you start talking, because you can't fight this alone."

"Fight?"

"Yes. Because that's what this'll take — brutal, hard and bloody. So, you better prepare, because whether you're ready or not, the road ahead won't be accommodating."

He was angry, but she had no idea if it was at her, or what he was alluding too.

"What do want?" she finally managed, realising this was the first question she should have asked. "I haven't agreed to anything."

"You're still standing here." Hooking a thumb in his jean pocket, he challenged, "Tell me why that is."

"I ..." There was no way to answer that without sounding like a fool.

"Is there something controlling your actions? Provoking you to act uncharacteristically?" He touched a hand to his head. "A presence?"

"Presence?"

"A dominating one." Cole looked her over, focusing on her eyes. "Does it reach out and influence you at critical moments?"

"No ..." Ebony shook her head, terrified at the thought. But he was serious, she could see that. Looking for escape, she took a step back. "Since one of us is on the point of a psychotic break—"

"Don't believe me?" asked Cole. "Try and walk away."

She could see Xavier's car, the doctor leaning against it, watching. "Fine, your words not mine."

The moment she turned, her muscles tensed, fighting her to the point she wanted to scream with fury, the burning returning to her spine, controlling her actions.

"What's happening? Why won't my legs move?" she wailed, then spun on him. "They shot me with some weapon, is that the cause? Has it made me submissive?"

"Playing the fool is only going to make this harder," Cole spat. "You know the answer, but are too afraid to confront it."

Out of options, the panic attack she had been fighting rose again.

"Control yourself," he ordered.

His tone did not help, Ebony's breathing becoming erratic to the point she felt dizzy, frozen in place.

"If you keep hyperventilating, you'll end up on the ground, and this time I won't catch you," he warned.

"Why can't I move?!"

"I can teach you how to communicate with it, before your time runs dry and it gains control."

"Control?" Of all he had said, this shocked her the most.

"Does this sound familiar," asked Cole. *"Looking upon my reflection, I'm haunted by a ghost, a stranger. She feels somehow familiar, something lost in my past."*

Ebony swallowed over the lump in her throat, blinking at the water filling her eyes as she shook her head. "Xavier says what's happening to me connects to my abduction."

"Everything connects," Cole said cryptically. "And if your condition is left unchecked, you're not only risking your own life, but the lives of everyone you know. Can you accept that, Ebony? Live with those consequences?"

Cornered, she groped to identify fact from fiction. How could she believe anything so outlandish? Then she remembered the Zheng house, what had happened there. Her mobile, what had happened with it. Was this so far removed?

"I don't know what to think anymore." She looked again at Xavier's car, the raw need to run scuttling through her system. "How am I supposed to trust you?"

"I'm all that's left, Ebony." Cole pulled a face. "Your final hope of surviving any of this. So, are you in or out? I prefer to do this with you willingly."

A clock ticked at the back of her mind, wound by the speed of her racing heart. The moment he turned, picking up his helmet, a desperate feeling grabbed at her, driving her to stand beside him when he mounted the bike.

"You're leaving?"

Helmet gripped, he paused, waiting.

Fingers sweaty, she wiped them against her jeans, searching for an answer, trying to think clearly over the panic that wanted to dominate. What choice did she have? She needed answers, and maybe this way Jevon and Nina were out of it, and her family was safe.

"Alright," she mumbled.

"I can't hear you?"

"I said, I'm in!" Throat raw, she glared at his face, surprised at the intense relief flooding her system.

Cole looked over his shoulder, eyeing those at the car while absently turning the helmet in his hands. "From here on out, we do this my way, understood?"

His way. Ebony chewed anxiously at her lip trying to imagine herself as a docile companion. That was never going to happen.

"The lie that surrounds your situation is layered." Shoving the helmet back on his bike, he stood, turning back to her. "All that must be stripped away until you learn what your family was a part of."

"My family?" If this was heading where she thought it was, her father would not be happy. "The Casteel—"

"Not your prior caretakers." For a moment the two glared at one another, his bold blue eyes telling her this was fact. "Your birth family."

"They're dead."

"Your passing to the Casteel family was a final, desperate act of necessity rather than choice."

"This is insane, all of it!"

"Our families were once allies that shared a common cause. A cause that will change many lives, not only ours. That's why I'm here, to honour old debts."

"No." She shook her head vigorously. "They're dead."

"No more evasion, only the truth." Stepping forward his expression held more than anger. It held resolve. "Your birth parents, Ebony, are alive."

The steady hum of a grav-lift drew his attention, Kaze spotting more Enforcers approaching. Knees locked, he gave his exhausted body orders to stay upright. There was no way he was giving anyone the satisfaction of seeing him collapse.

The group of heavily armed Enforcers stepped off the lift, crossing the rubble to join Noremar before it had fully powered down. Narrow-eyed, Rajek watched them, absently triggering a self-conditioning protocol on his armour to begin repairing his damaged clasp activators.

Unnerved at their appearance, Kaze rubbed his chest. "I might have ..." distracting tightness grew with every word, "... overcommitted a little back there. Feeling the over-burn."

Hand-shaking, he tried to activate his porta-tool, then groaned sinking to one knee, his armour powering down and tele-warping into his stasis-loader. Wiping sweat from eyes, he struggled to generate a screen, the simple task daunting. Blinking hard, he eyed his sync-pulse on the wave-guide screen. It didn't look good.

"Your pulse's retraction and expansion flow indicator is increasing exponentially," Zozes said. "You need to take control or it'll fall into rapid-dysfunction."

"Get that Blade on his feet!" Noremar snapped. "Utilise Alpha Green's spawn-net to assist the AI unit to rebalance the fusion interactions between Trone and sorge-spawn types."

Looking stunned and disgusted, Zozes stepped before his brother, deactivating his own armour. "He needs more time for his pulse to synchronise to base-form operations!"

Noremar looked over the telemetry on her porta-tool, while taking an aggressive step forward. "All Blades have been ordered to the main combat platform for a joint battle."

The words struck a light in Kaze's mind, not one of anger, but of memory. Before him lay a deep fog rolling and billowing, beckoning his approach. Taking a mental step forward, he searched harder, urging with his mind for it to part ... and there she stood, the Alpha Chief.

"What comes after the Trials will be your true test."

The image distorted, like it was moving out of sync to be replaced by ...

... Kaze felt weightless, surrounded by a liquefied substance. Vision blurred, he looked ahead to see three silhouetted figures standing before him. They seemed to be studying him intently, one stepped forward to reach out, the hand bringing the form into focus revealing the Major ...

An instant later he was jerked back, fully present on the platform, kneeling beside his brother while looking up at Rajek.

A strange fatigue racked his body, each breath scoring his chest, but his mind was working hard, scrambling to make sense of what he had just witnessed. It felt like he was being haunted by his own subconscious. Why did he keep conjuring images of their Alpha Chief, and how was the Major part of this?

Confused, he looked back at his brother, desperately wanting to share what had happened, but Zozes always cut him down, dismissed anything relating to seeing the Chief as a residual neurological by-product of their dual-pairing with the Link-Trone.

Maybe he was right, Kaze thought. But it did not feel like a past memory. Could it be the Chief's past memory patterns were resurfacing within the AI unit? The possibility struck Kaze as absurd, but he had a feeling Zozes would disagree.

"Take deep, controlled breaths, then release," advised the Major, ignoring Noremar who was motioning for Zozes to force Kaze up. "Like your brother stated, young Alpha, your pulse requires synchronisation, to stabilise so you can control your base-form operations."

Several Enforcers joined Noremar on the platform, indicating she needed to get them moving.

"Major Rajek!" she bellowed. "Assist in transferring the Blade to the grav-lift now, and prepare your mobile tele-warp badge for immediate evacuation to the hangar bay for departure."

"Lieutenant," snapped the Major, "he can barely move, let alone stand."

Noremar signalled the Enforcers behind her. "Warp out now! I won't be far behind."

At her order, one Enforcer threw out an expanding tele-warp rim, which took position above the assembled officers, the device levitating in place. After triggering their mobile teleportation badges, warp-orbs surrounded each and they were gone, shifting into the rim which remained open, still powered.

"Our orders are clear, Major. If you don't leave with me now, you'll be cut off. The moment this joint battle commences, a Blackout Protocol will engage, one that cannot be lifted."

"Blackout Protocol?" Kaze shook his head, her words vibrating through his mind. "Someone mind explaining any of this?" A sharp pain stabbed his chest, the last of his words dissolving in a coughing fit.

Rajek looked from Noremar to the Blades, clearly fighting something deep. After detaching the teleportation badge from his utility belt, he looked down at the device, watching the control screen flash from red to green.

"You condemn yourself by staying," Noremar warned. "Your progress within Astral Guard will take a fatal blow, as will the Commodore's arrangement with the Archetype!" She took a step forward, staring hard into his eyes. "Come with me, Sir. It is the only way."

Gaze still on the device, Rajek gripped it with a sudden intensity, destroying the tele-warp disc in one decisive jerk. Turning his hand, the remains fell on the deck, joining the rubble.

"Take your departure." His gaze cut back to Noremar carrying an authority earned over countless battles. "Flee to your Astral Guard lair where cowardice and folly battle for superiority. My place is here, with these Blades. For what is to come, their victory must be fulfilled and their title recognised."

Eyes narrowed, Noremar triggered her tele-warp badge, teleportation orbs breaking her into energised trace fibres. "Remember," her final words vibrated through the air, "standing with them means standing alone."

Mind working overtime, Kaze watched his brother walk to the edge of their platform, eyeing the Blades passing on grav-lifts to where they were gathering, a horrible sense of foreboding invading his system. One that tightened his airways, crippling with each breath drawn.

Rajek knelt before him, speaking calmly. "Re-centre your breathing cycle. Slow the flow of the oxygen moving in and out your body, time it with the beat of your heart in counts of five, slow and steady."

Kaze began to cough, "Slow and steady … isn't helping, Sir." Looking at the deck, he felt as if his chest was being crushed, gripped within a vice.

Annoyed, Rajek jerked his chin back up. "To overcome this, you must first attain the ability to listen, act on what I say."

Kaze nodded, closing his eyes, trying to focus on the Major's voice, knowing he was trying to help, and started to count.

"Yes, now breathe in, hold the count," Rajek watched carefully, "and slowly release on the count."

It took several more breaths but Kaze could feel the difference, how the Major's technique brought back balance between him and the sync-pulse. After a few more moments, the tingling numbness left his chest, hands and feet, his limbs once again growing in strength.

"His spawn-net sync-pulse is stabilising," Zozes said. "Realigning to base-form operations."

Though still unsteady, Kaze found his feet, shaking out his hands and legs, while watching the Major's expression. "You're going to say stuff now."

"The difference between you, your brother, and me, is control over the emotional state. You react without thought, without deliberation, and most times without all the facts."

"Sir." Kaze shook his head, laughing at the pins and needles riding his body. "This mental reconditioning talk is wasted on me. I'm just not built that way. Artificial methods of pure control are restricted to a set of rules, an area I've never paid much attention to."

"That's why it's learnt," Rajek said. "Your inner psyche is more a part of you than you care to acknowledge, and a strong means for controlling spawn technology."

Zozes turned, walking back to add, "Mental control is key to controlling spawns. Absolute acts of emotional force weaken our link to the Trone—"

"—forming ripples in the sync pulse," finished Kaze. "I heard you the first time. The starring question we should all ask is who the vok made this all so complicated?"

"Your untrained mind's a liability," Rajek said, as if Kaze had never spoken. "One that wears on your body. It is something that cannot be endured long term."

"Let me guess," griped Kaze sarcastically. "There'll be more happy consequences?"

"Your lifespan will be shortened. I lost many comrades following the Second Galactic War."

Zozes looked at Rajek. "Blade Mark Ones?"

"Indeed." Rajek never took his eyes off Kaze. "Tell me, young Alpha, how many Blade Mark Ones survived after the war with the Kadra?"

This seemed a pointless question to Kaze. "Thousands."

"And how many have lived since?"

Kaze looked at his brother, frowning in confusion, but he too seemed lost.

"Only twelve," the Major said, a shadow seeming to cloud his face when speaking of the past. "A restricted classification was placed around those who enlisted in the Mark One program, something that ended tragically. Many believed that the Blades who served were cursed."

"Then why," Kaze swallowed uncomfortably, glancing at his brother, "break shielding the truth to us now, Sir?"

Grim, the Major looked at each like he was fighting an internal war between speaking and staying silent.

"Are you saying ..." Zozes paused, like he could not believe what he was to ask. "You're one of the original chosen by the Archetype himself?"

Obviously still torn, Rajek spoke slowly. "The title of Blade came after commencement of the Galactic War. Individuals of leadership races were chosen from the Galaxy's Astral States. After the Actrix Covenant freed the Archetype, it was he who made this choice, passing on a legacy that saw the rise and fall of the Primordials."

"The rise and fall," said Kaze incredulously. "You speak as if the Archetype came from a time that predates the Primordial race."

Rajek neither confirmed or denied this. "What we term as spawn technology is but the first steps in a far more complicated tapestry, something I came to realise long ago. The Kadra," Rajek held up a hand, forestalling each brother's instinctive sneer, "wove their concept within this faith, using its guidance to understand the Kraph. The Primordial race termed the spawn as an intra-dimensional particle, a vital component in controlling the Actrix Stones."

"The origin of all creation is linked to the Actrix Stones," Zozes accepted readily.

"But our understanding surpasses all before," Kaze said. "We shape the spawns, have a realistic approach. We're no longer clouded by those who used to worship them, treating them like some type of faith."

"The Archetype's original teachings to the First Twelve were …" Rajek paused, struggling to complete the sentence, "different. It is this difference that kept us alive, and destroyed all those who came after."

"Teachings that were later integrated into the Blade Mark Two Command Training?" guessed Zozes.

"Only what the Planetary Allegiance deemed necessary was included. The Original Twelve," Rajek lifted his chin, "were not chosen because we were combat effective."

"Take a step back there." Kaze goggled at this. "You weren't always a solider?"

At Rajek's brief head-shake, Zozes' eyes narrowed. "And yet The Planetary Allegiance chose to weaponise the Archetype's teachings."

The Major looked past both, seeming lost to memory. "The Mark Ones that came after the Original Twelve were the best combat potentials the Planetary Allegiance had to offer. They shared your ideal, Alpha Blue, to punch their way through and force control over spawn technology." There was no mistaking the pain on his face. "By the time it was realised this was a mistake, countless had died in ways I will never speak of."

"Which led," Zozes said, "to the official ruling of Command Training for the Blade Mark Two program."

"The Archetype used a similar approach to identify between what was termed as internal and external perception based minds." Earnest now, Rajek looked at Kaze. "You, young Alpha, share many of the fallen Mark Ones' traits."

"Meaning without change," Zozes said, "your life will close without choice."

"Like theirs," said Rajek.

They were both concerned, Kaze could see that, but he was battling an inner instinct that told him what he was going through was different.

"There has to be more to this," he reasoned. "Why would the Chief make me an Alpha knowing it would be the seal on a death sentence?"

When Zozes' eyebrows met, Kaze knew his brother was wrestling with the same question. Why had she ordered them to form a dual-pairing, linking them with an AI Trone? No one else could answer this, only their Alpha Chief, and she was gone.

Freq-com alerted, the Major swiftly activated his porta-tool, opening the channel so both Kaze and Zozes could hear. The Star-Key identifier, Kaze noticed on the Major's forearm cyber-display, was marked as Alpha Commander Balota, his voice broken by the sound of battle and explosions.

"Joint battle commencing ... identify target ... class three identified ... Blade NE-squad five and ..." Weapons fire took over the channel, drowning anything audible.

A cascade of high-grade explosions erupted, the three looking up toward the arena's main combat platform, the deep rumbling impacts shaking all within the reinforced netted grid-shield.

Another crackle then freq-com's channel momentarily cleared, "... havoc-strike countermeasures ... spawn ..."

A high-yield detonation struck the main combat platform, violent enough to jolt the entire arena. Open-mouthed, Kaze swung, fighting to stay upright eyeing the sparking grid-shield, no longer clear but a jumble of colours. Almost on top came a submicro-count that collapsed the sector's combined net, a red beam ripping through the shield, exploding the platform's upper pylon.

The carnage drew Kaze and Zozes to the edge of their training quarter.

"That blast took out the platform's primary grav-nacelles," said Kaze.

The anti-gravitational device powered down, breaking away from the platform's assembly struts. The large, orb-shaped grav-nacelle went into freefall, crashing upon a lower power-distribution array. Within moments the arena's energy flow connecting to the upper sector affected neighbouring training quarters, turning them dark.

All that was left was the sound of raging battle, the arena sounding like a warzone.

"What the vok are they facing up there?" Kaze bellowed.

Rajek's jaw clenched, seeming torn with how he should answer.

"Major!"

The group braced as their own training quarter again felt the effects, lighting emitters shutting down, grid-shields struggling to stay active as their beam-nets deactivated, powering down defensive barriers. Reserve power flashed once before coming online, illuminating the training quarter in red emergency lighting.

Rajek signalled for the two to follow him to their grav-lift.

"Sir." Before stepping on, Zozes halted. "Is this the reason why Noremar wanted you out of the final fight? The Trials—"

"No longer have meaning," declared Rajek. "Astral Guard have used these Trials as a camouflage operation."

"For what?" Kaze demanded.

Rajek activated the grav-lift, opening the command panel. "To attain your full vindication against the Kadra."

"Wait, what?" Kaze tried to make sense of the words. "We're Kadra hunters not sympathisers! You're saying our loyalty is on the line along with our abilities?"

The Major worked the control panel, loading a new trajectory path. When he finally answered, each word was carefully considered. "It's more complicated than you. There are agendas that far exceed the launching of Global Reach on Earth. Powers working against one another, which have placed the Blades at the heart."

"You're saying Astral Guard needs us to more than fail," realised Zozes, eyeing the fighting Blades.

"They want us dead," Kaze spat.

"There's only so much I can do to protect you. I was told if you survived the Trials, your part in this would have been concluded, but now ..." The three braced as another high-grade explosion detonated above. Kaze watched as a small group of Blades were thrown from a combat platform, each body alight with fire, plummeting to their death upon the training quarters below.

Rajek immediately began priming the grav-lift's systems. One of the Blade officers engulfed in red fire had crashed onto their platform, spreading embers across the deck.

Zozes broke off, racing across, Kaze only a step behind. Side by side, the two examined the body, assessing the destructive assault.

"Keep your distance," Rajek yelled, jogging across. "These flames form a radiant energy field!"

Trust in his words had both brothers stepping back, waiting for the Major's next directive.

"Alpha Green, have LT reset your shield's repulse-field to align its flow-rate modulation cycle to my own wave guides."

On a nod, Zozes complied, relaying the orders manually through his porta-tool's cyber-controller.

Rajek generated a digital overview through his porta-tool, a structural outlay of the arena. He assembled the data through his map-scouter, highlighting an emergency wave-path. "Right now, my prime objective is to get you both to the fall-back emergency zone."

"Fall-back?" Zozes looked at his brother aghast. "Those Blades up there need us, Sir!"

"Their fate is not your responsibility," Rajek stated flatly, finishing the action on the porta-tool. "I will not allow Vae'gon's false fears to eliminate you all."

Kaze trailed the Major back to the grav-lift, halting next to Zozes who looked at him with a look he knew all too well.

"We can't do that, Sir," Kaze said. "We need to understand what's going on."

The Major turned, clearly measuring each brother's resolve, an energy shimmer flashing from head to toe indicating his clasp-activator's repair cycle had finalised. Rajek's Trone systems were now fully restored and bridged to his power armour.

"So be it." Glancing down, he eyed his forehand's damaged phaser-gauntlet, clenching a fist. "Do you think the humans are the only augmented sleepers targeted by the Kadra?"

Kaze swallowed this with difficulty, watching his brother glance back at the burning body.

"The Kadra are now targeting Blades?"

"In the same way they're targeting Earth humans? Ebony Casteel?" Kaze shook his head. "As much as I'd enjoy sharing some commonalities with her particularly, it just isn't possible. Our spawn-net makes us immune to any Kadra genetic overhaul."

"Never believe in absolutes," cautioned Rajek, bracing himself as the platform shook. "Astral Guard have identified Blade operatives within our own ranks."

"The Blades here?" Zozes turned, looking over the battlefield. "They've been identified?"

"What the vok?" Kaze was beyond incensed. "Marked us as targets?"

"Because of the Chief." Zozes looked staggered as the realisation hit.

"Initiating an unregistered dual-pairing—" began Rajek.

Visibly shaking with anger, Kaze snarled a deeply held knowledge. "She gave her life trying to save every Blade on our ship!"

"But Astral Guard," Zozes forced himself to focus, put aside his own anger, "are clearly working off a theoretical claim that she was what? Somehow was captured and repurposed by the Kadra?"

"Vok their theories!" Kaze roared. "She'd die before yielding!"

"A belief I share, Alpha Blue, but now is not the time for measured clarification. We need to make for an evac-route."

When Rajek stepped onto the grav-lift neither of the brothers followed. Kaze activated the cyber-controller on his porta-tool, trying to control his anger while cycling through several subspace freq-com channels, noting that all were blocked, no hope calling for aid.

"Every channel's jammed," he said to his brother.

"Fall in!" Rajek bellowed, for the first time showing real anger. "That's an order!"

Kaze looked at his brother, their Link-Trone hovering close, obviously aware of the tense atmosphere.

His spawn-net's sync-pulse was once again stable, and all base-form operations were back online. His cyber-optics shimmered over his eyes, before uploading the AI's tactical analysis, receiving sensor data on the battle raging around them. If they had to battle, he was ready.

The Link-Trone's optical-sensors directed Kaze's focus to a massive energy beam shooting across the south quadrant of the main combat platform. It detonated against a secondary anti-gravity port-nacelle, the unit losing structural integrity, sending the large platform into a slow descent wreaking havoc on the training quarters below.

Everything seemed to be happening in slow motion, Kaze's vision shifting and blurring, an overwhelming fog closing in on his mind. Claustrophobic, he stepped forward mentally, forcing it to shift only to find ...

... an active spawn-pod. No, he was in an active spawn-pod, he could feel the streams of cryo-liquid surrounding him, and when he looked up, there was a hand touching the hatch's screen. Outside the pod were dark figures, silhouetted against ... then the Major came into focus ... his hand reaching toward him ... and ... and ... there was no going further, not before the mist closed in. Then came the Alpha Chief's voice, so close it felt as if she was standing beside him ...

"... what comes after the Trials will be your true test ..."

With an abrupt yank, he was back, standing on the arena, watching his brother step onto the grav-lift. Though unnerved, Kaze followed, his body seeming to know what it had to do, taking position beside his brother.

"Any Blade that survives," Zozes said, generating a reserve sorge-rifle from his stasis-holder, "we take with us. Understood?"

"And the Augments?" Kaze asked.

Before Zozes could answer, the Link-Trone hovered close, relaying an emergency signifier on an incoming combat platform crashing through another training quarter.

"Warning, warning!" the Trone screeched. "Multiple approximation descent path collisions detected, evasion countermeasures uploading."

The primary combat platform was now losing stability, crashing through the main wall, taking out another training quarter. The Trone uploaded an approximate trajectory on their map-scouters, displaying multiple incoming projectiles.

"They're not giving in!" Kaze yelled, watching energy rounds firing, everything inside him saying he should be out there, sorge-beams blasting as it detonated along the arena's Ops-Station.

Dust and wreckage cramped his vision, the destructive force of the main combat platform descending towards them completing the devastation of the arena, the entire area beginning to shake violently, burning debris raining down, embers lighting up the darkness as they fell to the lower decks.

There looked to be no means of escape, not for the Blades engaged in battle.

Like something had sparked inside him, the Major glanced back, eyeing each brother with an unreadable expression, with not one hint of fear as he silently initiated the crawl of his hybrid battle armour.

"We hold the line alone — together!" he vowed, lifting an arm, powering his plasma cannon.

The battle cry set fire to Kaze's mind. Initiating Blade-Gear, he stood shoulder to shoulder beside his brother, each covered in power-armour. Demagnetising his sorge-rifle, Kaze looked hard at Zozes, seeing an expression identical to the Major's.

Together, they thrust their weapons high, declaring the last of the Blades' refrain. "Till the end!"

Acknowledgements

ROSE

A book this long in the making inevitably gathers an extensive list to thank. Where to start? How about the first person who knew I was even attempting to write: my husband, Rick. Thank you for your unwavering belief that I could accomplish this dream. For answering endless 'out there' questions, while handling an array of hysterical writer emotions that I'm told come hand in hand with the craft. This would not be a reality without you.

To my eldest girl, Keisha. I'll never forget watching you devour an early draft, becoming so invested that you closed the door of your room to finish it. To my youngest, Tahnee. The day you trapped me on the phone trying to predict what was coming was wonderful. And your critiques have been invaluable! How can I thank you both? You've both bolstered and consoled, laughed and cried while ordering me to just 'get it done!' Every word you said was true.

To my long-suffering friends and family – a heartfelt thank you! Chris ... the encouraging chats, the dragging you to every writer's event – none of it will be forgotten. Shaz and Taylor, you are two of the best! Liz Watt of Collins Booksellers, thank you for your unwavering support over many years.

What gave me the confidence to bring this all together was four people in the end. Dr Bob Rich who edited very early drafts and taught me how to write action scenes while killing info-dumps. Fiona McIntosh and her wonderful Masterclass. Spending a week with you and other writers gave me the confidence to turn that final corner where I found Joel Naoum of Critical Mass. His practical approach to publishing while answering endless emails made this process possible. Thanks also for finding our final editor Libby Turner, a fellow sci-fi lover.

The last I need to thank is the most important. Kane, my son, and co-writer. What can I say? You brought the world I dreamt up to vibrant life. We've laughed and commiserated, we've argued and apologised – a lot! We've talked for *hours* on the phone almost every day for years turning an idea I had so long ago into something beyond my imaginings. Without you, The Actrix Stone would not have become a reality and the full ride it is now. Thank you, mate. For everything.

KANE

It began in a galaxy far, far away, a four-year-old fanboy watching starships and lightsabres, learning what it takes to be a hero. I bow to honour my first inspiration. Without Star Wars and George Lucas, our world would never have come to fruition.

To my family who has endured countless years of development from character creation to plotting storylines. Those who know us well understand the highs and lows endured to get to the end. To my dad Rick. Thanks for instilling a strong work ethic to get the job done. Years of living a rural life from farm boy to adult will never be forgotten.

To Keisha – thanks for all your plans in wanting to spread the word of The Actrix Stone. Bet in ten years you're reading this with pearly whites – a job well done.

Who can forget the up and coming actress? Tahnee, in many ways creatively you are my mirror image. I see so much of myself in you it makes me step back and say ... oh sh!t. Your critiques in the final stages made all the difference.

To our artist Angel Angelov. From the rough designs and references, you brought to life our characters in a way that is light years beyond our expectations. Without your artwork and creative network, Ivan Sarov never would have come on board, bringing to life a mind-blowing book trailer.

To my friend, Christian Baczyk. I will never forget the day you were recommended. Your gift is creating music, a talent that should never be cast aside. The track 'Destiny' will never get old. It was a privilege to work with you. Hopefully, our paths will cross in the future.

To my friends new and old. The majority are still probably scratching their heads wondering why this took over half a decade of my life. I challenge you to read this and see what the world of The Actrix Stone demands – time.

I will end this by honouring the one and only ... my mother, Rose. You have an extraordinary imagination and talent for bringing originality back into storytelling. You are unquestionably the sole reason why The Actrix Stone has become a reality.

Your fascination for life in the stars and belief that humans can one day achieve a state of understanding that may change our perception of what it means to exist has endured, as has your vision of what will come in the end. My world building may have reset the clock, but the players are all present and remain consistent.

Let's bring it home. One day in the future many will understand. Thank you, Rose, for letting me into your world.

From book one to twelve and beyond. 'We hold the line alone – together. Till the end.'

www.ingramcontent.com/pod-product-compliance
Lightning Source LLC
Chambersburg PA
CBHW052349110726
47901CB00005B/1416